PARADISE FOUND

BOOK 3 - THE PARADISE CLUB SERIES

JA LOW

Copyright © 2021 by JA Low

All rights reserved. No part of this eBook or paperback book may be reproduced or transmitted in any form, including electronic or mechanical, without written permission from the publisher, except in the case of brief quotations embodied in critical articles or reviews.

This is a work of fiction. Names, characters, businesses, places, events, and incidents are either the products of the author's imagination or used in a fictitious manner. Any resemblance to actual persons, living or dead, or actual events is purely coincidental. JA low is in no way affiliated with any brands, songs, musicians, or artists mentioned in this book.

This eBook is licensed for your personal enjoyment only. This eBook may not be re-sold or given away to other people. If you would like to share this eBook with another person, please purchase an additional copy for each person you share it with. If you are reading this eBook and did not purchase it, or it was not purchased for your use only, then you should return it to the seller and purchase your own copy.

Thank you for respecting the author's work.

In memory of Tash from Outlined with Love who designed this cover but was unable to finalize it before her passing.

Huge thank you to Sly Fox Cover Designs for finalizing this cover for me and helping Tash's vision live on.

Editor by Swish Design & Editing
Proofing by More than words

❀ Created with Vellum

FOREWORD

Please note this book is extremely hot.
If you do not like lots of sex and sex with other people then do not pass go.

There may be triggers for some regarding childhood trauma.
Please proceed with caution if you have triggers.

1

ALISTAIR

One Year Earlier

"Hey, babe, where are you?" Miranda asks irritably as I pick up her call.

"I'm stuck in Mykonos. A storm has come through. I don't think we will be able to take off tonight," I explain softly to her, knowing how upset she will be with me. "I'm so sorry, babe, I tried everything, but I'm not going to be able to make it home in time for our anniversary dinner."

The line goes quiet.

Shit. I'm in trouble.

We're celebrating five years together, quite the milestone.

"You promised me you would be here," she says angrily.

"I know, but Mother Nature has other plans. I promise I'll make it up to you, sweetheart."

"You always do," she says with a sigh as if exhausted by this conversation already.

I understand her frustration. I didn't plan on the storm happening, and I did promise her come hell or high water that I would make it home to be with her tonight, but I've literally tried every conceivable way to get back there.

I've been away for the past two weeks finalizing the opening of my latest Mykonos club just before the summer season hits the island. It's important. I may not be saving lives like she does, but I am helping people escape from their lives. So that's the same, isn't it?

"The pilot thinks I'll be home by ten in the morning," I add hesitantly.

Miranda draws a breath before releasing it. I can imagine she's pinching the bridge of her nose. "I'm on the early shift. I won't see you till later that night." She sighs.

Miranda's a doctor and works emergency in one of the more superior hospitals in London. Our schedules frequently clash as I own nightclubs, which means most of my business is conducted at night. When we first started dating, and she was a resident, her hectic schedule kept us apart, but now she's a fully-fledged doctor and her shifts have stabilized—no graveyard shifts for her since she's the boss—things have become more normalized for us.

"We can celebrate tomorrow night. I won't go to work. I promise I'll make it up to you, Mir," I say, pacing around the private area of the terminal.

"I know you will," she says sadly.

She's so disappointed in me, I can tell by the tone of her voice, so I really need to make it up to her. "Love you, baby, with all my heart. Happy anniversary!"

"Happy anniversary to you too," she says less enthusiastically than me.

I know I'll need to be showering her with flowers and diamonds when I arrive home. "I'll be there just as soon as I can."

"Okay," she says before the lines go dead. *Yeah, I'm in the doghouse.*

The storm passed quicker than expected, and I can't believe we were able to leave Mykonos a couple of hours later. I tried to call Miranda to tell her, but she'd switched off her phone. I'm going to have to do some apologizing with my tongue all night long once I step through the door.

It's almost midnight by the time we touch down in London, but at least I made it before the night's over. Thankfully, the private airport isn't far from our home.

My driver heads straight there, and I might have one minute to spare of the actual day by the time we arrive.

I grab my bags and head inside my home. All the lights are off, and the house is quiet—of course, it would be—because Miranda needs to get up early.

I place my bags on the floor, kick off my shoes, and hang up my jacket. Then I walk through the living room and up the stairs to our bedroom. My hand presses against the wood of the bedroom door that's ajar and pushes it open. The light from the hallway filters through and illuminates the bed where Miranda is sleeping. The white sheet has slid down her side exposing her bare chest. My eyes slide down over her pert breasts and taut nipples until a snort catches my attention.

It's then I notice a second body in bed with her.

My entire body freezes.

My heart begins beating uncontrollably out of my chest.

Goddammit! *Is this what a heart attack feels like?*

I rub my eyes because they must be playing tricks on me—I don't believe what I'm seeing. There is no way in the world Miranda would have another man in her bed.

There's no way.

She's not like that.

I trust her.

She's never given me any reason not to trust her. Ever!

I take a step further, not believing my eyes, and I kick something on the floor that rattles. The sound bounces off the walls in the quiet bedroom.

Miranda sits up quickly and shakes her head trying to clear her sleep fog. "Ali?" Miranda gasps, her eyes widen with panic as she takes in that I am standing in *our* bedroom hours earlier than I said I would be.

I look over at the bedside clock, it's 11:59 p.m. *I made it.*

"What are you doing home so early?" she asks quickly, then swallows hard.

"Surprise," I say through gritted teeth.

The man beside her groans, shaking his dark hair as he sits up.

No.

No.

No.

Why him?

Of all the people you could have fucked. *Why him?*

I feel the moment my heart breaks inside my chest as the familiar brown eyes stare back at me. After all these years, I thought the rivalry would have stopped now we're fucking adults.

It seems I was wrong.

Dead wrong!

"Shit, Ali, you're home early," my brother grumbles as if my presence is an annoyance to him.

Anger bubbles through my veins as I launch myself at him. "You *fucking* asshole," I swear as I grab and then haul him from the bed, where I notice he's naked. My fist meets his jaw with a crunch multiple times as I lay into him.

"Ali, stop! Please stop," Miranda screams beside me.

"Why? Why her?" I yell as my brother fights back.

"She was mine first," he screams. "You fucking took her from *me*."

I took her from him?

Has he lost his mind?

As blind rage fills me, I continue to lay into my brother.

"Ali, please stop hurting George," Miranda yells at me.

She wants *me* to stop hurting *him*.

Fuck, no.

That fucker deserves every single fist in his face that he gets. He's done this to me my entire life. He doesn't give a shit if he hurts me.

He's in the wrong.

He's always in the wrong.

He's the one always fucking my girlfriends.

"Ali," Miranda lets out a blood-curdling scream which halts my assault on my brother.

I let go of the asshole, and he slumps to the floor with a groan before doubling over in panic as curses fall from his lips, but they are all white noise to me in this moment. I look at my bloodied knuckles and wipe the mess on my jeans. Then I feel the trickle of blood from my nose slide down over my lip, so I use the back of my hand to wipe it away. I look over at Miranda as tears stream down her cheeks, and for the first time, I notice how pale she looks as she holds her robe in front of her naked body.

"Why?" is all I ask her. She knows my history with my brother. With all the men she could have cheated on me with, it had to be him.

Does it really matter why? She still did it to you after knowing what he's done in the past.

"Get the fuck out of my house," I scream angrily at her.

Miranda flinches as she takes a step back at the ferociousness of my request. "Ali, please, let me explain." Remorse falls across Miranda's beautiful face as she implores me to listen to her pathetic excuse.

"There is nothing you can say that can justify you sleeping

with my brother," I tell her through clenched teeth as I try and reel in my anger.

"I know, Ali. Please, I thought you wouldn't be home tonight," she explains.

"Thank fuck I came home when I did then, right?" I say, giving my brother a sideways glance as he pulls himself up off the floor.

He angrily snatches his clothes that are scattered at the bottom of my bed and starts to get dressed.

"You weren't supposed to find out like this," Miranda adds quietly as she pulls the silk robe around her naked body and ties it closed.

I look up into Miranda's blue eyes that are ringed red with emotion. There is nothing in this world she could say that makes fucking my brother okay.

"Of all the people … *him*?" I ask as my shoulders sag. I'm sick of being fucked over by my brother. I'm surprised it took him this long to do it with Miranda if I am being honest with myself. I knew the time would come because it always does.

Miranda looks down at the floor. It's obvious she knows that of all the men she could have fucked around with, it being him was the one I could never forgive.

Ever.

I thought Miranda was different. I thought I'd finally found someone who my brother couldn't have taken away from me. *Fuck, was I wrong.*

"Tell him, Mir. He needs to know!" My brother sighs as he finishes getting dressed.

Tell me what? I'm no rocket scientist—I have two eyes and can see that you two have been fucking.

"No, I can't. Not like this," Miranda replies to my brother.

"I get it you two have been fucking around. There's nothing more to say, George." I turn and glare at my brother, whose face is looking pretty messed up, and that somehow makes me smile. His nose could be broken, and fuck, I hope it is. There's a line of dry blood smeared across his cheek. There are fresh droplets of blood scattered over his nice new white shirt.

"*Tell him*, Miranda," my brother says angrily.

Miranda blanches at my brother's words.

I hate them both right now, but how dare he talk to her like that. She'd never tolerate that bullshit from me.

"I didn't want you to find out this way, Ali. I ... I was going to tell you tonight," she says, stumbling over her words.

"You were going to tell me on our anniversary that you've been fucking my brother?" I ask bitterly.

Miranda frowns and wipes the fresh tears away from her cheeks. She then looks over to George for reassurance.

What the fuck is going on?

"She's pregnant, Ali, and it's mine," George tells me.

The entire room begins to spin, and I stumble physically from his words. It is as if he's reached out and slapped me across the face.

No.

It can't be true.

I don't believe it.

No.

Then I see the smirk on my brother's lips as he takes in my reaction. He knows he's just shoved a metaphorical knife through my heart, and the smile on his face shows me he's enjoying twisting it in my chest.

"You're pregnant?" I ask. The words tumble out of my mouth freely as the shock sets in.

"It wasn't planned. I'm sorry, Ali. I didn't mean to hurt you. It just happened," Miranda explains quickly as if that makes everything okay.

I literally stand there shaking my head, unable to process everything that has happened tonight.

"Get … the fuck … *out*," I scream at her, my hand shaking angrily as I point to the door.

"Ali, please! I'm so sorry," Miranda says, holding her hands to her chest.

"Get the fuck out of my home, my life, my everything. I fucking hate you both. I never want to see either of you again. You both make me sick," I roar as my entire body shakes.

"Calm down, Ali." George turns to me and bellows, "Don't talk to her like that."

I shuffle a couple of steps toward my brother as my hands ball into fists, and he quickly pulls Miranda behind him as if my intention is to hurt her. I would never lay a hand on a woman no matter what she has done to me.

But my brother? Fuck yeah! I would fuck him up, no questions asked.

That bastard deserves *everything* he gets.

"I love her, always have," George declares, his eyes narrowing on me as he tries to protect Miranda, who's huddled in behind him.

"How many times do I have to tell you? *Get the hell* out of my house. Get. Out," I shout at them both.

I've heard enough.

Love is not a reason to fuck over your family like this.

Miranda gives me a pained look as George grabs her hand and pulls her out of our home and into the early morning darkness.

I slump to the floor in shock.

2

ALISTAIR

"Is he dead?" I hear a voice.

"He smells dead," another voice adds.

"The guy just got his heart ripped out. Leave him alone," someone else says.

I blink a few times to try to crack open my eyes, but I seem to be having problems with it. A groan falls from my lips as it registers just how much my head throbs. Anguish. Pain. Agony. They all slam into me at once.

"Good, he's alive," a voice states.

The next thing I know, I'm drenched with water. "What the fuck?" I sit up, cursing at whatever asshole did this to me.

"Rise and shine." Jasper grins down at me.

I'm soaked to the bone from the bucket of water that was thrown on me and judging by the smirk on Jasper's face and the bucket in his hand, he's the asshole who did it.

"What the hell are you guys doing here?" I curse as I rub my temples with my fingers trying to get this hell in my head under control.

"Here," Daniel says, handing me two white pills and a glass of water.

I eagerly knock them back and hope the damn pain will subside soon.

"We heard what happened," Alex says, looking down at me with a frown as I'm slumped on my living room floor. There was no way in hell I was going to be sleeping in that bed—my bed—ever again after what I found. The entire thing needs to be burned.

"How?" I ask, rubbing my head, trying to get rid of this hangover. Once George and Miranda left, I drowned my sorrows with my friend vodka, who doesn't appear to be my friend this morning.

"Miranda sent me a message saying you guys broke up and to check in on you," Alex adds.

"That's all she said?" I ask because she seems to be missing a big chunk of the story.

Alex's eyes narrow on me for a moment. "Yeah, that's all she said."

"Guessing she broke up with you," Jasper adds.

I turn and glare at my friend.

"Don't be an insensitive ass," Daniel tells Jasper, who holds his hands up as if to say, *'Don't shoot the messenger'*.

Alex crouches beside me. "What happened?" he asks, as his eyes narrow on me in concern.

"She's pregnant," I tell my friends.

"Guessing you didn't take it well?" Daniel asks cautiously.

"That's not the reason you two broke up?" Alex questions me.

As if I would break up with someone because they were pregnant.

"No," I reply while looking at him angrily.

How dare he think I'd be that much of an asshole!

"It's the fact I'm *not* the damn father that did it!"

My friends all stare at me in silence, and no one dares say a word.

"I'm going to be an uncle instead," I add.

The silence stretches between us all, and it takes them a while to compute what I've said.

"Are you saying your brother is the father?" Jasper asks the dreaded question first.

"I caught them in bed together when I came home last night," I explain.

"Fuck!" Daniel curses.

"No wonder you smell like a brewery," Jasper adds, nodding as if it all makes sense.

"That's why your knuckles are fucked, and you have a black eye?" Alex questions while his eyes look over me with concern.

"Yeah, I lost my mind there for a moment," I tell them honestly.

"Don't blame you," Jasper says in agreement.

"I don't understand why Miranda would do that," Daniel states.

"I don't understand either." I sigh as I scrub my face trying to remove the images of them together in bed from my mind.

"You need a shower, some food, and then we'll talk some more. But we've got you, okay?" Alex tells me.

I nod, and he holds out a hand to help me off the floor. I'm a little shaky on my feet, but he steadies me and then pushes me toward the bathroom. Jumping into the shower, I let the warm water run over my body, easing my bruised muscles. I hope George feels as shitty as I do this morning. It's unbelievable what he has done to me again. Angrily, I thump my fist against the tiles of my shower. My shoulders sag while the weight of the life I thought I was headed toward crumbles in on me. As I slump to the shower floor, I let the water run cold.

"I did not sign up to see your dick today," Jasper grumbles as he helps me from the shower floor. Alex is also there with a towel and hands it to me. After wrapping it around my waist, I head to the guest room, slump into the armchair, and stare at my best friends. We've been through thick and thin, the four of us.

Alex—his fiancée had an affair with his enemy and used him to steal company secrets.

Jasper—he refuses to let a woman get close to him since his first love rejected his proposal and married his best friend.

Daniel—he's nowhere near ready to settle, if ever, after he witnessed his father blackmail his mother his entire life. It wasn't until she was on her death bed that his mother was able to tell Daniel about his half-brother. His dad had an affair with his secretary and then shipped her away out of sight. Daniel's father made him choose between his inheritance or finding his brother. He chose to find his brother because, for him, it was a no-brainer, and he ended up being the world-famous artist, Louis Marchant. Plus, the guy is French and enjoys women a little too much.

"Why the fuck did they do this to me?" I ponder more to myself, but it's come out as a question.

They all stand around shrugging their shoulders or giving me their best lost-for-words looks.

"Of all the people he could have fucked ... why her? Why *my girl?*"

"George has *always* been competitive," Alex suggests, knowing my family dynamics. I've known Alex for most of my life, except when his family moved to America for a short time.

"And a self-serving fuckhead," Jasper adds.

Yep, he's never been a fan of George. I've known Jasper since infancy, and our parents are still friends after all these years.

"What's happened has nothing to do with you," Daniel replies, hoping it will make me feel better. It doesn't. Daniel is the newest member of our friendship group. Jasper and I met him at university where Dan and I found out we were dating the same girl—we gave her the flick and became instant friends.

"It feels like it does with George," I say on a sigh, exhausted by everything.

The sound of keys rattling in the door has us all pausing.

Who the fuck is that?

My heart beats furiously in my chest as panic begins to travel through my veins when I hear Miranda call out my name.

"Get dressed and hear her out," Alex tells me.

"We'll run block," Jasper adds as my boys head downstairs.

Thank fuck for these guys. I'm glad I have them in my corner. Quickly, I get dressed and head on down where I hear voices being raised.

"You have a lot of nerve showing up here, you fucking asshole," Alex curses angrily.

"I'm here to support Miranda. I don't need to explain myself to you dickheads," my asshole brother argues back.

The hairs on the back of my neck rise as I rush downstairs. They are standing together, and instantly I'm filled with seething rage as I look at the two of them together.

Daniel reaches out and wraps his hand around my wrist, holding me in place.

Miranda appears pale, and I notice for the first time the dark circles under her eyes and the weight she has lost. Her blue eyes land on me, and there's remorse, but I don't give a shit. It's unforgivable what she has done. This woman knows the relationship I have with my older brother and how competitive he is with me. All my life, he has seen me as his greatest competition and will stop at nothing to be the best, to beat me at everything. There are only thirteen months between us, and we look like twins except that he has dark hair, and I have blond.

"What the hell are you two doing here? I thought I told you last night to fuck off," I yell at them.

Miranda flinches at my venom, but my brother simply smirks. He's looking happy with himself this morning knowing just how horribly he has hurt me.

"Suck it up, Ali. I'm here for Miranda. She's the one who's worried about you," George sneers in my direction.

What the hell is wrong with this asshole? He's the one who's been fucking my fiancée.

Miranda steps forward and tries to reach for me, but I pull my hands back—I don't want her touching me.

"I'm so sorry, Ali," she says as the tears begin to fall down her cheeks. "I never wanted to hurt you, but I know I did."

Never wanted to hurt me!

NEVER WANTED TO HURT ME!

What the hell! She didn't think getting knocked up by my brother would hurt me? I do *not* know who this woman is anymore.

"Why?" I ask.

"Because I'm the better man, that's why," George adds.

Jasper punches him in the stomach, and he buckles over.

"You asshole!" George groans as he holds his stomach. "What the fuck?"

"Stay fucking silent, or I ... will ... *end you*," Jasper growls.

George shuts up, but he continues to grumble words we can't quite hear.

"You were always away," Miranda states.

She's going to use it as an excuse for what she's done?

"You stole her from me first," George adds angrily.

What the HELL is he talking about?

Miranda looks over at my brother and then back to me.

"How the hell did I steal my own fiancée?" I yell at George.

Has the damn idiot lost his mind? What reality is he living in?

Miranda sighs. "I met George before I met you, Ali."

Huh? A frown forms on my face as I look over at Miranda.

Just how many secrets has she been keeping from me?

"We dated a long time ago before we ever met," Miranda states.

I look over and glare at George, confused by this news.

"We dated in university," George adds that missing piece of information.

My eyes flick to Miranda, who nods.

What the hell?

I don't understand.

Why did she keep this from me?

Why did they *both* keep this from me?

"George and I weren't serious in university, but we did date on and off for the entire time we were both there," Miranda confesses.

Years? They dated on and off for years?

That's something she should have fucking told me about. He wasn't some one-night-stand bullshit.

"We weren't ready to be together then. It wasn't our time," George adds, and his confession makes my stomach sink and roll as I try and hold back the bile that's creeping up my throat.

And now it is their time?

Is that what he's saying?

"I didn't realize you were related to George until you brought me home for the first time, and I met him at the dinner table," Miranda explains in a more quiet and measured tone.

"That was four years ago," I question.

"I should have told you then, but I didn't know how, and George was dating someone else, so it didn't matter. We agreed to keep it a secret for the sake of our partners," she explains.

"How long have the two of you been fucking around?" I ask through gritted teeth.

They both remain silent.

"*How. Fucking. Long?*" I ask, raising my voice.

Miranda jumps, and she blinks a few times before recovering her calm exterior.

"After that first family dinner," George adds, raising a brow at me in some sort of conquest. The smugness on his face as he drops that nugget of truth on me turns my seething lethal.

Miranda glares at him, then turns to me and nods once.

Four fucking years!

Practically our entire relationship.

"I couldn't believe you brought her home with you. I was so angry. She was the one who got away. The one woman I could never get out of my mind. I knew she was dating someone seriously, but I didn't know who. Then there she was at our family's dinner table with you," George tells me angrily.

How the hell is this my fault? I'm not fucking psychic.

"It was fate that brought her back into my life again that night. I had to know if she still felt the same way. So we slipped away, and when I questioned her about it, I knew she did, so I fucked her in my childhood bedroom," George confesses.

They fucked that night?

Miranda looks down at her feet sheepishly.

Are they fucking serious?

Why didn't she break up with me?

Why did she keep up this fucking charade for all these years?

What the hell did she think was going to happen when we got married?

Would George have stood up when the priest asked, *'If anyone objects ...'* and taken her away from me at that moment out of some sort of spite?

I can't listen to these two any longer. Miranda's as bad as my brother—she could have said no so many times, but she didn't. She kept fucking him, knowing just how much this would devastate me.

"Get out! Get the fuck out of my house! *Now*," I holler. "I hate you both. Go to hell," I continue to yell as Daniel holds me back, and Alex and Jasper show them the door.

Miranda rushes out in tears, but George lingers on the doorstep.

"Miranda is mine now. She's carrying my baby. You ever need to speak to her, you go through me. You hear me?" George points at me. "She lives with me now. We're going to be a family. My ring will be on her finger soon. Get used to it, Ali," George states as he walks out of my home with the woman I loved.

"That is some seriously fucked-up shit, Ali," Alex declares as he slams the door behind my brother.

"I need a drink," Jasper relays while shaking his head.

"You didn't deserve that. You don't deserve any of it," Daniel says quietly behind me.

"Fuck them! Let's get drunk," I declare.

3

ALISTAIR

"I know you might not be ready for this, but it's here if you want it," Alex says, sliding a black box across the table.

The boys have taken me out to celebrate my birthday, the first since breaking up with Miranda months ago. My brother was right, Miranda moved straight into his home, and instantly they started playing happy family as if I never existed.

The kicker was my parents siding with George and Miranda.

They said that what they did to me was unforgivable, but Miranda was having a baby, their first grandchild, and they didn't want any animosity over how the baby's parents got together to ruin the relationship they wanted to build with their grandchild. Which, reading between the lines, basically means that George had probably threatened them with not seeing the baby if they didn't support his relationship, and as the firstborn and the heir to the empire my parents have created, they must have folded.

This is the reason I never went to work with my father. I never wanted to be indebted to anyone in my family for money. Plus, I never wanted to work in finance nor have George as my boss. I used my trust fund money on my eighteenth birthday to buy into the nightclub I was working at and built my empire that way. I own some of the best nightclubs around the world.

The best part about my empire is that it was all me. *I* created my empire. No one handed me the keys to one already built.

George sent packers a couple of days after everything went down to collect Miranda's things after our altercation. He stated that day that he never wanted the two of us to be alone together again, probably scared that she might slip into her old ways and sleep with the other brother. She is, after all, a serial cheater.

She tried once when she came over during the day while George was out of the country. She gave me the tears, the sob story of being in love with both of us, that if she weren't pregnant, she would never have left, but she also let it slip that she wouldn't have stopped sleeping with George either.

Yeah, I didn't want to hear it, and the more I listened to her excuses, the more I realized that Miranda's a narcissist, and I was fooling myself all these years by thinking she was *the one* for me. She wasn't sorry for breaking my heart. What she really was sorry for was getting caught.

She did disclose that George is demanding a paternity test to make sure she truly is pregnant with *his* baby. I couldn't imagine anything worse than finding out that the baby is mine and not George's. Of course, I would be there for the baby, but I won't be tied to this woman anymore.

The results came back a couple of weeks later that George is the baby's father, and I don't think I've ever been happier.

Now, the two of them can go on and live the life they always wanted together without me being in the way.

"What is it?" I ask, staring down at the black box.

"Open it and see," Alex presses.

I open the box and stare down at the gold credit card, but there's nothing on it except my name and a number. I look up at Alex with a confused frown. Jasper chuckles excitedly beside us while Daniel sits there sipping his whiskey in silence.

"It's membership to The Paradise Club," Alex explains.

My eyes widen as I realize what this means. *Well, damn.* This is exactly what I need—full access to a secret society sex club. Alex doesn't talk about what his brother's business is but seeing as I've known the family my entire life, Alex talks about it with us. Nate explained his vision years ago, and now he's created this adult fantasyland for the wealthy. I never wanted to be a member because I was with Miranda and never thought I would ever need its services.

I stare down at the gold card and turn it over in my fingers. I'm waiting for angels to start singing or something. It's like I've stumbled upon the holy grail.

"That is going to get you over your heartbreak *really quickly.*" Jasper chuckles.

"Only when he's ready," Alex adds, not wanting to push me.

Fuck George.

Fuck Miranda.

I want to have some fun.

"Let's go check it out, now. You dickheads seem to enjoy going there. Maybe I'll give you all a run for your money," I joke.

"No one wants to see your dick. I already know mine's bigger anyway," Jasper says before bursting out laughing.

"You sure you're ready?" Alex asks with a frown.

"To have sex … yes. For a relationship … hell, no," I reply.

He, of all people, understands why I wouldn't want to rush into another relationship, but unlike Mr. Romantic, Alex, I don't think I'll ever be ready for another one. I hope I don't turn into Jasper though, because eventually, I would like to settle down, whereas Jasper is content to be a bachelor for the rest of his days.

Alex gives me a nod, and we head out of the restaurant and straight into his car. His driver takes us into the heart of the city before turning down an alleyway, and we hop out. There's nothing but darkness, and I'm wondering if we're about to get mugged in the seedy, rough area. Then Alex swipes his card against a reader attached to the bricks, and a beep bounces off the dark walls. A door opens as light streams out into the alleyway. We all step into the light and are greeted by a gorgeous blonde in a designer evening dress with a plunging neckline.

"Welcome, Mr. Lewis, Mr. Fox, Mr. DuPont," she says, smiling at my friends. "And Mr. King, welcome to The Paradise Club. We are incredibly happy that you have become a member. My name is Clara. I'm sure Mr. Lewis has explained how the club works."

My head spins to Alex, and he shrugs his shoulders.

What the hell has he forgotten to tell me?

Clara glances at Alex and then back to me.

"We're going to leave him with you, Clara. We'll meet you at the bar," Alex tells me as the boys walk through the golden door and disappear.

"My friends are assholes," I say, which brings a smile to Clara's lips. My eyes dip at how pink and glossy they are, and I wonder what it would be like to have them wrapped around my dick.

"Firstly, my bracelet is black, which sadly means I don't play," she explains as if she can read my mind. *Was I that obvious?* "There will be some staff inside the club who have colored bracelets which means they are willing to play. Each color means something different. Every member wears them, so it's easily identifiable what the individual is interested in," Clara states as she displays the bracelets before me. "It's your turn to pick what you're interested in. They are not set in stone, and you can change your preferences at any time."

Nerves begin to spark across my body as I stare down at the rainbow of colors before me, wondering what I want out of this experience.

"Pink is for exploring women, blue is for exploring men. White is no sexual intercourse, but all other play is okay. Red is intercourse, and all play is okay. Yellow is exploring with one person only. Green is if you want an experience with multiple people. Purple is okay with public play. Orange is if you prefer to play behind closed doors. And last, the black band is mainly for staff and anyone who doesn't want to play," she explains.

I pick my colors—pink, red, yellow, green, and purple.

Clara hands me my bracelets with a smile. "Bottom level of the club where the bar is located is strictly no play whatsoever. It's a place where you can meet people and mingle before taking it upstairs to the fun. The club does *not* allow drunkenness in any way. This is a safe environment." She looks at me for acknowledgment, and I nod.

"The levels of the club differ. The first level is the beginner level, still boundary-pushing but nothing extreme. The next level is medium and where most club members head. The top-level is our extreme play level, which is mainly for people who are into levels of play that the average person may not be into as well as fetishes and so on," Clara advises me.

Yeah, that may be a little out of my wheelhouse for a newbie.

"You can take a map if you wish," she says, handing me the slip of paper which has the layout of the club easily distinguishable. "Mr. Lewis has already sent through your sexual health report which is clean. Now go inside and enjoy your night, Mr. King." She smiles while holding open the golden door for me.

I step through and am instantly surrounded by dark leather, brass fixtures, and polished wooden tables—it looks like an underground speakeasy. There's a wall of bottles behind the large oval-shaped bar that stands in the middle of the room. Scattered around the area are booths with dimly lit lights in the middle of each table with people talking and laughing—it's as if this is any other London club. Walls are kept raw with brick, and in other areas, the wallpaper appears almost like leather. It's spectacular, luxurious, and welcoming.

My friends at the bar are all holding an old fashioned in their hands. As I approach, Daniel holds out one for me, and I take it from him.

"Look at this face. He seems overwhelmed," Jasper jokes, then he takes a sip of his drink.

"I'm not overwhelmed. I'm in awe of how amazing this place looks and can't wait to give things a try," I say, looking over at Alex.

"Yeah, Nate did a good job. You'd have no idea what lies above," Alex states, wiggling his brows.

I stare at the grand staircase that leads to the upper levels, trying to imagine what could possibly be behind those velvet ropes that security is standing beside.

"It's everything you can imagine," Daniel states, taking in where my eyes have fallen, his French accent swirling around the words emphasizing the insane thoughts running through my mind.

"Come on, then. I'm sure Ali is eager to check it out." Alex grins as we all throw back our drinks, and I follow my friends up the grand staircase.

Security scans our bracelets and lets us through.

My eyes widen as I see what's happening before my eyes. A glass cube stands in the middle of the floor, and there are people standing around in the darkness watching what's inside. *Is this a cult?* Then one of the guys elbows me, and I realize what everyone is looking at inside the cube. I'm not going to lie, my eyes widen as I watch a woman on her knees with a guy's dick in her mouth, his fingers are laced in her chocolate strands while she sits on the face of a woman lying down on the floor. That woman's hands are gripping the other woman's ass all the while her legs are wide open as another man is fucking her. Moans begin to echo through the room as I look around in the darkness wondering where the hell they are coming from. That's when I notice people all around me are in various states of play.

"There's a speaker," Daniel tells me as the moans begin to

bounce off the walls around us. My dick twitches to life, and I rearrange myself.

"You can stay and watch the show or head toward any of the doors marked with a green light and order whatever you want," Alex informs me as I see Jasper and Daniel walk off toward the doors. "Behind them are rooms for play … you have the option of people watching and listening if you want. There is also a menu so you can order anything you like from it," he explains to me.

"I'm not really hungry after dinner," I tell him, which has him chuckling.

"It's not just food you can order," Alex informs.

Well, damn.

"Go enjoy, let loose, and forget about your life for a couple of hours." Alex smiles as he claps me on the back, shoving me toward the rooms.

My hand lands on the knob of the first door that has a green light on, so I open, step in, and close it behind me. Instantly, the light turns red, which must mean it's now occupied while my eyes focus on what's around me.

It looks like a luxurious hotel room but with a little bit more. There is a large round bed in the middle of the room with faux furs thrown all over it. The walls are made to appear like ice, as if I might be in an ice palace. There's also a fireplace on one wall with two chairs that look like beds and another faux fur rug in front of the fake fire. On the other wall is an array of toys for the occupant to use—floggers, whips, chains, handcuffs, wax candles, and massage oils. Then on the other side, there's a wooden desk with a tablet on a stand in the middle. I pick it up and swipe it open. My bracelet lights up, and the tablet's voice welcomes me to the club. It then explains how the rooms work, that there is a button to open curtains and turn on microphones if I would like people to watch. Then it explains the different items on the menu from ordering food and drinks to toys, and all the way down to the different experiences I could be after. There was also a menu of gorgeous women on offer to help facilitate anything I desire.

This is seriously mind-blowing, and why have I not been here before?

Because Miranda would not have been interested in this.

True, but we wouldn't have had to share each other—it would have been fun just the two of us.

She was into sharing, just you weren't included.

My breath hitches in my chest as I try to shake the thoughts of Miranda from my mind.

Screw her.

Why am I allowing that bitch to affect my enjoyment of the club?

How dare she filter through my thoughts while I'm in a place like this. She made her bed, and she can damn well sleep in it with my brother.

I swipe through the different options, which has become overwhelming. Having all your desires laid out before you like a smorgasbord is a lot to take in all at once.

How do I even pick?

4

ELOISE

"Hey, Elle, you're needed up in room fifty-seven for Mr. King. He's a new member, first night, and is very good friends with Mr. Lewis," Sara informs me. Sara is the client resources manager, making sure all The Paradise Club clients' requests are met. She then hands me a tablet that contains all the details about Mr. King.

"Lucky bitch. I love getting the new members, and he's hot too," Lauren, my best friend, says over my shoulder while staring at my tablet. I glance down at the color photograph of Mr. King and take him in. He is gorgeous, Lauren isn't wrong there, with his sandy-colored hair that isn't cut or styled to perfection, unlike the many other suits that come in. It's a little longer and shaggier than the norm. He has a light stubble growing as if he didn't have enough time to be clean-cut, and I like it. He's tall as per his profile—six feet two—and he looks like he works out. He is trim and taut with well-defined muscles, but he's not a gym junkie. He has a nice sense of style in his profile pictures, likes to travel, obviously—there are some images with him in nothing but boardshorts looking like he's in Ibiza or somewhere equally as exotic with his six-pack abs on display. He has a tanned body as if he spends his days in the sun. One picture shows him with his arm slung around some male friends who are all equally as gorgeous as him. Now that I think about it, I've seen a couple of them in the club, but I've never had the pleasure of being with them.

I wonder why he's become a member now when I know the rest of the guys have been members since I've worked here, which has been the last couple of years. Maybe he is single again? Then again—as if being in a relationship stops some of the clients we get in here.

"You're drooling, Elle. Pick up your jaw," Lauren teases me.

Not all guests are as gorgeous as Mr. King, but that doesn't mean I don't have fun with the ones I may not be attracted to. You're not going to be sexually attracted to every person, but to be fair, the caliber of hot people who are part of this club sits high.

The Paradise Club vets its members, so the club is filled with the best people who are part of the one percent. They come here because it's safe, and they know that what happens in the club isn't going to be sold to the tabloids. There are, of course, some dickheads who slip through the cracks, but they are few and far between, and I've never once felt unsafe working here.

Not all the guests are here to live out weird and wild fetishes, there are some guests who don't even want sex. Sometimes they want me to sit and watch them with their partner, or they want me to teach them certain aspects of sex play. Then there are others who want to explore with another but don't want any entanglements after, so playing at the club is safer for them.

"Lauren, Eloise. Ruby would like to see you before your sessions quickly," Sara adds.

We both look at each other, and my heart begins beating quickly over the thought that our boss wants to speak to Lauren and me.

"Are we in trouble?" I turn and ask my friend.

"Hell no, you and I are the best. Probably a raise," she says while wiggling her brows at me.

Maybe she's right. I do love my job. I know it's not a job for everyone, but it suits me fine, plus the money is outstanding.

I don't consider myself a prostitute. I like sex. No, *I love sex*. And just because a guest requests me doesn't mean they automatically get sex. I have a choice whether to continue depending on the vibe between the guest and me. There hasn't been a case yet where I have turned someone down. I have, however, declined certain requests during a session and have found someone else to fulfill those particular needs. That's why I love working here—the company and the guests are so respectful.

Some days like any other job, you may not feel like having sex, and that's okay too. You let Sara know, and she places the black band on your wrist, and you will usually head on out to the bar or be a voyeur in certain situations. Everyone who comes to The Paradise Club respects the colored bands. You can't run a successful sex empire if people don't respect the rules.

This wasn't at all how I saw my life turning out—being someone's walking, talking sexual fantasy was not on my career list. I've always been sexually adventurous, but I grew up in an ultra-conservative home where I needed to dress and act a certain way in front of my family.

The old saying 'Kids should be seen and not heard' was me growing up, and as an only child, it was pushed upon me even more. As soon as I could, I rebelled against the constraints of my parents, especially at boarding school, where I was afforded much more freedom than if I were at home.

As soon as I graduated from high school, I moved out of my family home and in with Lauren, who I met at boarding school, and then fell into the modeling world. Lauren's family owned the agency, so I was in good hands, but I had to wait until my eighteenth birthday to sign with them as my parents forbade me from doing it.

It wasn't a respectable career!

But marrying some blue blood was.

When they found out I had signed with the agency, they cut me off, which was fine by me because I was making my own money, even if it was next to nothing. Let's be serious, I was no supermodel.

Lauren and I then spent the next five years traveling the world, living hand to mouth, working, wandering, and partying. Lauren has always been a free spirit and utterly unconventional which is why I love her. She started organizing these traveling sex parties for wealthy young people where she would hire luxury homes and basically get everyone drunk to have an orgy. Lauren knew all the right people and had access to hot, rich people. I knew what she was doing, but at the time, it wasn't for me. I wasn't really an orgy-loving kind of girl.

As the summers went on, the more my inhibitions started to disappear until I *was* that kind of girl—the kind who didn't mind fucking in public and didn't care if she was kissing a man or woman or whoever if she was feeling good. It was liberating. Never in my life have I ever felt as desired or as confident in myself as I did during those summers.

As the years went on, someone approached Lauren and me during one of her parties and asked if we would be interested in working full-time in something like we were doing already but instead of doing it for free, we would be paid. They explained how The Paradise Club worked and how much money we could be earning from doing essentially what we were giving away for free. They discussed the concept, that it was discreet, and no one would know who we were, and if they did, they would never say anything because they would risk their membership.

The last couple of years of partying and having fun with Lauren has been great and what I needed after having my life so heavily controlled, but I needed to work out what I wanted to do with all this freedom. I hadn't continued onto university to spite my parents. I didn't think partying, traveling, and having sex was an actual career either. I knew I needed to save for my future seeing as I had been cut off from my trust fund. I had dreams for a different life for myself.

The offer to work at The Paradise Club happened at the right time. Lauren and I agreed to work there for a short time to see if we could earn the kind of money they were saying we could. They told us we could quit at any time if we changed our minds. We took the opportunity, and here we are two years later. I think one more year here, and I will be at the goal amount for what I need to chase my dreams.

Lauren knocks on Ruby's office door.

Ruby calls out, "Come. Take a seat, ladies." She points to the two chairs in front of her desk. Nervously, I take a seat and try to calm my pounding heart.

Goddammit! This is it! I'm about to be fired.

They want me to do this one last guest, and then I'm being let go.

"I'll be quick as I know you're both scheduled upstairs," Ruby says seriously. "I had a meeting with Mr. Lewis earlier, and he asked for a couple more girls to join him on his new project at the resort in the Caribbean. He wanted me to suggest two girls who I thought would be best for the job. And that brings me to you two ..." she says while smiling at us.

Lauren and I glance at each other before looking back at Ruby.

"Would you be interested in working at the new Paradise Club resort?"

Lauren and I look at each other again, but neither one of us is game to speak because we don't believe what we're hearing.

"Are you asking if Eloise and I are willing to move to the Caribbean?" Lauren asks our boss.

"Yes, I think you girls are always up for an adventure. Plus, you will be getting a raise for going due to the island's remoteness." Ruby smirks.

"How much more?" I ask.

"Nearly double what you're earning now. You will be working longer hours compared to the club here, though. Everything is included ... meals, drinks, gym, beauty, and you'll have access to all the resort facilities on your day off free of charge," Ruby explains.

My mind is racing a hundred miles a minute as I take in everything Ruby is saying.

"How have we not said yes yet?" Lauren turns and smiles at me.

"It's going to be hard work. You will be at the guests' beck and call twenty-four hours a day until they leave the island," Ruby warns.

"No bills, Elle. You can save *all your money*," Lauren says, nodding enthusiastically. Lauren's right, if everything is paid for, then my entire wage is saved. I'm going to be that much closer to my dream.

"Hell, yeah, let's do it," I say, giving Lauren a wide smile.

"Fuck, yeah!" She squeals.

"Great! It's still a little while away regarding the move, but they wanted to finalize the number of staff who will be on the island. You'll have to share a villa with two other people," Ruby advises.

"But it's all-inclusive?" Lauren asks.

"Yes!" Ruby nods.

"Then I'm okay with sharing. As long as the two of us are together, that's all that matters," Lauren states.

"Don't worry, I've made a note of it on your files. If that's all, ladies, you're dismissed," she says with a smile, and we both stand and walk quickly out of her office. As soon as the door shuts behind us, we jump up and down like crazy people.

"I can't believe they chose us for the resort," I say to Lauren excitedly.

"See, I told you we had nothing to worry about. We are fricken awesome," Lauren states smugly as she gives me a tight hug.

"Girls, *enough* chitchat! Go to your guests," Sara calls down the corridor to us.

Shit! That's right, Mr. King is waiting for me.

"I'm so going to fuck the shit out of Mr. Fox when I get up there." Lauren squeals as she kisses my cheek and disappears down one of the dark tunnels that have been built behind the guest rooms to hide our entrance.

I can't keep the smile off my face as I walk along the tunnels toward the room. Tonight, Mr. King has asked for a happy ending massage which is tame for a beginner—I guess it's first-time jitters. It's the safest thing to choose if you're unsure of what The Paradise Club has to offer.

After I reach the door, I peek through the one-way window at the top, which allows me to see into the room without the guest knowing, just to check that everything is as it seems.

Mr. King is walking around the room raking his hands through his hair and muttering to himself. *Is this guy a hot nut case?* They should have mentioned that in his profile. I take in his large body which is dressed in jeans and a tailored white shirt with the sleeves rolled up on his thick, tanned, corded forearms. There's a platinum watch on his left hand which I can't quite make out the model, but I know the brand—expensive, at least fifty thousand pounds expensive.

Who the hell are you, Mr. King?

The longer I stay there, the more I realize he looks like he's moments away from bolting from the room, and I don't want that to happen. Not now that I have seen him in the flesh, and excited tingles are beginning to lace my body. Plus, I'm in the mood to celebrate, and I want to celebrate with him.

My hand pushes the door open, and I step into the room. The sound of the door unlocking from behind him has Mr. King turning around quickly. His hazel eyes flare with interest as they give me one long sweep up and down before a smile falls across his lips.

This is going to be fun.

5

ALISTAIR

Once I hit send on my request, I start to freak the fuck out. Not sure why but I get in my head that I've just ordered a prostitute. I've never done that before. Never once have I had to pay for sex. Technically, I know I'm not paying for sex, but the membership fee includes sex, so is that the same? But then again, I never paid for a membership so does that mean Alex bought me sex?

Yeah, I'm freaking out.

So what!

Who cares who did what and when?

Everything that's happened over these past months seems to have hit me all at once. I haven't been with anyone since finding out about Miranda. My only release has been found via my hand, which is sad.

But how can I trust another woman after what Miranda did to me?

How can I *ever* trust anyone else around my brother?

No. I need to stay single.

No good can ever come from being in a relationship.

So this club is better—no strings or expectations attached.

I can do that.

I think?

What happens if Miranda has fucked me up so much mentally that I won't be able to get it up with another woman?

What kind of loser can't get their dick hard at a sex club? Probably this loser here, who's having a panic attack like a princess.

Maybe I should cancel my order?

"She's not a fucking bag of fries, Ali," I curse at myself.

Okay, I'm officially losing it—I am talking to myself.

The sound of a door opening behind me has me turning around quickly, and my breath hitches at the gorgeous woman standing before me. My dick twitches to life, and the stress of the last ten minutes begins to subside from my shoulders as I take in this woman. She's tall, about five-nine in heels. She has a mane of strawberry blonde curls cascading around her like spun rose gold, then there are her jade green eyes that appear like jewels set against creamy porcelain skin.

My eyes shift further down over her body, taking in the black slip dress that is molded to her like a second skin. Her breasts look natural from here, the swell of her cleavage spilling over the low-cut neckline. My eyes travel further down over her svelte body to where the dress hits at the top of her thighs. I don't even think she could bend over in that dress without exposing herself. I wonder if she will show me? I bite my bottom lip as my eyes travel further to her incredibly long legs in a pair of killer black heels.

"You look a little stressed," the girl states as those green eyes do their own sweep of my body. A small smile falls across her lips, and I'm hoping that means she likes what she sees.

Shit, did she see my freak out?

"It's my birthday," I blurt out as if that makes the mental freak out I was having any damn better.

Her brows raise at my comment. "Then you've come to the

right place to celebrate," she says, her tongue running along her glossy pink lips.

"Didn't think wishes came true when you blew out the candles on your birthday cake, and yet, here you are," I tell her as my words make her smile widen.

"Guess I better make it count. No one wants bad luck on their birthday, do they?" she says, arching her brow at me.

"I've had enough bad luck to last a lifetime," I say, the words tumbling out before I realize what I've said. Good start, Ali, jump in there with your relationship trauma bullshit.

"My name's Elle, and it will be my pleasure tonight to make sure we give you nothing but good luck all night long," she says seductively.

I like the sound of that.

"Why don't you freshen up in the bathroom behind those doors while I set up your table for your massage," she says, pointing to a concealed door.

How did I not notice that before?

I give her a nod and walk over to where she gestured, place my hand on the wall, and a door opens, which leads to a concealed bathroom. I step in and close the door behind me. It's a decent-size bathroom with a large wooden tub and a two-person shower with stone seats inside the cubicle. Quickly, I get undressed and jump into the shower and under the cool water. Once I'm clean, I step out and grab a white towel to dry myself, then I wrap it around my waist because I'm about to get naked anyway, so why bother redressing. I step out of the bathroom and back into the room where there's a white massage table set up, but I notice there are two holes, one for my face and one for my ... *dick!*

He twitches again at the thought of what she's going to be doing that requires my dick to have its own special hole.

Elle looks up at me and smiles as I enter the room. She's

kicked off her heels and has tied her strawberry blonde hair up into a high ponytail.

"If you would like to lay either face up or face down," she says, waving her hand in front of the table.

"Which would you prefer?" I ask.

My question has her pausing for a moment as those green eyes roam over me again. "Face up for now," she states, giving me a warm smile.

Okay, then, she wants to see what I'm packing first. I'm down with that. I drop my towel and stand before her proudly because I know what I'm packing between my legs is a good solid length.

Elle licks her lips hungrily, which makes him jump under her watchful gaze, and she chuckles.

"He seems ready." Elle smirks, looking down at my dick.

Oh, he most certainly is.

I don't reply other than in my mind and jump onto the massage table and lay down.

Elle busies herself to the side setting up towels and smelling massage oils until she lands on one that she likes the scent of. I watch as she squirts a little onto her hands and rubs them together. The scent of French lavender fills the air, and I inhale deeply and feel my body almost instantly relax.

"Close your eyes," she says faintly. Soft hands fall against my chest as she spreads the lavender oil over my skin. "Take a deep breath in," she says, and I inhale the relaxing scent. "Now exhale out," she commands, and I do as I'm told.

The tension I was experiencing earlier begins to subside as her hands move over my body. Fingers dig into the tight muscles of my arms, shoulders, and thighs. My dick is standing to attention, but she keeps moving around it, which is goddamn torture.

"I want to help you relax before we have fun," she whispers in my ear as if she can read my thoughts.

A smile falls across my lips, and I settle in and enjoy her hands moving over my body. Didn't realize how much I needed this massage until the tension begins releasing, inch by inch, my muscles constricting and unleashing with the drama of the last couple of months seeming to disappear. My body has become putty in her hands, and my lids feel heavy the more I relax into her movements. Then her hand swipes along my dick, and my eyes flick open wide as a groan rumbles through my chest causing her to giggle at the sound.

"Seems like it's been a while since he's had any action," Elle purrs as she slides her hand over my dick, pulling another throaty groan from me.

"It has been. Fuck," I curse as she expertly grips my dick.

"I don't believe you. A man like you surely would have women falling at your feet." She chuckles.

"I wasn't ready."

Her hand stills while wrapped around my dick.

My eyes fly open at her sudden stop.

"If you tell me you're a virgin, I ..." she trails off, but there's seriousness in those green eyes looking at me.

I sit up onto my elbows. "What would you do if I was?" I arch a brow in her direction.

Her hand falls away from my dick, and I hate the feeling of loss that comes with it. She places her hands on her hips and looks at me seriously. "I don't sleep with virgins," she states.

Elle doesn't have time to react as I reach out and grab her, picking her up and depositing her over my dick, straddling me on the massage table.

"Lucky then, I'm no virgin," I growl as my fingers dig into her hips. "But it has been a while since I've fucked anything other than my hand for the last couple of months, thanks to finding out my ex was a cheating whore," I tell her honestly.

Those green eyes widen at my confession before a frown forms on her face. "Who the hell is cheating on a man like you?" she asks bluntly.

"Guess I should take that as a compliment," I tell her as my hands move up her sides. My dick presses against her warm silk-clad pussy.

"You should, you're gorgeous. Not that good-looking people can't get cheated on, but seriously, did this woman have rocks in her head?" she says honestly, which has me chuckling.

"Guess she did," I answer as my hands move further up her sides until my thumbs brush over her hardened nipples, which immediately has her biting down on her lower lip.

"It makes sense now why you were freaking out before I arrived," she muses.

"You saw that?"

Elle nods. "It makes sense. Do you still love her?" she asks.

I shake my head. "No, not anymore. Not now she's pregnant to another man."

"Oh ..." her brows shoot up high, "... that sucks," she adds.

I nod in agreement as my thumbs continue to roam over her nipples.

"Then I guess you've come to the right place to get over her." She grins.

"I think you're the medicine I want and need."

"I most certainly am." Her eyes sparkle as she rubs herself across my dick.

One of my hands moves up from her breasts and slides around her throat as she continues to dry hump me. A gasp falls from her lips, and those green eyes widen as my hand tightens ever so gently, but she doesn't stop me. We both stare at each other for a couple of moments as the electricity begins to crackle between us.

I want her.

No, I need her.

Elle's hand slides between her thighs, and her fingers wrap around my dick again. She uses the tip of my dick to move her underwear to the side as she runs it through her wet folds.

Teasing me.

Pushing me.

Waiting to see if I'll crack.

Her green eyes are filled with heat as she continues to torture me, her teeth have sunk into her bottom lip hard as she continues to glide the head of my dick through her wetness. Her pulse throbs against my hand, and I give her throat a tiny squeeze which makes it accelerate against my hand.

"Would you like a condom, or would you like to go bare?" she asks me.

The question stills me for a moment.

"We are tested regularly. All the women have IUDs. All guests are tested regularly before they come to the club. The choice is yours?" she explains before reaching between us and pulling out a condom from a secret compartment in the massage table.

"Condom, please," I reply before looking at the foil square she's holding between her fingers.

Elle gives me a grin and quickly rips open the foil then with practiced ease, she sheaths me. She then whips off her black slip dress, and before I have a chance to admire her naked body, she is impaling herself on my dick.

"Fuck," I hiss as I enter her.

It's been too long.

Far too long.

My hand is the poorest substitute for a woman's pussy.

"You feel so good," I tell her, as my hand stays wrapped around her throat.

Elle bites her bottom lip as she continues to ride me.

I stare up at this beautiful woman and commit to memory every curve of her body. The way her nipples harden and turn a darker pink, the more turned on she gets. The way her cunt tightens around my dick in time with my hand around her throat. She is exquisite. I watch as her green eyes go from light green to an almost precious jade color. The tiny mews that fall from her pouty lips make me want to taste them.

Maybe I should?

Is that against the rules?

"I want to kiss you?" I ask, unsure if that's something she wants.

"Stop thinking," she says, looking down at me with a smile falling playfully across her lips.

I'm momentarily distracted by her gorgeous tits bouncing in front of my eyes. Never have I been consumed by a woman before.

Is this how all men feel when they come here?

Is this normal?

Or is my dick that good?

"Stop it," Elle says, gritting her teeth as her pussy clamps down against my dick, and my eyes roll back inside my head. "I can see it all over your face … you're overthinking this. Don't! I want to fuck you. Your dick is magnificent, and as soon as I saw it, I wanted it inside me," she tells me. "I want this. I want you. When your request came through, I couldn't wait to get in here," she confesses.

"Really?" I ask, hating that I sound so damn needy. That's not me. Before Miranda, I would have grabbed a girl and fucked her until we both came and then do it all over again and again until neither one of us could walk. But ever since Miranda, I've lost my mojo. She's emasculated me by fucking my brother.

The next thing I know, Elle has slapped me across the face, and I still.

"Oh shit, I'm sorry. I um … needed you to stop freaking out, and I thought you might like it. I-I th … think I was wrong," she says quickly, stumbling over her words. Those green eyes are wide as she slowly stops riding me for the moment. "I'm sorry, I took that too far." She cups my face, her thumb running over the warm patch where her palm whacked my skin, soothing away the sting.

If I'm honest, it's exactly what I fucking needed. It's like she just reset me. She's right, I have been in my head. I've been freaking out about coming to a sex club. A club where I can do and be anyone I want to be. I have one of the most gorgeous women I've ever seen riding my dick, and here I am thinking about my ex like a pathetic loser.

Fuck Miranda.

Fuck George.

I need to reclaim Alistair King.

The man I was before.

The man I was when I was happy.

"Fuck it!" I curse as I pull her face to me and press my lips against her. Electricity zips around us as her hands land on my chest, holding herself against me as I catch her off guard with my kiss. Her mouth opens for me, and as soon as mine follows hers, she groans. Our tongues explore each other until it becomes a fight, each of us trying to get the upper hand in the kiss.

My hand wraps around her ponytail, and I pull her head back hard, which pulls a moan from her pouty lips. My mouth meets the thin skin of her neck as I begin to nip my way down her throat.

"Fuck." She moans loudly as she bucks against my dick.

She's intoxicating.

My mouth makes its way down her chest until my teeth tease a nipple. I roll the pink bud in my mouth, letting my tongue swirl around the sensitive skin. Her pussy tightens each time I suck hard on her nipple. I move my way over to the other one and do the same.

"Oh my god!" She groans as her hands fall to my shoulders, her nails digging into my skin as she fucks me harder, enjoying how my tongue is fondling her nipples.

I look up at her darkly, desire beginning to swirl thickly

around me as I let go of her hair and move my hand to her hips as I help Elle to fuck me harder.

She looks down at me, and there's a wide smile on her face. "Now you're out of your head!" She throws her head back and turns her bucking up a notch—

she must be getting closer. She's left her pussy wide open for me, so I slide my hand between her creamy thighs, and my thumb finds her aching clit, and once I slide it over the bud, her pussy begins to choke my dick.

"Yes. Just like that," I tell her with a hiss as her cunt continues to strangle my dick. My fingers continue to play with her clit, and she goes wild on top of me as I push her closer to the edge.

Elle begs me to fuck her harder, so I do. I give her what she's begging for, and my thumb moves across her clit, pushing her as far as I can toward the edge. I was never able to fuck Miranda like this. She would never be wild and free like Elle is with me. She hated fucking me anywhere that wasn't the bed, always had to have the lights off, and had to be quick so she could go to sleep.

I wonder what she's like with George?

"Stay with me," Elle commands, noticing my mind wandering somewhere else yet again. Her hands fall on either side of my face, pulling me from my rogue thoughts. "Fuck me, not her," she tells me.

I shake the ghost of Miranda from my mind with the quick agitation of my head.

"That's it! Yes, yes, stay with me," she tells me, and I do, my eyes never leaving hers as my thumb pushes her over the cliff, and she throws her head back in ecstasy. Elle arches her back as her pussy constricts around my dick. I continue to fuck her through her orgasm—her hands fall to my shoulders, and I move mine back to her hips. She meets me thrust for thrust until I can't hold on any longer and fall right over the edge into oblivion with her.

"Fuck," I curse as my orgasm begins to subside.

Elle giggles as she looks down at me.

"I liked that …" She grins. "We should do it again."

As my dick continues to twitch from aftershocks, I groan because I do want more of her. "Give me ten, and I might be ready again."

"Come, let's have a shower and clean up!" She smiles before leaning down and kissing me.

My hand captures her neck, and I pull her to me, then kiss her wildly, the electricity not dying even after we have come. My need for her is still there, sated but ready for round two as my fingers hold the back of her neck, keeping her lips against mine.

"Come on …" Elle grins as she pulls away from our kiss.

I grab her by the hips as I swing my legs off the table, which has her gasping. Her legs wrap around my hips tightly, and I carry her back to the bathroom, where I undressed earlier. I reach into the two-person shower and fiddle with the faucets until the water reaches the right temperature, then step in and let her finally disengage from me.

She slides down my taut body, kicks off her underwear, and steps under the water. I dispose of the condom, then stand back and watch as the water droplets cascade down over her breasts and stomach before disappearing between her thighs.

"You're so beautiful," I tell her as I reach out and run my finger between her cleavage.

Those green eyes watch me intently as water sprays between us.

"Here … turn around and let me wash you," she says, changing the subject.

I'm sure she hears that comment a million times a day.

She spins me around and begins soaping me up. Her fingers and hands run all over my body before I turn around, take a couple of steps forward, and push her up against the shower wall.

"Now, it's my turn," I say, taking the loofah from her hands and lathering up her body. My hands run along her chest, my fingers quickly finding a nipple to twist, which pulls a gasp from her lips. Then my hands run over her stomach before I fall to my knees in front of her.

Elle's green eyes follow my movements with curiosity. I run the loofah over her thighs, then each leg, before moving back up again, missing the spot I know she wants me to touch. I drop the loofah, pick up her leg, and throw it over my shoulder, which makes her gasp, then my tongue slides between her folds.

Elle's hands fall onto my shoulders, her fingers digging into my skin. Elle pleads, so I give her what she wants, which is my tongue against her clit. My fingers prod her ass cheeks as I continue to devour her from the inside out.

I let a finger slide between her thighs, then another, and her nails push further into my skin. I don't care if she leaves marks because I couldn't stop even if I wanted to—this woman tastes like heaven.

My fingers curl inside her, teasing the delicate nerves that have her pussy clenching against them.

"Fuck, yes," she hisses, and I know I've got her right where I want her. She's moments from coming all over my chin.

My rhythm increases, working her higher until she can't take it any longer and screams her release all over my fingers. I don't give her time to recover before I stand and flip her around, then push her up against the cool tiles of the shower. I kick her legs apart before sliding into her.

"Yes," she says through gritted teeth as I push myself in her further, her lolling back against my shoulder.

"I can't get enough of you!" I groan against her neck as I begin to thrust, my hands gripping her breasts as she pushes her peachy ass back against each one of my thrusts. "Your tits are magnificent," I state as I pinch the nipples between my fingers. "Your cunt is exquisite …" I push into her deeply, "… and those fucking lips are sinful," I tell her.

"Harder," she begs, and I give her what she asks for as I fuck her without control, hard against the shower tiles. I know I'm gripping her breasts probably too tightly and will probably bruise in the morning, but she doesn't seem to care.

"Nothing makes me harder than a woman who likes to be fucked hard," I curse against her neck.

"Your dick is magnificent," she purrs, turning her head, letting me see the smile that's fallen across her lips.

"Then fucking choke it, make me see stars when I come," I demand, and she clenches hard, making her pussy a tight little hole.

I swear she's blurring my vision with her magic, but I continue, both of us insane with need. We try and push closer to the edge of our release, attempting to hold off until it's too much, and we fall right over that edge into the abyss.

"Fuck," I curse as I rest my forehead against her shoulder.

6

ELOISE

Wow!
I wasn't expecting him to fuck me like that! Especially considering the way he was freaking out earlier. Once that man got out of his head and away from his ex, he knew exactly how to fuck and exactly what I like. The man has stamina and that tongue? He damn well knows how to use it. The way his hand instinctively wrapped around my throat had my pussy fluttering—it was the right amount of pressure, but then he disappeared into his mind again. Whoever his ex was, did a number on him because he retreated into a gentleman again.

Even though, yes, he fucked me hard and thoroughly which was perfect, it felt like something he had tried before and was told not to ever do it again. That he was shamed for liking it hard, rough, and demanding. His ex must be a Grade-A bitch because this man is fucking gorgeous, he knows how to fuck, and the stupid woman cheated on him and made him feel less than a king. *I don't like that.* He must be a good guy because I'm the first woman he's had sex with in months since breaking up with his ex. Most men are out fucking twenty-four hours after a breakup, but he was so heartbroken that he couldn't bring himself to touch anyone else. I mean, the guy was freaking out moments before I stepped into the room.

That kind of reaction doesn't come from being a fuck boy or a player. It comes from a guy who knows that it's for the best he moves on from her, but he's not a robot and can't turn off his feelings as easily. And it's the poor guy's birthday too. I need to make him realize he's worthy, that there are other women out there waiting for him, and that his ex cheating on him will be a blessing in disguise.

"So, it's your birthday," I say as we walk back out into the room.

"Yeah. My friends gave me a membership to the club," he adds, running his hand through his wet hair.

That's right, he's friends with Mr. Lewis, so I need to make sure I give him the best time of his life.

"That's very kind of them." I smile, giving him a seductive look as I run my hand along the massage table.

"They're good guys, but I'll deny it if you tell them I said that." He chuckles, giving me a heated look.

I pretend to lock my mouth up and throw away the key. "Seeing as it's your birthday …" I raise a brow. "Is there a special treat the birthday boy would like?"

"I thought you were my treat." He grins, looking over me hungrily.

"I'm the starter. I can deliver you any fantasy you have ever dreamed of for your entrée."

Mr. King's tongue slides along his deliciously plump bottom lip. "What happens if you're all the fantasy I need."

His words are sweet, but most men don't come to The Paradise Club to fuck one woman.

"It's your birthday, and it is the night where you can indulge in everything. Usually, when people come to The Paradise Club, they want to push their boundaries," I explain.

"Like what?" he asks.

"I can bring in another woman or man or multiple," I reply.

His eyes widen as he takes in my words. "I'm sure the men are hot, but they're not my thing."

Noted. He's straight, not curious at all.

"Another favorite is watching people in the cube. You may have seen it as you came in."

Mr. King nods his head.

"We can go outside and watch, you can join in if you like, or we can fuck in the shadows. Depends on if you are a voyeur or an exhibitionist?"

"I've done neither," he answers honestly.

"You've never had someone watch you?" He shakes his head. "And you've never stumbled upon someone out and about having sex?" He shakes his head again.

Well, damn! I would pay good money to watch that man have sex.

His ex must have been a prude because how the hell are you not jumping this man every damn moment of the day?

"What do you feel comfortable with?" I ask.

"Honestly, I'm not sure. This is all new to me," he states, running his hand through his hair. He looks so cute and overwhelmed. Usually, that would be a turn-off because those kinds of men don't know how to fuck. But I know with him that isn't the problem. Seems his ex has made him doubt himself. I'm sure he's super confident at work, but maybe she has made him doubt himself in the sexual sense. Women can do that to a man. If the woman was cheating on him, she also probably made him believe it was his fault. *Screw that.* If he was true to form, this guy should be one arrogant, cocky bastard considering the face and dick he has.

"Do you trust me?" I ask, which I know is asking a lot from a perfect stranger.

He bites his bottom lip and nods, giving me a blinding smile.

"We're going to go have some fun," I tell him.

I grab my black slip dress from the floor and pull it on. "You'll only need your pants," I tell him, handing them to him.

He slides them on commando style.

Hot.

I take his hand and lead him out of the room and back into the darkened hallways. I tug him to follow me down another corridor toward the voyeur room. This is a little more intimate than watching the cube outside in the main area. I push open the door and enter the room. Mr. King follows behind me as I tug him over the threshold into the old-style theater. The room is set up as an auditorium with seats curving around a stage, but unlike traditional auditoriums, these seats are leather daybeds.

There's one stage with a glass window stopping the audience from joining in—they can only watch from in here. The curtains are currently pulled, so we must have missed the show, but there will be another ready to go in a couple of moments. It's so much fun performing on the stage for the guests. Whichever staff member or members you're with in that moment, you just let go and have the best time with them, or multiple of them, depending on the scene that has been planned.

"Where are we?" Mr. King whispers as we step down the stairs toward our seats.

I tug him down into the darkness. There are a couple of other people in the room as well, but they're at the outer edges, so you can only see shadows dancing in the darkness.

"This is the voyeur theater," I whisper to him. "When the curtains pull back, you get to sit back, relax, and enjoy the show. It's like porn but in 3D."

Mr. King's eyes narrow as if trying to see through the thick red velvet curtains pulled across the stage.

"You never know what scene is going to play out when the curtains pull back. It could be a couple, it could be an orgy. There are surround-sound speakers throughout the theater, and every moan, groan, and thrust echoes through the room," I explain to him. "That's why there are these beds, so if the mood strikes, you can have some fun."

"There are other people here," he states as he looks around the black room and notices a few of the beds are occupied.

"Of course, you can watch them, the stage, or they can watch you," I tell him.

He nods slowly, taking it all in.

"If you don't feel comfortable, we can go." I don't want to freak him out as this is supposed to be fun.

"Oh no, I want to stay," he says, and I catch his wide grin underneath the dim lights. "You've made me curious now."

"It will be fun, I promise." Shifting, I reach over and touch his bare chest. "We don't have to wait for the show to start," I explain as my hand slides down his stomach and over the outside of his pants, gripping his dick through the fabric. "Looks like you might already be in the mood." I chuckle, cupping his hardening dick.

Mr. King doesn't get to answer me because the curtains move and pull back. The stage lights up, and there are two naked women and a man walking out on stage. Mr. King sits up, his attention pulled by the women in front of him. I know we are going to be in for a show with these three, as they're always in for a good time. There's a bed set up in the middle of the room and behind that is a table and chairs, and a sex swing is hanging in one corner.

Damon reaches out and wraps his hand around Layla's throat, pulling her to him, kissing her wildly. He then does the same to Vixen. Both women smile at him as he licks his lips looking them over, hunger beaming from his eyes. Damon looks at the bed and asks Layla to lay down. The theater is silent now, you can hear a pin drop, but the sexual anticipation is swirling around the room as everyone takes in the scene before them.

"Take off your pants," I whisper to Mr. King. He doesn't

even hesitate as he shimmies them off. I do the same and slide my black slip dress off and lay it beside his pants. "Lay back and enjoy the show," I tell him.

Mr. King's eyes are firmly held onto what's happening on stage. His dick is slowly becoming hard, so I'll wait a little bit before I start teasing him.

Layla, one of the girls, walks over to the bed and lays down, then she spreads her legs for the theater. Damon presses a button, and down from the ceiling comes chains.

Mr. King sucks in a harsh breath.

Vixen walks around and starts cuffing Layla's wrists and ankles, making sure she is secure.

Damon presses another button, and the chains begin to wind back, spreading Layla's arms wide out to the side and the same with her legs—she's completely spreadeagled.

Mr. King leans forward as if trying to get a better look, which makes me smile, before he lays back again, his dick now fully standing to attention.

I reach out and wrap my hand around his cock, making him hiss. "Do you like what you see?"

He turns and looks at me with wide eyes. "I do." He smiles before his attention is pulled back to the scene before us.

My hand lazily slides up and down his dick. I'm not trying to get him off yet, we have plenty of time for that, but I want to keep him there as it will make later so much more fun.

Damon moves around Layla's body inspecting her before stopping at the end of the bed where Vixen is standing. His dick is already hard, and Vixen reaches out and wraps her hand around it. The moan that falls from his lips at her touch echoes through the entire theater. Damon reaches out and kisses Vixen again as she begins to slide her hand up and down his dick.

I match her strokes, and Mr. King groans at the same moment as Damon does, which is hot.

They lose themselves in the kiss for a couple of moments and eventually break away. Damon nods in Layla's direction, and Vixen smiles. They both begin to trail fingers over Layla's exposed body. Vixen plucks a nipple which has Layla humming, and Damon slides a finger between her folds, which has her biting her bottom lip.

The two of them continue to lazily run their fingers all over Layla's skin as they move around her in a circle, each time touching or teasing another part of her body. Layla arches her back when Vixen slides a finger through her folds, but the chains hold her in place, and Vixen chuckles.

Damon then reaches out, grabs the sex swing, and helps Vixen into it. Once she's secure with her legs spread wide and her knees bent as if she is kneeling in the air, he moves her over the bed where Layla is lying. He positions her right over Layla's face, but she's about five feet above her in the air. He then kneels on the bed right beside her, his face disappearing between Vixen's thighs, and that's when her moans echo through the theater as he begins to eat her right above Layla's face. You can hear every lick and suck in stereo as it bounces off the walls around us.

Mr. King lets out the tiniest of groans as my hand continues to keep him hovering.

"She sounds so wet, doesn't she?" I whisper into his ear.

All Mr. King can do is nod. His eyes never leave what is happening on the stage. I must be careful because of the overstimulation that's happening right in front of him—men don't seem to last long in this situation.

"Can you hear how much she loves his tongue sucking on her clit?"

He nods, but still, no words come out.

"It reminds me of how well you suck on mine. Feel how wet I am from the memory," I say, grabbing his hand and sliding it between my folds.

"Fuck, Elle," he curses as his fingers sink inside me.

My eyes roll back in my head as his thick fingers slide through my wetness. I notice he's watching me now instead of the scene before us.

"Eyes on them," I tell him.

It takes all his effort to pull his attention from me, but he does just in time for Damon to pull away from Vixen, her wetness glistening under the stage lights all over his face. He then presses another hidden button which begins to lower her right over Layla's face. As soon as Layla makes the connection, Vixen is thrashing about wildly against her restraints as Damon keeps her poised over Layla's face. Vixen's moans and groans continue to echo throughout the theater.

It's not long until I hear others in their seats beginning to enjoy what's happening before them.

Damon grins mischievously as he presses the button and pulls Vixen off Layla's face while both girls are panting and groaning from the move. He then shoves his dick down Layla's throat as he stands over her, then his face disappears between Vixen's thighs again.

Things are really starting to heat up now as the three of them lose themselves on stage, the acting element now over as they all begin to give into their desires. I know it's not going to take them long before they reach their crescendos, and I want to make sure Mr. King reaches his at the same time. So, I move his hand from me, much to my pussy's horror, and then I straddle him reverse cowgirl style so he can fuck me while watching the stage.

I slide myself down over his glorious dick, which pulls a hiss from his lips, and the next thing I know, he's sitting up, pressing his chest into my back. His hands are gripping my tits as he begins to pump into me.

"Eyes on the stage," I tell him.

I can't see if he's obeying, but his thrusts begin to hasten.

Damon moves his dick from Layla's mouth and tugs Vixen as he moves down between Layla's legs. He positions himself between her thighs, and you can hear the moment he slides into her. Layla pushes against her restraints—the clanging of the chains fills the room as do Layla's gasps.

Damon then moves back to Vixen's pussy and continues eating her while fucking Layla. The sounds of Vixen's and Layla's slickness and Damon's slapping begin to filter through, and fuck, it's hot. My pussy tingles with excitement as Mr. King continues to fuck me into oblivion.

The theater descends into chaos as the sounds of people getting off trickle in around us. I can feel myself getting closer to the edge as Mr. King continues to give me exactly what I want and need.

One of his hands slides from my breast to my clit, and that's game over for me. I let out a primal scream as I fall over the edge, and Mr. King's teeth sink into my shoulder as he's not far behind me.

7

ELOISE

"You look like you've been thoroughly fucked," Lauren chuckles, meeting me in the locker room. She is also looking like she's had a good time.

"I have been. His dick is magnificent," I say, smirking.

"Hell, yeah," Lauren squeals, giving me a high five. "Mr. Fox fucked me up good. I love aristocratic men who look like they would be all uptight and tense, and then *boom,* they fuck you like a damn porn star." My brow rises at Lauren's choice of words, and we both burst out laughing.

"Tonight was a good night then, for both of us."

"No need for my vibrator! I'm going home completely satisfied, as I always do after fucking him." Lauren smirks. "If only I could find a man like him in real life who could fuck me like he does, then my single days would be over," she huffs out.

"You need to put yourself out there first," I remind her.

Lauren waves her hands in the air before she slips her leggings on. "Yeah, yeah … I know, but no one stacks up to Mr. Fox." She sighs.

There's a strict policy of no fraternization between guests and staff outside of the club.

Does it happen? Of course, it's human nature.

But if you want to keep your job and your membership, then you keep it at the club.

"There's no point dating now, not when we're about to head to the island," she adds.

This is true. I grab my backpack, and we walk out through the staff entrance to where a car is waiting. The club has drivers on standby to take staff members home after their shift. The majority are late at night, and with most of the staff being predominately women, the owner, Mr. Lewis, didn't want us walking along the streets late at night or catching the tube. Instead, he's hired a fleet of drivers for our safety. We open the door and slide onto the leathery seats.

"Evening, Paul," I call out to our driver.

He gives me a nod in the rearview mirror and waits for Lauren to close the door before pulling out into traffic.

"Have you social stalked Mr. King yet?" Lauren asks, pulling out her phone.

I glance up to where Paul is driving and frown while shaking my head.

Lauren catches my drift and gives me a smile as she puts her phone away again. We travel in silence all the way home, both of us exhausted from a fun night. As soon as the door to our home is shut, Lauren pulls out her phone and waves it in my face.

"Come on ... you can't tell me after you had some great dick that you aren't at all curious over who this Mr. King is?" Lauren asks.

"No. He's a client, and we're about to move halfway across the world to a tropical island. His dick isn't worth losing my job over. You know I need the money ... I'm so close to achieving my goal," I tell her. It's not my fault I haven't ever fallen for a guest like she has for Mr. Fox.

"You're right ..." She sighs. "What I will say is Mr. King is friends with Mr. Fox and Mr. Lewis, the brother, not the boss," she adds.

This bit of information catches my attention as I raise a brow at her.

"That's even worse. Knowing he's friends with the boss's brother, you would for sure lose your job if you did anything," I warn her.

"I know, I know. There's something about Mr. Fox that has gotten under my skin, and every time I'm with him, it burns brighter." She sighs.

"Maybe a move halfway across the ocean is what you need to rid yourself of this infatuation."

"You're right. I know you're right. Thank goodness he dumped that dumb blonde he was dating. She didn't deserve him," Lauren adds.

I shake my head at my friend. I know Lauren would never blur the lines regarding our job, and as much as she doesn't need the money thanks to her trust fund, she still loves her job.

"Fine! I need to stop thinking about him." She pouts.

"I'm off to bed, see you in the morning," I tell her.

"Night, Elle," she says as I disappear up the stairs of our townhouse and collapse onto my bed, thinking about my night with Mr. King. I let out a heavy sigh, roll over, and curl up into my pillow.

No dick is worth losing this job, I tell myself as I fall asleep to the images of hazel eyes and dirty words.

※※※※※※※※

I'm home alone this weekend as Lauren has gone away somewhere with a mystery man. I know it must be someone from the club. Otherwise, she would have told me about him. It's probably better I don't know. I keep telling her it's a bad idea, but Lauren doesn't need the job like I do. She has a healthy trust fund to fall back on, whereas I have nothing. *I need this job.* I need it to get that much closer to my goals. So, I let Lauren do her thing and hope no one finds out.

I head on out to my local café and order a coffee. I might head over to Hyde Park and have a lazy walk around the beautiful area this morning.

"Hey, Elle, your usual?" the barista calls out to me.

"Yes, thanks, Tommy," I call back.

It doesn't take long for my coffee to arrive, then I pay and say my goodbyes. Spinning, I step outside and right into someone, knocking my coffee out of my hand and right onto the ground, splashing both of us with hot liquid.

"Fuck," the deep voice curses.

"You need to watch where you're going," I tell the stranger as I stare at my coffee all over the ground. It's then I look up at those familiar hazel eyes staring back at me. He, too, is taken aback by my presence.

"Elle?" he questions.

Shit.

"Sorry, wrong person," I mumble and take off down the sidewalk.

I cannot be seen with someone from the club.

Does he not remember the rules?

He isn't supposed to acknowledge he knows me in public, and what he just did then breaks *all the rules*.

"Hey," he says, grabbing my arm and halting me. "I owe you a coffee. I'm so sorry, I was on my phone and wasn't paying attention," he states apologetically.

He is *so hot.*

Seeing him outside the club in natural light only highlights his handsomeness. *No, Elle.* Diffuse those thoughts. He is a guest, nothing more.

"I've got to go," I say, shaking myself from his grasp and taking off again. I take a sharp corner left down an alleyway and hope he walks right past. My chest is heaving with the stress of the situation, but he turns the corner and spots me straight away.

"Look, it's against the club rules to be seen together outside of those four walls. I *need* this job. Please, forget you ever saw me," I plead with him.

Mr. King looks taken aback by my abruptness at first, then reality sinks in, and he remembers. "I'm sorry, you're right. Here, take this ... I owe you for the coffee and the dry cleaning," he says, handing me a few bills.

My anxiety gets the best of me, and I grab the bills without thinking, just wishing for him to leave. He gives me a nod, turns on his heels, and exits the dark alley.

Shit. Why did I overreact like that?

I've run into guests plenty of times before and never lost my mind like I just did, and I've definitely not run down an alleyway to get away from them. I throw my head back against the bricks a couple of times, pissed off over my stupidity. He probably thinks you're the biggest freak. I look down at my hand where the crumpled notes are and realize he's given me two hundred pounds.

What in the fuck?

That's too much.

I run out onto the sidewalk to see if I can catch him, but he's gone.

※※※※※※※※

"Elle, you're in room thirty-four. Mr. King is back, and he's waiting for you," Sara states, looking down at her tablet.

He's back? Butterflies somersault in my stomach. I'm going to give him his money back—I still have it in my purse. I head over to my bag, pull the money out, and slide it into my bra before walking down the back corridor to his room. I suck in a deep breath as I stand outside the door, not sure why the hell I'm so nervous. He's just a guest like a million and one other guests you have seen over the years. He is a job, nothing more. Doesn't matter that he looks like a Greek fucking god with a magical dick. There have been many handsome men come through the club and many with equally magical dicks too.

So why am I freaking out about this one?

I peek through the window and see he's back to pacing again. Tonight, he's dressed in jeans and a white button-down shirt, his sandy blond hair is flopping in front of his face, and he keeps raking his fingers through it to get the strands to stay, but they don't.

It's cute.

No, it's not, Elle.

Shut up, brain.

My hand turns the door handle, and I step into his room with a sense of déjà vu as he looks up at me nervously, just like he did the last time I was here a couple of weeks ago.

"Elle," he says my name on a raspy growl, and it instantly sends shockwaves through my body.

"Mr. King, it is nice to see you again," I say.

Keep it professional, Elle.

Keep those walls up around you in place, no matter what.

"I didn't know if you would see me again after the other day," he confesses, and his face looks pained over the thought.

Crack. That's the sound of my wall breaking down, and one brick has now fallen to the ground. This wall is there for a reason, but upon seeing his pain … Fuck. I can't keep up the pretense.

"Here," I say out of nowhere, pulling the money from my bra and handing it back to him. "That was too much."

"It's the least I could do for causing you distress," he tells me.

"I'm not a prostitute," I say angrily, not sure why I'm getting upset over the money.

"I never insinuated you were," he replies while ignoring my hand, which is waving the bills in front of his face.

"Take it, p-please," I say as my voice cracks.

"Why?" he asks.

"I could lose my job over it. That's why."

Mr. King's eyes widen, and he reluctantly reaches out and takes the money from my hand and puts it in his back pocket.

"I think it might be best if I send someone else in here to look after you tonight."

"No."

"No?" I repeat his answer.

"That's what I said," he states categorically.

"This isn't going to work," I tell him and turn on my heels.

I don't get far until he's grabbing me and pushing me up against the wall. The sudden movement has my heart racing and my adrenaline pumping.

"I'm sorry about the other day, Elle," he says, running his nose along my neck. "I forgot myself for the moment. I thought I was doing the right thing, and I see now that I messed it all up. I don't want to mess things up," he confesses, and stupidly my stomach flip-flops over his words.

"Outside of these walls, we can only ever be strangers," I tell him.

"I get that now. It won't happen again. I promise," he says, staring down at me. Those hazel eyes drop to my lips before they move back up to my face. "I don't want to put your livelihood in jeopardy. I was shocked to see you at my local."

His local?

We must live close to one another.

Why have I never seen him before? I know I would have noticed someone like him there.

"That was my first time there. I was on my way to visit a friend," I lied.

He nods. "I'm truly sorry, Elle."

I know he is because I can see it on his face. Most men wouldn't give a shit over my concerns, but he listened to me and empathized. As far as I am concerned now, what's done is done. It's going to suck giving up that café, but it's for the best.

"Are you sorry?" I say, in a teasing tone raising a brow at him, hoping he catches my drift.

"*So* sorry. I'd do anything to make it up to you," he adds. The curve of his lip lets me know that he's caught on to the plan.

"Anything?" I ask.

"Yes, anything. I am your humble slave." He smirks.

"Then get on your knees," I command.

He does as he's told and instantly drops before me.

"What would happen if I brought another man in here to fuck me right in front of you as your penance?"

The deepest growl falls from his lips as he stares up at me.

Nope, he doesn't look too pleased with that idea.

"A woman then?" I tease him.

He doesn't say a thing, which gives me so many ideas as a smile falls across my face.

"Are you okay with being tied up?" I ask as I stare down at him.

"By you, yes, by someone else, no," he tells me honestly.

That's fair. "And you trust me?"

"Yes, I do."

"Good! Now get up and lay down on the bed," I command in a domineering tone. He does as he's told and scrambles onto the bed. "Take off your clothes." He does so quickly before kicking them off the bed. I press the hidden button, and chains fall down the posts of the four-poster bed. He swallows hard as he stares at the silver chains. "I promise you will like what I have planned. You watched something similar the last time we were together."

He nods absentmindedly as he looks down at where I begin cuffing his ankles to the bed.

"Are you okay with this?" I ask again as I cuff the other ankle.

"Yes," he answers, his voice gravelly with need as his dick stands to attention before me.

I walk around, grab his wrist, cuffing one, then walk over to the other side and do the same. I ask him again if he's okay, and he reassures me he is.

I press another hidden button that tightens the chains, spreading him out. I ask him again if this is okay, and he gives me a nod, but I can see he's dancing the fine line between panic and desire.

So, I grab the tablet off the side table and type in a message to Vixen, asking her to come join me. I know she's working tonight, and we always have fun together. I get a message right back letting me know she will be in the room in ten minutes.

I walk on over to the wall where all the toys are hanging, pick up the feather, and step back over to him. I drag the white feather up over his taut body, which has him straining against his cuffs. Mr. King bites his bottom lip as I tease his dick with the feather. I keep teasing him repeatedly until he curses me for it, which only makes me chuckle.

The door to the room opens, and Vixen walks in. She's dressed in the same black slip dress I am. Her jet-black hair is pulled up into a high pony. Her makeup is dark and dangerous with sleek winged eyeliner and red lips. She looks like a '40s bombshell.

"Oh, what do we have here?" Vixen grins as she sees Mr. King laid out on the bed. Mr. King's eyes widen as she steps into the room before they run down her hourglass figure. I'm guessing by the way he is licking his lips that he appreciates what he's seeing.

"Mr. King has been a naughty boy." I smirk as I stare down at the magnificence that is him spread out across the bed.

"Is that so?" Vixen turns to me and licks her lips.

"Yes, and this is his penance. He wasn't too happy about another man fucking me, but he didn't seem to mind another woman," I explain to her seductively.

"Oh, he has *no idea* how much that was the wrong decision to make. I get off on watching men beg while being denied." Vixen grins as she looks over him hungrily.

Mr. King's eyes widen like saucers as he swallows nervously. I can see he is rethinking his choices. *Too late, buddy.* This is going to be so much fun.

"Vixen, seeing as you like denying men, how about you take control?"

Vixen laughs. "You might be sorry you suggested that, Elle," she states, licking her lips.

I think I might.

8
ALISTAIR

This was not at all how I saw my night turning out, being strapped to a bed naked by two gorgeous women who are currently making out in front of me. I'm not mad over it. I'll take whatever begging this Vixen girl wants from me because I would rather see Elle being fucked by her than another man. Not that there's anything wrong with it, and maybe it's chauvinistic to be like that, but I know my dick, and it will get more pleasure out of two women enjoying themselves than watching Elle with some dude.

I lay back and watch Vixen pull Elle's black slip dress up and over her head. She then spins Elle around, so she's facing me at the end of the bed and unhooks Elle's black lacy bra. I watch it flutter to the floor. Vixen then plucks Elle's nipples, and Elle closes her eyes and lets out a small moan. My dick twitches over the sound.

Easy boy, more is about to happen, don't blow too soon.

Vixen then slides her hand over Elle's taut stomach and down beneath her black panties.

Oh shit.

Elle's legs shuffle open, and I watch as Vixen's hand moves between Elle's thighs.

Oh, shit again.

I tug at my restraints, trying to get a closer look. My eyes land on Elle's face which has a bright flush of pink to it, her eyes are closed, and her teeth have sunk into her bottom lip as her hands clench beside her.

Dammit. I want to see what Vixen's doing to her.

"Ready to beg yet?" Vixen asks, smirking at me over Elle's shoulder.

Yes. I am.

I'm not too proud to beg.

The words are on my lips before they are interrupted by Vixen.

"You start begging, and I'll stop what I'm doing and walk right out that door," Vixen warns me.

She sucker-punched me in the balls.

I suck in a deep breath and try counting to one hundred to ease my blue balls that seem to be increasing their throbbing. I watch Vixen's hand move back and forth, restricted by Elle's thong, but Elle doesn't seem to mind judging by the moaning coming from her. Moments later, Vixen's hand slips from between Elle's thighs, and I hear her audibly hiss at her for doing it, which makes Vixen laugh.

I think Vixen's a sadist.

"Take off your wet panties, Elle, and give them to me," Vixen directs, and Elle does as she's told and hands Vixen her underwear.

Then I see the smile that curls up across Vixen's red lips as she moves from Elle and walks over to me, dangling the black lace thong on her finger. She then lowers it and tickles my nose with the lace.

Fuck.

A growl falls from my lips as I smell Elle's arousal. Her

sweetness tickles my nose, and my dick throbs with need. He wants to be balls deep inside that sweetness.

"She smells good, doesn't she?" Vixen asks.

I nod enthusiastically because it's the truth.

"Here, taste her," Vixen says, placing the fingers she had in Elle's cunt into my mouth.

Fuck. Me. Dead!

I can taste Elle as if my tongue was getting it directly from the source. I suck Vixen's fingers into my mouth, swirling my tongue against her skin, licking her clean of Elle.

Vixen chuckles when I'm done. "He's such a good boy, Elle." Vixen grins before placing Elle's underwear on my chest, so I must continue to breathe in Elle's sweetness.

Fuck.

Vixen chuckles as she walks away toward my dick.

Oh no! What the hell does she have planned?

She looks down at the bead of precum that has pearled at the tip of my dick, and she runs her finger across it. Good God, I almost launch myself off the bed at her touch. She scoops up the pearl and passes her finger to Elle to lick it off.

Please don't come.

Please don't come.

Please don't come, I chant, watching Elle savor me.

"You two are such good little playthings," Vixen says, praising us, and I have no idea why that makes my dick throb.

Did I unlock a new kink? Who the hell knows?

Tonight is going way further than I ever thought I would, but I'm not mad about it. It's fucking hot, actually. I have no idea what's going to happen next, but the anticipation is killing me.

"Place a knee on either side of his face," Vixen commands Elle.

Elle moves from the end of the bed to my face and places a knee on either side of my head.

Fuck.

Her scent is intoxicating, and I'm so close yet so far. I was right! Vixen is a fucking sadist. I think she's trying to kill me.

I can feel the heat from Elle's pussy right above me. Then I feel Vixen jump onto the bed and she's flush against Elle's back.

"Make sure your wide open for him, Elle. I want him to be sure he can catch any drips." Vixen chuckles right before I watch her sink her long fingers into Elle's cunt. This is like a bird's-eye view of the action you see in porn, but much better. I watch as Vixen slides two fingers into Elle's cunt, curling her fingers so she hits her G-spot. There is no messing around with this woman as her thumb catch's Elle's clit.

This is such a fucking turn-on. I don't know how long I stare into the pink abyss of Elle's cunt. It's like her pussy is mesmerizing me the longer I stare at it. The first drip falls against my lips, pulling me from my delirium.

The room comes back into focus as Vixen is going to town on Elle's pussy, drawing I don't know what kind of magic from her, but I don't know if I've ever made a woman this wet before, and now, I feel lacking.

The next thing I know, Elle is coming.

Vixen's fingers are removed, and Elle's pussy is pushed over my face as she comes all over it. I lap at her pussy, drinking her all in as she continues to convulse over my chin. I don't stop. I'm like a starved man, and Elle's juicy cunt is my only nourishment. I can't get enough.

Elle continues to ride my face, screaming and panting as my tongue gives her exactly what she wants until she can't stand it anymore and slides off me. She rolls to the side, spent.

"Oh, dear …" Vixen smirks. "Seems someone couldn't hold it." Her eyes fall on my dick, and I look down. By some sort of voodoo magic, I've come all over myself.

How in the hell did I come and not realize it?

"It's been fun, guys. I'll leave Elle to clean up," Vixen states as she throws me a wink and disappears from the room.

Elle sits up and looks down at my dick.

"Oh dear, what a mess," she says with a grin, and before I know it, she is crawling down my body and licking up the mess I've made.

How does someone go back to normal sex after this?

"You're hard again," Elle muses.

Did Vixen slip me fucking Viagra or something? Because how the hell does one come and not know it and then get hard instantly afterward.

I watch as Elle slides herself down my dick and begins to ride me.

Fucking hell, she feels *so good.*

"I need to touch you, Elle." I groan.

She leans forward and unhooks my hands from the chains, leaving the cuffs around my wrists, and then she does the same with my ankles. Once I'm free, it's my turn to be in charge as I flip Elle over and wrap my hand around her throat while I fuck the living hell out of her.

"Your fucking cunt is addictive," I curse at her as I fuck her into oblivion.

We've turned animalistic with desire. It's as if Vixen has flicked some kind of primal switch in our minds, and only our base needs matter.

Elle's nails scrape down my back, and my hand tightens around her throat as if urging me on. I've never been able to let loose like this with a woman before. Never pushed the envelope this much.

Fucking hell, I love it.

We both come again, and I swear I see stars, fucking rainbows, and fucking unicorns when I come this time. I know I sound like some teenage girl, but it's so overwhelmingly sensual I have no other explanation for my thoughts.

I'm so exhausted that I slide off Elle and land in a sweaty pile beside her.

Both of us are unable to speak as we lay panting.

"Fuck. That was some of the best sex I've ever had." Elle groans as she looks over at me.

And coming from her, whose job it is to bring people's fantasies to life, that means something to me.

"I never knew sex could be like this," I say, reaching out and pulling her to me.

"Guessing you liked your punishment then?" she asks, smiling up at me.

"Maybe I need to be bad more often if this is my punishment," I reply as I lean forward and kiss her.

Elle sighs as we lose ourselves again. "Someone will be here ready and willing to dish it out," she states.

I still in her arms.

She said *someone else,* not her.

"You think that was because of a fantasy and not because of who it was with?" I ask her, confused.

"This is what The Paradise Club does, Mr. King. Any time you want it, night or day … your desires can be fulfilled," she explains.

I thought maybe it was different.

Am I being naïve?

"You think that someone else at the club can deliver what just happened?" I ask her as confusion swirls in my mind.

"Of course," she answers, not daring to look at me.

Maybe she's right.

"And you would be okay with someone else delivering it?" I ask.

God, I sound so desperate.

Elle probably gets this all the time—some guy gets his rocks off so good that he thinks he's falling for the woman whose job it is to do exactly that.

Elle pauses, hesitates for the moment, but finally answers.

"Anyone would be happy to make your fantasies come true, Mr. King."

But the only one *I* want to deliver them is *her*.

※※※※※※※※

"Mr. King, welcome back to The Paradise Club." Vixen grins, entering the room.

It doesn't feel right being here in this room without Elle. I know I'm being stupid, but I need to know if it's Elle who makes it feel this good or if it's the club in general.

I feel like I might be projecting my lust for her because she's the first woman since Miranda I've fucked. It's like I've imprinted on her somehow. That's not her fault, especially if she doesn't feel the same electricity between us as I do.

"It's nice to see you again," I tell Vixen. She's a gorgeous woman, and my dick appreciates what it sees, but my head doesn't seem to be in the game.

"You okay, Mr. King?" Vixen asks as she looks me over, sensing my inner thoughts.

"Sorry, been a hard day. Have a lot on my mind, that's all," I tell her, waving my hands in the air dramatically.

Yeah, I'm such a loser.

"Lucky you've come to the club then. I can take all your stress away. How does that sound?" she asks, then she licks her lips.

"Great," I mumble while my head flicks to images of Elle.

Stop it! I curse myself.

Concentrate on the beautiful woman before you instead of flicking your mind to Elle all the damn time.

"Take a seat, Mr. King, and relax," Vixen purrs, leading me over to an armchair.

I take a seat in the plush leather and close my eyes for the briefest of moments.

"Here ... looks like you might need this," she says, handing me a tumbler of amber liquid.

I knock it back in one large gulp, the whiskey burning down my throat.

Vixen's eyes widen at me shooting the whiskey, but she doesn't say anything. Then she falls to her knees in front of me and begins to unzip my pants.

I let her.

Her hands move swiftly, pulling me from my underwear.

Embarrassingly, my dick doesn't come to life.

"You really are stressed. I promise I'll make it *all* better," Vixen muses as she wraps her mouth around my dick and starts working her magic.

It's hard for my dick not to appreciate the hot little mouth trying to bring it back to life, and he, of course, starts to thicken with each bob of her head in my crotch, but my mind is elsewhere.

Look, Vixen is incredibly talented, and my dick is appreciating the shit out of the blow job, but my body keeps tensing because I know that's not the mouth I want to be wrapped around my dick.

Push through it, Ali. You cannot be losing your mind over a woman you can't have.

I look down and see Vixen's black hair, and it doesn't look right.

"Vixen," I call out her name as I tap her on the shoulder.

She lets go of my dick with a pop and looks up at me wide-eyed.

"I don't think I can switch off from work. I'm sorry. I don't want to waste your time."

"My ears work just as well as my mouth, you know." She gives me a wink as she slides my dick back into my pants.

"Am I weird for turning down your expert blow job?"

"Never. It makes you human, Mr. King. Sometimes a blow job won't fix things," she says, giving me a wide smile.

Elle's blow job would have. Stop it, brain.

"I better head back to the office. I'm sorry for wasting your time," I tell her as I hold out my hand to lift her off the floor. She takes it and pulls herself up, straightening herself out as I do the same.

"Just so you know, Mr. King, Elle isn't working this weekend, but she's back next Tuesday, I think."

I pause at Vixen's comment.

"Elle's a good girl. I wouldn't be telling you if it was anyone else," she whispers while biting her lip, worried she might be overstepping her mark.

"Then why are you?" I ask.

"You two looked like you had fun together the other day. I was surprised to see you here today on her day off," Vixen adds.

"I don't know her schedule."

"You know you can request certain people. You can make bookings for them via the secure app," she adds.

I had no idea.

"Ask the girls at the front desk to help set you up on your way out," Vixen tells me.

"Why?" I ask.

"Can I speak candidly? I can trust you, can't I, Mr. King?" Vixen asks as her dark eyes narrow on me with a warning to which I nod in agreement. "Elle is a gorgeous soul. I've known her for a long time. She has dreams, goals, and aspirations that are much bigger than this place. I'm hoping maybe one day she can achieve them."

And with that, Vixen walks out of the room, leaving me incredibly confused.

9

ELOISE

We arrive at one of the hottest clubs in the city, Minx. Lauren was able to book a booth in the VIP section tonight for our friend Kylie's birthday.

"This is exactly what I need. I have my dancing shoes on, and I'm ready to let loose." Kylie grins as we are led in by the ice queen door bitch, who looks us over with disdain and, judging by her uppity stare, she doesn't think we should be here. Lauren and I exchange eye rolls as we walk up the VIP staircase toward our booth.

"Here you go, ladies, your booth. Your hostess will be out in a moment to deliver your bottles." The ice queen smiles fakely.

"What a bitch," I murmur as she walks away.

"Who gives a shit about her? I'm ready to party." Lisa squeals as she jumps up and down.

"And maybe find a hot guy to take home," Lauren says, nudging Lisa a few times.

"Damn right," Lisa replies as they high-five.

Moments later, a beautiful redhead and blonde come out holding bottles of champagne above their heads with sparklers sitting on top of the bottles. "Happy Birthday, Kylie," they sing as they place the bottles in the ice bucket on the table while sparkles fly off everywhere.

They better not get on my new dress that I bought especially for tonight. It's a gorgeous pink sequin mini wrap dress that leaves nothing to the imagination as it hangs dangerously low in the front and crosses over at the back.

The hostess pops the bottles of champagne for us, and we take our glasses and wish Kylie the happiest of birthdays.

As the night rolls on, we have become considerably louder and maybe a little drunker. There's a table of assholes beside us, and all night they have been annoying us. They are trying to gain our attention with their small dicks and overinflated egos, which none of us are interested in.

The Paradise Club hires some of the hottest people in the world, and I know when a group of us go out together, we always gain attention, most of it unwanted. Men think a group of beautiful women is searching for a rich man. Not one of us sitting at this table is after that. We are independent women, and if we wanted a rich guy, we have a club full of them to whisk us away.

I haven't seen Mr. King at the club for the past couple of weeks. Stupidly, I checked his profile to see if he had been in, and someone else has had the pleasure of looking after him. Not that I'm jealous or anything, I just liked riding his dick.

He had an appointment with Vixen a couple of days after our fun.

Not going to lie—that stung.

But then I ran into Vixen, who told me nothing happened, that he wasn't into it, and they cut the session short. She said she sucked him off for a minute, and then he stopped it.

Not going to lie, that made me feel good.

Vixen joked that she thought he wasn't interested because I wasn't there. I call bullshit. Men can have off days when they aren't in the mood. Granted, they are a hell of a lot less than women, but I'm sure it happens.

Vixen thinks he's smitten with me.

I don't believe her.

I know some of the people I've worked with have ended up married to a client. There are some whose primary goal is to land a rich husband. That's not me. I couldn't imagine anything worse than relying on a man for money.

My mother was like that, and my father got away with treating her like trash. She was to look good on his arm, and that was all. I want my independence, that's why I've been working my ass off as I have been, so I have enough of a nest egg put aside to make my dream happen with no help from a man or my parents.

I shake all the thoughts of Mr. King from my mind. Although I find this difficult because every single time I need to come, it's his face I see, and as soon as I do, it's like fucking fireworks.

Please don't let me have a crush on a client.

Lauren definitely has a crush on one of hers, but I am trying so hard to maintain distance from Mr. King. That's the reason for my night out tonight, to get Mr. King from my mind and Mr. Fox from Lauren's. I need to hook up with a hot guy who isn't from The Paradise Club, do all the nasty things with him, and scrub Mr. King's face from my mind.

The music is thumping deep in my chest, so I allow it to take over me and begin to sway to the beat, letting myself get lost in the sounds. Hands wrap around my waist, and I ignore them, knowing it's probably Lauren behind me. I keep moving to the beat until I feel myself being pulled back against a hard body with a damn boner. *What the hell?*

"I knew you were interested. You like playing hard to get, don't you?"

I swing around in his arms. A tall, skinny guy grins down at me. He looks like one of those finance assholes who thinks money can get him free pussy. My eyes narrow, and I realize he's one of the assholes from the next table who have been harassing us all night.

"I told you I wasn't interested the first time," I declare while glaring at him.

Entitled rich guys think their flashy watch and suit make them a catch. Little boys, you have no idea how many men way richer than you I have fucked. Your net worth is probably what they spend in a year on underwear.

When I look around to see where my girls are, his friends are harassing them at the table again.

Why can't these assholes accept that *no means no*?

Why are they ruining my precious night off?

He reaches for me again, and I stumble back, trying to get out of his grasp, but unfortunately, he grabs me a second time.

"You looked pretty interested as you ground on my dick," he growls, pulling me into him, where I bounce off his bony chest.

"As *if*," I say, pushing him hard with both hands as I try to escape his touch. Unfortunately, his hand has a tight grip on my wrist, and I don't like it. "Let go of me," I scold while tugging my hand.

"Give me a kiss, and I'll let go." The asshole has the audacity to flash me a predatory grin.

"If you don't let go in *five seconds*, I'll kick you in the fucking balls."

His eyes turn dark at my words.

"Touch me, and I'll show you who's boss, whore," he sneers.

I'm moments away from kicking him in the balls when the creep is yanked out of my arms and slammed to the floor.

"She told you no, asshole. Learn some fucking respect, you piece of shit," the man yells, standing over the guy who's now on the floor.

"Who the fuck do you think you are? Do you know who I

am?" The guy on the floor screams out like a girl while curling his lip at the man.

"I don't give a shit who you are because what matters right now is who I am. This is *my fucking club*. I own this world, and you are not welcome. You hear me, asshole," the man bellows.

The guy on the floor's face turns pale as the realization sinks in on who he's talking to. "You're willing to kick me out because of that whore?" The guy doubles down on his assholeness as he looks over the man's shoulder at me.

"It's okay, boss, we've got this." One of the large security guys comes over and accidentally, on purpose, kicks the guy on the floor in the ribs with his shoe, which has him curling over in pain.

"You fucking asshole, you've broken my rib," he curses at the security guard.

"My foot slipped. It was an accident, and I doubt it's broken," the security guy replies before he picks him up by the scruff of the neck and begins to haul him out of the club.

"You're going to pay for this!" The guy begins a barrage of curses as the security guys escort his friends out too.

"I'm so sorry, miss, you should always feel safe in my clubs," the owner says as he turns around to look at me.

My breath hitches as I realize who's standing before me. His hazel eyes widen in realization too as he looks me over, assessing if the guy has hurt me or not.

"He grabbed my wrist, that's all." I hold it up for him to inspect and see that I'm fine.

He grabs my hand and checks the large bruise that's brewing across my skin. His hazel eyes turn dark as a growl falls from his lips. "I fucking should have made him pay!" He's cursing, the anger seeping from him as he turns my wrist over to inspect the bruise.

Our skin meets, and electricity crackles up my arm.

"He shouldn't have touched you like that, Elle." And as soon as my name falls from his lips, he drops my hand and takes a step back, running his fingers through his sandy-colored hair. There's a pained look on his face, and I'm not sure if it's from the attack or the realization that we aren't meant to know each other.

Lauren walks over, and her eyes widen when she notices Mr. King standing there before me. She looks at me, then back at him. "Thank you for coming to my friend's rescue, sir," Lauren says, acting as if he's a stranger.

"Women should be able to dance in my club without assholes invading their space. I'm sorry that this has happened to you. If you want to stay, which I hope you do, drinks are on the house for the rest of the evening," he says, giving us both a small smile.

"Thanks, but you don't have to do th—" I start before Lauren interrupts.

"Oh my god, you're the best. Thanks so much." She grins excitedly.

Mr. King gives her a tight smile, a curt nod, and bids us goodnight.

"He is *so much better* in real life." Lauren chuckles as we watch him stride through the crowd like the king he is. "Go after him," Lauren says, pushing me through the crowd.

"No, I can't! You know the rules," I hiss at my friend.

"The guy literally saved you from that asshole and was seconds from pummeling him. Go and say thank you, you know that's not against the rules." Lauren pushes me, and I go with a frown on my face.

I look back at her and shake my head, but she says, "Fuck off! Just do it."

He's at the bar talking to the staff, and they're nodding at whatever he's relaying to them, and then they disappear. He looks up as I walk through the crowd, gives me a shake of the head to follow him, then turns on his heel and takes off.

I'm not breaking any rules if I follow him, am I? All I'm

doing is saying thank you for saving me from that complete Grade-A asshole.

He pushes through a set of ornate wooden doors that reads 'Staff'.

Should I follow him? I'm not sure.

Maybe it's for the best if I don't.

The next thing I know, the doors open again, and he's standing there holding it wide for me. I suck in a deep breath and decide *fuck it* this time. I'll be halfway across the world soon, and this won't ever happen again. I step past him, and his scent of wood and earth filters through my nose while goosebumps lace my skin. *This is not good.* He doesn't say anything as he strides before me along a white corridor, the only sound is the clicking and echoing of my heels across the floor. He turns right, and there's a set of stairs, which he takes two at a time.

Yeah, not in these heels. I can't match his pace.

Slowly, I follow him up the stairs to another level which is like a mezzanine floor that overlooks the entire club, from the VIP section all the way down to the lower levels. He's walked through another door, and I find him standing in front of a desk which must be his office. He's dressed in dark denim jeans and a navy button-down shirt with the sleeves rolled up, exposing his tanned, muscular arms. There are a million and one monitors off to the right of his desk, paperwork strewn across it behind him. There are two gray armchairs on either side of the desk.

"Close the door," he commands, and a shiver creeps up my spine upon hearing his demanding voice.

I do as I'm told and shut the door behind me.

Now, this *is* crossing a line, one I swore I would never do.

A frown is deeply etched across his forehead. "I'm sorry that man touched you like he did." The anguish and anger are etched across his face.

"It's not your fault," I reassure.

"It happened on my watch," he growls, raking his hand through his hair in frustration.

"But you put a stop to it too," I say.

Those hazel eyes land on me, and my entire body shivers under his intense gaze.

This is not good.

This is *so* not good.

Just thank him and go, Elle.

"I just needed you to hear from me that I'm okay … well, I'll be okay. And please don't feel bad for what happened. It happens a lot, unfortunately," I explain. "That's all I wanted to say." As I turn and reach for the doorknob a few seconds later, he has me pushed up against the door, and his lips are caressing my ear.

"Seeing his hands on you made me want to rip his eyes out for daring to even look upon you." I close my eyes and soak in his warmth and strength for the tiniest of moments as his hand lightly runs down my side, sending a shiver over me. "Now you're here with me and dressed like pure and utter sin, I can't get you off my mind."

Shit.

"My dick hasn't gotten hard since that night, and now …" he presses his hard dick against me, "… you've fucking mesmerized it."

I can't stop thinking about him either or that night. *This is not good.*

I've had one too many champagnes, and I'm finding it hard to keep my distance as I close my eyes and lose myself against his hardness. It doesn't matter how much you may want this man, he is not worth you losing everything for.

"I should go …" I say the words, but they come out with no real emphasis or meaning.

"Don't," he says as his lips move against my skin.

"Being here with you *is* crossing a line," I tell him.

"I know." He sighs.

But he doesn't move away. Instead, he slides his hand down my side. His thumb catches my nipple as he works his way down.

"Tell me to stop, Elle." He moans in my ear.

I should tell him to stop, but I don't.

I will, though.

I won't let him go too far.

His hand moves further down my body until it reaches under the hem of my dress. His knuckle runs along the seam of my thong, and I bite my lip as a moan falls from my lips. He teases me with his knuckle, rubbing the seam against my clit, which makes my body feel like it's been set on fire.

Then, just like that, his hand is gone.

What? Why?

The next thing I know, he's ripping my panties from my skin, and I watch him bring my thong up to his nose and inhale deeply. My eyes are wide, and my mouth falls open—that's fucking hot.

"I need something to wrap around my dick later. And seeing as it can't be your cunt, I'll take these instead."

Okay.

Right.

Wow!

"See, didn't cross the line," he says with a smirk.

Oh, that one hundred percent *is* crossing the line, but I'm not mad about it.

"I've never been so close to crossing that line before," I tell him, honestly.

"Good to know." He smirks as he sucks in another deep smell of my panties.

"You can request people at the club," I tell him. "Not sure if you know that?"

"Is that so?" He quirks a brow at me.

I nod slowly.

"I'll be seeing you soon then, Elle." He grins.

I turn to walk out the door, but I stop and swing back to him. "I saw that you came back for Vixen."

Mr. King stills, then looks up at me through dark lashes. "I needed to know if it was the club or you," he explains.

What does that mean? My brows pull together in a frown.

"Good night, Elle. I'll see you again … *soon.*"

And with that, I walk out the door confused and aroused as fuck.

10

ELOISE

"What the hell are you doing?" Lauren asks as she comes downstairs, rubbing her eyes and trying to disperse her sleep. "Have you been baking all night?" Her eyes are focused on the mess I've made.

"Um, yeah," I say, looking up at her.

"What's going on? You haven't had one of these manic baking sessions in ages. Why are you so stressed?"

She's right, I haven't had a manic baking session since running into my parents at an event last year, and they pretended they didn't know who I was. That led me to bake hundreds of cupcakes and pastries, not that anyone at work was complaining.

"I wanted to try some new recipes, that's all," I lie.

Lauren's eyes narrow on me. The problem is she's known me long enough to realize when I'm bullshitting. And I'm definitely bullshitting right now.

"Really?" she questions, arching her brow as her voice raises unnaturally high.

"Yeah, I've made Prosecco and Margherita cupcakes, lavender, honey, and dark chocolate chili macarons, double choc fudge brownies, bread and butter pudding with whiskey, and a few other things I can't remember," I tell her.

Lauren's eyes widen as she looks at the baked goods laid out before me. I've loved baking my entire life, ever since Chef Marie taught me one school holiday while my parents were abroad. They left me with the nanny and the people who worked for us to take care of me while they were off galivanting at some gorgeous holiday destination.

My mother was always on a diet when I was growing up. She was obsessed with looking good for my father, making sure she looked her best at all times for him. I hated it because it meant I was never allowed to have any dessert or anything sweet as a child. My mother would pinch what she would deem fat on my body, telling me that if I didn't look after myself, they would never find me a husband from a well-to-do family if I looked anything less than what they said was perfection.

Thankfully, Chef Marie hated that my mother deprived me of dessert, and she would stash a few goodies in the kitchen, so I could come down in the middle of the night and enjoy a few delicacies. I would hide away in the pantry and eat my dessert with the biggest smile on my face.

As I got older, I took a vested interest in baking desserts, and the older I got, the more my parents would leave me at home by myself, which suited me fine. So, Chef Marie taught me everything she knew about baking desserts, which was a lot seeing as she was a Le Cordon Bleu-trained French chef, and as a French person, being deprived of happiness through sugar and butter was a sin. And that's the reason I've been working so hard ever since the day I turned eighteen when my family kicked me out of their home and cut off my trust fund because I wanted to become a model, while I saved every dime to one day be able to purchase my own bakery. I didn't care where it was as long as it was all mine, and no one could *ever* take it from me.

"You know I never say no to your sweets. But tell me …

what's bothering you?" Lauren asks while grabbing a macaron and taking a bite, then humming with delight. It's stupid, really, and I've been baking all night to try to forget about *him*, but I can't.

"Mr. King hasn't been into the club since that night at Minx." I huff the words out as I nervously start packing the treats away into takeout containers so I can bring them to work. I told him he could request me, and I thought he would have by now.

Lauren's brows raise high at my confession.

"Why the hell has this man gotten under my skin so easily?" I ask.

"I feel ya, babe. That's what it's like with me and Mr. Fox." She sighs.

I get it now, her obsession with a man she can't have.

"He demanded things from me that night that I wanted to give him, but …"

"You've come so far, Elle. You're so close to making your dreams come true, girl. One more year, and you will have everything you have ever dreamed of. And maybe if Mr. King is still single when you get back from the island, maybe you'll run into each other in the rain … because *hello, London* … and he realizes in that moment how much he's missed you, and he demands you to never leave him ever again. Then he whisks you off your feet, and you live happily ever after," Lauren says.

I stare at my friend, who I've always thought of as the least romantic woman I know, and slowly blink at her sentimental, idealistic fairy-tale image.

"What?" she asks, questioning me as she pops the other half of the macaron into her mouth. "Don't tell me that isn't what you've thought about?" She grins, eyeing off a cupcake.

"Is that what *you* think about?" I question.

Lauren stills, and her blue eyes narrow on me. "You can have a crush on someone and not wish for a happily ever after with that person, Elle," she tells me seriously.

I raise my brows in surprise at her tone.

Have I hit a nerve with her?

"Mr. Fox is a bit of fun. There are some guests you just gel with, and that's him," she explains.

"I wasn't implying anything, Lauren," I add quickly.

"I know, babe. Look, my infatuation with Mr. Fox is something to pass the time with. I don't have dreams like you do, Elle," Lauren explains as her face falls.

"What do you mean you don't have dreams?"

Lauren shrugs her shoulders. "I could work with my parents at the modeling agency if I wanted to, but how can I compete with Reed and Juliette ... the oh-so-perfect ones," she says, rolling her eyes over her siblings.

"Do you want to work at the agency?" I ask.

"No!" she replies, shaking her head. "I don't know what I want to do. Everyone else is doing well for themselves. Reed's running the New York branch of the agency, and Juliette's running Paris. Lennox is everywhere on the social pages. He's transitioning from modeling to acting, and then there's Ines, who's killing it as a DJ. Then there's me. What do I do great? Besides blow jobs ..."

I had no idea Lauren felt this way. She's never voiced any of these concerns with me before. "Oh, babe, don't put yourself down like that," I say, hating that she thinks so little of herself. She's more than her blow job skills. I rush around the kitchen island and wrap my arms around her tightly. "I love you, Loz. I think you're the bestest friend I could ever have asked for. You have been nothing but supportive of me in helping me reach my dreams. You saved me after school when my family turned their backs on me. Whatever you want to do, I'll support you."

Lauren hugs me back tightly. "That's the thing ... I don't know what I want. At twenty-five, you'd think I'd have my shit sorted, right?" She chuckles against my skin.

"You don't have to figure it all out just yet. There's time," I tell her.

"I'm lucky I have a trust fund to fall back on." She sighs.

"You're more than the sum of that fund," I tell her before a memory filters into my mind of a drunken conversation we had years ago, bubbling to the surface. "Not sure if you remember a conversation we had one night, and you confessed to me your dream would be to buy a house in the country and live a simple life."

Lauren's eyes widen as I tell her about the memory. "Oh my god, I remember that. Can't believe I said that out loud." She chuckles.

"Is that something you want to do?" I ask, curious now why she would hide this part of her away from us all.

"I know everyone sees me as this crazy party girl, and I am, but it feels like a character I play. People gravitate toward that persona because if I showed them the *real Lauren,* maybe they wouldn't like it so much," she confesses.

Oh, I had no idea she felt like this.

"Why have you never told me?"

"I don't know. I guess I was worried you'd think it crazy."

"Babe, I stayed up all night baking hundreds of sweets because I can't stop thinking about a man I can't have. Who's the crazy one in this house?" I joke with her. "You know I'm here for you?"

"I know you are. And I love you," she says, squeezing my hand. "For the moment, I'm happy helping you achieve your dreams while I try to figure out mine." I give Lauren another hug because I'm so proud of her for finally telling me her worries.

"You are my official taste tester, and that *is* a *serious* job," I say, grinning at her.

"Now that I can get behind." She chuckles, the dark cloud above her disappearing.

"I think I'm going to go for a run to clear this mind of mine," I tell her.

"Go you. I'm allergic to running, so I'm going to stay here. I think it's best I test some more of these treats, you know ... for quality control. I take my job seriously." She grins, which has me chuckling.

I give her a wave and head upstairs to get changed into my active wear.

Thankfully, Hyde Park isn't far from Lauren's house, and today I'm going to push myself and do the Kensington Palace jog, which is a good four miles around the park. It's a crisp end of Autumn morning, but thankfully, there's nothing but blue sky today as I head off.

As soon as I take off, my mind wanders to Mr. King.

Why am I letting this man consume my thoughts like this? Yes, he is hot and may have whispered dirty words in my ear while pinning me to the door, but plenty of other men over the years have done equally dirty things to me, but they've never lingered. My mind better not be falling for that broken-man bullshit those other women fall for. I am not the woman to put Mr. King back together again after having his heart broken. I have enough of my own baggage to deal with.

I push myself to the limit—my body is exhausted, my muscles ache, I'm drenched in sweat—but my mind is clearer after my run. I know what I've got to do now and that is to put Mr. King back into the client box, especially as I'll be moving halfway across the world in a couple of months.

I'm so lost in my thoughts that I don't hear someone shouting, "Watch out," until a soccer ball hits me square in the head and knocks me on my ass in the grass. I see stars for a couple of moments, wondering what the hell happened.

"Shit, I'm so sorry. I thought you heard me call out," the deep voice yells. "Elle?"

I look up, and standing before me, dressed in a white T-shirt that's drenched in sweat and clinging to his well-defined body, showing off every taut muscle, is the one man I'm trying to forget.

Universe, can I catch a break?

Mr. King is standing above me with his hand held out and a concerned look on his face. "Are you okay?" he asks, crouching down beside me while inspecting the impact on my head as I ignore his outstretched hand.

"I'm fine." I wave him away irritably.

"You took that ball to the head pretty hard," he says, trying to stop himself from smiling.

"You think it's funny kicking balls into unsuspecting women's heads?" I ask while raising my voice at him.

"Is she all right, Ali?" a voice calls out from behind him.

I glance over his broad shoulders and see a couple of men dressed in soccer gear looking over at where he's crouching with me.

"Go on without me," he calls out, throwing the soccer ball back toward the guys. That's when I notice one of the guys from the club standing there watching us with a frown on his face.

Shit.

"I've got to go. I can't be seen here. I don't want to lose my job," I tell him as panic races through my body.

Mr. King looks over his shoulder at his friends, who are kicking the ball to one another and not paying us any attention.

Then a dark look falls across his face as he stares back at me. "You know my friends?" he asks with a growl.

My eyes widen at the accusation he's throwing at me by that question.

"Fuck you," I say, pushing him hard. I must catch him off guard because he falls backward onto the grass. I get up and jog away.

How dare he look at me like that?

I thought he was different.

Even if I had slept with his friends, it doesn't matter because it's *my fucking job* to do that. *I haven't,* may I add.

"Elle, wait!" he calls out, but I ignore him. "Elle," he calls again.

"Stalking is a crime, Ali," someone states as he follows me.

While trying to push through my exhaustion to get away from him, I hear his thundering steps behind me, and seconds later, his enormous shadow falls across me. He doesn't say anything as he runs along beside me.

"Go away," I hiss and decide to run further through the park to get away from him.

"It's a public park. I'm not going anywhere," he answers.

I look over, and he has a smirk on his face.

Fuck him! I dig deep and cut through a thick forest section, but that wasn't the best idea because as soon as we are off the path and away from everyone, he pounces on me. He grabs my wrist and then pushes me up against a tree, making me squeal, and my heart thump even wilder in my chest.

"What the hell do you think you're doing?" I scream as he grabs my other wrist and pushes them high above me, holding them in his one large hand.

"I need to know, Elle … have you been with any of my friends?"

"What if I have?" I spit back.

"I don't care, but I need to know. It won't change the fact that I can't fucking stop thinking about you, or the fact that my hand doesn't satisfy the ache your pussy gives me …"

His filthy words have me swallowing hard against my dry throat. His dirty talk has set my body on fire, and the fact that I'm pinned against a tree by one of my clients outside of the club environment, should have me running for the hills or at least kneeing him in the balls, but I can't seem to find the strength to do that.

"I haven't been with any of your friends," I tell him in a semi-whisper because, for some reason, I want him to know.

"Thank fuck," he curses before launching himself at me.

As soon as his lips meet mine, I know I'm done for. I'm crossing a line that I said I *never* would. He pushes his hard self against me, and I feel the hardness of the tree's bark against my bare skin with only my sports bra protecting me from splinters. His hand runs up my side, and his thumb caresses underneath my breast, sending shivers down my spine.

"I haven't stopped thinking about you, Elle," he growls against my skin.

"I thought my underwear would have helped that."

"It's not enough. I don't feel satisfied when I come by my hand like I do in your cunt."

Fuck.

"You haven't come to the club."

"I know, I'm sorry. I've been away for work," he says as his lips run along my neck.

"I shouldn't be doing this. We both could be kicked out of the club," I warn him.

"You want me to stop?" he questions as his tongue swirls against the dip of my neck. A moan falls from my lips, and I can feel his smile.

"Stop!" I push him away from me.

"I can only imagine how wet your panties are right now. What I wouldn't give to take a souvenir home."

"Mr. King," I say, holding up my finger at him.

"Outside the club, it's Alistair or Ali, never Mr. King," he warns.

"There can't be anything … *outside the club*, Mr. King," I bite back.

The next thing I know, he's on me again, pushing me up against the tree, then his hands are down my pants which makes me squeal before he triumphantly pulls my thong from my leggings. *What in the Houdini trick was that?* Then his nose inhales the scent of my panties.

"Stop! Give me them back. They're all sweaty." I try to grab my panties back from him, but he holds them up high.

"They smell even sweeter."

"You have a problem."

"Yep!" He smiles as if stealing women's underwear is completely normal, then he shoves them into his shorts pocket.

"I'll be seeing you soon, Elle."

"You know where to find me, *Mr. King*," I call back, making him still.

He chuckles before turning around, pulling out my panties, and inhaling them again before putting them back into his pocket and jogging back out of the wilderness.

11

ALISTAIR

After my encounter with Elle, I head back to the guys to see if they're still playing soccer, but the only one there is Jasper.

"The others had to go," he says, packing up the last of his stuff into his backpack. "You wanna grab some lunch?"

"Yeah, I'm starved," I reply, rubbing my taut stomach with my hand.

Jasper grins, and we head on over across the road and into a luxury hotel for lunch.

"You know what you did today was incredibly stupid," Jasper warns as he takes a sip of his beer.

"Don't know what you're talking about," I tell him.

"Don't play stupid with me. That girl was from the club," Jasper states angrily. "Do you have any idea how much trouble she and you will get into if anyone saw? Lucky Alex wasn't here today. You don't know who is in and who isn't," he warns me.

"There's something about her …"

"Jesus, Ali, don't tell me you like the woman whose job it is to bring all your fantasies to life?"

"Of course not, but you can't tell me after all the years

you've been a member that a girl hasn't turned your damn head?" I question him.

"This isn't about me," he argues, taking a large gulp of his beer.

"Knew it! Here you are lecturing me, and you're probably doing the same with someone from the club. You are, aren't you?" I glare at him.

"Fuck you! No! I'm not stupid. No woman is worth giving up that fantasyland for."

"You're content with going to the club to get your fix?" I ask.

Does he not want more eventually?

"Hell, yeah, I am. You've seen the shit Alex has been through with women. And now you being fucked over by Miranda. Who the fuck wants to go through that?" He quirks a brow at me.

"You need to get over your ex, she's moved on, married someone else, and is popping out blue-bloodied babies," I tell him.

This was not *at all* how I thought lunch would go—I don't want to argue with Jasper.

"I couldn't give a shit about her. I wish her well!" He huffs while glaring at me.

"I'm not looking for a relationship. I'm happy to be single after the dumpster fire that is my love life," I tell him.

"Sounds like there's a but missing at the end of that statement," Jasper adds.

"Fine! *But* there is something about her that I like, and I don't know what it is," I tell him honestly.

"These women are experts at what they do. Do not misplace lust for something it's not, and don't think you're someone special to them," Jasper tells me coolly.

We sit in a silent standoff, neither one of us wanting to give in. We are both stubborn fuckers.

"Look ... I get it. There is one girl there that ... *does it for me*. And I catch myself wondering what the hell she's doing outside of the club now and then. But then I think is she like that with *all the other guys* who frequent the club? Or is it only that good with me? The thing is, I'll never know. It will drive you crazy thinking about it, so you need to put a wall up between the two of you. Enjoy everything you do in that moment but know that you can't recreate that again outside the club," Jasper warns.

"You're right," I say, sadly agreeing with him.

"I know!" He chuckles. "Look, at least you're getting back out there after a really shit time. How about I organize a double date for Friday night? You can enjoy the company of another woman and see if it's the magic of the club clouding your judgment?"

"Fine!" I huff the word out hoping it will shut him the hell up about Elle.

※※※※※※※※

"Heads up, they're here," Jasper says, elbowing me in the side.

I look up from the table and see two beautiful women walking through the door. Jasper had told me that the brunette is my date for the evening, and her name is Lila, and the blonde, Vicky, is his.

"Sweetheart, how are you," Jasper coos sweetly as he grabs Vicky's face and kisses her softly. She smiles up at him, fluttering her long lashes and pushing out her over-inflated breasts for him to appreciate.

Yeah, so not *my thing.*

"Hi, I'm Lila," the brunette says, introducing herself. She looks the opposite of the Barbie she arrived with. She's dressed in a skintight black dress and killer heels, her chest is in proportion with her body, and her dark eyes narrow on me as if assessing me to see if I'm worthy of her time. I watch as she looks over my suit, then down to my watch, before dipping to my shoes.

"I'm Alistair. It's a pleasure to meet you," I say, kissing her cheek before I pull out her chair for her.

"Ladies, the finest champagne for you both?" Jasper asks.

Vicky giggles beside him while Lila nods her head coolly. Jasper orders for the girls and then us before the waiter walks away.

"So, what is it you do, Alistair?" Lila asks, turning herself toward me, giving me her full attention.

"I work at a nightclub," I reply to the question, gauging to see whether she is still interested when she thinks I'm a lowly employee, not the boss. That cool demeanor flinches for the barest of moments, and that's when I know she's after a rich guy and isn't serious about meeting a man and forming a *real* connection.

"Oh, how nice," she says, looking away from me and over to where Jasper and Vicky are laughing together. Bet she's thinking she got the short end of the stick on this date.

"How about you? What is it you do?" I ask her because now it's awkward.

"I'm a model," she states, flipping her hair over her shoulder as if I should know who she is.

"Oh, how nice," I say, throwing her own words back at her. Her dark eyes narrow on me, trying to work out if I'm being sarcastic or not. "Would I have seen you in anything?" I ask as the waiter hands me my old-fashioned before popping the bottle of champagne for the ladies, to which Vicky squeals with delight.

"I've been in *Vogue, Harper's Bazaar, Elle* … all the major magazines. I currently have a billboard in Times Square," she adds, then takes a dainty sip of her champagne.

"Sounds like a big deal. Congrats!" I hold up my glass to her.

She plasters on a fake smile and then tries to insert herself into Jasper and Vicky's conversation.

The night continues in the same fashion—Lila ignoring me or giving me fake pleasantries while trying to capture Jasper's attention away from her friend, who doesn't appear too happy about Lila's sudden interest in her date.

Me? I can't wait for this shit to be over.

"Your shout, man." Jasper chuckles. He's had one too many whiskeys. "Ali here ... he's the richest amongst the group," he says, mock whispering.

Lila's eyes widen upon hearing Jasper's words.

Great.

I take out my black Amex and throw it down on the table for the staff. Lila's eyes take in the card before looking up at me. *Oh no, here it is.*

"So, Ali, you ready to take this party somewhere private?" she purrs, running her nails up my arm.

"Not really, I have somewhere else I would rather be." Her eyes widen at my rudeness, but the bitch has been an ice queen all night because she thought I wasn't rich enough, and as soon as she realized I had money, her entire demeanor changed. I pick up my credit card and place it back in my wallet.

"Jasper ... never invite me on a blind date *ever* again," I tell my friend loudly.

Lila huffs and mumbles curses under her breath while Vicky bursts out laughing.

Jasper stares at me as if I've lost my mind.

"I've got to go. I've got anywhere else to be," I tell them before turning and storming out of the restaurant. I grab my phone and call the number on the gold card and cross my fingers the person I would rather be spending my Friday night with is working.

12

ELOISE

"Hey, Eloise, you've been requested," Sara calls out.

My heart leaps inside my chest as I rush up to the tablet and look down to view who has requested me, stupidly hoping it is him even though I told myself to stop thinking about him.

Mr. King

The tablet flashes his name, and I try to contain my excitement seeing his name finally requesting me. It's been a week since our run-in at Hyde Park, and I was beginning to lose all hope. And because of that, I've been baking up a storm.

I hand the tablet back to Sara and hurry down the corridors to his room. I suck in a deep breath as I stand outside the door, then peek through the one-way window to see him standing there, pacing around the room, dare I say it, looking nervous.

Is that because he's excited to see me?

Or is it because he's going to tell me he can't see me anymore?

Only one way to find out, Eloise.

My hand touches the door, and I push it open. Mr. King turns around at the sound, and his entire face lights up upon seeing me.

Butterflies begin to dance in my stomach as my heart thunders in my chest—I'm surprised he's not able to hear it from where he's standing.

"Thank fuck! I'm so fucking happy to see you," he states, rushing to me and picking me up into his arms. He swings me around and kisses me until I'm dizzy. He then crashes us down against the bed in the middle of the room and rolls me under him. "I can't believe you're here," he says, staring at me in awe, those hazel eyes wide with excitement.

"I'm here, and we're allowed to touch finally," I tell him with a smile on my face, and this unfamiliar feeling of happiness bubbling underneath my skin. My fingernails run along his back, the softness of his shirt is the only barrier between us. A groan falls from his lips as I touch his back, the electricity crackles between us. The next thing I know, he's pulling up my black slip dress, exposing my lack of underwear, to which he lets out this deep, bone-tingling growl before he dives between my legs.

Oh shit.

I moan as the first swipe of his tongue slides along my slit. *Yes.* I squirm as I arch my back while he delves deeper, my fingers reaching out and tangling in his sandy-colored hair. He's feasting between my legs as if he's a starving man, and my pussy is the first meal he has eaten in weeks.

I sure as hell hope it is.

Not that you have a say, Eloise, you've slept with a heap of people since—*but that's my job.*

I haven't gone out and dated anyone or slept with anyone socially. There's a huge difference for me between club sex and outside-the-club sex. I know many people who are in relationships with people who work at the club, who can see the difference because to them, sex is sex. I'm not going to lie, some people I have slept with recently have been fantastic, but in my mind all I am thinking about is delivering their requests and making sure they're having fun. It's never about me. Guess I can't be upset if he's hooking up with people outside the club. He should because there's no option for us outside these four walls, and why would I hold him back? Plus, I'm about to move halfway across the world in the next couple of months. This is it! This right here is all you have with this man—these moments in the club where there's nothing but the two of us in our own little fantasyland, where I can pretend to feel what it would be like to be with him in an alternative world.

He slides two fingers into me, and I swear he knows the exact buttons to push to detonate me into oblivion. Every part of my body quakes as I come apart under his expert charms. He doesn't give me a moment to come down from my orgasmic high before he's turning me over and slapping my ass.

"Get on all fours, Elle," he commands, and I do as I'm told, pushing myself up from the bed and assuming the position. "Fuck, your ass is delicious." The next thing I know, Alistair's teeth sink into my ass cheek, and it should have hurt, but with the lingering effects of my orgasm still swirling around my body, it turns me on instead. He kisses the bite mark before giving it a good slap to push the last tingles of pain through my body and directing it all to my clit.

There's a mirror on the wall, which I've only noticed, and my eyes flick to the image of Alistair fully dressed behind me. His hazel eyes roam over me with heat. With quick fingers, he unbuttons the top button of his trousers, then begins sliding down the zipper to his suit pants slowly, all the while his eyes are on my ass. *I'm guessing Mr. King is an ass man.* His hand then knocks my knees apart, demanding me to open wider for him. He then pulls himself out of his pants, and my mouth waters as I catch a glimpse of his magnificent dick.

Alistair raises a brow as he gives himself a couple of tugs before sliding himself through my wetness. I close my eyes and suck in a gasp at the connection, and when I open them again, two hazel eyes are staring back at me through the mirror. His teeth have sunk into his bottom lip as he slowly pushes inside me.

"Don't close your eyes, Elle. Watch every last inch of me filling you." He grunts as I feel every inch of him. "Watch how perfectly I fit inside your cunt."

Dammit, he does, and he feels fantastic.

His fingers then dig into my hips as he pulls himself almost all the way out before slamming back into me. *Yes, he feels so deep like this.* "Keep watching, Elle," he commands as my eyes meet his again in the mirror. "I want to sear this memory of how perfect you look into my mind." So I do as he asks.

He keeps sliding into me agonizingly slow, savoring this moment.

My hand falls between my thighs as my fingers swirl around my clit.

"Don't!" He grunts. "It's my job to make you come," he demands as he knocks my hand out of the way, his thick fingers taking my place, sliding over my aching clit.

My teeth sink into my lip as the sensations begin to take over, and my legs quiver with each thrust and flick against my sensitive bud. With every moan falling from my lips, the harder and deeper his thrusts become, it's as if hearing me is his aphrodisiac.

"I own your fucking pleasure." He curses a few times as he furiously strums my clit, unlocking the secret code that only he knows as I feel myself moving closer to oblivion.

"Give it to me, Elle. Show me how easily I make you come."

And like a match to a tinderbox with one expert flick, he sets me off, and I clench down against his dick as his hand pushes me higher. I scream my release, and thankfully, the rooms are soundproof. Otherwise, we would have a group of eager watchers standing by our window wondering what kind of magic is happening in room twenty-four.

Grunts, groans, moans, and curses fall from his lips while he too chases his own entry into oblivion. His thrusts turn hurried as he fucks me close to his end until he can't hold it any longer and crashes over the edge, joining me in a sweaty mess on the bed.

"Fuck!" He chuckles as he pulls me into his arms.

"I know," I say, nestling into his chest.

We are both still dressed, and that makes what we did feel hotter as if we were so desperate to fuck each other we didn't have time to undress.

"How have I stayed away from you for so long?" he mumbles, running his fingers through my hair as my hand raises and rests on his chest, his heart beating wildly underneath my fingertips.

"I'm sure you've been busy," I say.

Silence falls between us before he speaks again, "With work not with anything else," he adds. He doesn't owe me an explanation, but he does let out a heavy sigh. "I was on a date earlier tonight, the first since my breakup," he confesses, and acid burns in my stomach at the thought of him dating someone else.

"Guessing it didn't go so well if you ended up here?"

"Hey," he says, lifting my chin to look at him. "You are *not* the consolation prize. My friend set me up with a gold digger. And that's not my thing," he says fiercely. "I went on the date because I was trying to stop thinking about *you*."

Those damn butterflies are back.

His hand cups my face. "I understand that all we have is what happens behind these walls ..." he trails off, his thumb running over my lip.

"It's the way it has to be," I tell him.

"I know." He smiles sadly, and damn him for making me question my stance on not crossing *that line*.

Be strong, Eloise. You can do it.

The problem is those hazel eyes are making my insides gooey.

"Did you know you can order food and drinks? Maybe next time we could have a date in here." And as soon as I say the words, I want to shove them right back into my mouth. "Or not, we don't have to do anything," I add quickly, which makes him laugh.

"Fuck it! Let's have a date right now," he says excitedly.

"Now?"

"Yes, now." He grins, and it makes my insides tingle.

"Okay," I say, shrugging my shoulders. Because why can't I have a date with the guy I like in the middle of a sex club?

"Go draw a bath, and I'll organize everything," he tells me, shoving me off the bed and into the bathroom.

"Okay, Mr. Bossy." I chuckle as I let him lead me into the bathroom.

"I'm going to date the hell out of you tonight." He grins before kissing me again.

"I'm sure you will, Mr. King," I reply while giving him a wink. Except those words have formed a frown on his face. *What did I say wrong?*

"It's either Alistair or Ali. *Not* Mr. King," he warns me.

I open my mouth to argue, but he places a finger against my lips.

"Please, let me have this," he asks gently, and I nod. "Thank you," he says, kissing me slowly again. "Now go. I have shit to do."

Fine! I roll my eyes, close the door behind me, and run myself a large bath, then turn on the jacuzzi jets. I never get to overindulge in the spa baths unless it's part of what the guest wants. So, taking the time for myself in the spa feels like a naughty luxury. I must doze off because a little while later, Alistair is nudging me awake.

"Hey, sleepyhead, I'm ready for you. But if you want to have an early night, I totally understand."

"No. Sorry, the bath was warm, and it lulled me off to sleep.

The next thing I know you're waking me up. I'm probably a giant prune now," I say, looking down at myself.

"Gorgeous prune," he says, kissing my nose. "I'll meet you outside." And then he's gone.

I pull the plug on the spa and jump out, and as I do, I catch a glimpse of myself in the mirror.

Ew. I am a giant prune. That's not sexy!

I quickly dry myself, then grab the black satin robe from the hook behind the door and wrap myself in it. I hang up the towel and head out into the room.

"Oh my god, Ali," I say as my hands cover my mouth in surprise. The entire room is decked out in fairy lights, making it look magical, and then there's a table set in the middle of the room with crystal glasses, porcelain plates with cloches, and a bottle of champagne chilling to the side.

"You like it?" he asks, seeming nervous as he shuffles from foot to foot.

"I love it. Thank you." I try to keep my emotions in check as I hug him because no one has ever gone to this much effort for me before.

"Good," he says, pulling out the chair for me. *Such a gentleman.* "Champagne?" he asks.

I nod, and he pops the cork and pours me a glass before taking a seat. He then takes the cloches off our dinner plates and right there in front of me is perfectly cooked lobster drizzled with herb butter. The smell is divine. It's served with thick fries on the side. Simple yet elegant. I look up to see Alistair watching me intently.

"Do you like lobster? I should have asked if you had an allergy. Maybe I should have gone for the steak," he rambles on.

"Ali," I say, reaching out across the table. "I love it, thank you."

"Cheers," he says, raising his champagne glass. I do the

same, and we clink them together. Then we fall into a happy silence as we eat our lobster.

The conversation flows after I told him we needed to set boundaries, and as much as I wish this was a proper date, it can't be. I'm not allowed to know anything about him, even though I may have stalked his socials. It took a couple of moments of negotiating, but in the end, he agreed. He spoke about the work I already knew about, owning Minx, regaling me with tales about the craziness that is running a nightclub. He then spoke about his other clubs and things that had been going on with those.

We spoke about our love of travel, and I told him how Lauren and I used to get paid to party at all the clubs around Greece and Ibiza. He was annoyed that he hadn't met me then as we were both there at the same time.

I told him about my modeling career that never took off and the crazy things photographers used to say to get the image they wanted.

In the end, it doesn't matter that we don't know about each other's families or past because I still felt like I have gotten to know who Alistair King is without any of that other stuff.

I don't think I've had a better date than this one.

13

ELOISE

For the last month, Alistair has been coming into the club for nearly every single one of my shifts, and we've had dinner and then spent the rest of the evening working it off. I know that his frequency at the club has been noticed, but I've assured Sara that everything is aboveboard. That he's having a stressful time at work and has recently had a breakup, and I'm helping him get back into the dating scene. That seems to have made Sara's concerns disappear because I'm doing a community service for one of our guests, which is not as uncommon as you would think.

"I love you, Elle, but this is too fucking early for me to be up on a Sunday." Lauren groans as I pack my treats into the car to take them to the local markets. For months, I've been applying to get into the local markets to sell my goods, but they had too many bakery stalls to accept me. Thankfully, as it turns out for me but not her, one of the stall holders broke her leg, and a spot has opened for the next eight weeks before she returns, which is fine by me because that works out well for my trip to the Caribbean.

"Would you stop moaning! I'll buy you a coffee when we get

there," I tell her as I carefully place the last box of goodies into the car. Nerves hit me as this is the first time I've sold my items publicly. Yes, I have a huge following on social media because I bake and post on there, but I'd been too scared to attempt to sell my sweet treats before.

Lauren dared me to do it. She was sick of hearing me talking about it. I've been so scared to make a go of my dream to be a baker, something I've aspired to be all my life, that no matter how much I wanted to do it, I couldn't bring myself to actually take the next step. My parents' words have rattled around in my head over the years, telling me I'll never be good enough, and those words have kept me from taking this leap, but when I was given the opportunity, how could I say no?

And what I need to know is *am I good enough?*

Yes, my friends and work friends tell me they love everything I bake when I bring in my goodies. But the general public? Now, that is scary stuff. What happens if all these years I've been working toward my dream, and I literally suck at it?

"Fine, you're lucky I love you." Lauren grins, jumping into the driver's seat, ignoring my internal crisis that's happening as we head out into the early Sunday morning traffic.

It takes us a while to set up my stall, put up the gazebo, and dress my stand to look pretty with bunting across the front. Then we carefully fill the display cabinets with all the treats.

Lauren starts building the treat boxes, so I don't have to do that while serving people. I double-check I have enough change in my pink money tin and that the credit card machine is working, then I suck in a deep breath as my nerves start to kick in.

"Here, enjoy this," Lauren says, handing me a coffee.

I thank her as I take a sip of the delicious, warm drink.

"You are going to do brilliantly. People will be looking for holiday treats because who the fuck wants to bake shit?" Lauren chuckles.

"I'm hoping a load of people don't want to bake *shit* ..." I laugh, "… and I sell out." I warm my hands against the mug of coffee.

"Sorry I can't stay all day, but I'll be back this afternoon to help pack up. I promise," Lauren says, sipping her coffee.

It's her dad's birthday, so I can't be upset that she isn't right beside me helping me all day today.

"Your dad's cake is in the fridge at home. Don't forget it, it's his favorite."

"He'll love it! Thanks, babe, for making me look like the best daughter ever," she says, blowing the steam off her coffee. "Oh, heads up … first customer coming." She grins as she jumps behind the counter.

"Hi, welcome to Cakeology. What can I get for you today?"

14

ALISTAIR

George and Miranda had their baby a couple of weeks ago, and I'm not sure how I'm feeling about it. On the one hand, I'm an uncle, and on the other, fuck them for betraying me. I've been summoned to meet the baby at my parents' house—neutral ground, some would say—and my mother has told me in no uncertain terms to suck it up and show up for the happy couple.

Why do I have to celebrate their betrayal? Yes, I know it's not the baby's fault, and I do want to meet my nephew, but why do I have to be the one told to not make things awkward? As if somehow this entire situation is my fault. They should be the ones walking around on eggshells after what they did, but I can't be mad at the baby—it's not his fault his parents are assholes.

I've decided to head to Hyde Park for a run this morning to clear my mind before heading over to my parents. I need to be Zen to get through this damn dinner.

As I enter the park, my mind wanders to Elle, and I think about the way I pushed her up against the tree as I pass it. Then that night at the club after my disastrous date, I had the perfect date with Elle and have been back to the club for the past month a couple of times a week. I'm a sucker, I know, trying to woo a woman who works at a sex club. But I do know there's something between Elle and me—there's something more. I'm a patient guy, but the more time I spend with her at the club, the more I wish things could be different.

How much does she need to reach her goal? Because I'm willing to pay if it means we can date outside the club.

I push myself running around the park until my legs ache, and I think I might have a heart attack, but I do feel better—clearer about everything that's going on in my life.

I can get through tonight with my family, I tell myself. *I think I can anyway.*

As I walk back to my home, I spy the local markets. They're set up every Sunday, but I never go in. Maybe I should get Miranda some flowers. After all, she did just birth a human. I let out a heavy sigh and cross the road to head into the bustling market. As I meander through the crowd, I spy the flower lady and order a bouquet of blue flowers, seeing as they had a boy. She adds a blue bunny and new-baby balloon to the assortment.

Once I have the assortment in my hand, I keep walking through the markets, thinking I might as well check it out while I'm here.

The scent of coffee and food captures my attention as my stomach rumbles. I head to the coffee van first and grab myself a hot drink, then I continue looking at all the different food on offer. There are tons of things available. I had no idea. Maybe I need to come down here more often. Then I spy towers of cupcakes in the distance with a line out the front. They must be good, so I head toward them. Maybe I should bring some dessert tonight? Make it look like I'm not bitter over the entire situation.

Let's face it, I am well and truly over Miranda. There isn't an ounce of attraction or love there for me anymore, but I know my brother is going to have his back up waiting to see if I'm going to try to steal his girl.

I don't care.

I want nothing to do with either of them.

Good riddance!

I'm happy for them.

They are now a family, but I don't want any part of whatever game my brother wants to play regarding Miranda.

It's done.

We're done.

He's won.

Game over!

The tension I seemed to have dispersed after my run is back again. Dammit! I might need to head to the gym back at my apartment to burn it off again. The closer I get to the cupcake stall, the hairs on the back of my neck begin to stand up as if there is static electricity in the air. The girl working at the stall is flat out serving people, and I think, *maybe I should come back when she's not so busy,* but then she turns around, and I realize who it is.

Elle.

My Elle.

What the hell is she doing serving cupcakes and sweets at my local markets?

Does she live around here?

Then my mind goes back to that time I ran into her at the coffee shop. She told me she was visiting a friend. Was that a lie? Does she actually live in this neighborhood?

The longer I stare at her, the more I realize how much she's in over her head by the sheer number of people she's trying to serve all by herself.

My feet pick up speed as I move to the side of her stall. "Need some help?" I ask.

She pauses, turning her head toward me, her jaw falling open as surprise flashes across her face. Her eyes look down at the bouquet of flowers in my hand, and a tiny frown forms on her face.

Is that jealousy? Sure as hell hope so.

It shouldn't make me feel good, but it does. It's as if she shakes the shock from her mind and continues serving people.

"What do you need me to do?" I ask.

"You want to help me?" she questions, turning again as she hands over the cash and gives someone back their change.

"You look like you need it. So tell me what I need to do?" I ask again, only this time my voice is stern.

"Right, thanks. Um … if you can pack the sweets into the box while I serve, that would be great," she says, giving me a relieved smile.

I can do this.

I've got her.

We work for the next couple of hours in perfect synchronicity as we move around each other, making a great team until the madness dies down and we can finally take a seat.

"Thanks so much for helping me. I wasn't expecting it to be this crazy." She sighs, taking a sip from her water bottle.

"Anytime. I couldn't stand there and watch you struggle like that." I grab a bottle of water for myself. "Did you make these?" I ask, pointing to the treats.

"Yeah, I did. Would you like to try one?" she asks, pointing at the last couple of cupcakes in the display cabinet.

"Sure."

She hands me what looks to be a chocolate cupcake with an incredible topper, and I take a bite into it. *Holy shit, this is good.* I take another bite, and before I know it, it's gone. She sits there staring at me waiting in anticipation for my thoughts.

"This was fucking delicious," I tell her honestly, her face lighting up by my compliment. "You're good. Like … really good," I add, which makes her laugh.

"Thanks. It's my love, my passion …"

"Well, you're born to do it. Can't wait to taste more. How come you don't do this full-time?"

Elle lets out a sigh. "I work where I work so I can save to buy my own bakery. It's something I've been working toward for a while now," she confesses.

"I'll be the first one there on opening day buying everything you make. Because this is damn good," I tell her.

"I appreciate the enthusiasm," she says with a smile.

"If you need any business advice, I'm happy to help. I've started many nightclubs and businesses over the years. I know the ins and outs."

She nods slowly. "You'd help me?"

"Of course!"

"Why?" she asks, and her question is like a punch to the gut, but I get what she's saying. She's being cautious of my intentions, and I understand that.

"Because when I see a business that looks like it's going to be a success, I'm willing to help them. I know how hard it is starting out. Believe me, I started small too. I've mentored many small business owners over the years."

Elle bites her bottom lip as she mulls over my offer. "We're not meant to have contact outside of the club, remember?"

"If we have to talk about it between those four walls of the club during our dates, then so be it," I tell her honestly.

"I don't want to be your charity case," she states.

"No! You've got me all wrong," I say, standing and walking over to her. "I wouldn't have mentioned my help if I didn't think you had the talent to make something of it. I don't offer my help to women I think are cute, that's not how I do business. Did you not see the lineup out the front of your stall?" I ask, reaching out and running my thumb across her cheek where there's a bit of icing smeared across it before licking it off my thumb. Her green eyes darken with arousal for the briefest of moments before she pushes it away.

"Here, let me give you a take-home pack to say thanks for helping me. I saved two packs, so I would love you to have one," she says, moving away from me.

I let her go even though I don't want her to, but I get it, she has this goal, and I'm kind of messing it up. I understand now why she's keeping me at a distance like she is. She hands me a dozen cupcakes in a white cardboard box, and I take it from her.

"Thanks again for helping me today, I appreciate it. But I don't want to keep you from your day," she says, eyeing the bouquet of flowers that I placed down on the chair while I helped. *Does she think they're for another woman?*

"My brother had a baby. This is for his partner, and the cupcakes will be for dessert tonight," I explain to her.

Elle nods and gives me a warm smile.

Right, I'm making her uncomfortable being near her in public.

"I'll get going. Congrats on a successful day." With a small wave, I turn on my heel and head for home.

※※※※※※※※

"You made it, sweetheart," my mother says, answering the door of my family home. She gives me a kiss on each cheek.

"I brought dessert. The cupcakes are some of the best," I say, handing her the take-home box. "I ate one when I got home, sorry."

"Aw, that's so thoughtful of you, my dear," she says, giving me a warm smile, but I can see the tension pulling against her face, wondering if I'm going to lose my mind or not. I promised I'd be on my best behavior tonight, no matter what my dickhead of a brother does to me.

"This is for Miranda." I show my mother the flowers.

"You didn't have to do that, but I appreciate it," she says, giving me a small smile as she takes the flowers from me.

"Alistair, my boy, good to see you," my dad calls out down the hallway as I shake off the rain from my coat, then I hang it up in the front entrance mudroom. He walks down the hallway to give me a welcoming hug.

Things have been strained in the family since the entire situation blew up, and I don't come around as much as I used to. This Christmas, I'm going to be sunning myself on the beaches of Australia, far, far away from here where I know the day will be about the first grandchild's first Christmas. No thanks, I'll pass this year. The baby has no idea what's happening around him, so I won't be missed.

"It's like a Band-Aid, rip it off, and then it won't hurt so much," my father whispers in my ear as he squeezes my shoulder and pushes me down the hallway to where I can hear the screams of a newborn baby.

Wow! That's so loud.

We walk into the living room, and my heart stops, and my stomach drops as I see Miranda rocking a little bundle in her arms, and the image feels like a dagger to the chest. Then I watch as my brother walks over and kisses Miranda on the forehead as he looks down lovingly at his baby.

I can't do this.

I can't be here and pretend these two didn't rip my heart out with their betrayal.

"Miranda, sweetheart, Ali got you these beautiful flowers," my mother says, pulling me from my thoughts.

Miranda looks up, and she gives me a bright smile as if she's happy to see me.

I can't do this.

My brother turns around, and I see the delight on his face as he takes in my pain.

I can't do this.

"Doesn't Miranda make the most beautiful new mother?" he says, kissing her temple while his eyes narrow on mine. "Didn't think she could get any more perfect, and then she produces me a boy. The next heir in the King family," he says with a wide grin, knowing he's beaten me to the next heir in the family.

Yep. I'm out.

"Sorry, Dad, can't deal with this shit," I whisper to him, and he nods in understanding.

"Congratulations, guys, on little Gabriel. He's very tiny. Unfortunately, I can't stay for dinner. There's a problem at work that I must sort out," I tell the room.

Miranda looks up at me with her face full of hurt and regret. Mum gasps beside me and tries to convince me to stay, but I'm not ready to accept all this.

"See, I told you, Mum, he'd make a scene." George moans as I step out of the room.

"George," my father's deep voice warns my brother.

Fuck this.

15

ELOISE

For the past month, I've been heading on down to the markets in Kensington, the ones where Alistair found me that day. And every weekend, like clockwork, he's come down to check in and help me with the stall. Every week is the same ...

"I've come to be of service." Alistair grinned as he walked around the stall and began helping me package the treats as if he'd done it a thousand times before.

And then, as soon as I've packed up for the day, he gave me a wave and continued on with his day. Never pushing for more. Come the next weekend, he was there again with a big smile on his face and a boiling hot cup of coffee for me, and we started the dance all over again.

Each passing week I'm becoming reliant on him to help me through this mad holiday season. I don't think I have baked so much in my entire life. There have been so many orders that I've had to take some time off from The Paradise Club to fulfill them all. Otherwise, I was working all through the night and not getting any sleep. Lauren's been helping me in the kitchen and at the markets but takes a break when Alistair is around giving us time to *'flirt over the icing'* as she says before coming back and helping again.

Lauren thinks it's fantastic that he's helping me.

"He's a busy guy, Elle. I know you haven't googled him, but the guy is a big deal. He owns some of the best clubs around the world. His family is rich too. They own some financing company, but he doesn't work there with them. Seems he bucked the family tradition and created his own way in the world, a bit like someone else I know." Lauren chuckled as I glared at her over a bucket of frosting. *"What I'm getting at is he must like you if he's coming down to the markets every Sunday in this shitty winter weather to help you out. Men don't do that kind of shit when they have pussy on tap as he does,"* she said, arching a brow at me.

"Doesn't matter, he's a client of the club, and that's the end of the story," I tell her.

"Quit then! You're making good money from your stall, yes? It's not like the money you're making at the club, but it's still good. I know you have this figure in your head, but there's more to life than numbers, babe," Lauren explained to me.

"I can't. I'm not willing to risk everything on him," I told her.

Lauren let out an exhausted sigh as it's the same fight we'd been having since Alistair started helping me out at the markets.

"I think he is worth the risk, babe," she said sadly.

"Doesn't matter, we're moving halfway across the world next month, so this is all a moot point."

"Don't go. Stay here and have little cupcake babies with that delicious man. What I would give to have a man give a shit about me like he does you." Lauren moaned out the words.

"Nothing is deviating me from my goal. No matter how gorgeous, kind, helpful Alistair is ... he is still a client."

"He sure hasn't been acting like a client. The guy hardly frequents the club now you're not there. You see him more outside of it than inside," Lauren stated.

"Like you said, he's a busy guy ..."

"Or maybe he's more interested in you than the hot sex you give him." *Lauren grinned.*

And I ignored her because her words were giving me hope that there might be something more between us, and I'd been trying to push down the feelings I got when I was around him, but it was hard.

"Thanks for helping again," I say, running my cold hands down my pants to warm them up as the winter chill bites into them.

"Any time! As long as you keep paying me with your baked goods, I'm all in," he says with a grin. "You've got me addicted to them, and like a junkie, I need my fix every Sunday."

"Now it all makes sense. Should I be calling for an intervention regarding your baked goods addiction?" I chuckle as I cup my hands in front of me and blow hot air on them.

Alistair frowns as he watches me before reaching out and taking my ice-cold fingers and rubbing them between his warm ones.

How is he so hot when I'm so cold? He then brings them up to his lips and blows hot air across my skin, and I feel it radiate through my entire body. I look up into his hazel eyes, and I'm drawn into the deep pools of molten heat as his lips touch my fingers, sending bolts of electricity through every nerve ending. My tongue runs along my bottom lip as my eyes fall to his, and everything around us falls away. His lips press together as he blows warm air across my skin again, and I swear I'm about to combust until he drops my hands suddenly.

"Oi, come back, fucking asshole," he bellows as he takes off through the market.

What the hell just happened?

Everyone standing around my booth looks over at me wondering too. I look around my stall, trying to work out what on earth happened, and then I look down and notice my pink money tin is gone. *No. Oh no.* As I rush out into the market to see if I can see where Alistair is, tears well in my eyes at the realization that everything I've worked for today has gone. Some asshole has stolen all my hard-earned cash. I sink down on my chair and stare at the empty dessert table, knowing this was the last weekend before Christmas and was my biggest yet.

Alistair walks back into the stall looking out of breath. "I tried to chase him, but I lost him in the crowd," he says, sucking in deep breaths before he rushes toward me. "I'm sorry, Elle, I tried to catch him," he says with a scowl on his face.

I'm unable to hold back the tears, thanks to my exhaustion, so they freely fall down my cheeks.

"Fuck," Alistair curses as he pulls me into his arms, and I wrap myself around him and cry. "I'm so sorry, baby girl, you don't deserve this. If I find that fucker, he's going to pay," he states against my neck.

I snuggle in tighter, absorbing his strength for a couple of moments before pulling away. "Thank you for trying," I tell him.

He wipes my tears away. "I'd do pretty much anything for you, Elle," he confesses.

Dammit! Why is he such a good guy? "I just want to go home," I tell him.

"I know, but you should report the robbery to the police."

"What are they going to be able to do? It was about one thousand pounds. It's not a lot for the police to give a shit about." I sniffle as I try to pack up my stall.

"But it's not right, Elle. He can't take your money and get away with it."

"Is everything okay?" The market organizer runs over and interrupts our conversation.

"Some guy stole her entire day's takings," Alistair explains to the organizer.

Her face falls as she sees my tear-soaked face. "I'm sorry, sweetheart, the police are on their way," she explains to me.

I let out a heavy sigh.

"It's happened a couple of times, so they are aware," the market organizer explains.

"Has anyone been able to get their money back?" I ask as the tiniest bit of hope burns brightly inside me.

She shakes her head.

That's what I thought.

So I turn back and finish packing up everything ready to take home.

Not long later, the police arrive, and I give them my statement. I know they think I'm a fool for turning my back on the tin like I did. It was stupid letting Alistair distract me in that moment.

My hands are shaking as I take my keys out of my bag, the adrenaline from the day now wearing off.

"I don't think you should drive," Alistair says, snatching the keys out of my hand. "You're in shock."

"I need to go home," I argue.

"I'll drive," he says, looking at me seriously as his brows pull together in a tight knot.

"No," I answer quickly.

Alistair raises a brow at me, surprised that I don't want his help. "Let me help you. I won't stay, I promise," he says softly.

I'm too exhausted to fight with him, so I nod and walk around to the passenger's side and slide in. I give him my address, he types it into his phone, and it begins giving him directions.

We drive in silence.

Once there, he helps me unload everything from the car into my home.

Lauren is away for the weekend, so the house is empty as I walk around in a daze putting everything away like I have done all the other weekends before this one. Alistair follows, putting the tables and gazebo away in the basement without saying a word.

"Thank you," I finally say once everything has been packed away. I'm sure he has a million and one other things he would rather be doing.

"I didn't do anything," he replies, shrugging his shoulders.

"You've done a lot. Maybe too much for me these past couple of weeks. And I don't know how to repay you for your kindness," I tell him through watery eyes.

"I did it for my own selfish reasons," he says, and I frown at his answer. "I got to hang out with you for the day."

A small smile falls across my lips as the tiniest of butterflies flutter inside my chest. "You can't say things like that," I declare, looking up at him.

Alistair stalks to me and backs me up against the wall in the living room. "Yes, I can, and I will." He glares down at me.

"No, you can't," I argue back.

"Yes, I fucking can … because it's the truth," he argues.

He's so frustrating. This man has no idea what it's like to have to work so hard for money. To build something from scratch, to have the world against you every step of the way, for people to judge you. Now the flutters have been replaced with anger, and I try and move around him, but he stops me at every corner.

"*No*, it's *not*," I argue stubbornly.

"You're not leaving until you understand that I'm going to compliment you every time I'm around you, and you're going to damn well like it," he curses at me.

"Fuck you," I throw back at him. "You don't get it. Nothing's been handed to me. I've had to work my ass off for everything, and here you are coming into my life, making me cross lines I never thought I would cross. Making it harder and harder to do my job because all I can do is think about you, and … I can't afford that. I can't afford to have some rich guy try to come in and sweep me off my feet. I've worked too damn hard for my independence, and I will *not* let anyone take that away from me," I scream, my anger and frustration from the day coming out in my toxic words.

"Your independence is one of the sexiest things about you, and I would never want to take it away from you," he roars back at me.

"Even if that means I'm fucking other men," I yell at him.

His body tenses over my words. He blinks slowly, then lets out a breath of air. "Even if it means you *must* fuck other men. As long as you know outside of the club walls, you're mine. I don't share you outside of that."

Oh.

A little bit of my anger subsides at that comment.

"I want you, Elle, and I can't explain it, and I know it's all fucked up, but I want you. I can't stop thinking about you. Every damn minute of my day is spent wondering what you're doing. Seeing that asshole take from you makes me want to kill him. I could offer you the money he took, but I know you would throw it back in my face or kick me in the balls for suggesting it."

He'd be right.

"I'm jealous as fuck that other men get to touch you, have you," he says while raking his hand through his hair. "But I'd never ask you to give up your job knowing you're so close to achieving your dreams. Not when you're so fucking brilliant at it. I'd never want to take that away from you," he tells me through ragged breaths as he thumps his chest. "Put me out of my misery, Elle. Tell me you feel whatever this is going on between us and that you will try to figure it out with me?" he pleads.

The look on his face stops me dead.

Alistair has ripped himself open for me.

He's laid it all on the line.

How can I say no when he's looking at me the way that he is? As if I'm the very air that he breathes.

I want him.

I want him so badly, but I can't.

He's standing there staring at me with those hazel eyes, and they are ripping through my walls.

"You know why I can't," I whisper.

"Babe, I do, but please just tell me you feel this," he asks as he grabs his hand and places it against his chest. His heart is thundering, and sparks of white-hot heat crackle beneath my fingertips.

"I do," I answer him honestly.

Alistair's eyes widen, and hope twinkles against a hazel backdrop. "Thank fuck!" He grins before launching himself at me, then wraps his hand around my neck and pulls me to his lips. As soon as our lips meet, I'm done for. I'm sick of fighting what's happening between us today, my walls have crumbled, and I'm giving in, just this time. So I kiss him back fiercely, and we become a tangle of limbs.

We begin to shed all our winter layers as we hop and kick around the living room—shoes, socks, belts, jacket—all the wintery breadcrumbs left over the floor until we are down to our underwear.

Alistair falls back onto the sofa and takes me with him. I straddle his lap while his warm fingers unhook my bra and throw it to the side, and then he's ripping my underwear clear from my hips.

As we continue to maul each other like rabid animals with teeth clashing and lips biting, my hand falls between us as I pull him from his underwear then wrap my hand around his hard cock. Sliding it up his shaft, pulling grunts and moans from his lips, at the same time his fingers are disappearing between my thighs as he begins working his magic on me.

"Fuck the foreplay, I need you," I tell him as I let go of his cock, and he curses at me.

"You owe me this wet pussy in the future," he states boldly.

I'm okay with that as he pushes and pulls his fingers out of me. I slide down onto him as he sucks my wetness from his fingers. "Show me what you've got, kitten." He quirks a brow, asking me to take the reins.

I place my hands on his shoulders and begin to buck like I've been bull riding my entire life. Alistair leans forward and begins sucking on my nipples which are my kryptonite. I slow my bucking. Otherwise, I'll throw him off my breasts, and no one wants that. So I begin to slowly grind against his dick while he teases me with his tongue.

My hand slides between my thighs, and I circle my clit, the sensation from the stimulations sending goosebumps over my body. The tension from the rest of the day eases as I draw closer to my orgasm. I throw my head back and bite my bottom lip as we work each other toward the edge.

"Yes … yes …" I groan as he pushes into me deeply, hitting the perfect spot time after time as my fingers reach their crescendo. I begin to crash over the edge and then back down to earth with Alistair not far behind me.

We both catch our breaths as we sag against one another.

"I'll never get tired of making you come, Elle," he says.

"It's Eloise. My name is Eloise." I've well and truly crossed that line, so I may as well tell him my *real* name.

Alistair pauses, and his hazel eyes land on mine. "Nice to meet you, Eloise." He grins which does all kinds of things to my body.

"Nice to meet you too, Alistair," I add, saying his name.

Tonight is about Eloise and Alistair having fun. There's no Paradise Club, no dark cloud of moving to the Caribbean, and certainly no threat of losing my job. It's just two people hanging out enjoying each other's company.

"I'm sorry about what happened today. I tried to catch him."

"It's not your fault," I tell him.

"I'll find that thug, and I'll make him pay," he tells me angrily.

"Don't worry about it. He obviously needed the money more than me." I mean, what could I do even if Alistair found him? The money would be long gone anyway, so there's no point worrying about it now.

"As there is not a threat to my balls because your cunt is tucked tightly around them, I'm happy to give you the money that asshole took. I'm the one who distracted you by trying to warm you up. If I hadn't tried to push my luck with you, the guy wouldn't have seen the opportunity to take your money."

"It's no one's fault but the person who took it. It sucks, but it's not going to break me," I tell him.

"It's so close to Christmas though, and I know you said today was your biggest day." He frowns at me.

"And it was, but I'll have other big days." I soothe away his frown with my fingers. "Please don't worry about me."

"You sure?" he asks.

"Yes, I am sure." I grin down at him.

He doesn't look convinced, but he stops pushing the subject. "What are your plans for Christmas?"

"Lauren and I are having the day with her family at their country estate … it's a holiday tradition."

"You don't spend it with your family?"

"No, they haven't been in my life since I was eighteen," I explain to him, and thankfully, he doesn't push for more of the story. "What about you?"

"I'm off to Australia for a couple of weeks. It's a mixture of business and holidays."

"You don't celebrate with your family?" I ask.

"Nope, not this year," he says with a shrug. "Do you think it would be okay if we caught up before I left? I could take you out on a date?"

"I don't know if that's a good idea," I answer sadly. "We have dates at the club, remember?"

"I know, but you're not there anymore. What if I brought the date to my house, then we wouldn't have to worry about being seen out," he asks.

"I think that would be awesome," I say because the days are counting down on my time left here in London, he just doesn't know it yet.

"Good. Now come here, I'm ready for round two." He grins then he kisses me.

16

ELOISE

"Hey, Elle, I know you said you needed some extra cash, so I was wondering if you might be able to come in tonight? It's become busier than normal. If Lauren is around, can you ask her if she wouldn't mind popping in too?" Sara, my boss asks.

"Sure," I reply as I turn to where Lauren is lazing on the couch. "Hey, Loz, Sara wants to know if we can help out tonight?" I call out to her.

"Yep," she replies, popping a macaron in her mouth.

"Give us an hour, and we'll be there."

"Love you guys. Thanks." And with those few words, she's gone.

"You're lucky I love you. I'll have to cancel my hot date," Lauren says, giving me a pointed look.

"Please! Your date was with a plate of macarons. I can assure you they'll still be there when you get home," I say, rolling my eyes.

"Fine." Lauren laughs.

"I'm exhausted." Lauren sighs as we get dressed after our shift. We watch as two of our friends, Sylvie and Camille, walk in and sit down beside us.

"Hey, Elle, you normally look after a Mr. King, don't you?" Camille asks me.

My body stills. "Yeah," I reply, as nerves begin to flutter beneath my skin, and a sinking feeling hits my stomach.

"Now I get why you're so excited when he comes in. That man knows how to fuck," she says, giggling.

Everything in me stops.

No.

She can't be talking about the same guy.

There's no way Alistair would do that to me.

Are you sure about that, Eloise?

No, Alistair is different, isn't he?

But there aren't two Kings in the system, I've checked, so it must be him. *Why?* He made me believe he was different. He made me believe I was special.

You work at a sex club, Eloise. You are not *special.*

The realization that Alistair has come in on my off day and fucked someone else hits me in the chest hard, and I struggle to breathe.

Camille ignores the internal struggle that's raging through my mind right now. "Let me know if he wants double trouble because I'm all-in." She smiles at me.

I give her a weak smile back as I try to fight my reaction because if they see how I really feel about him, then they're going to know something has been happening between us. The walls feel as if they're closing in, and panic begins racing all over my body as I struggle to breathe.

"Elle, we're running late. Come on! I want to get on the road before the traffic is bad," Lauren says, looking down at me and stomping her foot like an errant child. *Thank you, Loz.*

"You guys going away for the holidays?" Sylvie asks.

"Yeah, to my parents' house in the country. I want us to get the best room before the rest of my family arrives," Lauren states.

"My sister does that to me all the time. She's such a bitch," Camille adds.

Lauren nods but doesn't really take in what Camille is saying. Instead, she grabs me by the arm and wishes everyone happy holidays as she drags me out of the dressing room by the wrist. She doesn't say anything until we are in the car when she asks the driver to put up the privacy screen and then pulls me into her arms, where I break down.

"I'm so sorry, Elle. I had no idea he was coming to the club outside of your scheduled times. I would have told you if I knew. I can't believe him. What an asshole. You don't deserve that, sweetie. Men always think with their dicks not their brains. And how much of a bitch is Camille for rubbing it in your face. Urgh. I've never liked her. She thinks she's top shit. Goddammit! If I ever see him again, I'm going to punch him in the dick. No, I'm going to cut his balls off. Fuck him! How dare he do that to my bestie. I'm sorry, I really thought he was different. Thought he wouldn't be the kind of guy who would fuck you over. I'm even sorrier now that I pushed you to give that asshole a chance. He seemed so nice. I mean … who the hell helps at a cake stall in the middle of winter if you're cheating on your girl," Lauren says, filling in the time as the car drives us home.

Eventually, we make it home, and Lauren helps me out of the car and into the house. I throw my bag on the floor and slump on the couch.

Lauren is there instantly, wrapping her arms around me again as I fall to pieces.

"I thought he was different," I sob the words into her arms.

"He has a dick. They're all the same." She sighs.

"He made me think I was special."

"You were special. No, you *are* special, babe. I think he liked you, but the lure of the club may have been too much for him. Once men have a taste of Paradise, you know they will only want more."

Maybe she's right, but I honestly thought Alistair was different. I've seen so many men come and go through the club that I thought I could spot the problem guys easily. For once, I thought he saw me as a *real person* not someone's fantasy.

It seems I was mistaken.

"I could have lost everything because of that man. He would have been fine, he got his kicks, and I was a nice bonus. Never again. I'm done. This is what happens when I stray from *the plan*. The Universe is telling me I fucked up."

"Look … we can head early to my parents' place. We don't have to stick around. Unless you're going to confront him tomorrow night on your date?"

"Nope, I'm fine. I have no loyalty to this guy. We're not dating. He's not my boyfriend. He was just good dick. There's nothing more. I was swayed by the good D, Lauren, and that never happens."

"Good D will make you forget yourself," she says with a sigh.

"I'm going to take that early start date on the island Sara asked us about the other day too. I need to get the hell out of London."

Sara asked Lauren and me if we would be able to get to the island earlier than the original start date, and I had said no because I wanted extra time with Alistair.

What an idiot.

"Okay, I'm in too. Bring on the sunshine, right?" Lauren smiles.

"Thank you," I say to her through my tears. I couldn't ask for a better best friend than Lauren. She is my ride-or-die girl.

"No need to thank me. Us bitches need to stick together

because in our job, good dick is easy to find but friends, good friends, they are precious," she says.

I hug her tightly as tears roll down my cheeks.

17

ALISTAIR

Okay, I think I have everything ready for my date with Eloise tonight. I hired an event coordinator to put the entire thing together. There are a million and one candles lighting up the room and vases of red roses scattered all around. My dining room table has a large floral centerpiece with candles, a fine linen tablecloth with a silver setting, and crystal glasses. I've hired a chef to prepare dinner for us tonight, and it's all waiting in the ovens ready to go. I didn't want anyone around when Eloise arrived, I wanted the two of us to be alone together.

There's light jazz playing through the speakers, and the lights are dimmed to the perfect balance for romance. I'm pulling out all the stops for her tonight as I want her to know that I like her *a lot* and that I want to maybe try to see where this spark between us goes.

I nervously walk around my apartment, watching the clock counting down the minutes until she arrives. I've forced myself to not be a stalker and message her every two seconds to double-check she's still coming.

I continue to walk around and check to see if all the candles are still lit. Then I touch the roses because I'm fidgety with anticipation while I wait. I stalk back across my living room floor and stare out the windows that look over Hyde Park. It's a cold and miserable night, which isn't surprising for London. So I stand and stare at the droplets of water that are running down the glass.

Maybe I need to light a fire?

Why the hell did I not think of that earlier? It's romantic.

As I rush over to my fireplace and press the button on the fancy thing, it instantly springs to life with a swoosh that ignites the fire, warmth instantly radiating out.

I check my watch—it's past eight, so she should be here soon. I pace around my apartment again, wearing a path into my floorboards while watching the clock. I need to do something productive, so I head into the kitchen and plate up the starter. My eyes keep flicking to the clock in the living room as I watch the minutes tick by. I place the first course down at each of our places and walk back into the kitchen to double-check the champagne is chilled. I won't pop it yet as I'm not sure what she feels like.

It's now a quarter past, and she's still not here.

She is probably stuck in traffic, so I check my phone, but as I look down at the screen, it's empty. I'll wait a little longer, I'm sure she's not far.

I make another lap of the living room.

It's twenty past. Should I message her?

Yeah, I should.

I need to know she is all right.

Reaching out, I grab my phone and send her a quick text message, and it doesn't go through. A message pops up telling me I'm unable to contact this person. My heart leaps from my chest.

Has something happened?

Has she had a car accident on the way here?

Damn, I should have picked her up.

I call her number to see if it's just messages not going through but nothing. I'll try her socials that might indicate where she is, or perhaps I can contact her roommate to see what's going on. I type in her handle, and nothing comes up.

Huh? I don't understand what's happening?

What the hell is going on?

I pick up my phone and call Jasper.

"Hey, man, why the hell are you calling me? Shouldn't you be on your date?" he asks.

Seeing as Jasper is the one who busted Eloise and me months ago, he's the only one I can talk to about her.

"She hasn't shown up, and I can't get through to her on the phone. And all her social media has disappeared," I explain to him.

"That's fucking strange," he states.

"It is, isn't it? Something's happened to her, I can feel it in my bones."

"What's her handle?" he asks.

I tell him, and I hear him tapping away on his phone.

"That's weird, I can see it. She's down in Dorset with friends."

"What? She's in Dorset? There's no way in the world she's in Dorset," I tell him. My phone beeps as a screenshot comes through, and sure enough, it's a picture of her and her roommate sitting by a fire with cocktails in their hands.

What in the actual fuck?

"Why the hell is she there?"

"Did you have a fight?" he asks, sounding as confused as I do.

"Nope. I spoke to her yesterday morning, and she was excited. Well, I thought she was, but I haven't spoken to her since. What the hell does this mean?"

"I hate to say this, but I think she might be ghosting you," Jasper explains.

"Ghosting me?" I ask, raising my voice.

There's no way in hell she'd cut all contact unless …

Fuck! What happens if someone from her work finds out about this date and threatens her with her job. She told me that her job is important to her and that she's striving for her dream. That would make sense why she'd pull away, but why would she not tell me about it. Why has she blocked me everywhere?

"You okay, man?" Jasper asks.

"I'm so fucking confused. That's what I am."

"Look, I know you liked this girl, but you know what she does for a living. She may have used you, and once she got what she wanted, she bounced," he says.

"What did she get from me other than my time? I never gave her money. I never bought her anything. I helped her in a fucking cupcake stall. That's hardly gold digger material," I yell at Jasper, who's silent on the other end of the phone.

"I guess at least she's in Dorset with her friend and not with another guy," he says.

"I need to message her roommate," I tell him.

"No, Ali. *No*," he screams down the phone at me. "Do not do anything. She's blocked you, dude. She has disappeared. What more do you need to know?"

"Why?" I argue back.

"Does it matter why?"

"Yes, it does. I want to know what I did to make her disappear?"

"You did nothing. You're a fucking catch, Ali, and if she can't see that, then she's a fool," Jasper says quite angrily.

I'm thankful he thinks I'm a good guy, but I need to know what happened.

"I just want to know," I murmur.

"Fine! Give me five, I'll call you back. Let me find out for you," he says before hanging up.

I crash down onto my sofa and hang my head in my hands.

What the hell happened, Eloise?

I don't understand.

I sit there staring at the screenshot Jasper sent through, studying it, trying to see if there are any hidden clues. I zoom in and notice her eyes are bloodshot. Has she been crying? What is going on in her head?

My phone buzzes back and it's Jasper. "What did you find out?"

"Nothing. They refused to tell me anything. I'm sorry, but I think this might be the end of the road for you both," he says with a sigh.

"Thanks, man, I appreciate you helping me, and I think you might be right," I tell him sadly.

"Chin up. You're about to go to Australia, where there are hordes of gorgeous single women all ready and willing for you. Enjoy your holiday, Ali. London and all its drama will be here when you get back," he says.

We say our goodbyes, my head falls back against the sofa, and I let out a long deep breath. I must respect what Eloise wants because she's made it damn clear work is her priority. I can't fault her for that, but I do wish she had told me.

She did though, many times, but you kept pushing her.

My conscience is right, she did, but I was so excited I'd found a spark with someone after Miranda that I kept pushing.

18

ALISTAIR

Five Months Later ...

"Welcome back to The Paradise Club, Mr. King," a dark-haired man greets me as I step off the luxury boat. He's dressed in navy pants and a tight, white polo shirt stretched to within an inch of its life across his chest.

"Thank you, Lawrence," I reply, looking at his name badge.

"I trust you had a good journey, sir?" he asks as he ushers me toward a golf cart.

"It's been a long trip. I'm looking forward to relaxing," I answer him.

He gives me a knowing smile.

I'm going to be relaxing in the non-traditional sense. Nate invited the boys and me to the opening of The Paradise Club resort a couple of months ago, and it was wild, debaucherous, and exactly what I needed to heal my heart after Eloise walked out on me and disappeared into the night, never to be seen since.

At least I know she's not dead from the second account I've

set up for my online stalking I've been doing. She looks like she's sunning herself on a tropical island somewhere.

The next day I called the club, and they advised me they couldn't give any sort of information about their staff. I've tried everything to get in touch with her, except hire a private investigator, which Jasper told me was ridiculous. And he was right. I haven't been back to the London club since Eloise. I wasn't interested, but I have been to others around the world, thanks to throwing myself into traveling to get my mind off her.

Since coming back from Australia and finding out George proposed to Miranda over Christmas, I don't spend much time in London anymore. I'm traveling, visiting my clubs worldwide, and having fun.

That's how I've ended up here at The Paradise Resort. I've been in the states for work, and I need a holiday before going back to London for the first time in months to attend George and Miranda's wedding.

I need to prepare before attending that fabulous shitshow.

"Would you like the guided tour? Or would you prefer to go straight to your villa?" Lawrence asks, getting into the golf cart.

"Straight to the villa, please. I'm exhausted," I tell him.

We take off from the marina along the sandy paths through the dense tropical rainforest. Eventually, we pull up to a whitewashed villa. The sounds of the jungle are the first thing I hear once the golf cart is turned off.

Yes. This is exactly what I need.

The door to my villa opens, and the most beautiful woman steps out before me. Her white polo is stretched across her chest, exposing her generous cleavage. The last button on her polo is tentatively hanging on for dear life against the constraints of her breasts. Tight navy shorts that look like a second skin against toned, tanned legs that go on for miles. Her blonde hair is pulled back in a high ponytail. The images that rush through my mind of all the possibilities bombard me. Blue eyes, the color of the ocean behind us, and the tiniest smattering of freckles across her nose and cheeks, she is stunning.

"Welcome, Mr. King. My name is Sierra, and I will be your host for the duration of your stay. I'm here to cater to whatever you need while on the island." Of course, she is. I mean, that's the reason why I come to The Paradise Club is to have consensual sex with like-minded people, and that includes the staff. I double-check her wrists to be sure. At The Paradise Club, each person wears multicolored bands to indicate what they are sexually into, so there is absolutely no confusion, and it's the same on the island. Sierra is wearing pink, which indicates she plays with women, a blue band, which means she plays with men, a green band indicating multiple partners, and a purple for public play. All great answers.

"Your bags are inside, sir," Lawrence tells me. "Enjoy your stay," he adds before jumping back into his golf cart and heading into the rainforest.

"Would you like to follow me?" Sierra asks.

Of course, I would, so I follow her into the luxurious villa.

"This is your living area." Waving her hands through the air, she points out the large living area with its bright white oversized sofa and standard island wooden furniture with greenery in pots dotted around as if bringing the rainforest inside with you.

"Your bedroom." She points to the open bedroom just behind the living area, where a king-size wooden, four-poster bed sits on a raised platform with white linens and way too many decorative cushions spread out across it.

"Your bathroom and closet are behind the wall." She points to the white wall behind the bed.

Sierra takes a couple of steps toward the large glass sliding doors and pushes them back. I lick my lips as her shorts tighten even further with the movement while instantly, the sounds of the waves crashing on the beach and the squawking of the tropical birds that fly overhead fill my ears. "You have your own private pool and jacuzzi," Sierra explains while showing me my little private oasis. There are two large white walls covered in vines surrounding my private pool area, giving me privacy from the surrounding villas. Then behind that is the gorgeous backdrop of the white sandy beach and turquoise ocean.

Paradise.

"If you would like people to visit you, then you can put this flag up here ..." Sierra points out the tiny flagpole. "That will let them know you are happy for them to join you if that's what you desire." The way she says desire sends a thrill up my spine.

"Sounds fun."

She smiles at my remark, showing off bright white teeth set behind the most glorious, lush pink lips. I can't wait to see them wrapped around my dick.

"I hear you've been here before." A tiny smile falls across her lips as she looks up at me through thick, dark lashes.

"I've explored a couple of the clubs around the world and was here for the opening. Now that was a party," I say, except for the nightmare that happened with Alex's brother, which none of the staff knew about.

"It most certainly was," she says with a smile.

"As you know, but I will explain anyway, the island runs the same way as the city clubs, except for a few differences." I watch, mesmerized by her hips as she walks back inside the villa, her perfectly ripe ass filling out the navy shorts to perfection. They stretch even more as she bends over to pick up a tablet from the table. "On this tablet you can order all your meals and drinks." Turning the glowing device around for me to see, she points to the food icon. "We have the standard menu, but our chefs are here to cater to you. So, if you want something specific, they are only too happy to prepare it for you, any time of the day or night." Her finger moves to the next icon titled 'Toys.' "This is where you order your toys for solo or play with a partner."

"I'm hoping I'm all she will need." Yeah, that's me. I am reduced to cracking lame jokes.

"Toys are not a substitute ... they are an enhancement." Sierra's eyes meet my own. Heat is now swirling behind the blue pools.

Yes. I'm down for toys if she's going to look at me like that.

"Anything you can think of we have available." Her finger then slides to the next icon with the makeup icon. "This is where you will find massage and beauty services."

"Hopefully, I'm handsome enough that I don't need beauty services."

Stop with the lame jokes, Alistair.

What the hell are you doing? You're acting like a fool.

Jet lag is messing with my mind.

Sierra giggles. "You most certainly don't need any of them. But I am pretty sure you will be interested in the massage services we have available ... sexual and non-sexual." The flirtation flows through her words. "We have amazing masseuses who are happy to perform happy endings should you so desire." Her blue eyes look me up and down.

"But do you?" The question is out before I realize what I have asked.

"Yes, if you wish. I am a trained masseuse." Filing that little bit of information away for later, I smile. "Now this one ..." she points to the lip icon on the tablet, "... this one allows you to order any fantasy you so desire."

Sexual tension has entered the building, and it swirls around us like a tornado.

Feeling intrigued, I question her, "Anything?"

"Yes, anything." Her glossy pink lips pop over the word, insinuating so much without saying a thing, but then she adds, "Within reason, of course."

Yep, I bet there's a load of creeps ordering weird shit if absolutely anything was on the menu.

"The most requested fantasy by men is multiple women." Sierra raises a brow at me.

Is she testing me?

Teasing me?

Tempting me?

Does she want me to pick this one?

I mean, I am a male. Any straight male would fantasize about a group of beautiful women having their way with him.

"There's a drop-down menu for each of them." She starts pointing out the many fantasy options available at my fingertips at any time of the night or day. "Everything is included in your stay ... food, alcohol, day trips to fantasies. You can use as little or as much as you want."

There are so many possibilities that it's hard to pick where to start.

"The island also runs like any other resort where you have access to housekeeping, front desk, concierge, etc." Sierra moves away from the tablet and folds her hands in front of her.

I'm guessing the tour is over.

"Is there anything I can do for you now?" *Yes. So many things.* "You must be hungry after your long journey. Would you like me to organize something for you to eat?"

Eat.

Food.

Yes, that sounds great.

"Can I order a burger and a beer to start, please?"

"Of course, sir." She pulls out her phone and types into it. "Would there be anything else?" I stare at her for a couple of moments, but my mind has become blank. "You appear a little tense, Mr. King," Sierra adds.

Can she see the tension that's running over my skin?

"I am," I say, agreeing with her.

"Would you like me to organize a masseuse for you?" Those bright blue eyes stare at me expectantly.

"Yes."

"Great." Sierra smiles warmly, acknowledging my request with a single head nod. "Would you like a happy ending with that, sir?"

"Yes, please."

Sierra smiles again at my answer. "Is there anything else I can get you, Mr. King?"

"No thanks."

"Your lunch will be out in about fifteen, and I will be back in about forty-five." Sierra gives me a courteous nod and disappears out of my villa, and as soon as the front door clicks shut, I throw myself onto the living room couch and try to let the tension curling in my shoulders subside. My head falls back against the linen cushion, and the tropical breeze blows across me. The smell of rain, coconuts, and the ocean swirl around my nose. I need this break so much. Because in three weeks my brother is marrying my ex-fiancée.

Fuck my life!

19

ELOISE

"I am so looking forward to spending the day at the spa. I need some pampering ... these long days are killing me." Lauren groans as we get ready to head out on our day off.

It's been an adjustment working on the island. The long days, the wild nights with staff, and the drama that causes, it's like being back in high school some days. The money is great, and living in Paradise is an experience, but I've been working such long hours since arriving here that I haven't been able to concentrate on my baking. There's a part of me that regrets my decision to come here because my mind is on other things, and all I want to do is go back and start work on my business. Even after getting my money stolen, the rush of people coming and lining up for my goodies was the best feeling in the world. Yes, I have kept up with my social media, but there are so many people wanting to purchase my goodies from me back in London that if I had stayed, my business would be growing quickly and quite probably booming right now. I'd even settle on a market stall over a bricks-and-mortar shop after getting a taste for it before we left.

Thankfully, the chefs here let me come and play in the kitchens during quiet times, but it's not enough, and my hands itch with the need to bake and create. I promised Lauren I would stay here for six months when we arrived, and I realized as beautiful as this place is, it's isolating and intense. I also wasn't expecting to miss baking as much as I have.

The six months are almost up, and we need to have a conversation about whether she's going to stay behind or if she's going to step off the island with me. Lauren's having the best time here, and I feel bad for not enjoying it as much as she has been. I put a smile on my face for my girl because, after the support she has given me all these years, the least I can do is be there for her. Especially as I was the one who suggested we move halfway across the world in the first place.

Lauren and I set off from our villa we share with Sierra and Megan, who are two of the loveliest girls, and we are so grateful we were paired with them because there has been some nightmarish staff on the island. I don't think I would have lasted the full six months if we had to share a room with some of these other girls—they are competitive, and some are totally insane. If I'd been allotted rooms with them, I would probably have been escorted off the island in handcuffs months ago.

"I need hot rocks and maybe a deep cleansing sauna, my muscles are tight," Lauren states as we set off toward the spa area for our appointment.

After getting settled, I close my eyes, letting the professionals look after me for once, especially without the happy ending, unless it's one of the guys who has magic fingers, then I might be persuaded to finish with a bang.

We walk along the back of the staff area before heading back onto the main pathways of the resort. Lauren and I have our black bracelets on to make sure people know that we are staff and not here to play. I breathe in a deep breath of the fresh rainforest air, and my muscles begin to relax, and my mind clears.

"Is that Sierra on the ground?" I look over at Lauren, whose eyes widen as she takes in our roommate on the ground clutching her ankle.

"Sierra," I call out.

She looks up, and relief washes over her face as tears stream down her cheeks.

Lauren and I take off in a run to reach her.

"What happened?" Lauren asks, looking over at Sierra, whose face is twisted in pain.

"Stupidly, my foot got caught in a hole, and I ended up on my ass. I think I've broken it." She looks up at the two of us.

"Shit! Can you move? Maybe we can get you to the medic?" I ask.

She shakes her head as she grits her teeth through the pain. "I tried and almost died from the pain, and I have a guest waiting for me." She bursts out crying, more from the pain than the fact she is letting a guest down.

"Have you called anyone to come help you?" I ask.

When we're working, we have a small device that we can use to contact our boss or any services we need.

"My fat ass smashed it when I fell. It doesn't work. I've tried," she answers, bursting into tears.

"It's going to be okay. Don't worry. We're going to get you help. I'll take your client," I tell her.

Sierra shakes her head as more tears stream down her cheeks. "I can't let you do that. You've been looking forward to this time off for weeks."

"It's fine. Would you rather owe me a favor or Kelsey?" I question.

Sierra's eyes flare with fear, and she shakes her head quickly. No one ever wants to owe Kelsey a favor because she'll make your life a living hell. She thinks she's the queen bee of the staff on the island when really she's nothing more than a mean girl with an over-inflated ego.

"Right, well, hand me your bangles and give me your top," I tell Sierra.

We swap bracelets, and I pull on her staff polo. I'm not in work-issued shorts, but at least they look like they match the uniform. I only have my flip-flops on and no makeup, so I hope they like the natural look as this is what they are going to get.

"He's booked in a happy ending massage. I was on my way before I did this," Sierra states through gritted teeth.

That's easy. What's an hour out of my day to help a friend. "I can do that. We can sort out the rest of his stay once you've been looked after," I tell her.

"I owe you big time, Elle," Sierra says, looking up at me through her tear-soaked lashes.

"It's fine," I tell her waving her gratitude away. After all, it's what you do for your friends. "He better be cute?"

"The man is gorgeous, Elle. I'm so upset that I've done this because I was very much looking forward to spending the week with him." Sierra sighs.

Lauren's eyes widen as she looks up at me with a smile on her face. Guess if I'm giving up my day off, I am glad it's for a hottie. I blow them both a kiss, and they wish me luck.

As I head toward the villa Sierra told me her guest is staying in, all I know is he's booked in for a happy ending massage. While I get him set up, I will check the tablet to see what his other wants are so I can ensure he has a seamless Paradise Club experience. Once I arrive at the villa, I knock on the door and wait for the guest.

"Come in," the male's deep voice calls out to me.

I pause for the briefest of moments as icicles slide down my body.

No. That can't be right.

Memories of a once-familiar voice cascade through my mind —one that I have tried to forget about since leaving London. The ache and hurt from his betrayal rush through me, and I take a moment to try to compose myself.

There's no way it's him.

Fate wouldn't be so cruel.

He is a member. I still refuse to believe it could be him.

I've been thinking about going back home a lot recently, and that's the only reason why I'm thinking about him now. He's attached to London, and it's not because I've missed him or anything. There may have been times when my curiosity got the better of me, and I may have checked his socials. That ended in hurt, seeing the images of him out and about town with several beautiful women on his arm.

Guess I was easily replaced.

And I hate that it hurt me that much.

I hated that I let him slip through my defenses.

Never again.

I give myself a head shake to shake off the lingering hurt.

I have a job to do for Sierra—now, plaster on that Paradise Club smile and do what you must for your friend.

My hand turns the door handle, and I step into the beachfront villa while sucking in a deep breath. The gentleman is sitting in the pool, back turned toward me, staring out toward the ocean.

"I'm sorry to inform you, sir, but Miss Sierra has had an accident on her way to the villa." My eyes run over the broad, tanned shoulders exposed outside of the water—it appears he looks after himself. I wonder how gorgeous he really is. Sierra seems to think he's hot, and she usually has good taste. "She's fine. Looks like it might be a broken ankle, though. She is very sorry that she won't be able to continue to look after you during your stay," I explain to him. Not that it's going to be too much of a hardship for me, judging by the way he looks from behind. "I'll be your new host for the rest of the week. My name is Elle."

As soon as my name falls from my lips, he spins around, and that's when my world stops.

No.

This can't be happening.

He can't be here.

Is this a cruel joke?

Those hazel eyes flare with surprise before narrowing with anger. Why the hell would he be angry with me? I'm the one who's supposed to be angry. He's the asshole who promised me the world and then took it all away just as easily.

His sandy-colored hair is longer than it used to be. There's stubble growing across his square jaw as if he hasn't shaved in weeks. *I hate that I like it.* He's tanned, which means he's spent all his days in the sun. If his socials are anything to go by, he spends a lot of time with bikini-clad women draped all over him.

Large hands slap the edge of the pool as he hauls himself up and out of it. My eyes follow the water droplets running over his body as they sink into every deep line of his six-pack. It appears he's been working out with every muscle appearing like it's been cut from stone. He stands tall as those hazel eyes continue to glare at me.

Screw him! How dare he look at me as if I'm the villain in this story.

He grabs a towel from the basket and wraps it around his waist, then begins to walk toward me.

My heart is thundering in my chest. *Why is he so quiet?*

"And *you're* the replacement?" he asks, his voice is cold as ice as he looks me up and down with a raised brow. *Does he find me lacking now?*

Fuck you, buddy. My eyes narrow on the jerk. *How dare he look at me like that.* I can't believe I've wasted so much time thinking about this man for all these months.

"And you're here to massage me?"

I suck in a deep breath because as much as I want to chew this man out, he is still a client, and as the saying goes, 'the client is always right.'

"Yes, sir," I reply, putting on my sweetest work voice. "Where would you like me to set up?"

Alistair's eyes narrow on me again as if I'm a puzzle he's trying to work out.

"Out here," he answers curtly, pointing toward the pool.

I nod my head and disappear into the cupboard where we store the massage tables and gear, then go ahead and begin to set up out on the deck. As I work, I can feel his eyes on me every step of the way, and it makes my blood boil.

I *hate* that he looks this good.

No, better than when I last saw him.

There was a portion of me hoping, wishing that he had stacked on a few pounds and maybe lost all his hair and that he had been using photoshop on his social media photographs. Instead, he turns up looking like a fucking Adonis stepping out of the pool.

Fuck, life isn't fair sometimes.

There's a knock at the door, and his brows raise as he glares at me.

Is he expecting someone else?

I make my way to the villa door and pull it open to Roxana standing on the other side. Her eyes widen in surprise.

"What are you doing here?" Roxy whispers.

"Sierra had an accident, she's broken her ankle, and I've taken over her shift," I explain.

"Shit! Is she okay?" she asks.

"Not sure. Lauren's taken her to the medic. What are you doing here?"

"Sierra booked a two-person happy ending massage for Mr. King," she explains.

My stomach sinks at the realization of why she's here and what she is about to do with Alistair.

He's not yours anymore, Eloise.

He never was.

Treat him like any other client.

This is what he requested, and this is what you will have to provide for him, no matter how much the thought of Roxana touching him makes your stomach flip.

Switch off—do your job.

Luckily, I like Roxana. She's this gorgeous raven-haired ex-model from Poland. Not only is she beautiful, but she is also kind. We've played many times before and always have a great time. Roxana is bisexual but leans more toward women, and she is good at what she does.

"I'm glad it's you," I tell her.

"Me too. It's been a while since we've played," she purrs. Her lips are painted in her signature bright red lipstick as she looks me over with her hungry ice blue eyes. "I'm looking forward to it."

Maybe this isn't going to be so bad after all.

When I turn, Alistair is looking at the two of us with a frown on his face.

"Mr. King, this is Roxy, she will be helping with your massage today," I explain to him.

He raises a questioning brow as Roxana moves beside me. His eyes then flare with heat as he looks over the beauty standing beside me. *Shit.*

"Fuck, he's hot," Roxana mumbles under her breath, and it takes everything in me not to want to scratch her damn eyes out. I take in a deep breath as I try and control my emotions.

You can do this.

You're a consummate professional.

"Roxy, is it?" Alistair questions.

She nods and bites her bottom lip, putting on a performance for him.

"Come here," he commands as he curls his finger and beckons her over.

Roxana does as she is told and walks over to him, her hips seductively swaying.

You've got this. No matter what happens today, you can deal with it. I try and give myself a pep talk.

Alistair looks over Roxana's shoulder to me, and those hazel eyes never leave mine. He reaches out and wraps his hand around her throat, which makes her gasp before a giggle falls from her lips, his attention is then pulled back to Roxana. They stand like that for what feels like an eternity as I wait for him to make a move. A smirk falls across Alistair's face as he pulls Roxana to him and kisses her. The moment their lips meet is like a punch to the gut, but I don't look away. I will *not* let him see how much his actions are hurting me. As he kisses her, his eyes open and land on me and never leave.

Screw him.

I muster up my best-bored expression as I watch him kiss another woman.

I will not give him the satisfaction of reacting.

What does he expect me to do, run?

Storm out?

Make a scene?

Hell no. I will be fired.

I'm going to take it and push the pain all the way down inside me like I have with all my childhood trauma and pretend it never happened. That Alistair King never happened.

He pushes Roxana away from him. She stumbles a little bit from the intensity of his kiss, then looks over at me angrily as if upset by my lack of reaction. Roxana notices the tension that's swirling between the two of us, and a frown falls across her face in confusion. Panic runs inside my veins as Roxana gives me a questioning look. She's confused over why there's tension between Alistair and me, and I can't tell her the real reason.

That I let myself fall for a client.

Then he destroyed me.

Instead, I go on instinct and step forward and reach out to Roxana and pull her to me. I copy the exact move Alistair did and kiss Roxana, my eyes landing on him as her lips press against mine. With his anger now palpable, Roxana kisses me back, and I can't help but smile against her lips.

"You taste like raspberries," Roxana purrs as she licks her lips after our kiss. I give her a small smile, but my attention is pulled back to Alistair, who doesn't appear turned on like most guys would after our little display. Nope! He is one hundred percent furious. But he's the one who started this, and now I've turned the tables on him.

"I've changed my mind, Roxy. Thank you, but I won't be needing your services today," he says while looking at me intensely.

"If that is your wish," Roxana says to Alistair and gives him a nod. She turns her back on him, and I can see the questions on her face as she looks over at me. She mouths, "Are you okay?" and I give her a nod reassuring her that I am fine. She isn't going to push the subject in front of a client, but I know she's going to have questions when we're alone. I watch as she retreats from the villa, and as soon as the door clicks shut, my entire body begins to vibrate with tension.

"What the fuck, Eloise? What the hell are you doing here?" he asks, raising his voice as he runs his hand through his hair before he starts pacing the villa.

I'm taken aback by his questioning tone. "I'm here to do my job, Mr. King."

Using his formal name halts him, and he swings around and glares at me. "Don't you dare give me that Mr. King crap, do you hear me?" he says, pointing his finger at me. "You owe me more than that."

"Owe *you*? I owe *you* nothing," I argue back.

His eyes widen at my comment as if stunned by my reaction.

"Are you fucking serious? You owe me fucking answers," he demands.

"All I owe you is a massage with a happy ending, Mr. King," I say to him through gritted teeth.

Alistair looks like he's ready to punch a wall at my comment. I don't understand why he's so upset when he is the one in the wrong. He's the one who promised me the world, asked me to take a chance, and then fucked around with my work colleagues.

Alistair stops himself for a moment, sucks in a deep breath, then flicks those hazel eyes in my direction. "Guess you better do a good job then," he says, turning his back on me and walking over to the massage table.

Fuck him.

Do a good job? I'll show him.

I'm going to edge the shit out of him. He will be on his fucking knees begging me to make him come, and I'm going to enjoy the torture so much more. He has no idea what I am capable of.

He drops his towel, exposing his white, peachy ass. *Fucker.* He smirks over his shoulder, knowing that I'm checking him out before lying down on the massage table face up, showing his magnificent hard dick standing at attention for me.

Did our fight turn him on?

20

ALISTAIR

Seeing Eloise step through those villa doors, I thought I had seen a ghost. My brain exploded, unable to compute what it was seeing. I thought she was a mirage, something my subconscious dreamed up, but no, she is here, alive and looking as beautiful as ever, and I hate that I ache for her after everything that has happened between us.

How long has she been here?

Is this where she disappeared to?

Why didn't she tell me?

I don't understand why working here meant she had to ghost me. I would have understood. It might have torn at the edges of my heart to give her up, but this was her work, and I understood that from the start. She had goals, dreams, and aspirations that she wanted to achieve, and if this island could help her achieve them, then I would never have stood in her way.

I let my anger get the better of me when the other woman walked in, I saw Eloise's face drop, and rage bubbled inside me. How dare she get jealous of me being with another woman? She's the one who left me. She chose to disappear. She doesn't get to dictate who I can and can't sleep with. All I could think about in that moment was her leaving me alone in my apartment with a gorgeous meal prepared, a fire raging, and bouquets of roses all around me, looking like a fool as my heart disintegrated, knowing she wasn't coming.

After everything I had been through with Miranda, I took a chance on someone, someone I thought was worth it. So, seeing Roxy standing before Eloise and me looking panicked over the competition, I wanted her to know what it felt like when she ripped my heart out and betrayed me the way she did. I'm not proud of kissing that girl in front of her like I did, especially when I saw the hurt flash across Eloise's face.

Actually, I felt like an ass.

I'm not the kind of guy who goes all out for revenge. I won't hurt people like that. *What the hell was I thinking?*

Then she goes and does the same thing, throwing it right back in my face when she kissed that girl. *Yes, I totally deserved that.*

Then when she called me Mr. King, that was it for me. My damn pride and ego took a hit as if I was just like all the other men who had come before me. I refuse to let her lump me in with all those other men. They never deserved her. They never took the time to see behind The Paradise Club façade like I did. I saw how special she was. I saw the woman hidden behind her job.

Eloise felt something with me, I know she did.

I don't understand why she ran. Why she disappeared on me. *Did she not trust me?* I thought I did everything in my power to make her feel like she could trust me, that I was different, and that what I felt for her was real.

Maybe it wasn't enough.

Now here I am, acting like a complete dick, and I don't know how to stop.

"Are you going to take your clothes off?" I ask as I sit on the massage table and stare at her. I don't know what game I'm playing, but I know it's not going to end well for me.

Eloise stills at my request. "If you wish, Mr. King," she answers breezily as if she has not a care in the world.

My temperature rises at her formal use of my name. This woman knows how much I hate her using it. She's putting up impenetrable walls between us again, and I don't understand why?

"I do wish," I say stubbornly.

Eloise defiantly holds her chin up high and shimmies her white shorts down her tanned legs. She's wearing a white cotton thong which leaves nothing to the imagination. Then she pulls off her staff polo shirt, and it falls on the floor with the shorts, leaving her in a white cotton bra—a simple everyday bra—not what you would wear to seduce someone, or maybe it's that I don't know her anymore.

Eloise's hands move behind her back, her green eyes don't stray from mine as she unhooks her bra and holds it out to the side of her. She arches a stubborn brow at me as if to say, *'Nothing you do or request bothers me.'*

She's so fucking infuriating.

Her breasts bounce as they are freed, and my lips salivate as I take them in—dusty pink nipples that have turned into hard peaks. *Is she turned on?* I remember how they felt in my hands all those months ago. Her fingers then hook into the sides of her underwear, and she pulls them down slowly, exposing her bare pussy to me.

I try to stifle a groan that's threatening to escape my mouth—she doesn't need to know after all these months, she still turns me on. On the other hand, my dick stands to attention proudly between my thighs—can't hide that big fucker.

"Are you satisfied now, Mr. King?" she asks, taunting me.

Two can play this game, Elle. "Nowhere near satisfied, sweetheart," I answer her back.

Eloise lets out a frustrated huff at my comment, and I try not to burst out laughing because she looks as if she's moments away from blowing her cool.

"Then I guess you better lay down so I can *start* satisfying you. We pride ourselves on giving our guests the best experience at The Paradise Club," she states.

My left eye twitches at her professional words, but I decide not to bite *this time*. I do as I'm told and lay back. Closing my eyes, I try not to think about how naked she is beside me. How many nights have I dreamed of her being naked beside me again?

An oily hand slaps down hard against my chest, and I grit my teeth at the sting which pulls me from my lust-filled thought. I'll give you that one, Eloise, but come at me again like that, and you will not like how I seek out my own revenge. Her hands begin moving around my chest, over my shoulders, down my arm …

Has she noticed that I've been working out since the last time she saw me?

Is she impressed by my physique?

The only way I could get her out of my mind was to lock myself in the gym, but even then, she haunted my every thought.

Eloise's hand slides down my arm and back up over each defined muscle. Then her fingers slide down my ribs, and I wiggle against her touch—

I'm ticklish there, and she knows this because we've had discussions about it at the club in London. My eyes fly open as I realize she's tickling me on purpose. I catch the curve of a smile dancing across her lips before it disappears into a straight line again.

Eloise moves from my upper body down to my lower body, and I begin to recite the alphabet because I will *not* give her the satisfaction of my dick being hard for her. Well, harder than it already is, I mean. She continues down my thigh, over my calf, before sliding her fingers over my feet and running them up under the arch, which has me nearly launching myself off the massage table as she hits another ticklish spot.

This time when I open my eyes, I catch her smile as it tugs on her lips.

She tries to keep a straight face but is failing miserably.

"Try it again, Elle, and you're not going to like what happens," I tell her, specifically using her club name.

Eloise ignores me and continues massaging me as if my threats are idle, which they certainly are not. She works her way slowly up my other leg, her fingers skimming my inner thigh, making my dick jump. *Fucker, we're supposed to be playing it cool.* Then her fingers trail over my stomach and up my side, where she slides into the ticklish zone again, ignoring my earlier threats.

"I warned you," I say, grabbing her wrist and halting her movements. I sit up and glare at her. She refuses to look me in the eye, and I won't take that. I swing my legs off the massage table angrily and decide that enough is enough. We need to talk about what's happened between us. So, I pick her up off the ground, which makes her squeal, and throw her over my shoulder and carry her across the room.

"Mr. King," she calls out.

"I told you *not* to call me *that*," I grind out as my long legs eat up the distance between the pool deck and the bed. Then I throw her down onto my bed and watch as she bounces a couple of times before stopping. She sits up, her face is red with anger, and it's directed squarely at me.

"Have you lost your mind?" she questions.

"Yes … no … maybe. All I know is you drive me fucking crazy," I declare as my breath comes out ragged. "Pretending I'm a stranger. I'm not like these other men, and you damn well know that."

"Yes … you … are," she bites back at me.

Her answer stuns me for a moment. She seriously thinks I'm

like all those other men who come to this resort. Fuck that! Has she forgotten what it's like between us? Maybe I need to remind her.

"Open your legs," I demand.

Eloise hesitates for a second as she looks at my face trying to work out if I'm being serious. My eyes narrow on her, making it known I'm deadly serious. She lets her legs fall open for me, exposing her perfectly pink cunt. I reach out and grab her by the ankles and drag her to the end of the bed. She gasps which makes me smile, then I slide the tip of my dick through her folds.

"How can you forget the way you feel against my skin?" My dick slides back and forth between her. Eloise bites her bottom lip as I begin to tease her with the tip of my aching dick.

"Do you not remember the way my dick slides into you, inch by inch? The way your cunt tightens around it the further I go? The way your fingernails dig into my arm as I fill you up?"

She's soaked.

She can't hide her arousal from me.

I circle the tip of my dick around her clit. Her teeth sink further into the plumpness of her lower lip as she tries not to react to my teasing.

"Do you think I can erase your taste from my lips, Eloise? It's imprinted like a damn tattoo right across them." I let my finger slide through her wetness before bringing it to my lips, and my tongue slides along my finger as I savor her. Those green eyes flare with desire as she watches me enjoy her sweetness. "Fuck, you're even more delicious than I remember. Nothing in this world comes close to that taste. Nothing."

Eloise raises a brow at me as if she doesn't quite believe the words I'm saying to her.

"I know once I sink inside you again, there is nowhere in this world that you can run and hide that's going to be able to make me forget you," I tell her honestly as my dick slides between her wetness again. I pause at her entrance and look up at her through hooded eyes. "But it's worth it." Eloise stills at my confession. "You're worth it," I tell her as the tip of my dick now nudges her entrance. "If you don't want this, Eloise, I'll put my dick away, and you won't ever have to see me again," I tell her.

Eloise looks up at me through dark, long lashes, and I can see the internal struggle she's having with herself. "Whatever you want, Mr. King," she answers.

And just like that, I take a step back.

My dick isn't as excited as he once was.

I'm disappointed in how stubborn she's being, but maybe I don't know her as well as I thought I did. Maybe this fantasy I've had in my head about the two of us was just that—one carefully curated by The Paradise Club.

"I think we're done here. You can go," I tell her.

Eloise's eyes widen in shock at the sudden turn of events. Her mouth opens and closes a couple of times as if she has lost the ability to speak. I don't want to stick around, so I step away from the bed and into the bathroom, slamming the door shut with such force that it feels like the entire villa rattles.

I grab at my chest as the scar she left me with all those months ago reopens. I head toward the shower—a cold one will shock me back to reality. I thought there was a chance that the girl I fell for was still there. *I. Was. Wrong.* I turn the shower on and slump onto the shower floor, exhausted, trying to forget about what just happened.

What did I do for her to hate me this much? I ask myself as I shake the water from my hair. I sit there for I don't know how long before jumping up and finally turning off the shower. I grab a towel and dry myself before wrapping it around my waist. I head back out into the villa, knowing Eloise will be long gone and leaving it empty.

I step out of the bathroom and stop when I see her wrapped in a silky robe sitting cross-legged on my bed.

I'm stunned. *Why is she still here?* I don't understand.

"What the hell are you doing here?" I ask, not meaning to sound so damn rude, but the shock of seeing her there has caught me off-guard.

Before she can answer my question, my phone rings, I ignore it, but then it rings again. *Fuck off,* I internally curse at the stupid thing.

"If you need to answer that, it's okay, I can go … I shouldn't have stayed," she says as she moves to get off my bed.

"No, stay, give me a moment," I tell her because I'm intrigued. I want to know why she's still here.

The phone rings again, and this time, I see it's my mum. Grabbing the phone, I answer it, "Mum, hi …"

"I'm not interrupting anything, am I? You sound tense," she states.

Turning my head to the side, I look over at where Eloise is sitting on the bed, playing with a loose thread on her robe. "No, you're fine. My massage was canceled," I tell her.

Eloise looks up, and her cheeks turn pink at my comment.

"Are you having a nice holiday?" she asks.

Why is she calling me to see if I'm having a *nice holiday*? "It's been a rocky start so far, so I'm not sure if I am staying," I explain while keeping my eyes on Eloise, who shifts uncomfortably under my intense gaze.

"Oh, that's a shame," my mother answers after a slight pause. "Right … anyway, I was calling because we are finalizing the guestlist for the wedding, and I need to know if you're bringing someone?"

The wedding.

Of course, that's the reason she is calling me.

"I'll have a date for the wedding. Don't you worry, Mum," I answer my mother while watching Eloise trying not to react to that bit of information she's overhearing.

"That's good, sweetheart. If you're happy, then I am too."

"Was that all?" I ask.

"Yes, sweetie, it is. George will be so happy on the day … just remember that. He's worried you're going to make a scene," she rattles off, not realizing how much she's hurting me with her words, and I can't help but show that pain on my face.

"*Make a scene?*" my voice raises.

Eloise notices my reaction and frowns as she moves toward me a little more.

"I know you won't, sweetheart," my mother says, but her tone doesn't give me much conviction that she truly believes me incapable of not making one.

I feel Eloise's fingers lace with mine as she overhears the conversation heading south quickly.

"You think that when I see my ex-fiancée marrying my brother that I'm going to lose my mind and try and stop it? That I would want her back?" I ask defensively.

A small gasp falls from Eloise's mouth upon hearing that news. Her hand squeezes mine, letting me know she's right by my side in that moment.

"It's a fear George has, sweetheart. They are a family now," my mother adds.

Where was their concern when George was fucking my fiancée? Of course, my brother is worried because he thinks people are wired like him. And let's face it, Miranda cheated on me. Therefore, she's not innocent in this. It must make George wonder whether he can trust her.

I would *never* want Miranda back.

Trust—it's a two-way street, and there's no expectation that she could possibly be faithful to anyone, let alone me.

"Are you fucking serious right now?" I say, cursing at my mother.

"Ali, don't talk to your mother like that," my father calls out down the line.

Fuck them. I'm so angry.

How can they think so little of me when George is the one

who fucked it all up for me? He's the one they should be questioning. Where was their concern for me when my heart was fucking shattered after we broke up?

"You can't seriously think I'm the one who's going to be the problem? What about George? What about what he did to me? You've never once stuck up for me and my feelings in all this. You pushed me aside because he threatened to take your grandchild away from you. Miranda would never have allowed it. You let him manipulate you," I yell at my parents. All the pent-up hostility over the breakup is now coming out in this one phone call, but my questions are met with silence.

"It sounds like we might have caught you at a bad time, sweetheart. Let us know who the lovely woman is, so we can add her name to place cards because they are at the calligrapher as we speak. Have a wonderful holiday, and we will see you when you get home." And with that, my mother hangs up on me.

I'm in shock over that entire conversation.

With as much strength as I can muster, I throw my phone, and it hits the wall with a thud, then smashes to the floor.

I pull my hand from Eloise's.

I can't breathe.

I can't fucking breathe.

I need air.

The walls of the villa feel as if they're caving in on me.

I can't do this.

Not here.

Not with *her*.

Next thing I know, I'm turning on my heel and rushing out of the villa.

21

ELOISE

During that phone call with his mother, I watched Alistair's heart break into a million pieces. How could she not know what her insensitive questions were doing to him? No wonder he's bolted from the villa. His family obviously doesn't care that he's suffering.

And here I am being a bitch to him, for what? Hooking up with someone at a sex club where I work. Something I have done throughout our entire *whatever it is* that was happening between us. All the while, he was dealing with this.

What kind of lowlife brother knocks up his brother's fiancée? That's seriously fucked up. I'm surprised Alistair is still so open after being fucked over like that. I know for sure I would have built a huge wall around my heart if a sibling had done that to me. The fact that he isn't allowing the fucked-upness of the situation with his brother and ex keep him from his nephew shows what a good guy he is. I remember back to the first time he found me at the markets, and at that time, he was carrying a bouquet of flowers for his ex because she had given birth, and now I know it was his brother's child. Now, that *is* a good man.

Fuck.

Did I just add to his baggage by ghosting him? He doesn't deserve that.

Yes, I felt hurt by what he had done. But in the grand scheme of things, was it that bad? No. Certainly not fucking your brother's fiancée bad.

Honestly, I can't believe his mother had the audacity to question Alistair that way, thinking he would make a scene at the wedding. His brother is a fucking dick. Seems like he manipulates his parents to hurt Alistair. *How do they not see that?* He doesn't deserve any of this.

His ex is a one hundred percent bitch.

How could she be screwing Alistair's brother like that? Why didn't she have the balls to dump Alistair and then date his brother? I'll never understand why people do this type of thing. I hope whoever he takes as his date to the wedding is hot and makes Alistair feel secure because I can't imagine what that day will feel like for him. I'm sure the entire family will know that his brother is marrying his ex. Everyone's eyes will be on Alistair that day wondering if he's going to snap.

My stomach sinks at how I've just acted, denying him and punishing him for hurting me. When all I was truly thinking about was how much I missed him filling me. My walls have been up since stepping into this villa and seeing him before me. Stubbornly, I chose to put my head in the sand and run like I always do when faced with challenging situations, especially ones that could break my heart. And there he was dealing with the *ultimate betrayal*.

I need to make this right. Even if it means I'll never see him again, or perhaps, we can just be friends—I'd even accept acquaintances. I am hopeful for more, but I know I've ruined what we had, especially with ghosting him as I did.

Who the hell can forgive someone for that? *He could.*

Alistair wanted to earlier, and instead, I rejected him. All he wanted from me was *not* to call him Mr. King, and I wouldn't do it all because I was hurt over him kissing Roxana in front of me. Fucking hell! I've been incredibly immature over this entire situation.

I'm not great at letting my walls down, and when I did, I got hurt and ran like I always do. Dammit! I've been cruel, epically cruel, and I need to fix this mess right now. I need him to know that I'm sorry for treating him the way I have been and that I didn't mean any of it. He doesn't need me piling shit onto his already full platter.

So, I head outside. He's sitting alone on the beach looking out at the waves crashing on the shore. He's so lonely, so dejected, and his shoulders are slumped as if he has the world firmly loaded on them.

"Hey," I say, standing in front of him.

"I don't need your pity, Eloise." He glances up at me, and the look that he's giving me breaks my heart.

"Wasn't giving it," I answer back, which gets his attention. "Lay back, Ali, and look at the sky," I say, using his first name instead of baiting him by calling him Mr. King. His forehead crinkles in confusion but eventually, he does as I ask and falls back onto the sand. He looks up at the blue sky above and sucks in a couple of deep breaths trying to center himself.

I drop to my knees and unwrap his towel.

"What the?" he says, sitting straight back up.

I place a hand on his bare chest. Electricity tingles beneath my fingers as I push him back down.

"Eloise …"

As my hand wraps around his cock, I shake my head, pulling a grunt from his mouth. I give it a couple of tugs to get him hard before my mouth wraps around the head of his dick.

His hand stops me and pulls me off him, then he cups my chin as his hazel eyes soften. "You don't owe me this."

"I want to … no, I need to," I confess.

"You and I need to talk," he adds.

"And we will, but first I need to give you this. Please," I beg.

He thinks about it for a little longer but sees the determination in my eyes and relents. So, he lays back and slings an arm across his eyes as if to block out the world and any more hurt coming his way.

My mouth returns to his cock and slides down his length, taking him all the way to the back of my throat. Ali groans as my lips slide back up his shaft. My tongue swirls along the tip as my hands wrap around his girth. I give him every trick in the book, I cup his balls, I tickle his taint, I suck and gag on his dick while his fingers thread through my hair, and he punishes my mouth, letting me know how upset he is over me ghosting him, and I'll take it because I owe him that. The harder I suck, the more he fucks my mouth by pushing it deep down my throat, making me gag—my eyes water, salvia falls down my chin—but I don't care. All I want to do is make him happy.

"I'm going to come," he calls out, but he doesn't stop fucking my mouth.

Does he think I'm going to pull away? Hardly.

Then he lets out a mighty groan as I swallow all of him.

"Fuck," he curses as his dick falls from my lips with a pop. "Come here," he says, pulling me up to cuddle against his side in the sand. I lay my head against his beating heart and rest my hand over his abs. "Why did you leave me, Eloise?" he asks.

I owe him an explanation—the real one—not some bullshit one that I always thought I would tell him if I ever ran into him again.

"I was called into work the night before our date. At the end of my shift, one of my friends was raving about how much fun she had with Mr. King."

Alistair stills beside me and turns his head to look at me. "It wasn't me," he states categorically, and I want to believe him, but he is the only one on the system. I wish his words were true, but I know they're not.

"There is only one Mr. King in the system. My friend also said she understood why I kept you to myself, so even she thought it was you," I explain.

"Eloise, I'm telling you the truth, it was *not* me. I had a meeting that night at work and didn't leave there until late. I can show you my calendar back in the villa," he tells me, and I can see the honesty in his eyes which makes my brows scrunch.

I want to believe him so much. But how can my friend get it so wrong?

"I would never lie to you. I told you that. I despise liars, and after hearing that phone call earlier, you understand why. All this ..." he says, waving his hand around in the sky, "... I don't give a shit. The Paradise Club is nice, but I don't have some kind of kink that needs to be met. I don't crave sex that much that I need to come into the club every single day. Is the club fun? Yes, of course, it is. Do I need it as part of my regular sex life? Absolutely not. Why the hell would I want to go there on a day you're not working to sleep with some woman I don't want when the girl I do want had finally agreed to a date?" he asks me.

All that makes sense, but ...

Alistair reaches out and cups my face. "Please believe me."

If he's telling the truth, then ... *oh shit.*

His thumb runs down my cheek, wiping away the errant tears that seem to have fallen as the realization of what happened all those months ago hits me. If he's telling the truth, then I ran from him for no reason. All this pain I caused him was my fault.

"Hey, babe, don't cry."

"I ... I want to believe you," I splutter out.

Alistair's face falls at my honesty. "I get it. I understand why you didn't show up. I was asking you to take a leap of faith that night, and when you thought that I wasn't taking it too, you ran. I wish you had spoken to me because I would have been able to show you that it wasn't me. I don't know who it was, but it was not me at the club that night." Those hazel eyes implore me to believe him.

"I should have spoken to you. The way I handled that situation wasn't right. If only I had grown some lady balls earlier, all this shit could have been avoided. I've messed everything up," I confess to him.

"No, you didn't. I still think you're the most beautiful woman I know," he tells me as a smile dances across his lips.

"I don't deserve your kindness. I hurt you, all for the sake of my pride," I tell him.

"I get why. Just so you know, that date I had arranged for you was fucking perfect," he jokes, which makes me smile while making my stomach churn in knots thinking about the what-ifs.

If I had stayed, would we have been happy?

Would we have fizzled out?

Would my business be where I wanted it to be?

Would I still be working at The Paradise Club?

I feel like that moment when I chose to run changed the course of my life and not for the better.

"It hurt when you didn't show up. I thought something had happened to you, that you had been in an accident. I searched for you all night. I called everyone, and no one would tell me where you were." The anguish on his face is palpable as he relives the moment when I messed up big time. "Then you blocked me, and I was devastated. I didn't understand what I'd done."

Shit! I feel like even more of bitch, especially after listening to his phone call earlier. I hurt him. I made him think there was something wrong with him because of my reaction to getting hurt. It was cruel and unnecessary.

"I didn't understand how I had finally found you then lost you just as quickly," he confesses.

Tears stream down my face as my heart aches for him. How I treated him was worse than what I thought he had done to me. I ghosted him and ran halfway across the world, for what?

"I hurt you, Ali. There are *not* enough words to say that can make up for treating you like I did. I don't think I can apologize enough for hurting you the way that I have," I tell him honestly as I look up at him through tear-soaked lashes.

"That blow job was a pretty good apology," he jokes, which makes me smile. He wipes away my tears again. *How the hell did I walk away from this man?*

"When I get scared, I run," I tell him.

He runs his thumb across my lip. "Was I that scary?" he questions me with a smirk.

"For my heart, you were," I reply honestly. My confession stops him as if he wasn't quite sure he heard what I had said. "You made me want things that I had never wanted before …" I continue confessing my thoughts because I owe him that much, "… risking everything I had been working toward for all these years. No one ever made me do that before until you. Then when one of the girls told me about the good time she'd had with you, all my fears came true. And in that moment, I ran. No one could have talked me out of it … my flight instinct kicked in, and I was gone."

"I'm going to find out who this Mr. King is who fucked everything up for me," Alistair tells me. I can see it on his face that his words are serious. "I loathe that whoever it was broke what we had."

"That person didn't, though. *I did.* I blew up whatever was happening between us at that time. If I had just asked you about it that night, all this wouldn't have happened." That knot in my stomach twists a little tighter.

"Well, I'm sorry I made you doubt me," Alistair says.

He didn't do a damn thing. He owes me no apologies, I brought this on all myself. He set up a dream date, he waited for me, he looked for me, he made an effort, and I didn't. I took the easy way out. I roll over onto his chest so that I'm straddling him.

"You have nothing to apologize for," I tell him as I feel his dick twitch between us. *Is he hard again?* I rub myself along his length and feel him fully harden beneath my touch. "I'm the one who should be making it up to you," I tell him as I reach between us and slide his tip between my wet folds.

Alistair groans as I tease him against my entrance.

"I don't think I will stop until things are right between us," I say as I sink down on his length. We both hiss at the connection.

How have I gone so long without him?

He is only here for a week. That thought pops into my head as I begin to ride him. No. Whatever doubts you are having in your mind in this moment, they do not exist. I will not let them ruin this moment. They can cloud my mind when he's gone. I have no idea how I'm going to say goodbye to him for a second time.

"This feels right," he groans out. As he smiles up at me, my silky robe exposes my chest to him while his hands begin to caress my breasts. His fingers are plucking my nipples as I ride him.

"You like this apology?" I chuckle. My body breaks out in goosebumps as a breeze from the ocean slides across my skin.

"Fuck, yeah." He moans as we begin to lose ourselves in the moment once again. I arch my back and take him deeper, his dick hitting the exact spot inside me that makes my thighs quake.

Then Alistair sits up, so we are chest to chest, taking me deeper as he wraps his hand around the back of my neck and pulls me to his lips, connecting us at every point. We lose ourselves in the kiss as we slowly move to the natural rhythm between us, neither of us in any rush, both of us savoring the moments we have missed between each other until we can't hold on any longer, and we fall into oblivion together.

Alistair falls back and takes me with him, then rolls me onto my back getting sand everywhere. "Fuck, I've missed you," he says, kissing me again.

"Me too," I relay truthfully.

"Good! Now come on, let's get back to that villa and scrub this sand off us. Then let me show you all the ways I have missed you." He grins.

Alistair rolls off me and holds out his hand for me to take.

22

ELOISE

We walk back to the villa hand in hand, and as soon as we reach the outside of the villa, he lets go of my hand and runs toward the pool. He rolls himself up into a ball as he dive-bombs into the crystal blue water, making me laugh.

"Come on in. It's nice," he says, beckoning me in.

I shed my robe and leap into the warm water. He grabs me as soon as I pop up and pulls me into his arms. My legs wrap around his waist as we lazily float around the pool.

"You have no idea how many times I've wished for you to be back in my arms again," he whispers in my ear.

Damn him for being so sweet.

"Is this where you ran to after Christmas? he asks.

I nod my head, answering his question. "The island was always in the plans even before I met you. I had agreed to join their new team out here. It was the reason why I was reluctant to take things further with you …" I pause because this information is new, "… because I knew I was leaving."

"Guess I wore you down." He smiles as we continue to float

around in the water. "You know I would have understood if you had told me."

Why is this man so freaking perfect?

"It would have been my choice to continue what we had going on or to pause it till you got back," he states.

He's right. Guess I wasn't ready for a man who had his head screwed on like Alistair does.

"My walls were still up, even though they were beginning to crumble. My dreams meant more to me than any relationship, and in most ways, they still do," I tell him honestly.

Alistair absorbs my words. "You're a talented baker, Elle, and you deserve your dreams."

The sincerity in his eyes shines through. He's not saying it just because he wants to get into my pants. I lean forward and kiss him, which has him gripping me hard when he kisses me back.

"I would never get in the way of making those dreams of yours become a reality, Elle," he states seriously.

"I know ... I understand that now." I smile down at him.

"I've noticed you don't post as many photos as you used to on your business account," he states.

"You've been following me?"

"Of course, I have," he says, rolling his eyes with a smirk on his face.

Why does my heart expand upon hearing this? After everything I've put him through, he still wanted to check in on how I was doing.

"I created a second account, so I could watch and see if you were okay. If you were happy. I needed to know that you were all right."

This man.

"I may have done the same to you," I confess.

Alistair raises a brow, and a smirk falls across his lips.

"Really? What did you find?" he asks.

"There were a *lot* of beautiful women on your arm," I add, jealousy gnawing at my core.

"There were," he agrees with a smile.

"Which is fine because I'm the one who left you, and you're single, and ..." my words run away with me, so I trail off.

Alistair bursts out laughing and shakes his head.

"I didn't sleep with all of them. But I'm also not going to lie and tell you that since you left, I haven't been with other women. You vanished, and I thought I was never going to see you again."

I can't blame him for that because it's the truth.

"It made me so insanely jealous seeing those women on your arm and knowing they would be in your bed too," I tell him.

"I felt the same knowing you would be going to work every day, and another man or woman got to have you, and I couldn't do a thing about it."

"It seems we're as bad as each other."

He smiles while nodding in agreement.

"Least we have this week together," I say, wrapping myself tighter around him.

"The other girl won't be coming back?" he asks.

The pit in my stomach opens at his question. I thought we were getting somewhere. *Does he want Sierra?* I mean, that's who he was booked in with, so I understand.

"Hey," he says, pulling me from my wayward thoughts. "Where did you go?" he asks with a frown on his face.

"Inside my head."

"By the looks of it ... it didn't look good," he questions me.

"Do you want to spend your time with your original host?" I ask him honestly. I'm a big girl, and I can take whatever his answer is. I'll be okay with it. This is his holiday. He is the guest.

"What? No. Have I not made it clear enough that I want you?" he replies sincerely.

"I understand this is your holiday."

"Elle, come on ... I've just found you again after all this

time. I want to spend my time with you." His forehead crumples into a frown. "I didn't know if there was protocol or something about changing hosts. That's what I was worried about ... that maybe they would take you away from me again."

Oh. That flutter in my stomach is back, and this time it's because of happiness, not anxiety.

"It looks like Sierra might have broken her ankle. She won't be coming back."

"Is she okay? How did it happen?" Alistair asks, and the concern written on his face is so genuine.

"Her ankle twisted in a hole. It was lucky we found her as she had crushed her device and was unable to call out for help."

Alistair's eyes widen. "Now I feel bad for her ... that she was outside in pain, and I was in the pool."

"Lauren and I found her. She was lucky it was our day off, and we were on our way to the spa," I explain.

"Your day off?" he asks.

"Yeah, the hours are longer on the island than in the city," I answer, feeling a little weird talking about my job with him, even though he knows what I do.

"And now you have to work?" he asks with a frown on his face.

"Hey, who's getting inside their head now?" I say, looking down at him. I lean forward and press a kiss to his lips. "I would have given up all of my days off to be here with you."

"Really?" Alistair smirks.

I nod my head while biting my bottom lip. It's the truth. I would give up the day spa to spend the time with him. "Yep," I say, letting the word pop between my lips. "Are you okay spending your holiday with me?"

"I'm good with that." He grins as he moves us through the water.

"For the entire week?" I add.

"Hell, yes." He chuckles. "There's one condition, though."

My brows rise, curious over what that condition could be.

"You stay with me the entire time."

That is *not* at all what I thought he was going to ask.

"In my villa … just you and me. Are you up for that?"

"This is The Paradise Club. You sure you don't want to have any extra fun?" I'm genuinely curious because the point of the island is for all your fantasies to come true. Alistair pauses for a couple of seconds, mulling over my question.

"I don't want you fucking other men while I'm here," he adds seriously.

"Done," I answer. "What about women?"

Alistair's brows rise high as he contemplates my question.

"If you want to have another woman join us, I would be fine with it. It was fun last time," I say.

"You would be okay with me fucking another woman in front of you?" he asks me.

The tiniest flinch crosses my face, and a wide grin falls across his lips.

"I knew it! You don't want me fucking another woman as much as I don't want you fucking another man." He chuckles. "But I wouldn't mind watching you and another woman together, though. That image of you and Vixen still gets me hard," he tells me honestly, then bites his bottom lip.

I can feel his dick hardening from the image he has running through his mind.

"And you'd be okay with them touching me but not you?" Just want to be clear about where his boundaries are.

"Yes," he answers quickly. "I have no problem with a woman servicing you. Maybe it's a male thing … comparing myself to another guy, wondering if he is doing it better than me. My fragile male ego couldn't take it." He chuckles.

"And you think a woman wouldn't get me off as good?"

"Oh, I know she can. I could never compete with a woman. I might take some pointers, though." He grins.

This guy. He makes me laugh.

"Okay, I'm glad that's settled then."

He moves us toward the edge of the pool, then picks me up and positions me on the edge, pushes my legs open, and smiles up at me. "I've missed your cunt, Elle," he says, licking his lips as he admires me. I bite down on my bottom lip because I've missed his dirty mouth, and the way he's looking at me is doing all kinds of things to my body.

"Have you?"

"Yes." He moans as his fingers grip my thighs.

"Show me then."

"With pleasure." He grins before diving between my thighs.

The first swipe of his tongue against me has me falling back onto my elbows as my head lulls, letting the sun pour over my naked body warming the water droplets on my skin. Alistair continues to devour me, making up for all the lost months since the last time.

Yes. He hits my clit with the pad of his tongue while he slips a finger inside me, making my thighs shake. He then slides another finger inside me, curls it against my inner walls, and drags it along the sensitive nerve endings.

A moan falls from my lips as he continues to stroke me. *Oh yes.* I feel the tiniest nip of teeth against my clit, sending electric heat through my body. He does it again, and my arms can't hold my weight, so I adjust and lay flat against the pool deck.

Alistair doesn't stop eating me. He continues his rhythmic tongue action over my pussy until I'm unable to take it any longer. My stomach tenses as his fingers tantalize my inner walls, and I explode all over his tongue. I crash over the edge, pulled under by a tsunami of need that he doesn't let up on. He ignores my wiggling underneath his tongue, even though I don't think I can take any more.

"Ali, fuck," I curse, but he ignores my orgasm and continues to push me into delirium with his fingers and tongue. "I can't," I pant the words out, but he doesn't let up until I feel another wave begin to take shape—there's no way he can pull more from me. But he does.

He doesn't move from his steady rhythm until my thighs are clamped around his face, my fingers are lodged into his wet hair, and my back is arching off the deck as he pushes me so far over the edge that he makes me wet all over his face. Oh my god, it's been a long time since anyone has made me squirt and not like this. I've never been embarrassed before because sex is gratifying, but this man is drenched.

"Fuck, Elle," Alistair grins between my thighs. "You taste like the sweetest fucking nectar. I want to drown in the delicacy of your cunt." I'm panting as I stare down at him, my desire drenching his chin.

"I am pretty sure you nearly did drown," I say, cracking a joke which makes him laugh.

"Best way to fucking die." He grins, unfazed by what he made my body do.

"I should clean you up ... I seem to have made a mess." As I look around, I see a puddle.

Alistair stills when he notices me acting awkwardly. "Elle," he calls my name. "What's wrong?"

"Nothing," I reply.

"Did I do something wrong?"

"Hell, no. No one has ever made me come like that before," I explain.

A wide smile falls across his face at my statement. "Then what is it?" I can see his concern as his brows pull together.

Rip the Band-Aid off, Elle.

"I've never squirted like that before," I confess as I feel my cheeks begin to burn with embarrassment.

Alistair stares at me, his eyes are wide, and his mouth falls open as he struggles to say anything.

"Damn, I shouldn't have said anything," I say while shaking my head.

"Fuck that. Yes, you should have," he declares earnestly before reaching out and pulling me off the deck and back into the pool. "Do you have any idea how good I feel knowing that I have shared something with you that no one else has?" I shake my head. "You gave me a gift today. Something between you and me. And I'm going to cherish that."

"You are?" I ask, confused by this reaction.

"This is your job, Elle. I know that. I understand. There probably isn't much you haven't given to another. The fact that you gave me this one thing … something that happened between you and me. Not guest and employee."

He's right. Yes, I may be having sex with these people, but I've never let myself relax that much they were able to pull something so intimate from me.

"I can't wait to do it again." He grins before kissing me passionately.

23

ALISTAIR

"I think it's my turn now." She grins as we float around in the pool. My dick is hard as fucking steel, and each time I lick my lips, I taste her on them. I still can't quite believe she's here in my arms and back in my life again. I hate that a simple misunderstanding pulled us apart like it did.

"What do you have in mind?" I ask her.

I never want to let her go, not now that she is here with me. How can I ask her for more when she has been clear with me that her being here is about her chasing dreams? I can't ask her to give all this up again, not when I know how talented she is at baking.

All we have will be this week.

It's not our time.

I understand that now.

Fate can be a bitch sometimes.

She is the right woman for me, I know she is, but it's not our time yet. Now that I know she feels the same way about me, I'll wait. I'm a patient man, and if it means I have to move to the Caribbean for work, then maybe that's what I will do.

"I think I owe you that massage, don't you?" she states.

"Yes, please." Her hands on my body is exactly what I need. I float us back over to the stairs, and we exit the pool. There are two towels sitting on the sun loungers, and we each grab one to dry ourselves off. The massage table is still set up from earlier as we make our way over to it.

"Still want you naked," I tell her.

Eloise looks over her shoulder and drops her towel, then gives me a wink before turning back to the massage oil area.

"This time, I want you face down," she says, pointing to the table.

I frown as I stare at the massage table where there's a hole cut out for your dick. Is that going to hurt? Will my dick fit?

"I promise I will make it feel good," she assures me.

I have no doubt that she will. Ignoring my reservations, I jump onto the table and settle myself in, positioning my dick carefully in the hole. Then I place my face in its hole, close my eyes, and try to relax.

"I can see the tension in your shoulders," Eloise states as she runs her fingers along the tense muscles. They are tight—I didn't realize how much until she touched them. "This might be a little cold," Eloise warns me as I hear a squelching sound before a cool substance meets my skin. A hint of coconut and citrus dances in the air. Soon her fingers are digging into the fleshiness of my shoulder blades, manipulating the muscles to relax. I'm in heaven.

"Let me take your troubles away," she says in a soothing voice as her lips caress my ear.

I wish it were that easy, needing the stress of my life and this wedding kneaded from me permanently. Eloise loosens a knot in my shoulder, and my body begins to relax and turn to putty under her unbelievably strong hands. It could be the scent of the tropics lulling me further, the sounds of the ocean lapping the sands, the rainforest birds overhead squawking, or it could be the multiple orgasms I've had that begin to take over, and I fall asleep.

I wake with a start, shocked back into reality as Eloise chuckles behind me. I lift my head and look at her.

"You're so good at that. I think I really needed it," I mumble.

"You do. Now turn your head back. I'm not done with you yet," she tells me.

She's not finished. My body hasn't been this relaxed in, I don't know how long. She continues working on me for the next twenty minutes or so as I moan and groan against her expert hands.

"Hold on, let me grab something," she tells me.

I don't even bother answering as I float away on another blissful cloud of relaxation.

"Now, I'm going to relax you even more," she whispers in my ear. Not sure how she can do that because I feel incredibly relaxed now, but I'm not going to say no to whatever she has planned. There's some shuffling in a drawer or something and then I feel her grip my dick. *Hello! Yes, please.* Next thing I know she is encasing my dick in something.

"Elle?" I turn my head, and she's crouching beside me.

What the hell is she doing to my dick?

Eloise looks up at me, her hands still playing with whatever she has my dick wrapped in. "Trust me," she says, giving me a blinding smile.

I want to, but she's putting something strange around my dick, so any man would have concerns. I let out a long, nervous breath and trust that she knows what she's doing. I place my head back in its hole and stare down at the floor, wondering what's going to happen?

Then she turns it on, and I almost leap off the massage table. *What in the ever-loving hell?* The machine feels like someone has their mouth wrapped around my dick. It's bizarre. Like there's a mouth wrapped around my dick, sucking it while their hands are jerking me off.

The machine moves up a notch in speed, and I groan as the machine pumps away like I'm a dairy cow but a horny one. Eloise's hands come down on my muscles again and begin relaxing me, and the multiple sensations are confusing but feel fucking great. I'm not sure if I'm going to be able to hold on, as this machine is intense with its perfect rhythm. My eyes begin to roll back inside my head, my toes curl, and my body is a live wire as it tries to pull the impending orgasm from me. I hold out for as long as I can, but it's an epic battle between man and machine, and I know I'm losing as it continues to bring me closer to the edge.

"Let go, Ali," Eloise whispers in my ear.

And those three words ...

... do it.

I'm done.

Peace out, world.

I see the stars.

The heavens.

I've been transported through dimensions as I come hard.

Eloise's giggles pull me back to this world as I feel yanking on my sensitive dick then a towel wiping it off, but I don't have the energy to move. I'm exhausted, and this table is a comfortable place to lay my weary head.

"Looks like that was good for you," Eloise states.

"Humm ..." is all I can muster.

"Come on. You can nap in bed with me."

I groan because the thought of moving pains me, but if it means I can curl up against Eloise, then I'll find the strength somehow. It takes everything in me to get up off the massage table and stumble the couple of steps toward the bed where I face plant.

The next thing I know, I'm out.

"Hey there, sleepyhead." Eloise smiles at me as I open my eyes.

It takes me a couple of moments to realize I'm not dreaming and that she is truly here beside me again.

"Hey," I answer as my voice cracks from sleep. I reach out and caress her face to make sure she's truly here.

"Guess you're feeling relaxed now." She chuckles, which brings a smile to my lips.

"Not sure what voodoo magic you did to me, but I feel reborn."

"Yeah, that machine is worth its weight in gold. I'll send one home with you," she says with a grin.

I let out a disappointed smile at the thought of her sending me home with a machine rather than her.

"Are you okay?" She's obviously noticed my frown and the change in mood.

"Yeah, just realizing when I leave, you're not coming with me," I tell her honestly.

"Do you want to talk about that?"

"You're here, and I'm there," I say.

Eloise frowns. "I don't know how much longer I'll be here."

Hope blooms in my chest. "Are you thinking of leaving?"

"I think so." She sighs. "As much as I have loved living on the island with this weather, I haven't been able to do as much baking as I thought I would be able to. And I realize after doing those markets before I left that was what made me happy."

This makes *me* happy.

Not that Eloise is unhappy here, but because there's a chance she might be coming back to London.

"Would you continue with the club if you came back?" I ask cautiously. Hoping that the answer is no because then there would be nothing stopping me from asking her out on a date.

"Probably not," she says, shaking her head. "I want to start living my dream instead of thinking about it," she explains. "But …" she starts, and my stomach sinks. I don't know if it's going to be good or not for me. "I promised Lauren six months on the island, and it's only been five. She's having fun, so it wouldn't be right for me to just leave right now."

This is great news. What are four weeks in the scheme of things if it means Eloise is coming home?

"Lauren's been on this journey with me for so many years. She doesn't need to be working at the club, she has a trust fund that means she never has to work again, but she does it for me. I owe her so much. I feel bad asking her to leave something she likes because she has always followed me as I try and pursue my dreams," Eloise explains.

I can see the war she's fighting within herself. She wants to go back to London to start what she loves, but Lauren, who has been with her through everything, doesn't want to leave just yet.

"I'm sure Lauren wouldn't hold you back."

"No, she wouldn't, but I don't want to go back without her either," Eloise tells me honestly.

"I'd be happy if you came back to London," I tell her.

"You would?" she asks, sounding surprised.

I reach out and pull her on top of me, making her squeal. She looks down at me and brushes the hair away from my eyes. My poor dick wants to be hard, but he's exhausted.

"I would never pressure you to leave your job, but I would be damn happy if you came back to London," I tell her honestly. "I'd also happily wait the extra month till your time's up. As long as when you got back to London, you come find me."

"I'll find you," she says with a smile as she bends down and lightly kisses my lips. I will never get bored of kissing this woman.

"If you don't, you know I'm coming after you," I tell her.

"Stalker much." She chuckles.

"As long as you're okay with that."

Eloise pretends to think this over, but the smile on her face gives her true feelings away. "I think I could be."

Yes, I scream internally as I roll her over onto her back which makes her squeal with delight before my lips meet hers in a searing kiss.

24

ELOISE

We've spent all day in bed, napping, eating, watching television, and hanging out with each other. It was nice, and it's something we have never been able to do before. We didn't have to worry about sneaking around because of the island. We can spend the entire day in Alistair's villa without anyone caring.

I let out a groan as I stretch my muscles. "I have to head back to my place," I tell Alistair, who stiffens beside me in the bed.

"I thought you were staying?" he asks as his brows pull together. The disappointment on his face is so cute.

I lean in and place a light kiss against his lips. But Alistair won't have that, and next thing I know, he's flipping me onto my back and deepening the kiss. His hand is cupping my face as his tongue does wild things to my mouth. This man knows how to kiss. He's forceful yet tender.

Eventually, I pull myself away from him.

"Stay," he asks me tenderly.

"I am. I just need to grab my things," I tell him.

"You're not going to need anything. I can't imagine we are going to be in clothes much," he says, grinning down at me.

"Is that so?"

He nods as his mouth comes down and begins to kiss the tender skin across my neck. My body comes alive again under his lips, but I need to tell Lauren I won't be back, and I want to check in on Sierra. His mouth trails down over my collarbone and down between the valley of my breasts.

"Hold that thought," I tell him, stopping him from continuing further.

Alistair pouts his lips and gives me puppy dog eyes as he looks up at me.

"Let me do what I've got to do, then I'm all yours, okay?" He continues pouting. "Would you stop that?" I chuckle, trying not to give in to him because I can feel myself starting to.

His finger lazily moves around my nipple again as he bites his bottom lip and raises a brow at me, daring me to stop him.

"Alistair," I say, warning him.

He totally ignores me and continues teasing, but he says with a smile, "You can leave anytime."

"Then why are you making it so hard?"

"Why are you making it so hard?" He grins.

Oh my god, he's too much. I roll over on top of him and catch him off guard as I hold his wrists above his head. "Give me thirty, and I'll be back, and you can do whatever you want to me then." I lean down, pressing another kiss to his lips before jumping off him.

He lets out a groan of frustration as he watches me get dressed. "Fine, you win," he says, rolling his eyes. "I'll be here waiting for you, with a dick that doesn't seem to want to go down while he's around you."

"Good! I'll make great use of him when I get back." I smile as I give him a wave and rush out of his villa.

It's dark by the time I leave, and luckily, I know my way through the dense rainforest after all these months on the island. At first, it took me a while to get used to the island and the sounds at night from all the tropical birds. I was used to the city sounds of sirens, people shouting, and traffic. Also, it was hard to get used to how dark it is at night. Pure darkness can be disorientating. I don't think I've ever seen total darkness like this in London. And the stars are incredible, and when you look up and see the billions of tiny specks across the night sky, they are magnificent.

It doesn't take me long to get to my villa, and I can see the light is on. I open the door and walk inside. Lauren's sitting on the couch alone watching television, and she turns to see who has entered the villa. When she knows it's me, her eyes widen, and a grin falls across her face.

"You whore, where the hell have you been?" she asks.

"How's Sierra?" I ask first.

"She's fine! Flown to the mainland with a broken ankle. She'll be back in a couple of months," she explains.

"Well, damn, that sucks. I was hoping to check in on her. I'll have to send her a text."

"So?" Lauren asks, looking me up and down as she raises a brow. "You disappeared for hours. That massage sure was *looong*." She grins.

"You want a drink or something?" I ask as I head to our kitchen.

"Elle," Lauren calls out my name. "What is going on? My anxiety is through the roof after today," she calls out from the couch.

I grab myself a water, head back into the living room, and take a seat beside her on the couch. Her eyes are wide with questions as she stares at me like I've lost my mind.

"You're never going to believe who the guest is?" I say.

"Don't tell me he's some hot rock star? Movie star? Billionaire? Sheik? Royal?" Lauren asks, peppering me with suggestions.

"Alistair King."

Lauren's jaw falls open as I tell her, and silence fills the villa. "No ... *fucking* way. How the hell? I don't understand. Of all the people, it's him? Hang on, you didn't come back screaming and crying ..." She looks me over. "Actually, you look like you've been fucked sideways, Eloise?"

"So much has happened."

"I'm listening," she says, folding her arms across her ample chest.

"At first, I was shocked, angry, even vengeful." Lauren nods. "Then I overheard a phone call from his mum." Lauren moves forward, ready to hear what I have to say. "His ex is marrying his brother. That's who his ex cheated on him with."

Lauren blinks rapidly as she takes in the news. "No fucking way!"

"And he knocked her up too," I add.

Lauren shakes her head, her eyes wide with disbelief. "He was dealing with all of that at the same time as dealing with my drama. I felt like such a bitch."

"You didn't know, Elle. That's a lot," Lauren adds.

"I explained the reason why I left to him. About how someone told me they had fun with him back in London. He assured me it wasn't him. He even showed me his calendar from that day, and he was in a meeting on the other side of town. Why would he keep that in his calendar all these months if it wasn't true?"

"I agree. But there's only one Mr. King in the system in London," Lauren adds.

"At that time. Were we wrong?" I ask her.

Lauren shrugs her shoulders as a frown falls over her face. "Maybe we need to check again. Was it an admin error? Like it's weird, Elle."

"I know, but I believe him, Loz. I really do."

"Then that's all that matters," she says, giving me a small smile.

"I should have spoken to him when it happened. Would have saved me a ton of heartache."

"Hindsight is a wonderful thing. But you were leaving anyway," she adds.

"I know but—" I stop myself because the words were about to tumble out of my mouth, and I don't know if now is the time to be having this conversation with Lauren about my future.

"But what?" Lauren asks.

I sit there in silence, unable to work out how to tell her I'm unhappy here.

"Elle, you're worrying me. What's going on?" Lauren asks again, her voice rising with fear.

Emotions begin to well in my eyes as I confess my true feelings to her, "I'm not happy here, Loz."

"You're not? Why didn't you tell me?" she asks, seemingly confused.

"Because you are." Tears stream down my face at my confession.

"Oh, babe," she says, shuffling over to me and pulling me into a hug. "I would have understood. Of course, I'm having fun here, it's Paradise, but I can take it or leave it," she tells me.

"I dragged you halfway across the world," I say while sniffling against her shoulder.

"That's okay. You know I'm always up for an adventure. I wouldn't have cared," she reassures me.

"I know, but I promised you six months, and I owe you that," I tell her.

Lauren moves out of our embrace and wipes the tears from my cheeks. "Babe, you owe me nothing. If you were that unhappy, why did you not tell me? I would have understood. I know you haven't been able to bake as much as you like here, and I could see that was frustrating you. But then you reassured me you were so close to reaching your dream, so I didn't question you. Damn! Now, I wish I had. I never want to see you unhappy." I don't deserve Lauren as a best friend, so I do the only thing I can and wrap my arms around her neck again and hug her tightly.

"I'm so sorry I didn't tell you. I was upset that I had made this decision to leave because of Alistair hurting me, and I felt guilty that I dragged you away from London and away from your mystery man. That I made it seem like going to the island was the greatest thing ever, but I was so wrong."

"Why did you never tell me this? We could have left," she adds.

"I thought you loved it here?"

"Don't get me wrong, this is fun. But I can't keep doing this forever. I need to grow up and work out what the hell I want to do with my life," she confesses to me.

"I didn't know you were feeling this way."

"I didn't want to burden you with my concerns because I know you have a goal for your bakery, and I didn't want to destroy that goal," she tells me.

"We're a right pair, aren't we?" I say, chuckling beside her.

"We both thought we were being good friends by sucking it up, but in reality, we both aren't happy here," Lauren says, shaking her head. "So, what are we going to do?"

"I don't know."

"What are you going to do about Alistair?" Lauren asks curiously.

"He wants me to stay the week with him in his villa."

Lauren's face breaks out in a wide smile. "I think you should, and maybe by the end of the week you'll know if you want to go back to London with him," she adds.

"It's just fun in Paradise, nothing more," I say, rolling my eyes.

"Bullshit!" She nudges my shoulder. "You don't have to stay here anymore, Elle. If you want to go back to London and start that bakery ... *do it*. Take the leap."

"It all seems rather scary," I tell her honestly.

"That's life, babe." She gives me a small smile.

"What are you thinking of doing? Are you staying? Or are you going to come back to London too?"

"You're going to need someone to help you set up your bakery," Lauren says with a smile.

"You want to help me?"

"Bitch, I feel like this has been my dream as much as it has been yours. It's the only thing I've been working toward all these years," she says frankly.

"Really?"

"As soon as I tasted your cupcakes for the first time, I knew I had to help you bring your baking to the masses. I'd do anything to help you succeed, babe."

I knew she supported me, but I didn't realize how much. "I had no idea you felt that strongly about my business?"

"You're talented as fuck but not in the right headspace to take your dream to the next level. I knew what you needed was time and confidence to see your true worth. Don't forget, I've known you for half your life. I know what you came from and how far you have come from that scared little girl at boarding school. You needed to heal emotionally from all the damage your parents inflicted on you, and now I think you're ready."

She has me crying again—I'm not worthy of her as a best friend.

"Be my partner," I say, blurting out the statement.

Lauren's brows pull together in confusion. I don't know why I never thought about this before. Lauren's good at business and marketing, and I'm great at baking, but I have no idea how to run a business. We need to join forces and do this together. She has been with me from day one. She knows my vision and my business ideas and plans as well as I do. I had no idea she was as passionate about my bakery as I am.

"Why don't you and I create this business together. Let's

create the best motherfucking bakery in London, no England, no the world," I tell her.

Lauren's eyes widen. She seems surprised by my request. "You have been so adamant that you always wanted to do it yourself."

"I know because I didn't think anyone could love my business as much as I could, but I had no idea you loved the concept too," I explain to her.

"I've always had faith in you, Elle. I've always admired your drive to get to this dream and make it a reality, and I was willing to do anything to help you achieve it because I believed in it and you too," she says.

"Then join me. You and me against the world."

"You sure?" she asks.

"I'm so fucking sure, babe. I don't know why I never thought about it before. You and I have always made the best team."

"Friendship and business can be tricky."

"Then let's get a lawyer to do their thing. We sign a contract and make it all legal," I tell her excitedly.

"You're actually serious?" she questions.

"Never been *more* serious."

"I'm in," she says as tears begin to well in her eyes.

I launch myself at her, and we roll onto the floor in a fit of giggles.

"We're going to be such a kick-ass team." I chuckle as we lay on the floor.

"Fuck yeah, we are. My connections, your talent ... we're going to have the hottest bakery in London," Lauren says enthusiastically. "And Elle ... thank you."

"You don't need to thank me."

Lauren looks at me seriously. "I do. You've given me purpose," she says seriously. "I've never had that before."

I give my best friend a smile as I reach out and squeeze her hand. "We've got this!"

She gives me a nod as we help each other up off the floor.

"First things first though, you have a hot man to get back to. We can sort things out when you get back. Enjoy the week, and then we will work out what happens next," Lauren tells me.

"You sure?"

"Yes. The Universe is telling you to have fun with this man. How else do you explain Sierra's weird broken ankle?" Lauren wiggles her brows.

"Coincidence," I add.

"Nope, the Universe gave you two a second chance."

"Nothing is going to happen other than a great week of fun. He goes back to his life in London. You and I sort out our new life. It was probably the Universe giving us both closure so we can move on in new directions," I explain to her.

"If you say so," Lauren mumbles.

"Lauren," I say her name with a warning.

She holds up her hands and grins. "Go … pack! Do not leave that hot man waiting for one more second."

I give her one last hug and quickly pack my bag.

25

ALISTAIR

My dick is hard and unsatisfied as I watch Eloise leave my villa. I know I'm being unreasonable asking her to stay and not check in on her friend who's hurt or her roommate. I guess I'm worried because there's a small part of me that wonders if she'll come back. I'm worried she will disappear again, and I won't get a second or would it be a third chance to see her again.

I slide out of bed and roam around the villa, the anxiety of waiting for Elle to return has my body jittery. We've spent the day in bed watching television, fucking, and eating, and not always in that order. Honestly, it's been a great day.

There were never any awkward silences between us. It was as if we have always been this way. Everything is natural between us, and I don't want our time together to end.

This is her job. It's a roadblock we keep coming up against.

I don't know how I'm going to be able to leave the island after a week, and I know that as soon as I step off the island, she's going to be in another man's bed.

She's not yours.

Yet, I tell myself.

Maybe I should show her how it would be between us if she came back to London with me after this week. *You can't make her choose.* I know I can't, but I want to be an option because at the moment, I don't think I am. Yes, I believe Elle liked me all those months ago, but some fucker pretended to be me and fucked it all up. If I find out who that fucker is, I'm going to make him pay. It's hard to not think of the what-ifs if that hadn't played out the way it did.

My phone rings, pulling me from my thoughts. I look down and hope that it's not someone in my family ringing me about the fucking wedding. Jasper's name flashes, and relief floats over me.

I pick up his call. "Hey, man."

"What the hell are you doing picking up my call while at The Paradise Club?" he questions, which makes me laugh.

"I'm taking a break," I reply.

"Of course, you are, old man," he teases. "How's the island treating you? Hope you're relaxing like I told you to."

I guess I should be thanking Jasper since he's the reason I ended up at the island. He told me I needed to have a week of fun before having to deal with all the shit that's coming my way with my brother's wedding. If I hadn't taken his advice, I'm pretty sure he would have flown over here and dragged me to the island himself.

"Also, please tell me you're enjoying what is on offer? I know how you get inside your head sometimes," he adds, seemingly quite amused with himself if the chuckling is anything to go by.

He knows me so well. "I will say today has definitely not turned out the way I thought it would."

"Did she use a strap-on?"

"What? No!"

"Don't kink shame, Ali. That's not very progressive," Jasper says, chastising me.

What is he on about? "Your mind is a scary place," I tell him.

"You have no idea." He chuckles. "Don't leave me in suspense. If it wasn't a strap-on, then what happened?"

"I found her."

"Found who?"

"Elle." The line falls silent for a long while. "Jasper?"

"The girl that ghosted you?"

"Yes. But she had a valid reason."

"I'm sure she does," he grumbles down the line. "Ali, I'm worried about you. That girl broke your heart when she disappeared. I'm sure she has her reasons, but she hurt you. Fucking disappearing like that was cruel."

"Never knew you cared, big guy," I joke.

"Fuck you!" he spits back quickly.

"The night before our date, someone at the club told her they had just spent the night with me. She thought after I promised her I would only go to the club with her, that I'd been going there behind her back. She was risking her job to be with me."

"Were you there?" Jasper asks.

"Fuck no! I wasn't there, but they said there was a Mr. King, and one of the girls working there assumed it was me. Elle said there was only one King on the books, which was me," I explain to him.

"Did they type in the wrong name?" he asks.

"I have no idea. But it was convincing enough to make Elle bolt."

"That's strange," my friend adds. "We should ask Alex, see if he can find out who the guy was."

"He's loved-up with Ivy, I don't want to bother him. Plus, he's going to ask questions, and I can't get Elle fired from her job … she needs it."

"I have my ways. I can find out," Jasper tells me.

"Legal ways?"

"Do you really want to know?" He chuckles.

I shake my head. "I don't want Elle in trouble, but I do want to know who this fucker is that pretended to be me."

"Leave it with me," Jasper says. "How do you feel about her being back in your life?"

"I was angry at first, fucking furious. I didn't understand how she could walk away from what was happening between us. Just disappeared the way she did. Then Mum called me about the wedding, and it interrupted things."

"Oh, shit."

"Yeah. It was shit. George put her up to calling me and making sure that I wasn't going to turn up to his wedding and make a scene."

"That slimy fucker," Jasper curses.

"Right? The audacity of him after everything he has done to me," I say, shaking my head.

"What happened?" he asks.

"I walked out of the villa onto the beach and couldn't breathe. I felt like I was having a panic attack. Seeing Elle and then my own mother questioning me was all too much."

"What did Elle do?" Jasper asks.

"She was there for me. She didn't push me. She listened to me vent, and then she apologized. I could see how bad she felt about ghosting me while I was dealing with family stuff."

"*I bet she did.*" Jasper chuckles, but I don't appreciate the inflection in his voice.

"Fuck you! And don't speak about her like that," I warn him.

"Okay, okay … I get it. You're still into this girl. If you're that into her, why don't you invite her to the wedding?"

"Do you have better plans?" I ask him as he's supposed to be my wingman.

"Fuck, yeah. Anything is better than going to that farce of a wedding. I was only going to be your date because of the free food, but honestly, I think you should invite Elle."

"She will look better in a dress than you," I joke.

"Hey, I've got great legs, and you know I put out on the first date." He chuckles.

I shake my head at my best friend. "She's probably working on the island."

"I'm sure she gets holidays," Jasper pushes.

"You think she would?" The thought begins to percolate in my mind, and I become hopeful that maybe this will be a good thing.

"Only one way to find out," he states.

Would she want to come with me? I don't know if we're even at that level yet.

"I'll see how the week goes. I might suss her out a little more. Where she's at … it's only been one day."

"Good idea. Spend this week seeing if the spark you once had is still there and wasn't some figment of your overactive imagination," Jasper tells me.

"The spark is certainly there," I reply.

"As much as it pains me to say this, I'm not talking sexually," he adds.

"I know. I'll see what happens. I'll play it by ear," I tell him.

"Good. You know I only have your best interests at heart, don't you?"

This is the sincerest I think I've ever heard Jasper speak. "Yeah, man, I know. Thanks for looking out for me."

"No problem, brother. I'll let you go and enjoy Paradise. Also, there's no shame in trying a strap-on." And with that pearl of wisdom, he's gone.

With a shake of my head at my friend's parting words, I throw my phone onto my bed and head into the bathroom to shower and freshen up.

Once out of the shower and dressed in some boardshorts, I

grab the tablet and think about doing something nice for dinner. I don't think I'm ready to head out in public with Elle yet because I know once men lay their eyes on her, they will want to have a taste, and I'm not willing to share. I click through the options, and I hope that she's okay with what I have planned. I then grab my laptop and set it up at my desk—might as well catch up with some work while I wait for her to arrive.

A couple of hours later, the sound of the villa door opens, and Eloise steps across the threshold with a bag. Relief hits me—she's come back to me.

"Hey," she says, a wide smile dancing across her face when she sees me. I stand and stalk over to her, wrap my hands around her face and kiss her. "What was that for?" she questions.

"You came back."

"Did you *not* think I would come back?" she asks, a frown falling across her face.

I don't answer her, but my face probably says it all.

"I'm so sorry, Ali. If I could go back and change that night, I would," she tells me in all sincerity.

I reach out and cup her face. "I know you would. I don't mean to doubt you."

"It's my job to work at rebuilding the trust we once had together," she tells me honestly.

"Babe, you don't owe me anything." I don't want this to be a stumbling block between us.

"But I want to," she states clearly.

I lean down and kiss her again.

She drops her bag on the floor and wraps her arms around my neck. The kiss is heated yet sweet at the same time. With that kiss, she's showing me how much she regrets that night.

"Everything that happened before this moment, Elle, doesn't matter anymore, okay?" I try reassuring her that she doesn't have to keep apologizing or making things up to me.

"Okay," she declares, smiling up at me.

"Good! Now, I don't know about you, but I'm hungry." I grab her hand, pick up her bag, and walk her back through the villa, then place the bag on the bed. She eyes the freshly made bed, and I can see the desire flare behind her eyes. "That will be dessert," I tell her.

Elle looks up at me with a smile. I tug on her hand again and lead her out toward the deck, past the pool, and back down the pathway that leads to the beach where our dinner has been set up for us.

"Ali ..." Elle gasps as she notices the beach hut set up on the beach, which is surrounded by tiki torches. "This is so beautiful." She takes in the table set up with white linens, crystal glassware, and a large bouquet of tropical flowers in the center. No one is on the beach. We have it all to ourselves, with nothing but the crashing of the waves as ambiance and the millions of twinkling stars high above us for light. I asked for no staff as I didn't think Eloise would feel comfortable with them watching us because we won't be acting like normal guests and staff. I let go of her hand and pull out her chair for her. Elle bites her bottom lip and takes a seat.

Then I grab the bottle of champagne from the bucket set up on the side, pop it open, and pour each of us a glass. "Welcome to my restaurant," I say, waving my hand in front of me, making her giggle. "On the menu tonight is Oysters Rockefeller," I say, grabbing the dish from the pop-up kitchen set up and bringing them to the table.

"You know you don't need oysters to get me in the mood," Eloise jokes.

I place the plate in the middle of the table for us to share. "Thought I might hedge my bets just in case." I give her a wink as I take my seat.

"This is so beautiful, Ali," Eloise says as she looks out across the golden sand of the beach toward the inky black ocean and the endless darkness of the horizon, peppered with stars for as far as the eye can see. "No one has ever done anything so beautiful for me."

This pains me to hear. "You've been with the wrong men, then."

"Probably ..." She chuckles. "I haven't really dated since starting at The Paradise Club."

"Is that because men can't handle your job?" I ask before I throw back an oyster. I'm genuinely curious to hear her answer.

"Yes, but I also never tried because I felt guilty over my job," she explains.

"Did you feel that with us?" I ask, curious now as to where this conversation is leading.

Eloise is silent for a couple of seconds as she mulls over how to answer. "Yes. You scared me," she states.

Her answer catches me off-guard, and now I am all ears. "Why?"

"You were the first man I wanted to date who I was willing to give it all up for," she confesses as she slowly looks up at me through thick lashes.

My heart stops.

Dead!

"If I am being perfectly honest, I don't think I was ready, and I'm pretty sure that's why I bolted," she adds as she fidgets in her seat.

"You know I would never have asked you to give up your job."

"I know," she says, reaching out and touching my arm. I move my hand and link my fingers with hers. "You're secure in who you are. You understood there's a difference between what I do at the club and what we do at home."

I get what she's saying, and I would have supported her decision to stay. But if I'm honest, I don't know for how long. Because I do know if we had started dating, I would have fallen head over heels for her, and each time she left my bed to go to work, it would have chipped away at my heart.

"How long do you think you'll keep working here?" I need to know how long I must wait for her.

"I'm not sure anymore."

What does that mean? Hope begins to bloom in my chest.

"I promised Lauren six months, and that time is almost over."

And? I want to say the word, but I hold myself back.

"I thought she was happy here. I was willing to ride out the six months for her."

Why does it sound like there's a but coming?

"But we had a chat tonight when I went back to our villa, and as it turns out, we were both staying here for each other. We were both being loyal friends but hadn't asked the other what they wanted to do. We had made assumptions instead."

Okay, but what does that mean?

"Our chat tonight somehow ended up with us going into business together." Elle giggles. "Lauren's been there every step of the way, and I thought it was because she was being a good friend. Turns out it's because she believes in my dream too. So, we've decided to do it together," Elle states excitedly.

That's great, but what does that mean?

"We have so much business to talk about, but we will do that once you've left. I'm so excited, I can't believe it. I don't know why we didn't think about it sooner." She grins widely.

I can see the excitement lighting up her face making her look even more beautiful, so I squeeze her hand, showing my support. "Congratulations, that's brilliant news." I raise my glass in her direction. She does the same, and we clink them together.

"Firstly, we need to speak to a lawyer to write up a contract. We trust each other with our lives, but it's better to be safe, right?"

"Yes. I can give you my lawyer's number ... he deals in these matters all the time," I tell her.

"Thank you. Yeah, that would be great." Eloise grins. "Next thing I need to think about is ... do I continue markets, or do I take the leap and set up a proper bakery?"

"What is your dream?" I ask.

"I always envisioned this gorgeous girly style bakery. Pink and flowery-filled beautiful pastel cakes and other sweets. But maybe that isn't what sells," she adds, biting her lip as uncertainty begins to cross her mind.

"Who wouldn't want to buy cakes in a gorgeous shop. Will people be able to eat there?"

"Like a café?" she asks, and I nod. "Maybe. I hadn't even thought about that aspect." Her eyes widen as panic begins to take over. I know how overwhelming it can be starting from scratch.

"If you want, no pressure, I can put you in touch with some of the best shop fit-out designers. They can help bring your vision to life."

"Don't think I can afford them," she mumbles quietly.

"They will be happy to chat for free. I promise you they would love to help in whatever capacity," I reassure her.

"Thank you, Ali. I mean it," she says, reaching out again and squeezing my hand. "I've been so self-reliant for so long that I forget to ask for help. You're an expert when it comes to the hospitality industry. I'd be stupid to think that you don't know what you're talking about."

"I've always said, Elle, that I'm happy to help, and I'm not talking in a monetary kind of way. I'd love to be your sounding board. I can't wait to see things grow from an idea to reality right before my eyes. That shit gets me hard," I joke, which makes her smile. "I mean it. Don't think I'm helping because I want to keep whatever this is going on between us. Sure, that's a bonus, but I'd still help you even if you friend-zoned me. You can bake.

These past six months I have dreamed about your cupcakes as much as I have your pussy."

"Is that so?" Eloise raises a brow, not quite believing me.

"Who knew I'd have a thing for buttercream frosting."

Elle breaks out into laughter. "Don't give me ideas," she says.

"Now, you're the one giving me ideas. Didn't know frosting was on the cards." I chuckle.

"You're crazy," she declares, shaking her head at me.

"About you, yeah, I think I am," I confess.

She nervously takes a sip of champagne, and I notice the faint pinkness in her cheeks. Does she like knowing that she drives me crazy?

"I think the oysters are going to your head." She smiles.

"I think it's more the company than the oysters." Our jovial conversation begins to heat up as the sexual tension becomes like an inferno.

"It's not even been twenty-four hours since you've come back into my life, but it feels like a lifetime," she whispers as she looks down at her plate, embarrassed over her words.

"I feel it too," I tell her.

This has her looking up at me, and relief slides across her features.

"Whatever happens after this week, I'm glad that I got to spend it with you." The next thing I know, Elle is up out of her chair and is sitting on my lap.

"I'm glad I'm spending it with you too," she says. Elle wraps her arms around my neck and kisses me slowly.

We aren't in a hurry. We aren't waiting to take things further. It's nice to slow things down now that we know we have the week together, so there's no rush, unlike earlier today.

"I know I sound like a broken record, but I'm sorry about that night for leaving you the way I did," Elle apologizes again.

"You don't have to keep apologizing, baby." I look up at her and run my hand down her face. "The past is in the past." She slowly nods. "Are you ready for the next course?"

Elle moves to get off my lap, but I hold her closer to me. "You're not going anywhere. I like feeling your ass against my dick." Elle wiggles making me groan, the cheeky little thing. "I told you earlier, that's dessert," I whisper in her ear.

26

ELOISE

"I'm the kind of girl who likes dessert first," I tease, biting my lip, loving the thrill I get from hearing him groan beneath me.

"Elle!" Alistair says my name with a gravely warning before he picks me up, which makes me squeal in surprise, before placing me back down on his chair. He grabs the now empty oyster plate and takes it over to the pop-up kitchen set up beside the beach hut. I'm still in awe that he went to so much trouble for dinner tonight.

Is this our first date? It kind of feels like it is. Now I'm disappointed that I missed our *actual* first date if this is the standard he goes by.

He's dressed in a white polo with black linen pants, and it's only now that I notice he isn't wearing any underwear beneath those pants, judging by the thick dick print that's pressed against his zipper. *Hmm.* Alistair turns back around with two plates in his hands and walks over to where I'm sitting. He places both in front of me. *I'm not that hungry that I need two meals*, I think as I stare down at a plate that's filled with freshly cut steak, vegetables, and fries. *I'm hungry for a different kind of meat* I internally tell myself. Alistair then walks around and picks me up off his chair and places me back on his lap, but this time I'm facing directly toward the table.

"I want to feed you, Elle," he states, his voice all gravely with desire. No one has ever requested that of me before, but I'm not opposed to it.

"Okay," I answer him, but the smile that falls across his face is filled with mischief. *What is he up to?*

"Good, then stand up, bend over the table and take your panties off," he commands me.

The turn of events stuns me a little, and I obviously don't move quick enough before he picks me up off his lap and pushes me forward. My hands land on either side of the dinner plates on the table clattering the glassware and cutlery. He then flicks up the edge of my mini summer dress and pulls down my underwear but only gets my panties as far as my knees. My heart is thundering in my chest as need begins to throb between my thighs. I shimmy out of my panties and let them fall to the floor. Thankfully I'm wearing nothing more than a flimsy sundress. Otherwise, I'd be missing out on bliss.

Now what?

Alistair's hand squeezes one of my ass cheeks before he gives it a good slap. "Such a good girl." He chuckles behind me.

Yes. The sting of his hand against my skin sends goosebumps rampaging over my body. He then nudges my legs to open wider, and I do as he desires. Then his fingers slip between my folds, and I bite down on my lip as a moan escapes me.

"You're so fucking wet, Elle. Have you been this needy during the starters?"

A hum falls from my lips as his fingers slide inside me.

"This just won't do." He pulls his fingers from me, and the next thing I know he's lowering me onto his dick, slowly filling me until I'm nestled against him. He pulls me back against his chest as his hand snakes around my body, and his fingers slide across my clit. A hiss falls from my lips at connection.

The next thing I feel is food against my lips, and it pulls me away from the throbbing need between my thighs.

"Open, princess," Ali commands, and I do as I'm told. He slides the fork past my lips, and I bite into the succulent meat. It's so tender it melts in my mouth. Then I feel his other hand sliding across my clit again, and my body feels torn between enjoying the mouthful of food and the tenderness of his fingers against me.

What is happening? His dick is inside me, while his fingers play with my clit, while he fork-feeds me food. The tastes and sensations are overwhelming, and I don't know if I should come or praise the chef.

"Keep eating. You're going to need your strength," he warns me as I open for a mouthful of vegetables. Repeatedly, he feeds me in between bites for himself until there is nothing left on our plates. "Such a good girl," he coos behind me.

He has edged me toward a cliff, and I'm wound up like a spring. At any moment, I could tip over that edge and fall into the abyss of ecstasy.

He sighs as he finishes his last morsel of food, all the while lazily teasing me with his fingers between each bite.

The next thing I know, he's picking me up and depositing my bare ass on the table, and instantly I hate missing the fullness of him that I had moments ago. My eyes dip to where his thick dick is sticking out from his pants, standing to attention, ready for action. I lick my lips because I want him back inside me.

"Hold that thought," he says, looking me over. "I can see it on your face, dessert is coming," he states as he walks around me, grabbing our dinner plates off the table as well as the glasses. "Take your dress off unless you want to get it dirty," he calls out from the pop-up kitchen behind me.

Quickly, I do as I'm told and pull the dress off me and sit

naked, spread out before him. The next thing I know he's walking back with a platter of desserts, which he places beside me on the table and grabs the can of whipped cream. He gives it a good shake before taking the cap off and spraying it over my breast. It's cold, and the sensation makes me jump. His tongue is there to lick the cream from my nipple, and as he swirls it around, I close my eyes before he sucks it deep inside his mouth. He then repeats the action on the other breast.

"You're my favorite dessert." He grins as he squirts the cream down my stomach, and then his tongue follows, sliding along my skin. "I'll never get sick of eating you," he states as he squirts the cream at the top of my pelvis and then licks me clean before lowering his mouth further. He looks up at me from between my thighs, and I can see the desire swirling behind his eyes before he dips further and slides his tongue all the way up my slit. My head lulls back as my eyes close, and I suck in a breath because it feels so damn good.

"Morning," I say, walking out of the bedroom, feeling refreshed and relaxed after a good night's sleep. We didn't end up getting to bed until late after Alistair fucked me on the dinner table for dessert. Then he carried me back to the villa, where he unceremoniously dropped me into the pool and ate the remainder of his dessert from my body.

We then lazed around the pool before he dragged me back out of the water and laid me on the sun lounge. I remember curling up against his hard chest as we laid back and looked up at the stars. He pointed out all the constellations he could remember and whispered them against my ear, and then we fucked slowly underneath the stars.

Hours later, he carried me inside, where I promptly fell asleep tucked up next to him. It was the first time we had overnighted together, and it was the deepest sleep I've had in I don't know how long.

"Babe, I didn't know what you might like, so I ordered everything," he says, looking up from his phone while sipping his coffee. The breakfast table is filled with fresh fruit and pastries.

"You let me sleep in," I tell him as I walk outside and kiss him on his forehead before I take a seat beside him.

"You seemed exhausted," he replies before sipping his coffee slowly.

"I had the best night's sleep, thank you. I think you wore me out." I smile as I take a blueberry and pop it in my mouth.

"Need you to get your strength back for today," he says, giving me a wink.

"What do you have planned?" I ask, genuinely excited that we get to spend the day together.

"Other than you, not much. Thought I'd wait till you woke and plan out what we could do together." He gives me a wide smile.

Aw, that's so sweet.

"Is there something you want to do on the island but haven't yet?" he asks.

I plate up some fruit and grab a flaky chocolate croissant as I mull over his question. "I've always wanted to go on a boat and sail around the island. I've only ever seen the island from on land."

Alistair's eyes widen with delight. "That's perfect. Why didn't I think of that? Okay, let me organize it. We can disappear from the island and stay in our bubble for a little longer. Leave it with me." He stands quickly and places a kiss on my forehead before rushing inside and grabbing the tablet.

27

ALISTAIR

"Oh, wow!" Eloise's eyes widen as she sees the multimillion-pound yacht I have hired for the day. Thankfully, thanks to my boat license, we don't need anyone on the boat with us.

"Mr. King, the staff has filled the larder and the fridges with enough food for the day. The bar is also stocked. Hope you both have a great day," the concierge at the marina explains.

"Thanks, Doug," Eloise says, and the guy beams brightly at her.

I don't like it and throw daggers his way. He eventually pulls his attention away from my girl and realizes I'm staring at him.

"Right, well, let me take you to your boat," Doug states quickly and heads out of the marina office.

Elle shakes her head but is smiling, so I know all is okay. We follow Doug along the wooden walkway to where a line of yachts is bobbing in the ocean. He stops outside berth fourteen and indicates. He then proceeds to give me a rundown on the yacht, and I listen politely even though I have the same one at my place in Greece. Once he's finished his rambling, he gives Elle one last look before disappearing.

"He wants you," I tell her as she takes a seat.

"Who, Doug?" She frowns.

"Yeah, he can't keep his eyes off you."

"He used to hook up with Sierra. That's probably why. He came to our villa all the time. Are you jealous?" She chuckles.

"No," I say, shaking my head.

Of course, I'm fucking jealous.

The next thing I know, Elle is jumping into my arms and wrapping her legs around my waist, and I fall back against the daybed.

"It makes me hot seeing you jealous," she whispers in my ear as she starts to grind herself against my crotch. We haven't even left the marina yet, and I'm seconds away from fucking her right here.

"I can't believe I'm saying this, but I don't have time to fuck you just yet. Even though I want to … to make sure everyone at the fucking marina knows you're mine, I *would* rather be somewhere else with you than here."

"Righto, Captain, let's set sail," she says, giggling.

"You'll be bouncing on my buoy in no time," I tell her.

"That sounds *sooo* wrong." She squeals as she jumps off me.

"It does, doesn't it? I'll work on better nautical puns as I get us underway."

It takes about ten minutes to reverse out of the berth and putter away from the marina. I would love to put the sails up, but as there are only the two of us, and I don't think Elle is a sailor, it's going to be too hard to steer and pull the sails, so we will motor along the coast. It's a beautiful day out on the water, nothing but the turquoise ocean meeting the blue horizon with a smattering of wispy white clouds dancing across the sky.

Elle has stripped down to a red bikini, and I'm finding it hard to keep my eyes off her as I steer us around the island. The concierge told me there is a private island off the southern side of

Paradise Island where day-trippers can head out to. So, I'm following the course to that area.

It takes us another thirty minutes, but we eventually arrive. I drop anchor and join Elle on the daybed where she has been lying.

"Watching you steer this yacht is the sexiest thing I've ever seen," Elle tells me as she reaches out and pulls me to her. Of course, I go willingly.

"Was it now?" I say.

Note to self, *take her to Greece and show her more.*

She nods while biting her bottom lip. "Yep, it's like when men parallel park ..." *That's sexy?* "You put your arm around the passenger seat and then do your zippy reverse thing. It's hot."

Another note to self, *take her in my car and spend the day parallel parking. Who the hell needs oysters?*

"Never heard that before."

"Oops, giving away my gender secrets." She grins.

"Don't stop. I want to hear more."

"Like when you take off a T-shirt, and you grab it from the back and pull it up over your head type of thing?"

Taking T-shirts off is sexy? Who knew?

So, I do as she asks and grab the back of my T-shirt and tug it up over my head and let it fall to the floor beside us. Elle is biting her bottom lip quite hard as her eyes roam over my torso.

"So hot," she mumbles to herself.

What's got into Elle today? It's probably the sea air, or she's had a great night's sleep and is raring to go. Not that I'm complaining, she can stare at me all day long.

"How hot?" I ask.

Elle opens her legs, her red bikini bottoms on display. She then reaches out and takes my hand, pushes the fabric to the side, and slides my fingers through her wetness. She's soaked. "That hot," she purrs before letting go of my hand.

My fingers begin to move inside her, and Elle arches her

back while her hands run over her body with each flick of my thumb against her clit. I can't take my eyes off her as she looks like a wicked sea siren luring me into the depths of the ocean to ravage me, but I don't care. I'll gladly go. Her hand pulls her bikini top to the side as her fingers pluck at her nipples, all the while my fingers sink into her. *Fuck, she feels so good.*

"Yes, Ali, yes!" She begins to squirm as my fingers continue their steady course inside her. Her body arches as she thrusts her chest out, her eyes flutter shut again until I feel her body spasm over my fingers, and Elle's screams echo around the bay.

Eventually, I pull my fingers from her and lick her wetness from them—I'll never get sick of her sweetness.

Elle reaches for the tent in my shorts, but I halt her. "We have all day. I want to relax and enjoy your company," I tell her.

"Okay." She grins, pulling her bikini back into place.

I take the picnic basket and goodies the staff packed for us and help Elle into the tender, and then we head off to the island. We have to wade through knee-high water to get to the sand, but the water is crystal clear so we can see what's beneath us. I set up the picnic blanket and fold out the sunshade, then throw some cushions down for us to lounge on.

Elle starts unpacking the picnic basket and setting up the food. Once we're in our own little oasis, we both settle and enjoy the serenity.

"You can tell me to butt out of your business ..." Elle starts as she pops a grape in her mouth. We've enjoyed our lunch and are now lazily grazing on the cheese platter while sipping champagne.

"I'm an open book, Elle."

"You might not be open about this topic?" she adds while nibbling on her mouth nervously.

"It's about my ex, isn't it?"

Elle nods. "I don't understand how she could cheat on you with your brother. You're a freaking catch," she states flatly.

Her compliment warms me.

"How are you feeling about attending the wedding? I can't imagine how hard it must be for you?"

"Honestly, I don't want to go. It may sound petty or even mean, but I don't give a shit about their happiness. Just like they didn't give a shit about mine."

Elle reaches out and lays a hand on my arm in reassurance. "Do you still love her?" She peeks up at me through her dark lashes.

"Hell no," I tell her sternly. "Things between us weren't good for a while, but we were both so busy that we sort of swept it under the rug. Guess her rug was my brother." I sigh.

"It's a fucked-up thing they both did," she adds with a frown.

"If you knew my brother, you wouldn't be at all surprised." I sigh. "Now, he and my parents are demanding we all play happy families for the day. And I'm exhausted over the charade." I take a large sip of my beer to steady the anger that is bubbling to the surface as I talk about my brother. "Do you have any siblings?"

"Nope, an only child. My best friend, Lauren, is like a sister to me, though," she says, giving me a smile.

"You're lucky! But I do have my friends, who are more like brothers to me than *he* ever will be."

"Are you and your brother close in age?"

"We're thirteen months apart. He's older. Firstborn. We were always competitive growing up. He likes to one-up me where he can. I guess as most brothers do. But George takes it that much further. As the eldest, his birthday is before mine on the calendar. He would always find out what I desperately wanted for my birthday and ask for it so he would get it first. My parents wouldn't buy the same thing twice, so I always missed out."

Elle's eyes widen upon hearing that story.

"It started off with toys, and as we grew, it then became about girls. I don't think there was a girl I dated that he hadn't tried it on with. He's a charismatic guy, and they would always fall for his charms. He wanted what I had. Then came our first cars ... he chose my dream car, got it, and rubbed it in my face. He then got into the university I wanted to get into, knowing full well that I wouldn't go there because he would be there. The only thing that's mine is my business. My brother works for my father, so that gives me some sense of satisfaction because he's not the boss."

"Honestly, that doesn't sound like a stable person."

"You learn to live with it. I'm so used to his antics now. I had to carve my own way because, as firstborn, he will inherit the family estate from my parents. As tradition dictates, it will be passed down to the firstborn son. Not like I care, I could buy ten estates of equal if not more value than our family's, but the memories of growing up there he will taint them even more than he already has," I say, dumping my family baggage right into her lap.

"I'm sorry, that's horrible," she says, sounding shocked by the entire thing.

"It is what it is with him. Can't change your family, can you?" I say with a shrug.

"So true," Eloise agrees. "What I don't get is how those girls could fall for his antics? Most people know hooking up with your partner's brother is off-limits."

"Like I said, my brother can be charismatic." Frankly, I don't know what the girls I dated saw in him either.

"How did your ex fall for him? Especially considering as you two were engaged?"

"The explanation they gave me was they used to date at university." Elle's eyes widen in surprise over that tidbit of information. "They were never serious back then, but they did sleep with each other on and off their entire time at university. Once university was over, they went their separate ways until that fateful night I brought her home to meet the family. I thought there was no way George could use his usual antics, especially as he was serious about someone too. Miranda and I had been dating for over a year and a half before I felt comfortable bringing her home because of *him*." I let out a sigh. "Apparently, that night they fucked in my brother's childhood bedroom while his girlfriend and I were downstairs, seemingly unaware. He threw that fact in my face after we broke up."

"That's cruel," Eloise says, shaking her head.

"That's George."

"How did you find out?"

"It was our anniversary. I got stuck in Greece due to the weather, so I was going to miss it. She was so angry with me because I had promised her I would be there. Then, for some strange reason, the weather cleared quicker than we thought, and I was able to get out earlier than I'd told her. I didn't call her to let her know that I was coming home because I wanted to surprise her. You can imagine my surprise … finding my brother in our bed naked."

Elle gasps. "That's messed up." I nod my head. "Why do your parents not say anything? I mean, they can't excuse their son's behavior, can they?"

"My dad sticks up for me occasionally, but I think Mum pretends it's not happening because in her head, the image she always had of her family was a certain way, and because it's not, she can't handle it." I love my mum, but it's hard to get her not to straddle the fence. "Now that there's a baby involved, they don't want to rock the boat being it's a grandchild."

"If you can't count on your family, then who can you count on?"

"True. Are you close with your family?" I ask, changing the subject of my fucked-up family.

"Nope. I was cut off at eighteen because I chose the modeling contract over university, and I've never spoken to them since," she explains.

Well, damn, that's cold. We're more alike than I thought.

"Just like that! Done because of modeling?" I ask.

"Yep. I even saw them a couple of years ago at an event, and they pretended they didn't know me."

Well, that would have been painful.

"I'm sorry."

"It was never a great relationship. I always felt more like a tick off their list of things they should be doing as humans, not that they wanted to be parents," she adds.

For all my parents' faults, I felt loved.

"That's a horrible way to grow up," I add.

"It is, and I would never do that to my children. But it made me who I am today and has given me the strength to go after what I want in life and have the confidence in myself that I can achieve it."

"Like your baking?"

"Exactly, I know I'll succeed. It may have taken me longer, and I used an untraditional way to get where I needed to be, but at least I did it on my own. I never want to rely on a man for money. Some men wield too much power when they have a woman who is financially dependent on them. It's what my father did to my mother her entire life."

Like a light bulb moment, Elle's words about her childhood make everything fit into place. I get it now. I get why she's so set on doing everything herself. Why she stubbornly doesn't ask for my help. Why she never wanted any financial assistance from me. Why she has worked her ass off at The Paradise Club so she could reach that financial freedom she needed to chase her dreams. I have mad respect for this woman sitting beside me.

"You're going to make it," I tell her as I lean over and place a soft kiss against her cheek.

"Thank you. It's daunting, but I've never wanted anything so much as I do my bakery."

"Tell me more about it," I ask her.

"You really want to hear?" she asks, sounding skeptical.

"Babe, you know talking business gets me going." I chuckle.

"I'm told when I get on a roll, I can't stop, and that's usually when people tune out," she warns me.

"Tell me everything. I want to see Pinterest boards, menu ideas, recipes, paint colors, whatever you want to tell and show me. I want to listen and learn," I tell her excitedly because I truly am excited by this stuff.

We spend the next two hours literally talking about her business plan, and that must be the best foreplay known to man, watching a woman get excited about her dreams.

"I've bored you, haven't I?" she says, laughing.

"Fuck, no. I'm trying to work out when the appropriate time would be to fuck you. Because listening to you talk numbers has my dick throbbing," I tell her honestly.

"Show me," she says while raising a brow.

I quickly throw off my T-shirt, then kick off my boardshorts, and show her my dick in all its glory.

"You are hard." She smiles as she licks her lips.

"And it's all for you." I grin.

"I like that."

"Good, now lay back, Eloise," I tell her as I pick up the picnic gear and move it to the side. "I want to devour you," I tell her as my fingers dig into her fleshy thigh.

"Then do it," she challenges, opening her legs wider for me. She's still wearing her red bikini, so I reach up and untie the strings on either side of her bikini bottoms, which makes them fall away. Then I tug at the material, and they come free from her body, and I throw them to the side. Her bare pussy is now on display for me.

Where to start first?

Leaning forward, her body twitches with anticipation, waiting for the first swipe of my tongue against her aching clit. She knows me too well, so instead, I sink my teeth gently into her inner thigh, which makes her jump with surprise. She sits up on her elbows and looks down at me with eyes wide open—I guess she wasn't expecting that from me.

"Ali?"

"You look good enough to eat, princess. I couldn't help myself," I tell her before letting my tongue swirl around the tiny mark on her thigh, teasing the pain away.

My tongue travels along a path he knows oh so well and one he will never get sick of while she's waiting for me to devour her pussy like I always do. But not today, I'm in a teasing mood. Maybe I've had too much sun, and it's made me crazy.

My tongue continues a new path away from her slit and up over her pelvis before dipping down the other side. A tiny, frustrated huff falls from her lips as I miss the spot again as I continue doing circle work around the area she wants me to hit. I continue to frustrate her with my new path until her fingers latch onto my hair, and she shoves my face into her pussy.

"Stop playing with your food," she growls.

Her reaction has me chuckling for a microsecond until her sweetness takes over, and I lose my mind. I'm ravenous as my tongue explores all the areas she wants me to explore.

"Yes," she screams as she holds my face, not releasing me in case I stray from the well-worn path. My hands slide up under her peachy ass, and I grip her tightly as she decides to face fuck me with her pussy. *I don't care.* So I tilt her pelvis up so that I can devour every drop of her.

That's it, princess, give it to me.

Ride me.

Ride my fucking face.

My teeth scrape across her throbbing clit, and the moan that falls from her mouth has me almost coming.

"Fuck, Ali," she screams.

More.

I need to give her more.

I move one of my hands from her ass and slide a finger into

her cunt. She squeezes down as I suck on her throbbing clit. Elle is becoming frantic under my touch, thrashing around, so I add another finger.

"Oh my god." Her fingers dig harder into my hair as I fill her. "More. I need more," she pants.

This woman is exquisite.

So I add a third finger and press it against her ass, and she practically purrs for me. I do it again, pushing against the puckered center, teasing her, making her go crazy with need until it finally accepts me, and I push in.

That's it.

That's what sends her over the edge.

She screams so loudly as she comes all over my face. Her nectar is dripping down my chin as she rides her orgasm all the way through.

"Fuck me, Alistair," she curses as her legs continue to quake with her orgasmic aftershocks.

Who am I to deny this woman anything?

Reluctantly, I pull my mouth away and move up over her body, then with one swift thrust, I'm sinking inside her. We both groan at the connection.

"Fuck, Elle." She feels so fucking good as I begin to drive into her.

"More, Alistair, more," she pleads with me as her nails scrape down my back and her feet urge me into her deeper.

"You feel so ..."

The next thing I know, she's flipping us over and is on top of me. Holy hell, I'm even deeper inside her. She begins to ride me like a champion rodeo queen.

Those tits. Fuck. Watching them bounce as she fucks me is heaven, fucking heaven.

My fingers dig into her hips, holding her in place. "Fuck, Eloise," I yell as she squeezes my dick from the inside. *What voodoo magic is she doing to me?* She continues to ride and mesmerize me with her muscles that choke my dick.

"I want you to come, Alistair. I want to make you come so badly." She groans.

Me too, sweetheart, me too. She produces another couple of Kegel moves with her muscles, and that's it—that's the fucking spot. "Yes. Fuck, yes."

"Harder, fucking harder," she screams while squeezing the shit out of my dick.

We are both slick with sweat as we literally fuck each other into another dimension.

"Yes. Yes. Yes," Eloise screams and comes again all over my dick, squeezing it with her orgasm, which sets off my own.

She collapses on top of me, both of us breathless.

"Holy shit, that was …" she starts but can't seem to finish her sentence.

"The best." Tiny shockwaves are still hitting her, making her squeeze my dick. *Fuck me.*

"It was," she agrees, looking down at me.

Reaching out, I cup her face. She is so fucking gorgeous my chest aches just looking at her.

"Be my date for the wedding?" The words spill out of my mouth before I can stop them, let alone think about what they mean.

Eloise stills. "You want me to be your date?" she questions me.

"Yes."

"Are you sure?" Elle asks as a frown forms on her face.

"My dick is still inside you. It would be a shit thing to do if I wasn't serious, don't you think?"

She smiles. "Would you be offended if I say, can I think about it?"

Not going to lie, her answer slightly deflates my ego.

"Hey," she says, gripping my chin to gain my attention. "A lot has happened in the past forty-eight hours. I've finally found you again. Lauren and I have gone into business together. I don't know when I'm allowed to leave the island. But what I do know is I'm ready to go back to London. I just don't know when it will be."

That's not a no, then.

"The wedding is in three weeks," I tell her.

"Guess I better sort out my shit then," she says, leaning down and kissing me.

28

ALISTAIR

The sun filters through the windows waking me from my sleep. We were exhausted after exploring the island and making love under the sun and all over the boat. We came back to my villa, and both of us were out as soon as our heads hit the pillow.

I reach out for Eloise, but she's not there. Her side of the bed is cold like she's been missing for a while. Panic laces my body, and I sit up in bed, wide awake.

Where is she?

Did I push things too far yesterday by asking her to be my date to my brother's wedding, considering that's a lot of baggage to throw at someone?

Jumping out of bed, I look around the villa, wondering where she could be. Movement outside catches my attention, and I see her sitting in the jacuzzi with her head back and eyes closed, looking relaxed. I make my way over to her naked and join her in the jacuzzi.

"Ali," she squeals when I splash her.

"Morning, sweetheart," I say while pulling her to me. She

wraps her legs around my waist. "You weren't in bed when I woke," I say with a pout.

"You were snoring away. I didn't want to disturb you." She giggles as she moves my hair to the side out of my eyes.

"Lies," I say, tickling her sides which makes her wiggle and squeal.

"My muscles were sore from yesterday, so I wanted to loosen them up for today." She grins, giving me a knowing look.

How did I get so lucky? "Is that so?" I say, raising a brow at her.

"You know so. Is that ego not big enough yet?" she jokes.

"I think it could grow some more. Tell me again how well I fucked you yesterday," I tease.

Eloise shakes her head with a wide smile across her pink lips.

"Did you sleep well?" I ask, nuzzling into her neck.

"I did."

"Me too." I lick the water droplets off her neck as I float us both over to the edge of the jacuzzi before lifting her and placing her bare ass against the tiles. A rogue drop of water slides down over her breasts, and my tongue decides to follow it, swirling around her nipple as I go until I've sucked it into a tight peak. Then I do the same with the other one. Eloise lets out a hum of delight as I continue to use my tongue like a towel, licking up all the drops of water clinging to her sun-kissed skin.

"Don't look now, but we have an audience," Elle whispers to me as she looks over my shoulder.

I turn around and notice a young couple standing off the side of our villa watching us. He looks familiar, maybe an actor or something. He has dark brown hair, and his body is made of nothing but pure muscle. And the woman he's with is a gorgeous redhead with large tits and a svelte body. It could be worse than people watching us.

"Watching only. I don't share," I remind her.

Elle nods as she looks over at the voyeurs with heat in her eyes.

Is this turning her on?

"Watching only," I call out to them.

They both nod in understanding, and I turn my attention back to Elle.

"They're hot." Elle smirks as she looks down at me.

"I told you I won't share you with another man." The words come out in an almost growl.

"I know. I think they're voyeurs anyway, judging by their wrist bands," Elle says, licking her lips. "His hand has just slipped down the front of her bikini," she explains to me.

Oh, okay, they are eager. I turn back around to see the girl's hand is gripping her partner's dick through his boardshorts. "Guess we should put a show on for them?" I turn my attention back to Elle.

"I think so." She grins in agreement.

"Get on all fours, babe," I command, and Eloise does as she's told, flipping onto her knees. I get out of the water and position myself behind her. My hand slaps her perky white ass that's staring back at me, and the sound echoes throughout the villa. I turn and notice the couple has shed their clothes altogether and are now both naked. His fingers are inside her, and her hand is wrapped around his cock.

I pull my attention away from them and concentrate on Elle laid out before me. My hand slides between her folds which pulls a moan from her lips. I do it again, this time sinking my fingers inside her, getting her ready because my dick is hard as steel.

Who knew performing in front of a hot couple would get me going?

When I feel Elle is significantly wet, I pull my fingers from her cunt and then lick them clean, my eyes straying over to the couple who are still touching each other. With the weight of their eyes resting on my back, I don't look away from them as I slide into Elle from behind, and I watch them both bite their lips as I close my eyes as the sensation of filling Elle takes over.

Now that I am nestled deep inside her, I couldn't care less about our two watchers. I grab her hips and begin to fuck her, my fingers digging into her flesh as I pull her back hard against my cock. The sound of our flesh slapping mixes with the sound of our voyeurs moaning in appreciation of our performance. My hand comes out and slides around her front, and I begin to play with her clit.

"Fuck, Ali ..." My fingers do their job as I feel Elle's pussy wrap around my dick tighter while I continuously play with her. "Yes, oh fuck, yes." Elle begins to moan. "That's it, big boy, fuck me hard."

Huh? She's never said that kind of stuff before during sex.

"Oh, you're so big. Fuck me harder," she screams out.

"What the fuck are you doing?" I whisper-yell at Elle as I continue to fuck her.

"Putting on a show for those two," she says, turning her head to look back at me.

Right! Okay, I'm down for that.

"That's it, choke on my dick," I tell her.

"Harder! Fuck me harder, master."

Such a cheeky little thing. You want a master, then you'll get one. I pull my hand from her clit and use it to smack her ass hard. Isn't that what masters do? Isn't that what happens in that Fifty book Miranda read and told me about? I do it again, and Elle moans.

"That's it, Daddy," she says, and that one nearly sends me over the edge as I try hard not to burst out laughing. I need to concentrate. *Just think about her wet pussy wrapping around your dick, and nothing else matters.* She feels so good. Nice and tight and wet. That's it. The tingles begin to race up my spine as I get closer to finding my release. My fingers grip tighter as Elle's hand dips between her thighs, and she starts furiously rubbing her clit. I'm too far gone now as I feel myself begin to hurtle toward the edge. Elle begins to tighten around my dick, and that is the final straw as I fall over the edge, and we come at the same time, static electricity swirling around us.

I'll never get sick of fucking Elle.

I don't know if I'm willing to give her up after this week. I'm going to do everything in my power to make sure she's coming home with me. I don't think phenomenal sex is going to be enough. I pull myself from Elle and slide into the jacuzzi as does she.

When I finally look up, the couple who was standing there has gone. I hope they got to have the same kind of happy ending we did.

29

ELOISE

"Hey, you're up early," I say, seeing Alistair setting up his laptop on the sofa. He looks up at me, his sandy blond hair is disheveled, and a frown is pulled across his face. He looks stressed.

Alistair reaches for me and pulls me to his side. My fingers slide through his hair as he kisses my stomach.

"I'm sorry, babe, something's happened at work. Then I find out a deal is in jeopardy on a new space I've wanted for years. I'm going to be here for a couple of hours sorting it out," he tells me. The pained look on his face tells me exactly how sorry he really is.

"No need to apologize. You do what you've got to do. We have all day," I say, looking down at his handsome face as I run my hand along his tight jaw.

"You sure?" he asks, looking like he doesn't quite believe me.

I would never keep him from his work. He owns numerous businesses and each one would come with their own set of problems, and it must be bad if they are pulling in the big boss.

"Of course, I'm going to go catch up with Lauren. We can

talk about all the things we spoke about yesterday. And I need to check in with Sierra and her broken ankle," I tell him.

He looks relieved, but his shoulders sink as if my answer releases some of the tension in his body. "Thank you. I'll make it up to you when I'm done." He grins wolfishly.

"I'm sure you will," I say, leaning down and kissing him.

As soon as I leave his arms, he's back to work. I get dressed and text Lauren that I'm popping over for a couple of hours, then head to our villa.

"Oh my god, I miss you," Lauren says while pulling me into her arms as I enter our villa.

"I miss you too," I agree, hugging her back tightly.

"Let me look at you," Lauren states as she pulls away from the hug and looks me over. "You are glowing, girl. That D must be good," she says, then bursts out laughing.

"It's *so* good," I reply, which has us falling into fits of laughter.

Lauren makes me a coffee, and then we sit on the sofa together.

"Tell me everything," Lauren says, blowing the steam off her coffee.

I tell her what's been happening since leaving the villa. She tells me that Sierra is doing fine, bored but good. Then I tell her about my chat with Alistair and the business. How I showed him my prized Pinterest board, and he gave me great feedback on what would and wouldn't work and the general benchmark of costs, which made me rethink my grand designs. We talked about what kind of space I would need for a commercial kitchen and bakery display and if I wanted the added bonus of a café. I haven't even looked at all the commercial kitchen options. I've been so focused on saving money that I never planned all the other things. He made me think about issues I hadn't even thought about. He explained to me about staff and the law involved around that, then social media and advertising. It was a lot to take in, but I feel so much more prepared than I did before chatting with him.

Honestly, I thought I knew what I was doing, but there are so many little things I hadn't even thought of, and I'm so glad I had Alistair there to advise me. Then I told her about Alistair asking me to come back to London to be his date for his brother's wedding. Of course, I told her about what happened between Alistair, his brother, and the ex, and she was shocked like I was.

"Are you going to go?" she asks.

"I don't know. It's in three weeks, but I don't know if we're going to be finished here in time."

"Are you crazy?" Lauren shrieks at my answer. "You're going to miss out on something great with this guy for what? A couple of weeks of work?" She looks at me as if I've lost my mind.

"I can't just quit. I have to give notice."

"Then give notice now. Right this minute. Are you telling me once that man is gone, you're going to be okay going back to fucking other people?" Lauren questions as she narrows her eyes at me.

I don't know. Probably not but it is my job.

Over the years, I've dissociated from sex being sex and sex being a job. But I've never had someone I care about like Alistair before.

"You were heartbroken six months ago when you thought he had fucked someone else. You think you're going to be okay watching him walk out that door and away from a woman who's willing to not stop sleeping with other people?"

"This is my job," I argue with her, a little pissed that she's calling me out like that.

"*Was* your job. You and I are becoming bakery owners. We don't need all this anymore, Elle. We are about to take over the London bakery scene. That is what we need to be focusing on right now. If it means you get the guy too, then that's a fucking bonus."

Maybe Lauren is right. I've got enough money to live on, plus with Lauren coming in as my partner, we've just doubled the pot to start this business.

"I've been working toward this goal for so long that I forgot I need to start it. I'm used to working my ass off to save the money that I never thought it would ever happen."

"This is happening, Elle. You and me against the world," Lauren tells me.

"We have so much to do. It's overwhelming," I state as the anxiety begins to swirl in the pit of my stomach.

"I know. But let's figure it out back in London instead of halfway across the world," Lauren adds. "We've got this, Elle. I've got you. I know it's hard for you to rely on other people after everything with your family, but I've been your ride and die for half your life. I haven't let you down yet, have I?"

"No."

"Then will you trust me when I say *you've got this*? I won't let you fail, Elle. I promise." Tears well in my eyes over Lauren's heartfelt words, so I crawl over and hug her tightly.

"Thanks for believing in me."

"Of course, I believe in you. You're family, babe," Lauren states, hugging me back. "I can't wait to take over the world with you, Elle."

"I can't wait either."

We spend the next couple of hours talking business and planning our domination of the London bakery scene before it's time for me to make my way back to Alistair.

"You're back," Alistair says, looking up from his computer as I walk into the villa.

"Time flew away from us. We got into business planning mode, and the next thing I knew, it had been three hours. Did you sort everything out?" I ask.

Alistair places his laptop on the coffee table and holds out his arms for me. I go willingly into them and snuggle into his chest after a quick kiss. "How did it go?"

And I tell him.

I spilled everything Lauren and I had discussed today, and he sat and listened to everything I had to say. And then he told me about his day, everything that had gone wrong back in London, and then the hold-ups with permits for a new club he was creating. It was nice to lay down in his arms and talk shop with someone who gave a shit about my dreams.

"Come on, you need to get out of this villa and relax. I can feel how tense you are," I tell him, jumping out of his arms.

"All I need is you." He smirks.

"You *will* have me. But I think a trip to the waterfall is exactly what you need to dissolve all that tension I can see written all over your face," I tell him as I place a finger between his pulled brows.

"Fine! Take me to these magical waterfalls," he says.

"Come on, old man." I hold out my hand for him as I pull him up off the sofa with a groan.

"Who you calling old?" He chuckles as he tickles my side. "Actually, how old are you?" He stops and looks down at me.

"Twenty-five."

"Thirty-three … that's not too much of an age gap then, is it?" he asks.

"Eight years is nothing," I reply.

"Might be when I'm old and gray, and you're still this hot little thing running around in a bikini," he jokes.

My heart beats wildly in my chest at the thought of being with him when he's old and gray. *Is he planning on us being together long-term?*

"Come on then, let me enjoy you while you're still young and fresh," I joke.

After we pack our bags, we jump onto the golf buggy with

me in the driver's seat, and we head from the beachfront villas to the waterfall. We travel through the rainforest and wave to the people walking along the paths in various states of undress. I look over at Alistair, and he gives me a cheeky smile as we pass another naked couple. I pull up to the area beside the path that leads to the waterfall and park our buggy.

"Come on, it's just up here," I tell him as I grab his hand, and we start meandering along the path. The rainforest is packed densely around us, but I know up ahead it disappears and opens to a magnificent waterfall that has natural rockpools. I also know that built underneath the waterfall is a grotto that stretches for miles. Loads of people come here, have sex on the rocks, and the sound of their coupling echoes through the caves, which can be hot if you're into that kind of thing.

Eventually, the rainforest path leads us to the waterfall.

"Wow, this is gorgeous," Alistair states as he stares across the cascading water.

As it's later in the day, a lot more people are here in various stages of undress scattered across the lounging areas. There are pool umbrellas set up around the waterfall's rocky pools shading the occupants underneath them. There are also large lounge pods that fit up to ten people on them. You can leave the door open or closed if you want to keep your antics private.

There are people scattered throughout the pools, most are naked, and some are even having fun on the rocky edges. There is more than one couple having sex on the edges. We haven't explored the resort too much since he's arrived, mainly keeping to ourselves, except for that young couple who watched us have fun in the jacuzzi earlier.

I tug Alistair's hand, and we follow the path down to the pool area. I spy a couple of daybeds seated underneath an umbrella away from the rest of the crowds, and we place our bags down on them.

"There's a lot of people here," Alistair comments as he takes in the entire outdoor area.

"Does it make you uncomfortable? We can go somewhere else if you like?" I thought this would be relaxing for him, but I don't want to stress him out even more.

He reaches out for me and pulls me into his chest. "No. This looks like fun. I'm so fricken intrigued by everything that's going on. There's an orgy happening in one of those pods. There are people fucking on the edge of the pool, which I wasn't ready for. There are people lazing around the pool. Don't look now, but there's a guy over there getting a blow job while he sucks on a cocktail," he muses with a chuckle.

"Does that mean you're prepared to have a little poolside fun?" I ask.

"With you, hell, yeah." He grins as he kisses me.

"Shit, I left my phone in the golf buggy. Let me go get it. Then we can order some food and drinks and enjoy the show," I tell him as I pat his chest with my palm.

"Be quick, I'm starved." He grins.

30

ALISTAIR

"Hey there, sugar," a beautiful brunette calls from the pool's edge. She's lying naked on the little beach area, barely covering her amazing body.

Where did she come from? I didn't notice her earlier.

"Come in, cool off," she asks seductively.

As tempting as that sounds, I'm not interested. "I'm waiting for someone," I reply.

"Male or female?" she asks, raising a brow at me.

"Female," I answer.

"Is she as hot as you?" the naked woman asks while raising a manicured brow at me.

"Hotter," I tell her with a smirk.

"Can't wait to meet her," she purrs as she waves her colored bracelets in front of me. I notice she has a pink band for play with women, blue band for playing with men, red for sexual intercourse allowed, green happy to play with multiple people, and purple for public play.

Then I look down and realize I'm still wearing colored bands —pink, red, green, purple, and yellow which is happy to play with one person and white which is everything but intercourse.

Quickly, I take off the red—I do not want to fuck other women. The woman's eyes widen as she notices what I've done and nods in understanding.

"Things have changed," I add, feeling like I owe her an explanation.

"I'm fine with that, sugar. If you're okay with me looking, I don't need to touch," she says, giving me a wink.

There's no harm in that. I mean, I was in the process of undressing anyway, and it is rather hot outside. I strip off my T-shirt and throw it to the ground while the mystery woman licks her lips as she takes in my naked chest, and then her hungry eyes follow me, sliding off my shorts and underwear until I'm naked. The woman's face lights up as her eyes hone in on my dick.

"Your dick is glorious," she says, biting her lip.

"Thank you," I tell her, a little unsure about how to deal with that kind of compliment. I look up and see Elle walking across the pool area—she has a wide smile on her face as she takes in my naked body.

"Is that her? Fuck, she's gorgeous," the naked brunette states.

"Yeah, it is," I answer her absentmindedly.

Elle's eyes check the naked lady in the water, and then they move back up to me. I can see it on her face she has questions because when she left, I was fully clothed and alone, and now I'm naked with an admirer in the water.

"I want her," the woman states seriously from the water.

Wait! What did she say?

"I want a taste. I know you don't share, but does she?" the woman asks, sending me a wink.

"I, um …" I am a little lost for words.

"Found it," Elle states waving her phone at me. She looks between the mysterious brunette and me.

"You're beautiful," the woman tells Elle.

"Oh, thank you. You're so sweet," Elle says, touching her hand to her chest in surprise.

"Your man here, as hot as he is, told me that he isn't looking for fun. But I was kind of hoping you are," the brunette tells Elle as she licks her lips seductively. "Why don't you come on in? The water's nice," she purrs, giving Elle her best hungry eyes.

"The water does look inviting," Elle tells the woman before turning her attention back to me. Elle raises her brows in my direction.

I shrug my shoulders. I'm not sure what I'm supposed to say in this situation because my dick is twitching at the thought of watching them together.

"You can have one little taste," I tell the brunette over Elle's shoulder. "Is that okay?" I turn back to Elle.

"Are you okay with it?" she asks.

I nod and give her a smile. "I'll sit back here and watch." I point to the daybed.

"Guess I better put on a show then," Elle states, giving me a wink as she strips off her sundress and throws it to the side. The woman in the water gasps as she takes in Elle in her red bikini, looking like she's stepped off the cover of *Sports Illustrated*.

"You won't need your bikini." The woman giggles at Eloise from the water.

Eloise turns her back to me, undoes the strings that hold her bikini top up, and then drops it beside her. The woman's eyes widen as she takes in Elle's naked breasts. Then she unties the sides that hold her bikini bottoms together, and they fall to the ground. The woman licks her lips as she eyes a naked Elle in all her glory. I do the same because Elle naked is the most glorious thing to behold. Then Elle slides her fingers through her thighs, teasing the woman.

My dick springs to life, and I wrap my hand around it.

"Don't you dare touch yourself, Ali," Elle says as she turns around and saunters over to me. She places a knee on the daybed and then another as she crawls toward my dick. Elle looks up at me through lust-filled eyes before wrapping her mouth over my dick. Shit. Fuck. Yes. I hiss as her mouth sucks on me.

Movement behind Elle catches my attention as the gorgeous brunette moves from the water, her eyes squarely on Elle's perky little ass thrust high in the air.

"I bet his dick tastes good, doesn't it?" the woman purrs as she walks toward Elle. Her hand comes out and squeezes Elle's taut ass. "Your man has a glorious dick. Almost perfect," the woman tells Elle as she stands behind her, running her fingers over my girl's ass. "I bet he knows how to choke you with it, doesn't he?" she asks before looking over Elle to me. She gives me a wink before her fingers slide into Elle.

Elle's mouth hums against my dick, and it feels so fricken good. My eyes close, and a groan falls from my lips.

"The more you choke her with it, the wetter she's going to be against my mouth," the woman tells me as she drops to her knees. She doesn't remove her fingers from Elle's pussy for a couple of moments, and when she does, Elle groans at their loss, but it's not long until the woman is laying back and moving between Elle's thighs. She then places her fingers on either side of Elle's hips and pulls her pussy directly over her face.

"Fuck," Elle screams as her mouth falls from my dick. It takes her a couple of moments to adjust to the brunette between her thighs, but then a look of delirium comes over her face as her cheeks turn pink, and she dives back to my dick, but this time she goes to town.

I feel every hum, groan, and moan the woman is pulling from Elle's cunt as each note vibrates through to my balls. Fuck, this feels good. We've collected a bit of an audience, but I don't care because it feels so fucking good.

Elle continues sucking me until I'm unable to hold back any longer.

"I'm going to come, babe," I tell her, but she ignores me and continues sucking my dick all the way to the back of her throat.

I'm the first to fall over the edge. Elle swallows everything I give her, and she doesn't stop sucking while my mind goes blank—I've peaced out of this world.

Elle releases my dick from her mouth as she starts screaming a million and one curses as the woman pushes her over the edge into oblivion, and it takes Elle a couple of moments to come back down to earth.

The brunette slides from beneath Elle's thighs and wipes her face with triumph as she stands up and looks down at the two of us, exhausted from our orgasms as we snuggle on the daybed together.

"That was fun. Now, I better go find my husband so I can fuck him into next year, I'm so fricken horny. Thanks for the taste, sugar," she says to Elle, giving us both a wave before striding off between the crowd of mesmerized onlookers who have started to have their own fun thanks to us.

"Wow. That was …" Elle says, looking up at me from my side.

"Amazing, babe. So, fucking amazing," I tell her as I reach out and pull her face to mine, then kiss her passionately.

"Not how I saw the day going." Elle giggles.

"Bet you feel relaxed now?"

"Hell, yeah, I do, but the point of today was to relax you, not me." Elle chuckles.

"Pretty sure that blow job relaxed me," I say, moving the hair away from her face. "I feel pretty good, actually. I could do with a feed now. Get my energy stores back up again. I'm excited to explore this grotto you were telling me about."

"Let's get you fed. Because you're going to need it in there." Elle smiles, giving me a wink.

I couldn't be happier.

31

ELOISE

Yesterday was fun at the waterfall pool. All the tension Alistair had before he got there vanished by the time we left. We fucked all over the grotto—in the water, against the rocks—and we couldn't get enough of each other.

I thought he might be a little freaked out by the hot brunette touching me by the pool, but he reassured me he had a lot of fun.

If I quit my job here, will he still frequent the club? *You're not dating, Elle.*

But he invited me to his brother's wedding? *Because he didn't have a date, and he doesn't want to go to that shit show by himself.* No. Alistair isn't like that.

What happens after the wedding? My mind wonders.

I'm going to be busy building a bakery. Am I going to have time for him too? I know he's a busy guy, but what happens if we both become so busy we don't have time for each other?

Is this all doomed before it's even begun?

"What's going on in that head of yours?" Alistair asks, nuzzling into my neck. "Whatever it is, it's going to be okay," he reassures me.

Should I say something about my fears?

Should we talk about what's going on between us?

The week is almost over, and while we've both had fun together, Alistair hasn't asked me again for my answer about the wedding. *Maybe he regrets asking?* Before I can broach the subject, Alistair's phone rings. He groans and rolls over and answers the phone.

"Alistair speaking," he says, answering the phone without looking.

"Brother, have I caught you at a bad time," a deep voice booms through his phone. He must have accidentally hit speaker instead of answer when he picked up the phone.

Alistair sits bolt upright, and I can see all that tension I was able to get rid of yesterday is back again. "What do you want?" he asks his brother.

"Apparently, you upset Mum the other day when she phoned you about the wedding. I'm not impressed," his brother warns him down the phone.

"I didn't upset Mum. I just didn't agree with the conversation we were having. Two totally different things," Alistair sneers at his brother.

"Are we going to have a problem on the wedding day, Ali?" his brother asks.

"I couldn't give two rats about you and Miranda," Alistair answers angrily.

"Please, we all know how well Miranda sucks dick. There isn't anyone else quite like her." His brother chuckles down the line.

My mouth falls open in surprise at his brother's words about his fiancée. *What a fucking creep.*

"I've won, Ali. You know that. I know that. The family knows it," his brother gloats down the line.

"Not sure how marrying the woman that was fucking your brother is considered a win," Alistair bites back.

"You always did enjoy my sloppy seconds."

This guy is a creep. I can't imagine how women fall for him over Ali. He must drug them or something.

"How's the nightclub game going? Can't imagine you make great money. Did Dad tell you I was able to get the Patricks to sign with the firm? Nice million-pound commission to me," his brother gloats down the line. "While you're off sunning yourself on some tropical island, probably with only your hand for company, I was working hard on securing the deal. I guess that's why you couldn't hack working for the family business. Not everyone can be a success."

This guy is crazy.

"You have no idea how hard it was to land this deal. I worked especially hard on Mrs. Patrick, she was a hard nut to crack, but boy, when I did, it was glorious."

Ew, what kind of fucking asshole is this guy?

Gloating to his brother about fucking your client's wife while about to marry your brother's ex-fiancée, who you stole. Alistair's eyes widen as he reads through the none-too-subtle lines his brother is drawing.

"You're a fucking dick, George. What makes you think I'm not recording this call to play to Miranda?" Alistair growls angrily.

"Because Miranda loves me and believes *everything* I tell her, like the good woman she is," he adds offhandedly.

My jaw hits the floor at the audacity of this man. *How the hell have they come from the same family?*

"Guess you got what you wanted then." Alistair sighs.

"I always do, brother, you know that." His brother chuckles. "Mum says you're bringing a date to the wedding."

Alistair's hazel eyes land on me. "I am," he answers through gritted teeth.

"Anyone I would know?" his brother pushes.

"Doubt it."

"Who is it then? Wanna make sure I haven't fucked her … yet," his brother adds, bursting out laughing.

As if I would let that toad of a man fuck me.

Fuck him.

Then I still as a thought comes into my mind.

No. There's no way in the world the guy Camille was talking about was this guy. Could it be?

"What is it?" Alistair whispers to me.

"Could he be the second Mr. King?" I whisper back to him.

Alistair's eyes widen, and he mouths the word, 'fuck.'

"Ali, you there? Or are you crying into your cereal over the prospect of me fucking your date … *again*," his brother says, baiting him.

"There's no way in hell. She would never touch you," Alistair curses at him.

"Is that a challenge, brother?"

"You're repulsive. Thinking about trying to fuck someone else at your own wedding," Alistair spits at his brother.

I've heard enough of this conversation—it isn't going anywhere—so I reach over and press end.

Alistair's eyes widen as he stares at me in surprise.

"Sorry, I was sick of listening to his bullshit," I tell him with a shrug.

"Come here," he says with a smile on his face then he kisses me passionately. "Thank you."

"You don't need to thank me. I can assure you, your brother is disgusting. Sorry."

"He's horrid," Ali says sadly.

I can't imagine what it was like growing up with a sociopath.

"I get now why you don't want to go to the wedding. Not when he's going to rub it all in your face." Alistair doesn't deserve that. I'm glad Miranda fucked up because she never deserved a man like Alistair. She deserves a man like George.

"I can't believe he's already fucking around on her," Alistair says, shaking his head.

"Men like him think they deserve the world and don't care who they hurt to achieve it. I think your brother was the second Mr. King at the club," I explain to him.

"You think so? I didn't think Nate would accept him after what he did to me," Alistair adds.

"Maybe he doesn't know. Mr. Lewis isn't as hands-on as he used to be."

"What a fucker. I detest the asshole," Alistair says. "Speaking about the wedding, what are the chances of you being my date?" Those hazel eyes look up at me, and I can see worry swirling beneath his golden flecks. This man deserves to have someone in his corner at that wedding because no one else is going to stand up for him.

"I'm all in," I tell him.

Alistair stares at me in disbelief.

"I'm done with The Paradise Club. I'm ready to start my new life in London with you," I tell him honestly, and as soon as the words are out there, I know in my heart of hearts it's the right decision. I've never been surer in my life.

"You are?" he asks, unsure if he believes what I'm saying.

"Yep. I'm yours, Alistair King, if you'll have me."

"You are *all mine*." He growls as he reaches over and pulls me into his lap. "All ... fucking ... mine," he says as his lips meet mine.

32

ALISTAIR

I'm nervous as the concierge drives me to the marina. Eloise needed to pack her things and finalize her resignation before she is able to leave the island. But as the hours tick over, I'm starting to get anxious that she might have changed her mind and not come home with me.

"We hope you had a wonderful time at The Paradise Club, sir," the concierge tells me as we arrive at the marina for my boat transfer.

"It was great, thanks." *It would be better if I had a certain woman beside me.*

The concierge grabs my bags and takes them to the boat.

I look at my watch nervously as the clock ticks down, Elle's really cutting it close.

"The captain is ready when you are," the concierge tells me.

"A friend told me they thought they would be joining me on the transfer, but they aren't here yet," I tell the man, who gives me a nod. I look down again at my watch. It's five minutes to five. I told her she needed to be at the marina by five. Fuck! Hope is beginning to sink. "I might make a quick phone call to hurry them up," I tell him, trying to save face as I grab my phone and pretend to call Elle. Goddammit! I don't even have her phone number. If she makes it, I'm going to need to fix that. Nervously, I look down at my watch again, and the five minutes are up. *She's not here.*

Turning on my heel, I head aboard the luxury boat, and my heart begins to crack.

"Welcome, Mr. King. We trust you had an enjoyable stay at The Paradise Club," the bronzed captain asks me.

"Yeah. Great," I answer, not sounding too enthusiastic, which could be a first for someone leaving the island.

"We will be heading off in a couple of moments. Just sit back, relax, and enjoy the beautiful sunset. There is a minibar to your left if you would like a beverage," he advises me before heading back to his cabin.

I thought things would go my way this time.

I was wrong.

Laying my head back against the cream-colored leather seats of the boat, I close my eyes and contemplate what happened.

"Hey, Cap. Do you have room for one more?"

That voice.

Sitting up quickly, I turn around to see Eloise walking onto the boat with a wide smile.

"You made it," I say.

"I did," she says, dropping her bag as she launches herself into my arms. I swing her around, unable to believe she's here with me finally.

"Sorry, I'm late. My goodbyes took a lot longer than I thought," she tells me.

I notice her puffy eyes as she slides down my body, and it pains me to see her upset like that.

"I'm sorry," I say, feeling bad I've taken her away from all her friends.

"Don't be. I'm so ready to be going home," she says with a big smile, and my heart skips a beat.

"And by home, you mean with me, don't you? I want you to come back to my place," I stress.

Elle stills at my comment, and I can see her mind processing my statement. Before she gets to say anything, the boat takes off, and we both lose our footing and fall back against the leather couch in a tangle of limbs.

"I want you to come home with me until the wedding is over. There are a million and one family things leading up to the wedding that we must go to," I explain. It's the truth, but she doesn't have to stay with me for them.

"Lauren won't be back until after the wedding. I'd rather stay with you than be by myself," she says, agreeing with my request.

That was easy. I thought she was going to fight me so much more than that. "No second thoughts?" I ask, my vulnerability shining through.

"Never," she says, kissing me again.

"You?" she asks.

I shake my head and link our fingers together as I bring her hand to my lips. "I couldn't be happier, Elle."

We both sit back and enjoy the stunning sunset, our last for a while as we head back to London. Elle snuggles into my side as the orange and pink streaks float across the sky.

We board our plane back to London. Two first-class tickets. Usually, I would have my private plane, but as it was just me coming to the island, it seemed like a waste. We head on in, where the plane has suites in first class where two people can sit together in a secluded cabin.

"Wow," Eloise says, admiring the plush surroundings.

She's probably never flown first class, and I like watching her excitement as she takes it all in.

"Who knew commercial flights were like this now. I'm used to flying private," she states.

I almost choke on my drink because that's not at all what I thought she was going to say. *Nice assumption there, Ali.*

It's not long until we are up in the air, and we've had our three-course meal. Eloise is glowing after a couple of glasses of champagne, and we have now settled in to watch a movie.

"Have you ever joined the mile-high club?" Eloise asks, giving me a sideways glance.

"No. Can't say I have."

"How thick do you think these walls are?" she asks, reaching out and touching the walls of our cabin.

"Probably not as thick as we might think. We do have a full bathroom through that door, remember. It's probably a lot quieter in there," I say, pointing to the white door.

"I like your thinking, Mr. King," Eloise says, wiggling her eyebrows. As she gets up out of her chair and sways her hips seductively, she sashays toward the bathroom. She stops and looks over her shoulder at the door. "You coming?" she asks, curling her finger at me.

Hell, yeah, I am. I jump out of my chair and head toward the bathroom, slamming the bathroom door shut behind me.

"You ready to join the mile-high club with me?" I ask as I push her back toward the vanity. Elle wraps her arms around my neck as I pick her up and place her ass onto the marble vanity. Thank fuck she's wearing a maxi dress for easy access. My hands roll up the dress's hem to her waist. She's wearing the tiniest bit of fabric, and we stare at each other for a couple of beats taking in each other.

"I don't think I could be happier than I am in this moment. Thank you for giving me a second chance," I confess.

Her eyes soften at my words. "I think you're the one who gave me a second chance."

"As horrible as it is … I'm kind of glad your friend broke her ankle. Otherwise, I would have never known you were even on the island. It was a real sliding doors kind of moment," I comment, shaking my head.

Elle nods in agreement as her legs wrap around my hips. "I haven't been happier," she confesses.

"We probably should have talked about things before getting on this plane. But now that we're off the island … I don't share. Not even with women," I advise her before leaning forward and nuzzling her neck.

"I'm okay with that. I'm happy to be putting The Paradise Club Elle to bed. I'm looking forward to finding out who Eloise the baker is," she says with a bright smile curling on her lips.

"And I'll be here every step of the way," I urge, stroking the hair from her face.

"Does this mean we're dating?" she asks, biting her lip nervously.

"Will you freak out if I call you my girlfriend at the wedding?" I state firmly.

Elle's eyes widen, and a pink blush falls across her cheeks as she shakes her head slowly.

"Good, because I was going to do it anyway," I tell her, which makes her giggle, and that sound is the best sound in the world.

Hold on, no. It's the second-best sound because the sound of her coming all over my dick is by far the best. I unzip myself and slide my dick between her folds.

33

ELOISE

After spending the entire flight christening every inch of our luxurious suite, we eventually passed out. When we finally wake, we are landing at London's Heathrow Airport. It's strange being back again after all these months. Of course, we are welcomed back by a typical British summer—rain.

Alistair takes my hand as we walk out of customs together, and I couldn't be happier.

A man wearing a suit is holding up Alistair's name. "Welcome home, sir," he greets us.

"Thanks, Bernard," Alistair says, shaking the man's hand. "I would like you to meet Miss Eloise Muller, my girlfriend."

The tiniest bit of surprise filters across his face before he hides it again. "Lovely to meet you, Miss Muller," he says, shaking my hand.

We follow Bernard toward a black town car. Alistair opens the door for me, such a gentleman, and I slide in. Then moments later, we are merging into the heavy traffic out of Heathrow.

"Is it strange being back?" Alistair asks as he links his hand with mine.

"It is. Living on an island, you get used to no traffic. Also, there's the constant sunshine, quiet, and blue skies," I say, looking out through the raindrops on the car window.

"We can always head to my place in Greece for our injection of sunshine and blue skies," he states eagerly.

"I'd like that," I say, curling further into his side.

Alistair's phone rings, and he gives me a small smile.

"It's fine," I declare while giving him a nod.

He answers, and the phone call turns tense. Alistair's mood darkens as the phone call continues, and I notice Bernard look in the rearview mirror a couple of times, checking on him.

Eventually, he hangs up, looking exhausted.

"Whatever you have to do, do it," I tell him, squeezing his hand.

"Huh." He looks at me distractedly.

"You phone call, it seems important," I say.

Alistair shakes his head as if coming out of a trance. "No. I can't leave you. We've just arrived. That's not fair. Especially not after I just made you fly halfway across the world," he says, leaning forward and placing a tender kiss on my lips.

"I'm a big girl. But just to clarify, I might go snooping around your apartment while you're gone," I say, giving him a grin, hoping to lighten his mood.

"I've moved. I used to live in South Kensington, near you. But I moved just after you left to be closer to work in Chelsea," he informs me.

There's a small pang of guilt sliding over my body. I hope he didn't move because of me. *Elle, get over yourself, as if he would pack and move because you didn't turn up for your date.*

"I have nothing to hide," he says, smiling at me. "I won't be long, I promise. I need to go to the club to sort out this mess. Can you give me two hours? Max?" I promise.

"Don't rush on my account. Business comes first," I tell him.

Alistair stares at me in silence, and I'm wondering if I've

said something wrong. "Are you sure?" he asks, double-checking with me.

"Yes, of course. I'm going to grab a shower and crash in your bed," I tell him.

"Naked, please. So when I slide between the sheets, I can slip inside you when I get home," he whispers eagerly in my ear.

I bite my bottom lip and nod because that sounds delicious.

"Bernard, I have to go to the office. Can you drop me there first, then take Eloise home? That would be great."

"Yes, sir," his driver says as he changes his route.

We arrive at the back of his club, Minx, where he rescued me from that group of assholes one night. It's amazing how much has happened since that moment between us.

"Thanks for this," he says, leaning over and kissing me one more time.

"Go. Sort out what needs to be done. I'll be home waiting for you."

He gives me a nod and jumps out of the car, then a small wave before he heads inside the club. Bernard takes off and merges back into the traffic again.

"That was very kind of you, Miss," Bernard says as he looks up at me through the rearview mirror, and I can see the concern on his face that he might have spoken out of turn.

"It seemed important. I can wait," I reply, shrugging my shoulders as if it's no big deal because it is not.

Bernard gives me a small smile and looks back at the road.

Silence falls between us again, but now that I know Bernard is a little chatty, I want to see if I can find out more about Alistair because I haven't met his friends or family yet.

"How long have you worked for Alistair?" I query him gently.

"Since he was a teen, Miss," he answers naturally.

A memory of my own driver, Terry, hits me in the chest. When I left my parents, I left all the staff behind to cut away from that entire life. A pang of regret hits me because the staff was more like family than my own flesh and blood. Did they miss me when I left? Do they still miss me? I should really try to find them and see how they're going. Do they still work for my parents? Or did they move on? Are they okay?

"I'm assuming you know his brother?" I ask cautiously, pushing the sensitive subject.

"Yes, Miss, I do," he answers matter of factly, looking back at me through the mirror. His gray eyes have narrowed on me as if trying to work out what my angle might be.

"Is he really that much of a dick as he sounds on the phone?" I ask honestly.

Bernard tries not to laugh at my question, but I can see the faint curl of his lips through the mirror.

"He is an *interesting* character," he finally answers me diplomatically.

That's the polite way to say he's the world's biggest dick. "What about his ex? Is she crazy too?"

"Miranda was ..." Bernard begins to talk but then shuts his mouth.

"I won't tell Ali anything you say in this car," I promise him.

Bernard eyes me suspiciously. I can tell he's unsure whether he can trust me or not, and I guess rightly so. He answers with, "She wasn't the right person for him, Miss."

I can read between those lines—*she was a bitch*.

"I don't think it was fair what they did to him," I say, meeting his eyes in the mirror.

"No, it wasn't," Bernard agrees.

"I don't think he should have to see the smug-ass face of his brother marrying his ex next week without someone on his arm who has his best interests at heart," I confess to him.

"That's very kind of you, Miss," he says, but I can tell he's unsure what my motives are by the way his eyes narrow when he talks.

"I'm not a gold digger if that's what you're thinking," I explain. The last time he dropped his boss at the airport, he was single, and now he isn't. I'd be suspicious too.

There's silence.

Bernard doesn't say anything, but he thinks it.

I get it.

"Alistair and I met over six months ago. We lost touch and found each other again on the island," I add, not sure if Bernard knows that Alistair frequents The Paradise Club or not.

"He's spoken of you before," Bernard states honestly.

Oh, well, that surprises me.

"It was a misunderstanding between us, and that's why we lost touch," I say, attempting to explain myself.

"Not my place, Miss," he adds. But those eyes tell me he knows I broke Alistair's heart when I left.

"It was purely by accident we ran into each other. I had no idea he was on the island." *Why do I feel the need to explain myself to this man?*

Bernard nods and continues driving. I can see I need to convince him a little more that I'm not after Alistair because he's rich. I'm sure he's probably dealt with a heap of gold diggers during his time working for Alistair.

"I grew up here," I say, pointing to the familiar terraces of Chelsea.

"London, Miss," Bernard asks.

"No, Chelsea," I answer. "My family home isn't far from here," I add. Hating the fact that driving through these once-familiar streets brings back so many memories.

Bernard schools his reaction before speaking again, "Would you like me to drive past your family home, Miss? I'm happy to make a detour if you wish."

Do I? I try not to come down here in case I run into them.

"I'm not sure, Bernard. It wasn't a good place for me," I confess to him.

"Sometimes, seeing those memories are only bricks and mortar can be liberating. But I don't want to push you, Miss," he adds.

"You can call me Eloise," I say.

Bernard gives me a nod and a smile, but I know he won't do such a thing. He's definitely old school.

Maybe I should drive past. Bernard's right. In the cold light of day, what happened behind those walls can't get me if I don't give the memories life. If I see my family home for what it is, simply random bricks and mortar, then perhaps I can move past the old memories I have locked away in my mind, and maybe I might have room to create new ones. So, I give Bernard the address, and he changes direction and heads toward my family home. I can feel my heart beating wildly in my chest, my stomach is churning in knots, and I don't know if I'm going to be sick or run for the hills.

Bernard pulls up out the front of the red and white brick terrace home. The front garden has changed, and the trees in the front courtyard have grown so much bigger than I remember. The black front door with the gold street number on its front still catches the eye. The private garden across from my home, where only residents can walk amongst its gorgeous floral displays, is still there. The light in the front room, which overlooks the street, is switched on, and I just know my father is sitting at his desk going through paperwork.

"Are you okay, Eloise?" Bernard asks, using my first name.

I must look bad if he's broken with protocol. That's when I realize the tears are streaming down my face.

"We can go now," I tell him.

He gives me a nod and pulls back out into traffic as my family home disappears behind me.

A little while later, Bernard arrives at Alistair's home. It wasn't at all what I was expecting. I thought he might have bought a modern apartment on the Chelsea embankment overlooking the Thames. Instead, he's pulled up out the front of a historic mews house. This gorgeous little cottage is in the middle of the city.

I remember walking past these cottages growing up and falling in love with the image of them, with their quaint little cobblestone laneways and picture-perfect window boxes with colorful flowers growing in them. I always imagined that the people who lived in these homes had perfect lives.

"Not what you were expecting, Miss?" Bernard asks as he studies my reaction in the review mirror.

"Actually, no. But it is perfect. Somehow it feels more Alistair than some slick modern apartment would," I tell him.

Bernard gives me a bright smile through the rearview mirror. "I'll go grab your bags." And with that, he jumps out of the car, opens the side door for me, then continues to the back, where he opens the trunk and grabs my bags. I step out onto the sidewalk and suck in that London air. It feels like home.

"Thank you," I say as I wait for him to open the front door. He gives me a smile before pushing the door open and carrying my bags through into the hallway.

The house is gorgeous. It's masculine yet homey. Creamy white walls with toffee-colored furniture. Gorgeous polished wooden floors with Persian rugs scattered around. The kitchen is small but appears state of the art. There's a glass staircase that takes you to the next floor, where beautiful exposed whitewashed walls follow you up to the next level.

"On this level are his office and spare bedrooms. Mr. King's room is on the top floor. I will take your bags to his room," Bernard explains.

I follow him up to the third level, where Alistair's master suite is located.

There's a large wooden bed in the middle, and again the whole room is in a coffee-colored palette. Gorgeous skylights above let in natural light. There is a huge walk-in closet and marble en-suite.

"You must be tired from your journey. I'll let you rest," Bernard states as he begins to quickly back out of Alistair's room.

"Bernard," I call out after him.

He stops and turns around waiting for my request.

"Thank you," I tell him.

His eyes widen as if surprised by my words. "You're very welcome, Miss," he says with a nod and begins to turn on his heel but hesitates and turns back to me. "Please don't break his heart!"

And with that little bombshell, he exits the room.

34

ALISTAIR

Four hours later, goddammit! I didn't mean to stay away from Eloise for so long, but one thing after the other happened.

"Did Eloise get settled in all right?" I ask Bernard as I slide into the car.

"Yes, she did."

Good, I want her to feel like my home is hers while she's staying with me.

"And what do you think of her? I trust your judgment, old man," I ask him with a chuckle.

Bernard has been with my family forever and has been my private driver since I was a teenager. He knows all my secrets. He's been privy to all the chaos George would inflict on me. He was the one person I could vent to back then, and I know no matter what, he would never betray my trust. He felt more like a father to me than my own. Not that I had a bad father, but he and George were close because they work together. They have spent every waking moment together for their entire lives, and I always felt like the third wheel anytime we were together. I was never privy to their private jokes.

"She seems lovely, Ali."

He's not giving much away.

"Lovely?" I question with a frown. That's not at all what I thought he was going to say.

"Yes."

"That's all?" I ask, pushing him further. His opinion means the world to me. And Elle means something to me.

"Do I believe she's a gold digger with ulterior motives? No, I don't, sir. Not when she showed me her family home," he adds.

"Wait! Her family home?"

Bernard's eyes widen in the rearview mirror. "I didn't realize you didn't know, Ali," he says.

"It's a subject she doesn't like talking about, so I've never pushed it. All I know is her family cut her off when she chose to model over university, and she's been on her own ever since. She's also an only child," I explain to him.

"Miss Muller comes from money, it seems. Her family owns a terrace home in Carlyle Square," Bernard tells me.

My eyes widen in surprise. "That's an expensive area," I say to Bernard. A terrace in that area is about twenty million pounds. If Elle comes from a family like that, then why the hell is she working at a sex resort? I always assumed she didn't come from money because of her work.

She was cut off, remember? Fuck, no wonder she has been so dead against me helping her in any way. She's been cut off from extreme wealth, and I guess she wants to prove to her parents that she did make something of herself, and she didn't need their money to do it. I must admire her determination.

"She's also protective of you," Bernard adds.

"How so?" I question him, intrigued by that thought.

"She doesn't like George very much," he says with a grin.

That makes me smile. "She overheard an interesting phone call from my brother while we were away. He was trying to rub my nose in a deal he'd done through sleeping with the client."

Bernard's brows rise high. "Fatherhood hasn't changed him at all," I say, rolling my eyes. "I like her, Bernard. And I think Elle might just be the first girl who won't fall for George's charms."

"I believe you could be right. She didn't have anything nice to say about him. She looked angry while talking about the entire situation," Bernard says with a smirk on his face.

That gives me hope, thinking about Elle championing for me with Bernard.

"Was she okay that I had to work tonight? Should I stop and get flowers, chocolates, diamonds?" I ask.

"Miss Muller was more than happy when she arrived at your home. She understands that your work's important to you and that things sometimes arise that can't be helped," Bernard tells me.

"It's all so new at the moment. What happens in a year's time when I'm called in, or five years? I'm not sure if she's going to be as understanding then, is she?" I say as worry sets in.

"Maybe … maybe not. Just because Miranda became unhappy about it doesn't mean Miss Muller will," Bernard explains.

Maybe he's right. I shouldn't put my past baggage onto Elle, just like she did with me when she ran all those months ago.

"You're right. Can we stop and get some flowers? I think it might be nice to show her that I appreciate her patience."

"Sure thing, sir." Bernard nods.

It's not long until we are pulling into my driveaway. Stepping from the car, the most delicious aroma is wafting from my home. I look over at Bernard, and he gives me a wide smile and a thumbs up. I grab my keys and notice that Elle hasn't pulled the front curtains. You can see directly into my house all the way to the kitchen, where Elle is currently dancing around as if she's on stage at Glastonbury. Her strawberry blonde hair is up in a messy ponytail, she has on a tight top that clings to her breasts which hypnotizes me as she bounces around the place. She's wearing an apron, and I have no idea where the hell that came from. She's a vision. This is something I could get used to seeing every day when I get home from work.

Upon opening the door, the music is pumping. Whatever Eloise is cooking, the smell hits me instantly. Dropping my stuff by the door, I slam it shut. The sound makes Eloise jump.

"You're home," she squeals out as she rushes toward me. I have a couple of moments to brace myself as she wraps her arms around my neck and kisses me. My heart thuds in my chest at how happy she is to see me walk through that front door. *I could get used to this.* "Did you get everything sorted?" she asks once she disentangles herself.

"I did, thanks. Here, I got these for you. I'm sorry it took me longer than I anticipated," I tell her, thrusting the bouquet of flowers into her hands.

"You didn't need to do that. But thank you anyway. These are stunning," she says, smiling as she walks back into my home and into my kitchen, looking as if she belongs here. She opens a couple of cupboards and finds a vase for the flowers, fills it with water, and then places them into the vase and puts them on the dining room table.

"What are you cooking? It smells delicious," I ask.

"Nothing special. Once I saw your kitchen, I had to explore. It's state of the art, and the oven is so sexy," she says with a wide grin.

"Don't think I've been told I have a sexy oven before." As I reach out and pull her to me, I look down at her gorgeous face that has been washed clean of makeup, and I don't think she's looked more beautiful than she does in this moment. I pick her up, walk a couple of steps back, and place her ass on my marble countertop. "I didn't realize I had a Betty Crocker fetish until I came home and saw you in this apron," I tell her, flicking the frilly edge of it with my finger.

"It's my lucky apron. I travel everywhere with it. You never know when the mood to bake will strike." She grins ecstatically.

"I like it," I tell her, running my finger along the frills that hug her breasts. Elle bites her bottom lip as my finger continues south, and I pluck a nipple which makes her hiss.

"How long until dinner?" I ask.

"Ten minutes."

"Don't think that's enough time for me to do all the things I want to do to you," I tell her as she wraps her legs around my waist, pulling me closer.

"I'm sure you can be quick when you want to be," Elle purrs as she licks her lips hungrily.

"You'd be okay with a quickie before dinner?" I question.

"I'm happy whenever I get your dick."

Who the hell can say no to that?

"First things first, let me pull the curtains. It was cute watching you dance your ass around from outside, but I don't want the neighbors to know how cute your bare ass is," I tell her, untangling myself from her legs.

Elle giggles. "That's going to take a bit of getting used to. I'm so used to seeing naked people everywhere that I've forgotten normal society isn't."

I pull the curtains and stride back to where she's sitting. My hands slide up her thighs and pull down her leggings and underwear in one go.

"Leave the apron on, I like it," I tell her through a growl.

Elle nods and smiles up at me. I push her legs wider for me, then lick my fingers before sliding them into her needy pussy. I curl my fingers deep inside her and caress the sensitive nerves.

"Yes …" She groans the word as she throws her head back. I'll never get sick of hearing her appreciate my fingers in her cunt. I can feel her wetness on my hand, and I know she's ready.

"I think you're going to have to turn around for this, sweetness. The angle isn't right," I say, pulling my fingers from her.

She does as I ask, hops down, and folds herself over the marble countertop. I unzip my jeans and coat my dick in her wetness before rubbing the tip between her folds. Elle wiggles her ass as I tease her. As much as I would like to pull this out, I won't because I don't want to ruin the dinner she has prepared for me tonight. So I slide right in, and there's no better feeling than when I am balls deep inside Elle. I wrap my hand around her ponytail and tug her against my chest, angling my dick deeper into her.

"Ali," she hisses.

"Touch yourself, Elle. I need you to come for me. We have seven minutes left. I don't want dinner to burn."

Her hand moves from the counter to between her thighs. I can feel her fingers against her clit as I thrust into her. She begins to work herself over as I steadily pump into her.

"That's it, my little Betty Crocker whore. Choke my cock with your cunt and make me frost that pussy."

"Wait! What?" Elle stills, turning her face to me.

"I was trying to come up with dirty baking terms. I failed, I see that now," I tell her, and I see her lips curling in a smile.

"Just fuck me, Ali. I don't need anything other than your dick pounding me," Elle says.

Right! I'll give the woman what she wants as I start to thrust into her again. My hand tightens on her ponytail as her fingers move swiftly over her clit, and we get back into that steady rhythm.

"We have three minutes left, Elle. You need to come," I tell her.

"I would have come if you hadn't asked me to frost my pussy." She giggles as her pussy clenches. She's getting close. I'm never going to live that down, I don't think.

"Two minutes," I yell out, the time constraint now getting to me.

Can I make it happen in time?

"Fuck, yes," Elle curses as she makes herself come all over my dick, and as soon as her pussy clenches down on me, I'm done for.

We finish in synchronization with the timer of the oven.

"Guess we're cooked." Elle turns, chuckling.

"Hold steady, let me clean you up," I tell her as I grab some paper towels and clean up the mess we've made between us, then I help her get dressed again.

"Go ... have a quick shower. You must be exhausted after the flight and work. Dinner will be on the table when you get down," Elle tells me.

"You sure?"

Elle nods and pushes me out of the kitchen as she prepares dinner. I quickly run upstairs and undress. I have the world's quickest shower, grab a T-shirt and track pants, and head back downstairs just as Elle finishes placing the plates on the table.

"Want me to grab some wine?" I ask.

"Sure! It's chicken, so maybe white," she calls out.

I pull out a sauvignon blanc and head back to the table where it's all set out and looks incredible.

"For dinner, we have chicken confit with vegetables and mash. Dessert is apple tart tarin," Elle explains to me.

I don't care what it is, it smells delicious, looks amazing, and to top it off, I didn't have to cook.

35

ALISTAIR

This week with Eloise has been fantastic. She likes my kitchen, and I've been loving coming home to a gourmet meal every night. Seeing her happily dance around the kitchen with the biggest smile on her face when I come home makes having to leave her that little bit more bearable. I've put on a couple of pounds because of her food, but luckily, we work most of it off at night. While I'm at work, she's been spending time creating new recipes and making content for her socials, letting everyone know she is back in the UK. Then once I get home and we sit down for dinner, we talk about each other's day, and we also discuss her business. She shows me shopfronts she's interested in, and then we talk about the pros and cons. We have decided to check them out after the wedding next week.

I've never had such a sense of normalcy before in a relationship, and I like it. This little bubble we've been living in for the week is coming to an end with the wedding now looming around the corner.

It's Friday afternoon, and we're heading to Hertfordshire to my family's country estate, where the wedding is being held. I refuse to be there for a day longer than necessary.

"Relax," Eloise says, squeezing my hand as we head on out to the countryside, the city giving away to the green rolling hills of my childhood. "Ali, I've got you this weekend, okay? We can leave anytime you want. I can try to run block between you and your brother …"

The tension in my body subsides as I bring her hand up to my lips and kiss the top of her hand. She has no idea how much I appreciate her support during this time and especially after everything.

"My family's estate can be overwhelming because of its size, but my parents are down-to-earth people, which you might not believe after the way I have painted them," I explain to her.

"It will be fine, Ali. I promise I won't embarrass you."

"Babe, that's not what I meant." I look over at her with a frown on my face, I hope she didn't think she wouldn't fit into my rich family's lifestyle.

"I know, Ali," she says, giving me a wide smile. "I promise, you don't have to worry about me. I'll make sure I'm the perfect girlfriend."

"I want you to be yourself, Elle, which *is perfect*," I tell her.

Eloise chuckles. "You're tying yourself up in knots, Ali. I'm trying to calm you down, but I feel like I'm making it worse," she says, squeezing my hand again.

"I'm freaking out, aren't I?"

Eloise nods but gives me a reassuring smile. "It's going to be fine," she tries to reassure me.

"I'm going to apologize in advance for my brother. I know he's going to say or do something completely inappropriate."

"I'm a big girl, Ali. I can handle myself. I've also dealt with far worse people than your brother over the years, let me tell you."

Maybe she's right. Maybe The Paradise Club was the best

training ground for her to deal with assholes like George. I shouldn't be worrying about Elle. She's telling me she's got this, and I need to believe her. I just don't want my family scaring her off, not after I've found her again.

We make our way down the country lanes until we get to the imposing gates of my family's estate. Pressing the code to get in, we wait as the large ornate gates slowly open for us, then we proceed along the long gravel road through the woodland forest. We arrive at the red brick, the three-story sprawling mansion which rises from the rolling hills. I look over at Eloise to check if she is okay, but I notice she's a little pale.

"Are you okay?" I ask with concern as I park the car out the front of the home.

"Yeah, I feel like I've been here before, which is strange. Must have been somewhere that looked like this that my parents dragged me to," she says, shaking her head as if dismissing whatever thoughts had filtered through her mind.

Paul, my family's butler, is at my door before I have a chance to press the issue further.

"Mr. King, welcome home, sir," Paul greets me.

"Thank you, Paul. It's been a while," I say, nodding in his direction.

"It's been too long, sir," he replies while giving me a small smile before walking around to Eloise's door.

"Miss Muller, welcome to Moore Place Estate," Paul says, greeting Elle.

"Thank you," she says, taking his hand as he helps her out of the car.

The rest of the staff rush out and open the car's trunk and start pulling out our bags.

"Your bags will be taken up to your room, sir," Paul explains.

"Thank you. I'm assuming it's a madhouse inside?" I ask as I reach out and take Elle's hand in mine.

A flicker of amusement falls across Paul's normally professional face. "You could say that, sir."

"Ready?" I turn and look at Elle, and she gives me a bright smile and a determined nod. "Right, lead the way, Paul. Let's get this over and done with."

Paul nods and asks us to follow him. We step over the threshold of my family home, and it seems relatively quiet down the long corridors.

"They are out the back, sir," Paul tells us.

We turn left down the corridor from the entry, past the antique paintings that line the walls, past the library, the parlor room, and a drawing-room until we finally get to the conservatory, which leads us out to the garden area. As soon as Paul opens the glass doors, my ears are assaulted with noise.

Banging.

Clanging.

Yelling.

There's a large white marquee that has been set up on the formal lawn. Staff is madly running around looking stressed. There are trucks reversing up the seventeenth-century path unloading their contents onto the gravel terrace, and people scattering like ants grabbing what they need and moving on their way.

"Last chance, babe. We can run, and no one will be the wiser." I turn and look down at Elle.

"It's one weekend, Ali. We can do this," she says, reassuring me.

She's right. Just one weekend. It's maybe fifty hours, and some of that we will be asleep for if I have my way.

I *can* do it.

We can do it.

"Let's do this," I say, taking her hand. As soon as we walk inside the massive marquee, I find my mother and Miranda standing there with frowns on their faces talking to a couple of women with tablets in their hands.

"Hope I'm not intruding," I say, interrupting the intense discussion.

Everyone turns, and they look surprised to see me. I notice Miranda's eyes widen as she takes in Elle standing beside me. Her eyes dip to where our hands are linked, and a frown forms on her face.

Oh dear, she doesn't look happy about Elle being here with me—*suck it up!*

"Sweetheart, you made it." Mum smiles as she moves away from the group and pulls me into a warm hug. "You look lovely and tanned after your holiday," she states while overexaggerating, brushing some imaginary lint from my shoulders as mothers do. Then my mother notices Eloise standing beside me, she tilts her head to the side as her eyes roam over Elle, assessing her, seeing if she's up to the King standard. I don't care if they think she isn't because it is none of their business who I date. As far as I'm concerned, their standards are shit anyway if they are allowing Miranda into the family.

"Mother, Miranda ... let me introduce you to Eloise, my girlfriend," I say happily.

Eloise steps forward with her hand out. "It's such a pleasure to meet you, Mrs. King."

My mother takes her hand warmly.

Eloise then turns her attention toward Miranda, and I brace myself. "Congratulations on your wedding," Elle says, greeting Miranda as she holds out her hand. Miranda's eyes darken, but she politely shakes Elle's hand. Elle continues to give Miranda a bright smile, ignoring the daggers my ex is sending her way.

"Alistair, it's lovely to see you again," Miranda says, turning her back on Elle and walking over and pulling me into an embrace. She kisses each of my cheeks slowly and hugs me tightly.

This game will NOT work, Miranda.

"You must be so excited to be marrying the man of your dreams?" Elle adds, not letting the slight go.

And I almost burst out laughing at her comment.

Miranda's eyes narrow on Elle, and she understands the subtle undertone of Elle's comment, especially after that territorial display she just tried on with me.

"Of course, I am. George is a wonderful father, and I can't wait for our family to be one. It's going to be a beautiful weekend. I've heard they believe it's going to be the society wedding of the year," Miranda brags to Elle.

"That's exciting. Is *Tatler* magazine covering it? They love society weddings," Elle asks curiously.

Miranda's eyes narrow on Elle—she knows Elle is biting back. "My wedding planner has it all covered. She knows everyone."

"Of course, she would. But if she doesn't, my cousin is the editor, so I can give her a call if need be. She owes me a favor or two," Elle says, then gives her a blinding smile.

Miranda's jaw falls open at Elle's name drop, but she quickly recovers. My mother thinks this is exciting and is gushing all over Elle. And I am blown away because this is another fascinating tidbit about Eloise that I did not know.

"We didn't know you were dating anyone, Alistair?" Miranda adds as if she's trying to dismiss Elle like she is nothing.

"He mentioned it to me when he got back from vacation," my mother declares, not realizing she's in the middle of some tension.

"How long have you been together?" Miranda asks.

Eloise places a reassuring hand on my arm as if letting me know she's got this. "I've known Alistair on and off for a while now," Eloise says, looking up at me. "Unfortunately, work took me to the other side of the world for the past six months. But we reconnected again recently, and this time we decided we were sick of having an ocean between us, so I moved back to London to be with him."

"Elle lives with me," I add.

"Oh, this is wonderful. I'm so happy for you two. It might be your wedding we are planning next," my mother says with a wide smile.

Slow your roll there, Mother. I just got Elle to come back to London with me, I don't think we are ready for that step just yet.

"Might be a while before that happens," Elle answers with a deep chuckle. "I have some career goals to meet first."

"What is it you do?" Miranda questions Eloise.

"I'm a baker. I create decadent cakes and sweets," Elle replies.

"That sounds like fun. Would I have seen you anywhere? You look familiar, and I can't quite place it?" my mother questions Elle.

Eloise tenses beside me. "I don't think so. Perhaps I have one of those faces."

"A common one," Miranda adds bitchily.

"I swear you look like a friend's daughter, but to be fair, I haven't seen her in probably ten years," my mother muses.

"Must have a doppelgänger," Elle answers, but I can see the tension that's written across her face.

That's awfully strange for my mother to say something like that.

"Sorry, can you excuse us for a moment? We have a couple of questions we'd like to ask," the wedding planner says, interrupting our conversation.

Perfect.

Saved by the bell.

"We'll leave you to it. I'm going to take Eloise for a walk before getting ready for dinner," I tell my mother, giving her a kiss on the cheek as we say our goodbyes. I take Elle's hand and pull her out of the marquee and away from Miranda's frostiness. We walk in silence, removing ourselves from the chaos of wedding preparations. It's not until we are deep inside the formal gardens that I push Elle up against one of the stone walls and kiss the shit out of her.

"You did so well. Especially when Miranda was coming for you," I tell her as I run a hand down her cheek.

"I knew she would say something. I'm sure she wants you to stay unhappy to make herself feel better. I was surprised at how bold she was at dismissing me. She probably thinks she can get away with it because your family wouldn't pull her up on it, especially not during her wedding weekend," Elle states, and I can tell she's not upset over it, even though it makes me feel like shit that she must endure Miranda's bitchiness. "How are you, though?" she asks me.

"First hurdle down. Next one is my brother," I tell her on a sigh.

"There's nothing he can do or say that will make me fall for whatever charm he thinks he has," Elle says, reassuring me as if she can read my mind.

"I know you won't." I run my thumb against her cheek. "It's just men with those kinds of egos, the ones who are never told no, they don't understand the word when they hear it."

"I'm a big girl, Ali. Also, I'm trained in self-defense. I'm not above kicking him in his balls at his wedding if he decides to get handsy," she tells me, which makes me smile.

"I'd fucking pay to see that," I tell her, chuckling.

"Let's hope it doesn't come to that." She grins.

"Thanks for doing this for me."

"I'd pretty much do anything for you, Alistair King, if you hadn't guessed by now."

"Anything?" I question as my mind wanders to all the things I want to do to her right now.

Elle's hand slides between us and rests on my dick, giving it a good squeeze. "Anything."

Fuck, this woman is something. "Then lift that dress and slide those panties to the side so I can fuck this tension from my body."

Elle does as she's told, and thank fuck, she is wearing a gorgeous navy sundress and her next-to-nothing thong, so when she slides her underwear to the side for me, there is nothing between us.

I unzip myself from my jeans and lick my fingers, then I slide between her folds. She's ready for me. I replace my fingers with my dick, and I sink inside her in the middle of my family's garden.

"Yes," she hisses as I enter her.

This is what I need, to be deep inside Elle, where everything feels right in the world. It doesn't matter what's happening outside of us because right here, when we are joined, it's paradise. And I know I've found paradise with Elle, and I'll do everything in my power not to lose these feelings. In this moment, something has changed between us. It's as if fucking her in my parents' gardens has brought us closer. My heart expands when I look down at her, and those green eyes look back up at me.

"I love you, Elle," I tell her.

She stills beneath me.

"You don't have to say a thing, but in this moment, I don't think I've ever been happier," I confess to her.

"Ali …"

I shake my head. "You don't have to say it, Elle." As I begin to thrust slowly into her, I continue, "Not yet. I want you to know that I'm already there. I'm not going anywhere, no matter what." The words tumble out of me as I begin to make love to her.

"I don't want anyone else, Ali, but you," she tells me, and that's all I need to know right now.

It's too soon for her, and I respect that. I'll wait forever to hear those words come back to me. I don't care how long it takes.

"You're mine, Elle," I whisper into her ear as I push myself deep inside her until she's falling apart on a gasp, and I'm not far behind her. "You look so beautiful when you come all over my cock," I say, holding her face and caressing her skin. "Come with me. I had something planned for us this afternoon, but I can't seem to keep my hands off you or my dick out of you." So I tug her further into the gardens.

36

ELOISE

He loves me!

I wasn't expecting his declarations of love while he fucked me in his parents' garden. I wanted to say that I felt the same way as him in that moment, but the words got stuck in my throat. I hesitated, worried because what I feel for him is so overwhelming, and I'm concerned if I go all in that if things don't work out between us, it's going to crush me.

"There's an abandoned cottage up ahead," Alistair says, pulling me off the path and through the meadow toward a thatched cottage. It appears out of nowhere like something out of a fairy tale. "This was my favorite place to get away from my brother when I was younger. He never came this far into the woods, not once I filled his head with ghost stories." Alistair chuckles, remembering a strong memory.

We reach the cottage, and Alistair lets go of my hand and gives the rusted door handle a turn. It seems to turn easily enough, but who knows what's behind that wooden door? There are probably a million and one spider webs. Not my idea of sexy, but he wants me to share his special place, and that's kind of cute, and I guess worth running into spiders for.

The door slowly creaks open. "Let me double-check there are no rouge animals in here," he tells me, disappearing behind the door, and moments later, he comes back out with a smile on his face. "All good, come on in," he says, inviting me into his private space.

Stepping over the threshold and into the semi-darkness of the cottage, I pause when I see what is in front of me. What in the world? The cottage has been transformed into a magical wonderland. Fairy lights are strung along the wooden beams, there's a table with a gorgeous bouquet of flowers in the middle, and a platter of chocolate-dipped strawberries and assorted cheeses. A bottle of champagne with two crystal glasses is beside the beautiful flowers.

My eyes look further into the cottage, where a gorgeous wooden four-poster bed sits with white material draped around the sides. Large pillows are stacked neatly against the headboard, a fluffy navy duvet sits on top of the bed.

"Alistair," I say his name shocked at what I'm seeing before me. "You …" My chest constricts at what he has created for me.

"I called Paul earlier in the week and asked him to help me. I knew this weekend was going to be tough, and I wanted a place where we could get away from it all. Just the two of us."

My hand covers my mouth in awe. No one has ever gone to this much effort for me. "I love it."

"This is where I was wanting to take you. But after what happened in the marquee, I needed you right there and then," he confesses.

"You never have to apologize for fucking me against a stone wall," I reply, making him grin.

"Come lay down and let me feed you," he says.

"Sounds great, but firstly is there a bathroom?" I ask, needing a refresh.

"Down the hall." He points.

I head down the short hall and freshen up, and by the time I get back, he's lying in bed with the platter of chocolate-dipped strawberries beside him and a glass of champagne in his hand. There's a glass waiting for me on the side table, so I kick off my heels and jump into bed with him before picking it up and taking a sip, letting the bubbles flow through me.

"Open wide ..." He offers me a strawberry, and I do as I'm told, biting into the fruit. It tastes delicious. I hum in delight as I nibble on the chocolatey goodness. "This is where I wanted to tell you my feelings," Ali explains.

Did he plan all this so he could tell me he loves me? Oh, my goodness, can this man get any more charming?

"I liked you telling me when your dick was still in me," I say, grinning over a strawberry.

"Is that so?" Ali raises a brow.

"Everything feels better when your dick is inside me." I chuckle.

"Good to know." He reaches out and pulls me into the crook of his neck, where we stay in silence, enjoying each other's company.

"Wasn't it strange that Mum thought you reminded her of someone?" he muses.

Well, damn! I was kind of hoping he had forgotten that conversation.

"And you thought you'd been here before?"

Urgh. He picks up on everything.

The problem is I have a sneaking suspicion that I *have* been here before, a long time ago with my parents, but I am praying that there are a million other red-bricked country estates dotted around here that all look the same.

"Do you think the Universe is telling us we're meant to be together?" he asks.

Phew. That makes me happy that he doesn't suspect anything else. I left this world for a reason, and it's just my luck that this world—this world I abandoned long ago—has found me again.

"Fuck!" Alistair wakes with a start. "We fell asleep, and now we're late for the rehearsal."

I sit up with a jolt and look out the window, which has gone from blue clouds to a twinkling, inky black sky, then stare down at my watch and realize it's late.

"We've got to go. My mother is going to have a heart attack if we miss this thing," Alistair states.

"Right then, let's go."

We make it back down in record time. We've missed the actual ceremony rehearsal, which is fine, as Alistair wasn't chosen to stand by his brother anyway. George chose not to have him as his best man or even groomsman.

We step into the grand ballroom inside the home, and thankfully, it's cocktail hour with the bride and groom's friends and family, so there are only about sixty people milling around.

"Where the hell have you been?" an older gentleman curses as we enter the ballroom. I'm assuming it's his father as they have the same eyes and jaw.

"Sorry, fell asleep and forgot to set the alarm," Alistair states as he slaps his father on the back. The older man narrows his eyes at his son and shakes his head before he notices me standing there. His eyes widen, and he does a quick sweep over me.

Thankfully, I'm wearing formal cocktail attire that Ali insisted I purchase for this weekend. In his exact words, 'It's going to be an over-the-top formal weekend, and people will judge you on your outfit.' I didn't want to embarrass Ali, but I also didn't want to take his money either, but Ali is very persuasive. Now I feel so much better about relenting and letting him buy me what he wanted. Ali chose a gorgeous forest green cocktail dress that's fitted at the top, cinched in at the waist before flaring out into a semi-ballgown style, but it stops at my calf.

The material is sheer over the bodice with sequins arranged in a pattern. It's simple yet gorgeous.

"Oh, you must be Ali's mystery girlfriend," he says, reaching out and shaking my hand.

"I'm Eloise. It's a pleasure to meet you, Mr. King." I reach out, take his hand, and shake it.

A waiter walks by, and we grab a glass of champagne—I need it to settle my nerves.

"My wife tells me you're a baker?" his father asks me.

"Yes, self-taught. But I've been told my cakes are delicious," I answer.

"Eloise made those cupcakes you raved about when meeting Gabriel for the first time," Ali explains to his father before looking down at me and showing how proud he is to say the words.

"Really? They were amazing. I might need to put in a request as I haven't been able to find anything like them since." His father's high praise makes me smile. "Oh, excuse me, I need to see Robert over there," his father states before darting off to catch up with someone.

"That went well," I say to Ali, then take another sip of champagne.

"He never stopped talking about your cupcakes, so I knew it would win him over telling him you made them," Ali says before leaning over and kissing my lips.

"Well, well, well ... long time no see, brother," a deep voice interrupts our moment as a hand slaps Alistair on the back so hard it forces his champagne to slosh over the edge and drip down his fingers.

I glance up to an uglier version of Alistair standing before me. *Seriously, this is what women are falling for?* Where Alistair is light, his brother is dark, like yin and yang, except these two do not make a whole.

"Miranda told me you had a girlfriend, but I didn't believe

her. Had to come over and see it with my own eyes." He laughs as his beady little eyes look over me with interest.

For goodness sake. Ew. I'll need a shower after this.

Alistair's face is pulled into a strained frown, his shoulders are tense, and his hand curled into a fist, ready to strike.

"You must be Eloise," his brother says while holding out his hand for me to take. "You look familiar. Have we met before?"

"I'm certain we haven't. And you are?" I ask even though I know he introduced himself as Alastair's brother, I don't want to give him anything.

He frowns for a moment as if he can't believe what I've said to him. "George ... his older, richer, and more handsome brother," he says as he takes my hand and kisses it.

I want to throw up.

How dare he do that to me.

I pull my hand away instantly, which surprises him, judging by the confused frown he has on his face.

"Right! I haven't heard much about you," I add.

"That's because he doesn't like the competition," George says and gives me a wink.

What fucking competition, you wanker? You are an inferior copy of Alistair.

Someone calls out Alistair's brother's name, and he gives them a wave, plastering on a politician-like smile. He turns back to me and states, "Eloise, I look forward to welcoming you to the family ... later." The innuendo drips with each word, and I can't help but turn up my lip in disgust.

No. Thank. You.

And before Alistair can say anything more, he's gone.

"You okay?" Alistair asks, looking me over as if George has physically hurt me.

"I feel like I need a shower where I can slather myself in disinfectant after that. I don't get it. Why are women attracted to *that*? There's no appeal there ... *at all*," I say to Alistair. "Sorry, that was mean. He is your family, but …"

Alistair bursts out laughing and moves closer to me, cups my face, and kisses me deeply. "If I hadn't told you that I loved you earlier, I would have right now," he states, those hazel eyes burning with hunger as he looks down at me.

Thankfully, after that, the night went on without incident. We sat through his brother's long-winded speech about how much he loves Miranda, how they met at university, and how he always knew she was the one, completely ignoring the fact she was engaged to his brother for some of that time.

"I can't wait to get you into bed," Alistair says as he nuzzles my neck while we walk down the corridor away from the ballroom toward our room which is at the top of the grand staircase.

"The things I'm going to do to you," I whisper back, giggling, as I may have had a couple more champagnes than I should have.

"Son, do you have a moment?" Alistair's dad calls out to him, interrupting us.

Alistair looks down at me, then up to his father, and he hesitates.

"Go! Catch up with your dad. I'll meet you in our room. I can entertain myself till you get back," I tease, patting his hard chest.

Alistair growls before he places a kiss on my lips and heads off down the corridor with his father. He glances back at me before disappearing into one of the rooms off the corridor.

"My brother really shouldn't leave his toys lying around. You never know who might try and steal them," George says. The bastard scares me as he steps out from the darkness.

"Goodnight," I reply, turning on my heel and walking away from him, but I hear footsteps following me.

"Wait! I want to get to know my brother's girlfriend better," he says, sliding up to me, blocking my exit.

"I think that's something we can do with Alistair here, don't you?" I narrow my eyes on him. I'm not like the other girls who have come before me. I won't fall for your bullshit.

"You sure?" he asks, raising his brow.

"Yeah, I'm positive." I attempt to move around him, but he blocks my path again.

"I thought you looked familiar, and it's been bugging me. So, I did a little digging into you, Eloise Muller, the baker, and it was most certainly interesting." He smirks as he places a hand on the wall next to my head as his eyes leer on me. The asshole has the audacity to lick his lips hungrily, but I'm not intimidated by a creep like him.

"I'd have assumed you'd have more pressing things to worry about the night before your wedding than little old me," I reply, giving him my most innocent voice.

"My brother's happiness is important. I needed to make sure who he was bringing around is worthy of being a part of this family," he says snidely.

"Like your soon-to-be-bride who was supposed to be marrying your brother," I throw back at him.

"She was mine to begin with!" He spits the words out while his face turns bright red with anger.

Touched a nerve, I see. "I don't have time for this." I roll my eyes and try to move around him again, but he's not having any of it.

"Oh, you'll have time for me," he says smugly as he reaches out and runs a finger down my arm.

What a creep. I grab his wrist and flick it away to stop him. "Touch me again, and I'll break a finger," I warn.

"Who knew threatening me with violence would get my dick hard, but look at that …" he points, "… seems it does."

This time I push him away from me.

This man is a pig.

"You realize you have a wife-to-be and a child here?"

"Please! Miranda fucks whoever she wants to fuck as well. We aren't monogamous," he states.

"Oh, is that why she was flirting with Alistair earlier? Now it all makes sense. I thought it was because she still had feelings for him and may have been having second thoughts about the wedding," I declare.

George thumps his hand on the wall high above my head and glares at me. "Listen bitch, she can have whoever she wants, just not my brother," he seethes.

"You sure about that?" I tease, which is probably stupid of me, but I can't help it. No one stands up to this guy. He isn't God. He's a spoiled rotten rich guy who thinks the world should be bowing down to a man like him simply because of the car he drives, the home he lives in, or job he has. *Screw him.*

"Spill whatever you think you need to spill. I'm sick of this charade," I assert.

"Mistress Elle from The Paradise Club," George states with a grin.

"You have the wrong person," I tell him.

What the fuck! The first rule of The Paradise Club is you don't talk about it.

"Is that so?" he says as he pulls out his phone and connects to The Paradise Club's secure app. Then he turns the phone around and shows me working there.

Shit. I am going to have to let HR know that a client showed me this—they won't appreciate the fact that he is using it like this.

"My friend wouldn't stop talking about you. How much fun you had together, and then he showed me your photo, and I locked it away for the next time I was to be at the club. I wanted to see what all the fuss was about. Wish you were scheduled each time I'd been there. We could have had some fun."

Fuck him.

Now it makes sense why there are two Mr. Kings on file.

"You do realize this is grounds for termination of your membership ... harassing me like this," I articulate while raising a brow.

"You think they would listen to a slut like you over me?" he spits back.

I laugh in his face. "You really have no idea what the club is about if you think they are going to side with you over me."

"Don't you fucking dare say a thing," he barks and grabs me.

"I don't think so. You started this, but I'm going to finish it!"

His face turns red with anger again. "You really shouldn't try me. I have the best people on my payroll, and the things they can find out at the drop of a hat ..." He grins. "Amazing."

"Nothing you can say will upset me. So, go ahead, give it your best shot."

George smiles sadistically. "Is that so, Lady Eloise Miller of Winchester," he says, stating a name I've long forgotten about.

Everything in me stops. The bad part about all this is the fact I can see it on his face how much he's enjoying catching me off-guard like this. "Who knew *you* are a Lady? Would never have guessed," he says, looking me up and down with disdain. "You left home as soon as you could, not because you wanted to be a model but because good old Uncle Henry wouldn't keep his creepy hands to himself. And so many times you told people, but they all said, 'Little Eloise has such a vivid imagination' and ignored your cries for help."

Fuck.

I can feel my brick walls crumbling as this asshole is taking me back to a time I had long forgotten. *How the fuck did he find out about this?* The only person outside of my parents I told was the therapist they sent me to because they thought it was all lies. Turns out she was on their payroll, and so she tried to convince me I was making it all up because Uncle Henry is a respectable man and couldn't possibly do anything so disrespectful to a young lady.

"Fuck you!" I try my hardest not to fall apart in front of this psycho.

"Oh, I truly hope you do," he says, licking his lips. "Come to my room tonight, and I'll make sure no one finds out about your dirty little secret."

"Never."

"I'm a patient man, but the deal's up at midnight." He turns on his heel and chuckles darkly, and then he walks away from me.

37

ALISTAIR

Eloise was asleep when I got back to our room after speaking with my dad. He wanted to check in on me and see if I was okay with the wedding. I told him I didn't care, and especially not now that I have Eloise. We spoke about my feelings for her and how surprised I was that they happened so quickly. Of course, I gave the watered-down version of our relationship.

He told me he thought she seemed a perfect fit for me, and he had never seen me happier, even when I was with Miranda. I told him Eloise is the one, which scared the shit out of me but also made me feel at peace for the first time in my life.

When I woke up this morning and rolled over and saw Eloise lying there in my arms, I don't think I've ever been happier.

"Hey, sleepyhead," she says, rolling over and wrapping her arms around me. *I could get used to this.* The next thing I know, she has me on my back and is sinking her pussy over my morning wood. Hell, yeah, that is exactly how I want to wake up in the mornings, every single day for the rest of my life.

The thought should terrify me, but it doesn't.

We fuck in relative quiet, simply enjoying each other.

"Morning," Eloise says, smiling at me.

"Good morning to you too."

"What can I say, I can't keep my hands to myself," she states, placing a chaste kiss on my lips.

"Me either, babe. But we better jump in the shower. Have you seen our itinerary?" I point at the book on the coffee table. "We have a strict schedule to adhere to."

Elle groans as she pulls the covers back over her head. "Do we have to go? I'd rather spend all day in bed with you."

"There is no place I would rather be, but alas, my parents want me to show up and perform," I tell her.

Elle rolls her eyes, but she nods her head.

Thankfully, I wasn't in the wedding party, so I didn't need to hang out with George and Miranda. I still had to join in with the family photographs, which was a pain in the ass. George was in fine form all day, loving the spotlight and enjoying that absolutely everything was about him. He was at his most obnoxious self today. Thankfully, he left me alone, and there were no more crude remarks about Eloise. I wasn't above giving him a black eye on his wedding day. Actually, I was looking forward to it if the time was right, but it never came.

We made it through the wedding ceremony where they said their vows, which we know mean nothing, then headed on to the lavish reception.

Eloise and I had fun at the reception—we danced, we drank, we laughed.

During a dance with my mother, she peppered me with questions about Eloise and our future together. It's still a little soon, but what I do know is I don't want her moving back in with her best friend. I've enjoyed coming home to her puttering around the house, and I've loved being her sounding board for her business. But above all, I've relished simply laying on the couch and watching television with her, enjoying all the mundane couple things that I never did with Miranda.

Looking down at my watch, it's past midnight, and Eloise hasn't come back from the bathroom. It's been a while—I should check on her. I head out of the wedding marquee and into the darkness. I follow the lights along the path to where the luxury portable bathrooms are located. The doors are all open on the ladies' toilets, so where the hell is she?

"Eloise," I call out, sticking my head in each cubicle to make sure she's not there.

"Missing someone," Miranda asks as she slides up to me in her wedding dress, then she runs her hand down my arm. For fuck's sake, this woman just married the man of her dreams. What the hell is wrong with her?

"Have you seen, Eloise?" I ask reluctantly. She's the last person I want any help from, especially where Eloise is concerned, but I can't help but be a little concerned.

"You mean your whore?" Miranda spits.

What the hell did she say? I turn my head and stare at her.

"George said she's a whore, and you hired her to be your date. Did you think I would be jealous of a girl like that? You need someone a hell of a lot better than her to make me jealous. She is no competition to me," Miranda says as she lays her hands on my chest.

"Don't touch me," I yell as I take a giant step back. "I'm trying to find Elle, and if you don't know where she is, then I don't have time for your toxic bullshit. This is your wedding day. Shouldn't you be with your husband?"

"Please! We all know he's probably fucking one of the catering girls as we speak," she says, slurring her words. "We aren't traditional, Ali. We can fuck whoever we want."

"Good for you, but leave me out of it," I reply, stepping back a couple more steps.

"I wouldn't be surprised if George is fucking your date right now. He told me she propositioned him last night," she adds.

"Fuck off! George is the biggest liar known to man. I know for a fact Elle wouldn't touch him."

Miranda shrugs her shoulders in a blasé manner.

"I'm so glad you fucked my brother. Because quite honestly, seeing you here like this makes me realize how wrong you were for me," I tell her honestly.

Miranda's a little taken back by my words because her jaw drops in surprise, but she quickly recovers. "You'll come crawling back when your whore fucks you over," she spits.

"Congrats on your new life, Miranda. I hope it brings you *sooo* much happiness." I turn on my heel, head back into the party, and come across my mum. "Mum, have you seen Eloise? I can't find her anywhere."

"No, sweetie, I haven't. Maybe she's gone to get changed or perhaps she's gone to bed, like I probably should," she says, swaying against me.

Looks like Mum's had one too many champagnes.

Maybe she's right. I'll go check our bedroom, but it seems strange as I'm sure Elle would have waited for me. But then again, perhaps she couldn't find me and went back to my room and fell asleep while waiting for me.

Making my way inside, I step up the grand staircase and into our room. As I walk through the door, I switch the light on and stop.

No, Eloise.

I step into the bathroom.

Nothing.

Where the hell is she?

Then I notice the empty basin, where her makeup was spilled everywhere before we left. It's gone. *Did she clean up?*

Walking back into the bedroom, I look it over again and notice her phone that she left charging is gone along with the charger. Rounding the bed, I open up the closet, and everything of mine is there, but everything of hers is not.

Fuck.

Running my hand through my hair, I realize *she's gone.*

No. This can't be happening.

She wouldn't leave me.

No, I don't believe it.

Frantically, I check the room, and every single trace of her is gone, except a note on the floor under the desk. It must have fallen.

Alistair,
 I'm sorry.
 This isn't going to work.
 Eloise.

The letter has tear stains on it, so she was crying while she was writing it.

What the hell is going on?

Why would she have just left me like that?

I don't understand.

Rushing back into the wedding reception to double-check she's not in there, and I've missed her somehow, most of the partygoers have left for the night. Then I see George sitting in the corner with his asshole friends. He grabs a waitress's ass as she passes by, his friends all cheering his actions on.

The poor girl looks scared and rushes away, forgetting her tray.

I see red.

I rush at my brother and tackle him to the floor. Then I start laying into him. He tries to fight back, but he's never been one to work out. His groomsmen eventually pull me off him, and we're both bloodied.

"What did you do to her?" I scream at him while my chest

heaves with the anxiety that's building inside me. It takes him a couple of moments to get up off the floor with blood streaming from his lip. He spits some of it to the side.

"What didn't I do?" He smirks at me. "I will say she was worth every single penny. She's the best of all the girls you've brought around." He chuckles.

I try and lunge at him, but George's friends hold me back.

"Get the fuck off me," I scream at them. "Don't think my brother hasn't fucked your wives," I say, pointing at every one of them.

A couple of their faces drop, and their eyes narrow on my brother.

"What the hell's going on in here?" Dad asks as he walks in, looking at the two of us.

"Brother here is upset that I found out his woman wasn't who she said she is. Did you know she's a prostitute?" my brother says to my father.

My father turns and raises a brow, and I shake my head because she wasn't a prostitute.

"He's upset because she propositioned me before my wedding. I thought he needed to know," he says to my father.

The lying, conniving sack of shit.

"Come on, son. Let's get you cleaned up," Dad says, pulling me out of George's groomsmen's grasps.

We walk silently back into the house, and he takes me to the mudroom to clean me up, so none of the guests can see.

"Seems like your brother is worse off than you," he states with the tiniest of smirks. He pulls a first-aid kit out of the closet with a bottle of scotch. "Think you might need this more," he says, handing me the bottle.

I open the lid and throw back the golden liquid courage, feeling the burn slide down my throat.

"Want to tell me what happened?" he asks, looking up at me.

I give him the look of *hell no* before silence falls between us again.

"I don't care if Eloise isn't your real girlfriend," my father adds.

"She is, though. We may not have had a conventional start, but what we have between us is real."

My father nods, takes the seat beside me, and grabs the scotch bottle from my hand then throws it back himself. "I don't believe for one minute she would have propositioned your brother," he says, handing the bottle back to me.

"She's gone, Dad. She left me a note saying sorry. All her stuff is missing too."

He claps me on the back. "Maybe she thought you were better off without her. Especially with George spreading lies about her."

"She's not an escort. It wasn't like that," I plead my case with my father.

"Maybe you should start from the beginning, son," he says, tapping me on the knee.

Maybe I should.

So, I do.

I tell him everything about Eloise and me.

38

ELOISE

The wedding was beautiful even if it was the devil himself getting married. I made sure I kept my distance from George. I wasn't going to be the girl to ruin the wedding, no matter how much I wanted to. I've plastered on a smile and bided my time. As soon as we get home and away from his psycho brother, I'll tell Alistair everything his brother did to me this weekend. And I'll tell him who I truly am also. He deserves to know the reasons why I am hiding my identity.

Tonight has been fun, and I've danced the night away in Alistair's arms. He whispered all the dirty things he wanted to do to me when the night was over, and I couldn't wait.

"Sweetheart, over here," Alistair's mother calls out.

We walk over to where his mother is standing, chatting animatedly at a table. When I get close, my entire body pauses. *No.* What the hell are they doing here?

"I can't remember the last time you might have seen Ali. It's probably been eight years or longer," Alistair's mum explains to the older couple. "Sweetie, do you remember the Marquis and Marchioness of Winchester? They are our neighbors across the road. They had a gorgeous little girl called Eloise, and I always thought you two would be great together." She sighs. Little does she know how right she is. "And funnily enough, Ali's new girlfriend is called Eloise, so I guess in some way it came true," she babbles on.

"It's a pleasure to see you both again," Alistair says, shaking my parents' hands.

Both are staring at me as if they have seen a ghost.

"This is my beautiful girlfriend, Eloise," Alistair says, proudly introducing me to my own parents.

My heart is thundering in my chest, my palms are sweaty, and they are looking at me, wondering what I'm going to do, and I'm doing the same.

"It's a pleasure to meet you both." I place the fakest of smiles on my face as I pretend to not know my parents.

"I swear this Eloise looks so similar to yours, don't you think?" Alistair's mum asks my parents.

"I don't think so," my mother adds while looking me over, and I can see her top lip curling in disgust.

"I'm sorry, will you excuse me?" I say, interrupting the family get-together to head for the ladies' room. I need to get away from them. I haven't seen them in years, and they are starting to age.

"Do you need me to come?" Alistair asks.

"No, stay here. Catch up with your parents' friends. I won't be long," I tell him. He kisses my forehead, and I make my hasty retreat from my past.

I head out the back along the darkened path to where the luxury portable bathrooms are located. *Who knew there was such a thing?* I suck in a couple of deep breaths because seeing them here, in this space and so close to me, has thrown me for a loop. Now I realize why I remember this place. We've popped in on occasions, but most of the time, I was never invited.

After doing my business, I walk out and straight into George.

Seriously, could this night get any worse? Just touching him makes me physically recoil.

"Aren't you going to congratulate me?" he goads.

"It was a lovely ceremony," I say while gritting my teeth.

"I couldn't stop thinking about you." The asshole has the nerve to lean into me, the stench of alcohol on his breath is overwhelming.

"If you'll excuse me," I ask, not engaging in whatever he thinks this is.

As I try and move away from him, he sneers, "Not so fast. I want to show you something." He grabs my arm forcibly.

"Let go of me," I yell as I try and get away from his grasp.

"I did warn you last night, Eloise. If you didn't come to my room that I *would* retaliate," he says, leading me off the path near some bushes.

"And I warned you too," I reply, rubbing my arm where he held me. I am sure there will be bruise marks in the shape of his fingers tomorrow.

"Oh, Eloise. It really is you," a familiar voice echoes from the bushes.

No.

No.

No, no, no!

Swirling around, I see the man who made my life a living hell.

"It's Uncle Henry, sweetheart," George coos as he moves toward me.

"No. Stay away from me," I yell at him as I take a couple of steps back while panic laces my body. I hear George's sadistic chuckling off in the distance.

"You've grown up into a beautiful woman, Eloise," he says as his creepy eyes roam over my body.

I want to hurl.

Literally be physically ill, right here, right now.

"Leave me alone, you sick man," I shout.

"The family misses you, sweetheart. You need to come back home," he states.

"Leave me the fuck alone. I hate you. I fucking hate you. You ruined my life," I scream and stumble as I try to get away quickly from these two pieces of shit they call men.

"You seem to be doing well for yourself," my uncle spits back.

I turn on my heel and run toward the main house.

I have to get out of here.

I have to get away.

The panic attack I know is coming is creeping up fast through my body, and its sharp claws are starting to dig into my throat, constricting it, making it harder and harder to breathe.

I must get away from this place.

From these vile people.

From my past.

I'm sorry, Alistair, but your family is crazy, and I can't be around them.

How cruel do you have to be to bring someone's monster back into their life?

No, I can't do it anymore.

I escaped this life.

I will *not* be dragged back here again.

Reaching the door, I rush down the corridor, up the grand staircase, and into Alistair's bedroom. Looking down at my beautiful dress, it's covered in mud and ripped. I catch a glimpse of myself in the mirror, and my face is pale, my eyes are rimmed with red, and my body is shaking. Quickly, I remove my clothes and jump into the shower, scrubbing myself until I am almost bleeding.

I have an innate need to get that man's eyes off me.

Grabbing some leggings and a top, I throw them on. Then I grab the rest of my stuff in the cupboard and pack my bag.

Seeing the notepaper on the desk, I quickly scribble out a note for Alistair—I don't want him to worry. Tears run down my cheeks as I say goodbye to him.

But I value myself more.

I will not be subjected to that kind of terror ever again.

I stuff my dress into the bottom drawer of the closet—I don't want to see that thing ever again.

And without a second glance, I'm gone.

39

ALISTAIR

"Hey, Ali, baby," Miranda says as she leans against the wall. Her eyes widen, and her face flushes pink as she sees my father step out of the mudroom behind me. I watch as she swallows harshly, her carefully curated façade beginning to fall.

My father's eyes narrow on Miranda—I know he heard her. "Sweetheart, do you happen to know where Eloise is? She seems to have gone missing," my father asks her softly.

Miranda shakes her head as she bites her lower lips.

Yeah, that was always her tell when she lied to my face.

"Yes, you do."

"It's very important, Miranda," my father says sternly.

"Honestly, I have no idea," she answers, trying to sound innocent.

"Don't fucking believe her," my father mumbles under his breath.

"Neither do I," I add.

"If you think George is scary, then you haven't seen me angry. I need to know *right this moment*, Miranda. *Do. You.*

Know … what happened to Eloise?" my father asks, raising his voice.

Miranda swallows hard again. "All I know is George found out something about your girlfriend. That she wasn't who she said she was. That's all I know."

If she thinks I don't know Elle used to work at The Paradise Club, and it's some big secret, then they are sorely mistaken.

"There's a file in his room on Eloise," she adds quietly.

Why the hell does he have a file on my girlfriend in his room? This is insane.

My father looks over at me, and the next thing I know, he's striding down the corridor, looking angry. He walks into the kitchen and finds Paul, our butler, who jumps up and stands to attention when he sees us enter. "Evening, gentlemen," he says, greeting us.

"Paul, have you seen Eloise come through here?" I ask.

"No, sir."

Shit. Then she must be here. There's nowhere for her to have gone.

"Come on, let's see if we can find out what George seems to be blackmailing Eloise with," my father says as we head back up the stairs to George's room. We pull back the door, turn on the lights, and search his room high and low, but we can't find this stupid file. Even his safe is empty.

"Slippery little fucker," my father curses. "I'm sorry, son, for everything that's happened this past year," my dad says, clapping me on the shoulder, and I see the sincerity and pain written on his face.

"I understand."

"But you shouldn't have had to. What George and Miranda did to you was deplorable. He's been a shit his entire life, and your mother and I have indulged him. He's never had to be accountable for anything. We should have been more sympathetic to you, Ali. I'm sorry."

I give him a nod just as the door to George's room swings open, and Paul is standing there out of breath.

"She was picked up about an hour ago via private car. The front gate found the footage. I texted it to you," he states.

I pull out my phone and see the images of Eloise being hugged by her best friend, Lauren. It looks like she's crying.

What the hell has happened?

What has George done?

"I promise whatever George has done to push Eloise away, I *will* find out, and I *will* fix it, I promise," my father tells me seriously. "Now go get some rest, and in the morning, we'll deal with that little asswipe."

I head back toward my empty room, safe in the knowledge that Eloise is with Lauren. Opening the door, I walk back inside with a heavy heart as I stare at the tangled sheets from our lovemaking only hours ago. I fall backward onto the bed, wondering what the hell happened.

I stare up at the ornate ceiling for a long time, trying to work it all out.

What secret did George find out about Eloise? It must be more than The Paradise Club because I can't imagine she would be upset over that unless he tried to blackmail her into sleeping with him. My hands ball into fists as I punch the crap out of my pillow. I'm done with him and Miranda. They're as bad as each other.

At some point, I must fall asleep for a couple of hours, as I am startled awake when I hear a knock at my door. Instantly, I think it's Eloise and jump out of bed, then realize it won't be her. I head on over to my door and pull it open. Paul and my father are standing there.

"Can we come in?" my father asks.

I move aside and let them in.

"We found this," my father states, handing over the manila folder. "George's friend, Fred, handed it to me this morning when I interrogated his good for nothing bunch of friends."

Opening it up, I see Eloise's birth certificate.

Lady Eloise Victoria Miller.

Wait! What? She's royal? And her surname isn't Muller?

"I can't believe it. Her parents were at the wedding last night. They are good friends of ours, the Marquis and Marchioness of Winchester. We had no idea your Eloise was their Eloise, and what's worse is they never said a word."

"Oh my god, we met them last night. Eloise even introduced herself to them as if they were strangers, and they acted the same way. Why the hell would they do that?" I ask him.

"I have no idea, son. All I know is over the years, they had a wayward daughter, Eloise, who they said had a lot of mental health problems, and she had decided she didn't want anything to do with them," he explains to me.

"Does Eloise seem to you to have mental health problems?" I ask him, my voice rising as the anger begins to bubble away under the surface.

My father shakes his head.

"She must have had good reason to hide her past like that. To change her name. She told me her parents cut her off because she wanted to model. Do you think they would really do something like that?"

"Who knows, son."

Then a sheet of paper falls out of the folder. It was hidden underneath some others, and I stare down and look at a psychologist's notes. I begin reading, and my stomach turns.

No.

Oh my god.

No.

I hand the paper to my father, and his face pales as he reads the report.

"Her uncle was here last night. We're friends with him. This is absolutely disgusting. I can't believe it. I can't believe they didn't protect this little girl."

"George used this against her. That's why she ran. He tried to blackmail her into sleeping with him, and when she wouldn't, he did something, and she ran. Fuck! I'm going to kill him," I scream as I rake my hands through my hair. "I'm going back to London, Dad. I have to find her."

"Go, son, go get her. I can't apologize enough for what has happened. This isn't right, Ali. I'll be dealing with George myself," my father tells me angrily as I start heading for the door.

Good, looks like karma is coming for my brother.

The problem is, I hate that it is at the expense of my girl.

I've driven like a maniac back to London and have rocked up to her old home and knocked on her door. *Please talk to me, baby.* I don't care about her past. I just care about her. I want to make everything all right. I don't want this wall up between us.

The door opens, and Lauren's standing there.

"Alistair?" she answers, seemingly shocked to see me.

"I know she's there with you. Please, will you let me come in? I need to talk to Elle. I need her to know I still love her and that I'm going to murder my brother. And that whatever it takes, I want her to know that I'll keep her safe," I explain to Lauren, whose face softens at my request.

"She's not ready yet, it's still so raw. What your brother did ... ambushing her with her uncle, the man who used to haunt her nightmares, is unforgivable. He's ruined her. She's back at square one again, the fragile little bird she used to be. I helped her out of that hole once before, and I'll do it again," she tells me angrily.

"I'm so sorry. I had no idea my brother was this crazy or that he had this much of a vendetta against me," I try and explain to her.

"Your brother knocked up your fiancée, for fuck's sake. How did you *not* think he would be capable of such things?"

She's right. Am I so used to my brother's antics that I haven't taken into consideration how seriously messed up he is? How he's been blackmailing my past girlfriends to sleep with him. And for what? To be better than me? To ruin me? I don't understand why he hates me so much.

"I love her, Lauren, with all my heart. She's it for me. I don't want anyone else. I love you, Elle," I scream down Lauren's hallway.

Lauren blinks a few times and looks at me sadly. "I know you do, Alistair, but you need to give her time."

"I'll wait an eternity if it means I get to spend one more moment with her."

Lauren nods. "I'll let her know you popped round," she says before closing the door in my face.

40

ELOISE

"Oh my god, Ellie, did you hear him? That man is heartbroken. I really think you should talk to him," Lauren tells me as she comes back inside after talking with Alistair.

"I can't, Lauren." I shake my head as tears begin to roll down my cheeks again, thinking of what his family put me through hours earlier.

"He's not like his brother, Elle. That man loves you, and it looks like he would move mountains to be with you. One day I wish to find a guy who loves me like that," Lauren tells me.

"I need time. Please just give me time to process this." I curl into a ball—my mind is not willing to discuss something so traumatic from my childhood.

"I know, babe. I also think you should talk to someone. This time someone who isn't on your parents' payroll," she tells me.

"Not today. I don't want to deal with it today. Please don't make me."

"That's fine. You don't have to do anything today."

I snuggle into the couch and begin to flick the channels on

the television, trying to find something to numb the excruciating pain I'm in.

"Another bouquet," Lauren states as she brings in another gorgeous arrangement of flowers.

Alistair has sent me a bouquet of flowers every single day for the past month. Lauren's house looks like a funeral parlor, but it's kind of cute. I've been sending a thank you message every single time a bouquet has arrived—I'm not that much of a heartless monster. I've also been baking up a storm because it's what I do when I'm stressed. Not that Lauren's complaining. I've also started going to therapy, trying to work through my childhood trauma. Every single day for the past couple of weeks I've been going, and I feel better for it. This time I know I'm getting the help I deserve.

"When are you going to put this man out of his misery and take him back?" Lauren asks.

"I'm trying to get myself better, so I deserve a man like him," I reply.

"Babe, please, you deserve him just like he deserves you."

"I don't know what to say to him. I'm embarrassed and heartbroken all at the same time," I explain to Lauren.

"You can say anything. The man just wants to love you," she says with a smile.

Maybe she's right. "Fine! I better message him to say thanks for the flowers and go from there."

"There you go, that a girl," Lauren replies, giving me two thumbs up.

I head upstairs to my bedroom, flop down on my bed, and grab my phone. I nervously bite my lip as I begin a message to him.

Eloise: Thank you so much for the gorgeous flowers. You don't have to keep sending them to me.

Alistair: If it means I get to hear from you, it's worth it.

Aw, that was sweet.

Alistair: Also, thanks for the cupcakes. My staff thinks I'm the best because of them.

Lauren suggested that I start sending Alistair the excess items I was baking as thanks for the flowers. So, I've been doing that.

Eloise: I'm glad they have been enjoying them.

Alistair: They have been asking me where they can purchase them. So I told them to contact you via socials. Hope that was okay?

Eloise: OMG that was you? I was wondering where I was getting all these requests from.

Alistair: You know I've always thought you were talented. The world is crying out for your gift.

Eloise: I know. I need to get my ass into gear. I finished another week of therapy today.

I bite my lip, hoping he doesn't think something is wrong with me.

Alistair: I'm so proud of you. It must have been a big step to do that.

Alistair: Just so you know. My father demoted George from CEO of the company down to an entry-level advisor. He told him while on his honeymoon, he wasn't impressed. Finally, my father has put his foot down with my brother's antics. My family can't apologize enough for what happened. They have also cut ties with your parents. They were horrified to know they refused to help you.

Well, shit! I don't feel bad for George losing his job, he deserves so much more than that, but I understand it's hard when he's the heir to the family business. I appreciate them cutting off my parents, but they didn't need to do that. However, the gesture is kind. I feel bad that I've affected their family so much with my baggage. I know people will say it's not my fault, but still, if I hadn't walked into their life, their entire family wouldn't have imploded. When I think about it, *it should have imploded when George knocked Miranda up.* Maybe I was the straw that broke the camel's back.

Eloise: I'm sorry.

Alistair: You have nothing to apologize for. George had this coming for a very long time.

Maybe he's right.

Alistair: I know I might be pushing my luck, as this is the most we have spoken in weeks, but I was wondering if you could meet me somewhere next week. I found the perfect spot for your business.

Even through all this, he's still thinking about my business. I truly don't deserve this man.

Eloise: Okay. Send me the details.

Alistair: I thought I would have had to work a little harder than that, but I'll take it.

I smile down at my phone.

Eloise: See you then.

Alistair: Can't wait.

※※※※※※※※

I'm nervous as I turn up to the address Alistair sent through to me in Kensington, and I know instantly I can't afford something as gorgeous as this. It's perfection. A blank canvas to work with, in a great location, and there's no other bakery shop like it in the area. The building has character. It's on the corner with a large outside area where people could sit and relax while enjoying a coffee and a sweet treat. I peek my eyes through the windows, but I can't see what it looks like inside.

"What do you think?" Alistair asks, making me jump upon hearing his voice.

I spin around, and there he is, looking utterly handsome. He's dressed casually today in jeans, a navy blazer, and a white business shirt. His sandy blond hair is a little disheveled, he has scruff across his square jaw, and he's giving me a bright white smile. I've missed him so much. I'm itching to jump into his arms and hug him because in this moment, I've realized how much I've missed him. Tears well in my eyes as my emotions seem to take over me.

"Babe, is everything okay?" he asks, hesitating to reach out to me.

Screw it. I rush toward him and wrap my arms around his body and cry. "I've missed you so much," I mumble into his hard chest.

"I've missed you too," he says, holding me tightly.

We stay like that for a little while until I pull away and look up into his handsome face. Alistair wipes my tears away with his thumbs and smiles down at me.

"I really want to kiss you, but I will always respect your boundaries, Elle," he states firmly.

"Kiss me," I request.

"With pleasure." Alistair smiles as he cups my face and brings it to his. His lips meet mine, and all the tension and stress from the past couple of weeks begins to fade away. His lips are soft as he slowly kisses me. He's in no hurry, it's as if he's savoring every second of our kiss. My mouth opens for him, and his tongue slides against mine, and that's when my body comes alive.

Oh, how I've missed him.

"I could kiss you all day, but I need to show you inside," he states, winking at me.

That's right, that's why we're here—to look at this space for my bakery.

Alistair pulls out the keys and opens the doors to the space. *How did he get the keys?* I guess rich people don't need real estate agents. We enter, and the area is phenomenal. It's exactly like the spaces I showed him I was after on Pinterest.

He listened.

He totally understood my vision.

"It's perfect, isn't it?" he asks me.

"It truly is. But I can't afford the space. This location is highly sought after, and I know the rental prices are astronomical," I explain as I take in the space before me, and my mind runs wild with ideas.

"Lucky I know the owner, and they will give it to you for a good rate," he tells me.

"No." I gasp. "Still, it will be too expensive."

"I'm sure the landlord would happily trade sexual favors and cupcakes for rent," he says, giving me a wink.

He what now? And then my jaw falls as the penny drops, and Alistair starts laughing. No. There is *no way* in this world that he bought this shop. "Are you the owner?" I ask hesitantly.

"Yep. I saw it months ago and was able to negotiate a great deal. It closed this week, and I bought it for you, Elle," he explains.

Who the hell buys someone a shop?

"I know you will want to pay me rent, but how about this? "You don't start paying me rent until you start making a profit," he adds.

"Ali..."

"I won't take no for an answer, Elle. This is where you're meant to be. In this space, with hopefully, me by your side," he says.

"This is too much."

Ali shakes his head. "Nothing is too much for the woman I love." He grins. "I believe in you. Always have. From the moment I tasted your cupcakes, I knew this is what you were born to do. Now *do it*!"

"Okay. Let's do this," I agree.

"Seriously?" he asks, not quite believing I've agreed to his demands this easily.

"Yes, seriously. How am I supposed to say no to the man I love?" I grin.

"You ... love me?"

"With all of my heart," I say as I jump into his arms and almost knock him over with my enthusiasm. "I love you, Alistair King."

"I love you too, Eloise Muller. Wait! Is it Muller or Miller?"

"Miller is my *real* surname, but that's another person. I don't know who Eloise Miller is anymore," I tell him.

"That's okay because one day it's going to be Eloise King. So it doesn't really matter, does it?" he replies cheekily.

"One day," I say, agreeing with him.

"Can't wait." He grins as he cups my face and kisses me passionately.

Behind me a throat clears, and Alistair and I break apart in surprise. There standing before us is Alexander Lewis, my old boss's brother, and a gorgeous blonde. What are they doing here?

"Alex, Ivy, thank you so much for coming," Alistair greets them excitedly, shaking their hands. "Let me introduce you both to Eloise." He turns back and gives me a wide smile.

"We have heard so much about you, Eloise," Alex states while shaking my hand.

"All good, I hope," I say with a chuckle as I look over his shoulder at Alistair.

"This guy never shuts up about you," Alex declares with a smile.

His comment makes my heart flutter.

"Hi, I'm Ivy," the gorgeous blonde says, introducing herself to me.

I reach out and shake her hand.

"Sorry. This is the love of my life, Ivy Starr. She is also the world's best interior designer," Alex states confidently as he wraps his arm around Ivy's waist and pulls her to him, then places a kiss on her cheek, making her blush.

"Not going to deny it. I am one of the best," Ivy relays while giving me a wink. *I like her.* "Alistair has hired me to bring your dream to a reality."

He did what? I look up at him as my mouth falls open.

"I see he may have forgotten to tell you." Ivy chuckles.

"He also forgot to mention he purchased this shop … I'm still trying to comprehend it all," I tell them both.

Alistair walks over and reaches out for me, then pulls me into his side. "I'd do anything for the woman I love."

Swoon. There goes my heart again.

"Aw, you big softie." Ivy grins. "Well, I hope you don't mind, but he also shared with me your Pinterest boards, and I've created some mock-ups for you to have a look at. Three months is going to be a tight timeframe, but Alistair has said to spare no expense on the project, so I'm confident we will get it done," she explains to me.

"Ali!" I gasp.

"I want you to be in your shop doing what you love, sooner rather than later," he says, looking down at me and giving me puppy dog eyes.

How can I be mad at this man?

EPILOGUE

"I think I'm going to be sick," I grumble to Lauren as I look up from the state-of-the-art commercial kitchen.

"It's opening day jitters, Elle. It's going to be fine. Have you seen the lineup outside? It's all the way around the block," Lauren explains to me.

"What happens if I haven't made enough for everyone. I don't want to disappoint my customers. That's not a good look on opening day," I moan to Lauren as I try to quell the unease that's continually rising in my stomach.

"Elle, please don't stress. We've got this," Lauren tries to reassure me.

"And I've got you too," Alistair says, walking into the kitchen with a wide smile on his face. "You are going to kill it today. London is going to fall in love with your cupcakes just like I have." He leans down as he pulls me into his arms. "I told you I would never let you fall, and I mean it," he says as he grabs my chin and brings our lips together. Alistair kisses me ever so softly, trying to give me the strength I need to deal with my opening day jitters.

"Okay, let's do this," I tell them both, trying to drum up the confidence that I'm severely lacking in this moment.

I step outside the kitchen, where I've been all morning with the other staff, and am greeted by Alistair's friends, Alex, Jasper, Daniel, and Ivy. They all wish me well for the opening.

"Oh my god ... this place is gorgeous," a female voice says behind me as the sound of the door slamming shut echoes through the shop.

I turn around and stop dead. *Is that Axel Taylor from Dirty Texas in my fucking shop?* I look over at Lauren, and her mouth has fallen open as well. She then mouths *'what the fuck'* to me as she stares at the rock star.

"This is my best friend, Olivia, and her husband, Axel," Ivy explains.

"We've just moved back to London from LA. Ivy has been raving about your cakes for months now, and I had to come and see for myself. Congratulations on your grand opening. I can't wait to taste one of everything," Olivia says with a smile as she gives me a welcoming hug.

"Sorry, but Ginny was having a tantrum outside," a stunning brunette walks in with ... *is that the ex-President of France?*

Am I asleep? Because this seems awfully like some weird anxiety-driven dream I'd be having before opening day.

"This is my sister, Penny, and her partner, Julien," Olivia says, introducing the couple to us.

"Your shop is amazing," Penny declares, giving me a bright smile as she wrangles a wiggly child on her hip.

"Thank you all for coming. I'm overwhelmed by everything," I say honestly.

"We are here to help." Olivia smiles. "Babe, go take some photos with the cakes and post them online. Your fans will love it," she tells her uber-famous husband, who kisses her and starts taking snapshots in front of the cake displays with the other guys.

"What the fuck is going on?" Lauren whispers to me. "You know that's fucking Axel Taylor from Dirty Texas?" I nod my head, unable to speak. "And isn't he that French politician who was into kinky stuff," Lauren adds in a whisper.

"He was the President of France," I mumble back.

"Fuck," Lauren curses. "This is going to be the best PR for the shop." She smirks excitedly as we watch everyone taking photos and generally having a good time.

"Sorry I'm late. Fuck me! There's a line that goes all the way around the block," another gorgeous blonde woman curses as she enters the kitchen.

"You made it," Ivy squeals and runs to hug her.

Then my eyes widen, and I reach out and grab Lauren's arm and squeeze it tight as we both stare at the owner of The Paradise Club, Nate Lewis. *What the hell is he doing here?*

"Eloise, Lauren … congratulations on your grand opening," Nate says, holding out his hand for the both of us.

Lauren and I shake his hand in stunned silence because this is more than a little bit surreal. When I worked at The Paradise Club, Mr. Lewis was an enigma, you never really saw him, and now he's here in *my shop*.

Ivy skips over, dragging the other blonde, and smiles. "This is my sister, Camryn. She is the world's best event planner. Camryn lives in New York with her partner, Nate," Ivy explains.

"My sister has been raving about your shop, and we were in town for the weekend, so I had to see the finished product. And … it's fucking awesome. My sister is so talented."

"She truly is. Never in my wildest dreams did I ever expect what I had in my mind could ever be created almost exactly as I envisioned it would be," I tell them both.

"That's why she's the best," Camryn states with a bright smile on her face.

"She truly is. This is a dream come true for me. Looking around and seeing everything she has been able to create, the execution is phenomenal. I don't know if anyone else could ever have done it," I say as tears well in my eyes.

Ivy and I, over the past couple of months, have become quite close working on this project together. Also, Alistair and Alex being best friends means we spent time together outside of work, and Lauren and I have happily welcomed her into our circle.

"It's been my pleasure," Ivy says as she gives Lauren and me a hug.

"It's time, guys," Alistair calls out, breaking up our hug.

"You ready?" Lauren asks me, grabbing my hand as we stare at the excited faces of the people standing outside.

"So fucking ready. *Let's do this!*"

THE END

ACKNOWLEDGMENTS

Thanks for finishing this book.
Really hope you enjoyed it.
Why not check out my other books.
Have a fantastic day !

Don't forget to leave a review.
xoxo

ABOUT THE AUTHOR

JA Low lives on the Gold Coast in Australia. When she's not writing steamy scenes and admiring hot surfers, she's tending to her husband and two sons and running after her chickens while dreaming up the next epic romance.

Come follow her

Facebook: www.facebook.com/jalowbooks
TikTok: www.tiktok.com/@jalowbooks
Instagram: www.instagram.com/jalowbooks
Pinterest: www.pinterest.com/jalowbooks
Website: www.jalowbooks.com
Goodreads: https://www.goodreads.com/author/show/14918059.J_A_Low
BookBub: https://www.bookbub.com/authors/ja-low

ABOUT THE AUTHOR

Come join JA Low's Block
www.facebook.com/groups/1682783088643205/

🌴🌴🌴🌴🌴🌴🌴🌴

www.jalowbooks.com
jalowbooks@gmail.com

INTERCONNECTING

You will find characters in this story also in

The Arrogant Artist - Standalone - The International Bad Boys Set

Playing the Player - Book 2 - The Hartford Brothers Series

Paradise - Book 1 - The Paradise Club Series

Lost in Paradise - Book 2 - The Paradise Club series

INTERCONNECTING SERIES

Reading order for interconnected characters.

Dirty Texas Series

Suddenly Dirty

Suddenly Together

Suddenly Bound

Suddenly Trouble

Suddenly Broken

Paradise Club Series

Paradise

Lost in Paradise

Playboys of New York

Off Limits

Strictly Forbidden

The Merger

Without Warning

The Hartford Brother's Series

Tempting the Billionaire

ALSO BY JA LOW

Playboys of New York

Off Limits - Book 1

Strictly Forbidden - Book 2

The Merger - Book 3

Taking Control - Book 4

Without Warning - Book 5

ALSO BY JA LOW

The Dirty Texas Box Set

Five full length novels and Five Novellas included in the set.

One band. Five dirty talking rock stars and the women that bring them to their knees.

Suddenly Dirty

A workplace romance with your celebrity hall pass.

Suddenly Together

A best friend to lover's romance with the one man who's off limits.

Suddenly Bound

An opposites attract romance with family loyalty tested to its limits.

Suddenly Trouble

A brother's best friend romance with a twist.

Suddenly Broken

A friend's with benefits romance that takes a wild ride.

One little taste can't hurt; can it?

If you like your rock stars dirty talking, alpha's with hearts of gold this series is for you.

ALSO BY JA LOW

International Bad Boys Set

Standalone Books

Book 1 - The Sexy Stranger (Italian)

Book 2 - The Arrogant Artist (French)

Book 3 - The Hotshot Chef (Spanish)

ALSO BY JA LOW

The Hartford Brothers Series

Book 1 - Tempting the Billionaire

Book 2 - Playing the Player

Book 3 - Seducing the Doctor

ALSO BY JA LOW

Reading order for Interconnecting Series

Bratva Jewels Series (Now on Wattpad)

The Sexy Stranger

Printed in Great Britain
by Amazon